The Russian Debutante's Handbook

"Uproarious and highly entertaining ... Vladimir Girshkin [is] what Kingsley Amis's Lucky Jim would be, if he were a Russian emigre trying to cope with the confusions of life in America of the 1990s and the incessant demands of an ambitious and endlessly aggrieved mother. ... [Shteyngart] uses Vladimir's picaresque adventures to satirize Americans' and Russians' preconceptions about their former cold war enemies and to send up their illusions about themselves. Like Salman Rushdie and Bharati Mukherjee, Mr. Shteyngart uses his appraising outsider's eye to examine the bizarre weightless state of exile; and like Viktor Pelevin, he proves himself a nimble cultural magpie, borrowing street argot from both the East and West to create a wonderfully idiomatic, jet-fueled prose. His voice, however, is thoroughly his own, by turns ironic and earnest, farcical and melancholy, as attuned to the exhilarating possibilities of the English language as Martin Amis, as deadpan funny as the young Evelyn Waugh. ... An equally wicked and comic hand ... the very talented Mr. Shteyngart expose[s] the absurdities that exist on either side of the former iron curtain."
—Michiko Kakutani, *The New York Times*

"As first novels go, Shteyngart's tops Saul Bellow's for bounce and Philip Roth's for wit. By any standard, he is sharp about love, wise about death, and hilarious beyond belief."
—*Entertainment Weekly*

"Vladimir is an irresistible hero, bumbling and ruthless yet eager to please. *The Russian Debutante's Handbook* is often hilarious, and Mr. Shteyngart crafts his sentences with evident relish for language. 'Part P. T. Barnum, part V. I. Lenin,' Vladimir's story is not to be missed."
— *The Wall Street Journal*

"Gary Shteyngart, a young Russian American, has produced a sardonic, moving, and ingeniously crafted update of earlier sagas of upward-struggling American newcomers. And in Vladimir Girshkin, the wise-cracking, lovelorn, desperately self-reinventing protagonist, Shteyngart has given us a literary symbol for this new immigrant age, much as Saul Bellow or Henry Roth did in theirs. ... Space does not permit doing full

continued ...

justice to the scope of the intrigue or to the breathless pace and supple humor of Shteyngart's prose, which is especially strong in rapid-fire, unself-consciously satirical dialogue. Suffice it to say that *The Russian Debutante's Handbook* is that most unlikely of new millennial creations—a heartfelt lunge into the ever-shifting politics of cultural identity and a mordant fable of making it, American- and Russian-style."
—*The Washington Post*

"Hilarious . . . Few recent novels can claim to be as funny as this wildly imaginative fantasy . . . [an] epic search for that most American of dreams—a meaningful identity . . . As you watch Vladimir conquer what his soulfully funny creator refers to as 'the wrong half' of Europe, you realize that for all the fun it provides, Shteyngart's debut is as serious as it is funny. With dizzy pacing and satiric acidity reminiscent of Bulgakov, his tale of Vladimir's ascent—descent?—is transformed into a rich moral and political parable about the tragicomedy of post–cold war culture. . . . Rich, complicated, and humorous."
—*New York Magazine*

"[A] satisfying skewering all round, as funny and wicked as Waugh."
—*Time*

"When I began reading the first pages of *The Russian Debutante's Handbook*, I thought immediately of writers like Bellow and Nabokov and Malamud. Here was sparkling and ebullient prose, possessed of a vital and far-ranging intelligence and infused with exquisite delight in the uses of language. . . . [Shteyngart's] novel—like all the very best work in our literature—continues to surprise and challenge, continues to instruct me about how our language really works in all its possibilities, and how that shows on our human condition."
—Chang-rae Lee, author of *A Gesture Life* and *Native Speaker*

"[An] energetic, sparkling, often hysterical first novel . . . The fantastical transformation of a soft-chested, Oberlin-educated young man into a Mafiaso furthers Shteyngart's idea of how fantasies of America create their own reality. . . . Shteyngart's descriptive and ironic language, comic sense and eye for detail are . . . very much in evidence . . . impressive."
—*Los Angeles Times*

"Shteyngart has rewritten the classic immigrant narrative—starring a sarcastic slacker instead of a grateful striver. . . . *The Russian Debutante's Handbook* is a rambunctious satire that upends one of the most solemn traditions in American literature: the immigrant novel. . . . Shteyngart revels in detailing the debased behavior of fictional conationals. The cast of seedy ex-Soviets includes everyone from Kalashnikov-toting casino managers to Pushkin-quoting prostitutes. . . . It is a world he knows with surprising intimacy. . . ." —*The New York Times Magazine*

"*The Russian Debutante's Handbook* is one of the year's more accomplished debut novels, combining the comic wit of Joseph Heller with a knack for storytelling that's worthy of the Russian tradition of episodic, labyrinth tales." —*Pittsburgh Tribune-Review*

"Energetic, ambitious . . . *The Russian Debutante's Handbook* is like a precisely measured map drawn by one of Nabokov's whimsical madmen. . . . Shteyngart's playful, carnivalesque sensibility fits within a Russian satirical-fantastic tradition that stretches from Nikolai Gogol in the nineteenth century to Mikhail Bulgakov in the Stalin period and Vassily Aksyonov in the Soviet twilight. . . . Madcap inventiveness . . . bitter hilarity . . . a magpie's nest of allusions and observations, full of note-perfect parodies. . ." —A. O. Scott, *The New York Times Book Review*

"This Girshkin—call him a distant cousin of Augie March and Alexander Portnoy—is the winningly resilient comic hero of Gary Shteyngart's remarkable debut. . . . A picaresque, sprawling story, so precisely imagined that you can't help giving in to the pleasure of it and losing yourself in the improbabilities of its 480-page span. Girshkin's narrative mixes acerbic observations of mid-90's post-collegiate culture, obsessive insecurity and irrepressible libido with an affecting longing to be a fully realized American. It's a strong, tasty cocktail. . . . Mr. Shteyngart has introduced himself as one of the most talented and entertaining writers of his generation . . . a stylish writer, adept at sentences that combine sensitivity of observation with great comic timing. . . . After all the rambunctious action, we're left with a serious and moving portrait." —*New York Observer*

continued . . .

"There is no shortage of targets for Shteyngart's scathing satire. Girshkin bounces from one absurd capitalist escapade to another."
—*Newsday*

"The rampaging narrative is festooned on every page with glittering one-liners, improbably apt similes, and other miniature pleasures ... incisive [and] uproarious."
—*Elle*

"A brilliant, funny debut describing the vicissitudes of immigration today."
—*Harper's Bazaar*

"Darkly fun ... First-time novelist Gary Shteyngart, himself a Russian immigrant, ups the deftly-handled daffiness in this reeling, rollicking and often hilarious read. Succumbing to the mayhem, we just go along for the joyride. ... [A] melting-pot hodgepodge of Russian, East European and American impulses."
—*San Diego Union-Tribune*

"*The Russian Debutante's Handbook* is that rare find: a truly engaging comic novel from an unknown author. ... Shteyngart tells Vladimir's story with energy and wit, plunging him into a series of unlikely events, surrounded by a cast of remarkably ingenious characters. ... Vladimir's adventures are an endless source of amusement, and Shteyngart relates them in an energetic prose style that has its own appeal. His takes on both America and Eastern Europe capture the enduring paradoxes of this post–cold war, post-capitalist era."
—*Sun-Sentinel*

"Gary Shteyngart has a wickedly acute eye and ear, and the manic humor of the deeply melancholy. As the criminal mastermind of his own imagined New Yorkistan, he manages, in some post-Einsteinian way, to get way outside and way inside the place and its inhabitants at the same time."
—David Gates, author of *Jernigan*

"An exuberant literary debut."
—*Pages*

"Shteyngart limns the expat experience from the other way around, through the eyes of a hapless Russian immigrant who tries to be a capitalist in New York City. The author, originally from the Soviet Union, captures the ecstasy and heartbreak of discovering a 'boundless world.'"
—*Details*

"A broadly comic tale delivered in an exuberant, omniscient narrative voice [and] sprinkled with literary allusions . . . As Girshkin leaves New York, he, like Joan Didion, thinks, 'Goodbye to All That.' He becomes 'Our Man in Prava,' along the lines of Graham Greene's 'Our Man in Havana.' Chapters have titles such as 'The Unbearable Whiteness of Being,' drawing on Milan Kundera, and creative writing programs are exposed as just another brand of pyramid scheme. . . . Shteyngart's book is in the tradition of narrative that Sir Walter Scott once dubbed 'a romance of roguery,' inviting the audience to identify with a central character branded the underdog and yet who is simultaneously—subversively—in charge, living by his wits as he makes his gloriously unfettered way in an unwelcoming world." —*The Sunday Oregonian*

"[Shteyngart's] sense of the exploded past and volatile present suffuses this gifted first novel. Its roguish young hero, Vladimir, moves from a surreal America to central Europe and finds himself ensnared in a series of political and sexual misadventures in Shteyngart's tender and hilarious émigré's romance." —*O, The Oprah Magazine*

"This moving and funny debut novel offers a fresh take on the oft-told story of the immigrant longing for an authentic sense of place. This is a complex and impressive work, full of humanistic touches and worldly humor." —*Book Magazine*

"*The Russian Debutante's Handbook* is often laugh-out-loud funny. Gary Shteyngart, who came to the United States at age seven and, like his protagonist, spent time in Prague in the early 1990s, modulates between sly and antic humor as he explores the bewilderments of the immigrant identity. . . . What Shteyngart does so well is convey the immigrant's divided sensibility in language that's fresh, wry and witty." —*Houston Chronicle*

"Yes, friends, it's been a while since we who value Nabokov and Brodsky have waited for a new literary hero to emerge from the ranks of Russian-speaking immigrants in America. We have waited—and now he is here. Recently, the work of the young Russian writer Gary Shteyngart began

continued. . . .

appearing on the shelves of American bookstores . . . and New York's literary beau monde immediately took note."

—*Novoye Russkoye Slovo*

"[T]he spirits that Shteyngart explicitly summons belong to Raymond Carver and Ernest Hemingway, both practiced vodka drinkers. The novel itself is an exuberant riff on American innocence and imagination, as set to the music of ABBA but filtered through an alcoholic haze."

—*The Boston Globe*

"*The Russian Debutante's Handbook,* the extraordinary debut novel of thirty-year-old Gary Shteyngart, chronicles Vladimir's whirlwind odyssey of self-discovery with flair, wit and an enviable command of the English language. Shteyngart's energetic prose infuses Vladimir with a vibrant and complex personality, making him the kind of character you remember long after his story is over. . . . Shteyngart has made a grand leap onto the literary scene with this impressive debut. He also demonstrates the qualities of a postmodern Gogol or Dostoevski by making a fictional world marked by despair and alienation humorous, engaging and enlightening. . . . Shteyngart is a young writer to watch."

—*Rocky Mountain News*

"Shteyngart is a young writer to watch. His writing style brims with a piquancy most readers will relish. There are very few great first novels, but this one just might be worthy of that description."

—*Fort Worth Star-Telegram*

"Shteyngart, whose book has generated fine reviews and lots of buzz, has been compared to Vladimir Nabokov and Saul Bellow, Franz Kafka and Woody Allen. Which means he's Russian, Jewish, darkly comic and funny. He's also immensely talented."   —*The Star-Ledger*

"[T]he kind of book that could have been written by few other young, Jewish authors, many of whom lament not having been part of the immigrant experiences that spawned the likes of Saul Bellow, Bernard Malamud and Norman Mailer."   —*Forward*

"Shteyngart skewers New York's Bohemian scene in baroque prose worthy of Bellow. . . . Humorous—okay, hysterically, laugh-out-loud

funny—though it may be, the novel addresses Shteyngart's sense of being 'divided' between three cultures: Russian, American and Jewish."
—*Shout*

"In the grand gallery of Jewish schlemiel-heroes, Vladimir recalls *Catch-22*'s Yossarian—if Yossarian ever tried to sell out and save himself by becoming a manic opportunist such as Milo Minderbinder. . . ."
—*The Dallas Morning News*

"[B]road humor and biting satire . . . Even as [Shteyngart] exposes the absurdities of late capitalism in the United States and too-late capitalism in Eastern Europe, he can never be accused of taking himself too seriously. Shteyngart is not burdened with the challenge of getting the foreign backdrop exactly right, nor is he obliged to create fictional political crises in real European countries, as Franzen does in *The Corrections*. Instead, Shteyngart creates an entire fictional country, the Republic of Stolovaya (Russian for 'cafeteria'), whose chic but dilapidated capital, Prava, suggests a neutral territory between Pravda and Prada. Implicitly, Shteyngart recognizes that the romantic haven of free-thinking and free love to which these young Americans flock ('It's the Paris of the 90s!') has always been a fantasy projection, less like Mitteleuropa and more like Middle Earth."
—Eliot Borenstein, *The Nation*

"Shteyngart explores what he calls the 'unholy netherworld of Assimilation Gone Wrong.' He navigates with vodka and explosives and a range of humor. . . . In this first novel, Shteyngart resembles Bellow and Malamud, but he also follows Faulkner."
—*Boulder Camera*

"A wonderful farce of one man's coming of age entangled with literary poseurs, addled Russian immigrants, and gangsters. . . . This is the first epic novel about the young Russian-American experience, and it truly sings. Shteyngart has developed a brilliant comic hero in Vladimir Girshkin."
—*Milwaukee Journal Sentinel*

"A far more unruly Everyman than Kafka ever invented. . . Shteyngart can certainly turn a phrase."
—*The Seattle Times*

continued. . . .

"[Shteyngart's] writing is energetic, full of inventiveness and wisdom, brimming with atmosphere. The 480-page novel is fast reading, although laugh-out-loud moments slow the pace. He leaves the reader with an engaging and memorable cast of characters, and much to ponder about alienation, identity, exile, and contrasts between East and West."
— *Jewish Week*

"[A] smart debut novel . . . Shteyngart's Vladimir [is] an impressive piece of work, an amoral buffoon who energizes this remarkably mature work."
— *Publishers Weekly*

"Sort of like an old-fashioned hero, Vladimir Girshkin comes of age out of necessity . . . and, possibly, [steps] into the ranks of the most beloved heroes of preposterous fiction. . . . *The Russian Debutante's Handbook* is truly a masterpiece of prose that may even be worthy of comparison to Nabokov. Certainly, Shteyngart shares Nabokov's love and understanding of Americana, if of a very different age . . . loaded with dry wit [and] filled with real tenderness and pathos."
— *Flak* magazine

"Shteyngart mercilessly exposes the moral ambiguities of late-twentieth-century life under whatever form of government. . . . Ambitious, funny, intelligent, in love with irony and literary allusions, as if by a lighter Nabokov."
— *Kirkus Reviews* (starred review)

"If Henry Miller were Russian, this is a book he might have written. . . . Fueled by wry humor, biting cultural commentary, and charming, oddball characters, [*The Russian Debutante's Handbook*] transcends its personal genesis to become an all-around great American story."
— *Time Out New York*

THE
RUSSIAN
DEBUTANTE'S
HANDBOOK

GARY
SHTEYNGART

RIVERHEAD BOOKS

NEW YORK

RIVERHEAD BOOKS
Published by The Berkley Publishing Group
A division of Penguin Group (USA) Inc.
375 Hudson Street
New York, New York 10014

The author gratefully acknowledges permission
to quote lyrics from the following:
"Route 66" by Bobby Troup. Used by permission of
Londontown Music, Inc., and Edwin H. Morris & Company,
a division of MPL Communications, Inc.
"You're the Top" by Cole Porter. © 1934 (renewed) Warner Bros. Inc.
All rights reserved. Used by permission of Warner Bros.
Publications U.S. Inc., Miami, FL 33104.

First Riverhead hardcover edition: June 2002
First Riverhead trade paperback edition: May 2003
Riverhead trade paperback ISBN: 1-57322-988-1

The Library of Congress has catalogued the Riverhead hardcover edition as follows:

Shteyngart, Gary.
The Russian debutante's handbook / Gary Shteyngart.
p. cm.
ISBN 1-57322-213-5
1. Russian Americans—Fiction. 2. New York (N.Y.)—Fiction.
3. Immigrants—Fiction. 4. Young men—Fiction. I. Title.
PS3619.H79 R87 2002   2001047676
813'.6—dc21

Printed in the United States of America

To My Parents

AUTHOR'S NOTE

"Volodya" and "Volodechka" are diminutives
of the Russian name Vladimir.

THE
RUSSIAN
DEBUTANTE'S
HANDBOOK

PART I

NEW YORK, 1993

1. THE STORY OF
VLADIMIR GIRSHKIN

THE STORY OF VLADIMIR GIRSHKIN—PART P. T. BAR-
num, part V. I. Lenin, the man who would conquer half of Europe
(albeit the wrong half)—begins the way so many other things
begin. On a Monday morning. In an office. With the first cup of
instant coffee gurgling to life in the common lounge.

His story begins in New York, on the corner of Broadway and
Battery Place, the most disheveled, godforsaken, not-for-profit
corner of New York's financial district. On the tenth floor, the
Emma Lazarus Immigrant Absorption Society greeted its clients
with the familiar yellow water-stained walls and dying hydran-
geas of a sad Third World government office. In the reception
room, under the gentle but insistent prodding of trained Assimilation Facilitators, Turks and Kurds called a truce, Tutsis queued
patiently behind Hutus, Serbs chatted up Croats by the demilita-
rized water fountain.

Meanwhile, in the cluttered back office, junior clerk Vladimir
Girshkin—the immigrant's immigrant, the expatriate's expatriate,
enduring victim of every practical joke the late twentieth century
had to offer and an unlikely hero for our times—was going at it
with the morning's first double-cured-spicy-soppressata-and-
avocado sandwich. How Vladimir loved the unforgiving hardness

of the soppressata and the fatty undertow of the tender avocado! The proliferation of this kind of Janus-faced sandwich, as far as he was concerned, was the best thing about Manhattan in the summer of 1993.

VLADIMIR WAS TWENTY-FIVE TODAY. He had lived in Russia for twelve years, and then there were the thirteen years spent here. That was his life—it added up. And now it was falling apart.

This would be the worst birthday of his life. Vladimir's best friend Baobab was down in Florida covering his rent, doing unspeakable things with unmentionable people. Mother, roused by the meager achievements of Vladimir's first quarter-century, was officially on the warpath. And, in possibly the worst development yet, 1993 was the Year of the Girlfriend. A downcast, heavyset American girlfriend whose bright orange hair was strewn across his Alphabet City hovel as if a cadre of Angora rabbits had visited. A girlfriend whose sickly-sweet incense and musky perfume coated Vladimir's unwashed skin, perhaps to remind him of what he could expect on this, the night of his birthday: Sex. Every week, once a week, they had to have sex, as both he and this large pale woman, this Challah, perceived that without weekly sex their relationship would fold up according to some unspecified law of relationships.

Yes, sex night with Challah. Challah with the bulging cheeks and determined radish of a nose, looking ever matronly and suburban, despite all the torn black shirts, gothic bracelets, and crucifixes that downtown Manhattan's goofiest shops managed to sell to her. Sex night—an offer Vladimir dared not refuse, given the prospect of waking up in a bed entirely empty; well, empty save for lonely Vladimir. How did that work again? You open your eyes, turn, and stare into the face of…the alarm clock. A busy and unforgiving face that, unlike a lover's, will say only "tick tock."

Suddenly, Vladimir heard the frenzied croaking of an elderly Russian out in the reception room: "Opa! Opa! *Tovarisch* Girshkin! Ai! Ai! Ai!"

The problem clients. They would come first thing Monday morning, having spent the weekend rehearsing their problems with their loathsome friends, practicing angry postures in front of the bathroom mirrors of their Brighton Beach studios.

It was time to act. Vladimir braced himself against the desk and stood up. All alone in the back office, with no point of reference other than the kindergarten-sized chairs and desks that comprised the furniture, he suddenly felt himself remarkably tall. A twenty-five-year-old man in an oxford shirt gone yellow under the armpits, frayed slacks with the cuffs coming comically undone, and wing tips that bore the black traces of a house fire, he dwarfed his surroundings like the lone skyscraper they built in Queens, right across the East River. But it wasn't true: Vladimir was short.

In the reception room, Vladimir found the bantam security guard from Lima pinioned against the wall. A chunky old Russian gent sporting the traditional flea market attire and six-dollar crew cut had trapped the poor fellow with his crutches and was now slowly leaning in on his prey, trying to bite him with his silver teeth. Alas, at the first hint of internecine violence, the native-born Assimilation Facilitators had ignobly fled the scene, leaving behind their Harlem, U.S.A., coffee mugs and Brooklyn Museum tote bags. Only junior clerk Vladimir Girshkin remained to assimilate the masses. "*Nyet! Nyet! Nyet!*" he shouted to the Russian. "We *never* do that to the guard."

The madman turned to face him. "Girshkin!" he sputtered. "It's you!" He pushed himself away from the guard in one remarkable motion and started limping toward Vladimir. He was a man of small stature, made smaller by a weighty green rucksack bearing down on him. One side of his azure guayabera shirt was filled bosom to navel with Soviet war medals, and their weight pulled down one collar, exposing a veined lump of neck.

"What do you want from me?" Vladimir said.

"What do I want from you?" the Russian shouted. "My God, what haughtiness!" A shaking crutch was quickly lifted into place between them. The lunatic executed a practice jab: On guard!

"I spoke to you on the phone last month," the crutch-bearer complained. "You sounded very cultured on the phone, remember?"

Cultured, yes. That would be him. Vladimir examined the man who was killing his morning. He had a broad Slavic (as opposed to Jewish) face, with a web of creases so deep they could have been carved with a pocketknife. Bushy Brezhnevian eyebrows were overtaking his forehead. A small island of hair, still blond, was moored at the geographical center of his pate. "We spoke, heh?" Vladimir said, in the devil-may-care tone of Soviet officialdom. He was a big fan of the syllable "heh."

"Oh, yes!" the old man enthused.

"And what did I say to you, heh?"

"You said to come over. Miss Harosset said to come over. The fan said to come over. So I took the number five train to Bowling Green like you said." He looked pleased with himself.

Vladimir took a tentative step back toward his office. The guard was settling back on his perch, rebuttoning his shirt, and mumbling something in his language. Still, something was amiss. Let's tally up: angry Slav; cowering security guard; low-paying, absurdist job; misspent youth; sex night with Challah. Oh, yes. "What's this fan?" Vladimir asked.

"It's the one in my bedroom," the fellow said, smirking at a question so obvious. "I have two fans."

"The fan said to come over," Vladimir said. And he has two fans. Right then, on the spot, Vladimir recognized that this wasn't a problem client. This was a *fun* client. A loop-de-loop client. The kind of client that turned on your morning switch and kept you brisk and agitated all day. "Listen," Vladimir said to this Fan Man, "Why don't we step into my office and you tell me everything."

"Bravo, young one!" The Fan Man gave a victory salute to his erstwhile victim the security guard. He limped into the back office, where he lowered himself onto one of the cold plastic chairs. Painfully, he removed the green beast of a rucksack.

"So, what's your name? We'll start with that."

"Rybakov," said the Fan Man. "Aleksander. Or just Aleks."

"Please . . . Tell me about yourself. If you're comfortable—"

"I'm psychotic," Rybakov said. His enormous eyebrows twitched in confirmation, and he smiled with false modesty, like a kid who brings in his father the astronaut on career day.

"Psychotic!" Vladimir said. He tried to look encouraging. It was not uncommon for the mad Russians to give him their diagnosis right off the bat; some treated it almost like a profession or a calling in life. "And you've been diagnosed?"

"By many people. I'm under observation as we speak," said Mr. Rybakov, peering under Vladimir's desk. "Look, I even wrote a letter to the president in the *New York Times*."

He produced a crumpled piece of paper reeking of alcohol, tea, and his own wet palm. "Dear Mr. President," read Vladimir. "I am a retired Russian sailor, a proud combatant against the Nazi terror in the Second World War and a diagnosed paranoid schizophrenic. I have lived in your wonderful country for more than five years and have received much moral and financial support from the warm and highly sexed American people (in particular, my thoughts alight on the women skating around Central Park with just a bit of cloth wrapped around their breasts). Back in Russia, senior citizens with mental disabilities are kept in dilapidated hospitals and humiliated on a daily basis by young hooligans who have scarcely heard of the Great Patriotic War and have no sympathy for their elders who fought tooth and nail to keep out the murderous Krauts. In America, I am able to lead a full, satisfactory life. I select and purchase groceries at the Sloan's supermarket on Eighty-ninth Street and Lexington. I watch television, specifically the show about the comical black midget on channel five. And I help defend America by investing part of my social security income into companies such as Martin Marietta and United Technologies. Soon I will become a citizen of this great nation and will be able to choose my leaders (not like in Russia). So I wish you, Mr. President, and your desirable American wife and developing young daughter, a very healthy, happy New Year. Respectfully, Aleksander Rybakov."

"Your English is impeccable."

"Oh, I can't take credit for that," the Fan Man said. "That was Miss Harosset's translation. She was faithful to the original, you can believe me. She wanted to put 'German' instead of 'Kraut,' but I insisted. You have to write what you feel inside, I told her."

"And the *New York Times* actually *published* this letter?" Vladimir asked.

"Those cretinous editors crossed out half my words," Mr. Rybakov said, shaking a symbolic pen at Vladimir. "It's American censorship, my friend. You don't blot out the words of a poet! Well, I've instructed Miss Harosset to commence a lawsuit on this matter as well. Her little sister is thrashing around with an important state prosecutor, so I think we're in good hands."

Miss Harosset. That must be his social worker. Vladimir looked down at the blank form on which he should have been jotting down information. A rich and particular psychosis was taking shape before him, threatening to upset the meager line allotted for "client's mental state." He grew restless, attributing it to the coffee settling within his abdomen, and started tapping out "The Internationale" on his metal desk, a nervous habit inherited from his father. Outside the nonexistent windows of the back office, the canyons of the financial district were awash with rationalism and dull commercial hope: suburban secretaries explored bargains on cosmetics and hose; Ivy Leaguers swallowed entire pieces of yellow-tail in one satisfied gulp. But here it was just Vladimir the twenty-five-year-old and the poor huddled masses yearning to breathe free. Vladimir looked up from his thoughts—his client was wheezing and sputtering like an overtaxed radiator. "Look, Rybakov," he said. "You are a model immigrant. You collect Social Security. You publish in the *Times*. What can I possibly do for you?"

"The crooks!" Rybakov shouted, grabbing once again for his crutch. "The awful crooks! They won't give me my citizenship! They've read the letter in the *Times*. And they know about the fan. They know about *both* fans. You know how some summer nights the blades get a little rusty and you have to grease them with corn oil? So they've heard the *trikka trikka* and the *krik krak,* and they're scared! An old invalid, they're scared of! There are cowards in every country, even in New York."

"That's true enough," Vladimir agreed. "But I think what you need, Mr. Rybakov, is an immigration lawyer...For unfortunately, I am not..."

"Oh, I know who you are, little goose," Mr. Rybakov said.

"Pardon?" Vladimir said. The last time he had been called "little goose" was twenty years ago, when he was, indeed, a diminutive, unsteady creature, his head covered with a smattering of golden down.

"The Fan sang an epic song for me the other night," said Rybakov. "It was called 'The Tale of Vladimir Girshkin and Yelena Petrovna, His Mama.'"

"Mother," Vladimir whispered. He didn't know what else to say. That word, when spoken in the company of Russian men, was sacred in itself. "You know my mother?"

"We haven't had the pleasure of being formally introduced,"

Rybakov said. "But I read about her in the business section of the *New Russian Word*. What a Jewess! The pride of your people. A capitalist she-wolf. Scourge of the hedge funds. Ruthless czarina. Oh, my dear, dear Yelena Petrovna. And here I am chatting with her son! Surely he knows the right people, fellow Hebrews perhaps, among the dastardly agents of the Immigration and Naturalization Service."

Vladimir scrunched up his hairy upper lip so as to smell its animal fragrance—a soothing pastime. "But you're mistaken," he said. "There is nothing I can do for you. I lack Mother's cunning, I have no friends in the INS...I have no friends anywhere. The apple has fallen far from the apple tree, as they say. Mother may be a she-wolf, but look at me..." Vladimir gestured expansively at the deprivation around him.

Just then the double doors opened, and, twenty minutes late for work, the Chinese and Haitian women—Vladimir's fellow junior clerks in the back office—walked in from the streets, laden with buttered rolls and coffee. They retreated behind the desks labeled CHINA and HAITI, tucking in their long, gauzy summer skirts. When Vladimir's gaze returned to his client, ten hundred-dollar bills, ten portraits of purse-lipped Benjamin Franklin, were unfurled on the table to form a paper fan.

"Ai!" Vladimir cried. Instinctively, he grabbed the hard currency and deposited it inside his shirt pocket. He glanced at his international colleagues. Oblivious of the crime just committed, they were stuffing themselves with morning rolls, bantering about recipes for Haitian crackers and how to know if a man was decent. "Mr. Rybakov!" Vladimir whispered. "What are you doing? You cannot give me money. This is not Russia!"

"Everywhere is Russia," said Mr. Rybakov philosophically. "Everywhere you go...Russia."

"Now I want you to place your upturned palm on the table,"

Vladimir instructed. "I will quickly throw the money in there, you put the money in your wallet, and we shall consider this matter closed."

"I would prefer not to," said Aleksander Rybakov, the Soviet Bartleby. "Look," he said. "Here's what we'll do. Come on over to my house. We'll talk. The Fan likes his tea early on Mondays. Oh, and we'll have Jack Daniel's, and beluga, and luscious sturgeon, too. I live on Eighty-seventh Street, right next to the Guggenheim Museum, that eyesore. But it's a nice penthouse, views of the park, a Sub-Zero refrigerator...A lot more civilized than this place, you'll see...Forget about your duties here. Helping Equadorians move to America, it's a pointless task. Come, let's be friends!"

"You live on the Upper East Side...?" Vladimir babbled. "A penthouse? On Social Security? But how can it be?" He had the dizzy impression that the room had begun to sway. The only enjoyment Vladimir derived from his job was encountering foreigners even more flummoxed by American society than he was. But today this simple pleasure was proving highly elusive. "Where did you get the money?" Vladimir demanded of his client. "Who bought you this zero refrigerator?"

The Fan Man reached over and pinched Vladimir's nose between thumb and forefinger, a familiar Russian gesture reserved for small children. "I'm psychotic," the Fan Man explained. "But I'm no idiot."

2. YELENA PETROVNA,
HIS MOTHER

ON THIS MONDAY MORNING, LIKE ALL MONDAY MORN-
ings, the Emma Lazarus Society experienced a state of misdirected
frenzy. Lonely social workers were opening up their hearts to one
another; the agency's Acculturation Czar, a homesick, suicidal Pole,
was bellowing through his introductory course on America ("Selfish People, Selfish Land"); and the weekly immigrants' pet show
was underway in the International Lounge, a Bengali turtle leading
the pack this time.

Surrounded by such polyglot commotion, it was easy for
Vladimir to abandon his post—the so-called Russia Desk, covered
with bureaucratic ink stains and newspaper clippings about Soviet
Jews in distress. But before Vladimir could accompany Mr. Rybakov
to his penthouse, an impassioned well-wisher rang him at the office.

"DEAREST VOLODECHKA!" Mother shouted. "Happy birthday...! Happy new beginning...! Your father and I wish you a brilliant future...! Much success...! You're a talented young man...!
The economy's improving...! We gave you all our love as a child...!
Everything we had, to the very last...!"

Vladimir turned down the volume on the headset. He knew what was coming, and, indeed, seven exclamation marks down the road, Mother broke down and started wailing God's name in the possessive: *"Bozhe moi! Bozhe moi!"*

"Why did I get you that job, Vladimir?" she cried. "What was I thinking? You promised me you would stay no more than one summer—it's been four years! I've stagnated my own son, my one and only. Oh, how did this transpire? We brought you to this country, and for what? Even the stupid native-born do better than you…"

On and on she went, through a barrage of tears, gurgling and explosive nasal contretemps, about the joys of going to college and then law school, the lack of status in being a desk slave for a nonprofit agency, *working for eight dollars an hour* while his contemporaries were going full steam ahead with their professional educations. Gradually, her soft, steady wail increased in tempo and pitch, until she reminded Vladimir of a devout woman at a Middle Eastern funeral the moment her son's coffin is lowered into the ground.

Vladimir sat back and sighed loudly in protest. She couldn't stop, not even on his birthday.

It had taken his own father a year of courtship and a decade of marriage to adapt to Mother's talent of bawling at will. "Don't cry. Oh, why are you crying, little porcupine?" the young Dr. Girshkin would whisper to his wife in their dim Leningrad apartment as he ran his hands through her hair, hair darker than the exhaust hanging over the city, hair which even strong Western hair-curlers could not curl (they called her *Mongolka,* and she was, indeed, one-eighth Mongolian). Intermittent flashes of neon would illuminate the tears descending her oblong face as the meat-store sign positioned directly below their flat struggled to keep alight in the erratic power grid. He would never forgive her for not responding to his caresses until late into the night, when she fell asleep and instinctively curled into his shoulder, long after somebody had mercifully put out the MEAT sign and the streets surrendered to the foggy and indiscernible Petersburg darkness.

Vladimir, as well, suffered under his mother's accusative wails as B-plus report cards were ceremonially burned in the fireplace; as china was sent flying for chess-club prizes not won; as he once caught her in her study sobbing at three in the morning, cradling a photo of the three-year-old Vladimir playing with a toy abacus, so bright-eyed, so enterprising, so full of hope...But the coup de grace took place during the wedding of a California Girshkin when Mother publicly broke down and accused Vladimir—shyly disco-dancing with a fat cousin—of having "the hips of a homosexual." Oh, those sensuous hips!

Guilt-ridden and confused, Vladimir looked to his father for reinforcement, or at least an explanation, but one was not forth-coming until his early teens, when his father took him on a long autumn walk through swampy, gaseous Alley Pond Park—Queens' gift to the nation's forests—allowing his mouth to expel the word "divorce" for the first of many times.

"Your mother suffers from a kind of madness," he had said. "In a very real and medical way."

And Vladimir, young and tiny but already a child of America, said, "Aren't there pills she can take?" But the holistic-minded Dr. Girshkin did not believe in pills. A strenuous alcohol rubdown and a hot *banya* were his universal prescriptions.

Even now, when Vladimir felt more detached from her sobs than ever, he remained at a loss for what to say in order to bring them to an end. His father had never figured it out either. Nor did he ever gather the courage to go through with his meticulously planned divorce. Mother was, for all her faults, his sole friend and confidante in the New World.

"*Bozhe moi,* Vladimir," wept Vladimir's mother, and then she stopped abruptly. She did something with the phone: it beeped. For a moment there was nothing. "I'm putting you on hold, Vladimir," she said finally. "There's a call from Singapore. It could be important."

An instrumental version of "Michael, Row Your Boat Ashore" blared from the electronic bowels of Mother's corporation and into Vladimir's ear.

It was time to go. Mr. Rybakov, left unattended, had stumbled back into the reception room and was terrorizing the security guard once more. Vladimir was close to hanging up when Mother returned with a whimper. Vladimir cut her off: "So how are things with you?"

"Terrible," said Mother, switching to English, which meant job-talk. She blew her nose. "I have to fire someone in office."

"Good for you," Vladimir said.

"Is big complication," groaned Mother. "He is American African. I am nervous I will say something wrong. My English not so good. You must teach me to be sensitive to Africans this weekend. It is important skill, no?"

"I'm coming over this weekend?" said Vladimir.

His mother made an effort to laugh and told him how insane it would be not to have a birthday barbecue. "You're only twenty-five once," she said. "And you are not a—How you say? A complete loss."

"I'm not on crack, for one thing," Vladimir volunteered cheerfully.

"And you're not homo," said his mother. "Hmm?"

"Why do you always—"

"Still with Jewish girl. Little Challah-bread."

"Yes," Vladimir reassured her. Yes, yes, yes.

Mother exhaled deeply. "Well, that's good," she said. She told him to bring his swimming trunks on Saturday because the pool might be fixed by then. She managed to both sigh and kiss Vladimir good-bye at the same time. "Be strong," was her last, enigmatic bit of advice.

THE LOBBY OF MR. RYBAKOV'S BUILDING, the Dorchester Towers, was centered around a tapestry depicting the Dorchester coat of arms, a double-headed eagle clutching a scroll in one beak and a dagger in the other—the graphic story of New Money and how it got that way. Two doormen opened the door for Vladimir and his client. A third one gave Vladimir a piece of candy.

Displays of wealth, American-style, always made Vladimir feel as if Mother was behind him, whispering into his ear her favorite bilingual nickname for him: *Failurchka.* Little Failure. Woozy with spite, he leaned against an elevator wall, trying to ignore the rich red glow of Burmese Padauk wood, praying that Rybakov's apartment would be one hovel of a penthouse, government-subsidized and littered with crap.

But the elevator doors opened to reveal a sunny, cream-colored waiting hall, outfitted with sleek Alvar Aalto chairs and an ingenious wrought-iron torchiere. "Right this way, pork chop…" said Rybakov. "Follow me…"

They gained the living room, which was also inoffensively cream-colored except for what looked like a Kandinsky triptych taking up an entire wall. Beneath the Kandinsky, two sets of sofas and recliners were arranged around a projection television. Beyond was a dining room where an overextended chandelier hung centimeters above a grand rosewood table. As big as the apartment was, the furniture seemed destined for a place even bigger. Just wait and see, said the furniture.

Vladimir took in this tableau as slowly as he could, his gaze settling, of course, on the Kandinsky. "The painting…" Vladimir managed to say.

"Oh, *that*. It's just something Miss Harosset picked up at auction. She keeps trying to sell me on abstract expressionism. But just look at that thing! This Kanunsky guy was obviously some sort of a pederast. Ah, let me tell you, Volodya, I'm a simple man. I ride the subway and iron my own shirts. I don't need money or modern art! A cozy outhouse, some dried fish, a young woman to call out my name… This is my philosophy!"

"Miss Harosset," Vladimir said. "She's… your social worker?"

Mr. Rybakov laughed brightly. "Yeah, social worker," he said. "That's it exactly. Ah, Volodya, you're lucky to be so young. Now sit down. I'll make tea. Don't let these fool you." He waved a crutch at Vladimir. "I'm a sailor!"

He disappeared through a pair of French doors. Vladimir sat down at one end of the table, more appropriate for a state dinner than for a sip of tea, and looked around. A string instrument not unlike a Russian balalaika hung on one wall along with several yellowing military certificates. On the opposite wall, there was only a framed black-and-white photograph showing the face of a frowning young man bearing the Fan Man's thick brows and light green eyes. A cold sore stretched along much of his pouted lower lip like an excavation in progress.

Beneath the photo stood a simple nightstand on which perched a wide-blade fan, its metal chassis gleaming.

"I see introductions are in order," Rybakov said, wheeling in a cart with a miniature samovar, a bottle of vodka, and plates filled with matjes herring and Riga sprats. "Fan, this is Vladimir. Vladimir, Fan."

"It's a pleasure to meet you," Vladimir said to the Fan. "I've heard such wonderful things."

The Fan said not a word.

"The Fan's a little tired," Mr. Rybakov said, stroking the blades with a velvet cloth. "We spent all last night drinking and singing hooligan songs. 'Murka, oh, my Murka…Oh, my darling Murka… Hello my Murka and goodbye!' Do you know that one?"

"You betrayed our romance…" Vladimir sang. "Oh, my darling Murka…And for that, my Murka, you will die!"

"What a beautiful voice you have," Mr. Rybakov cheered. "Maybe we can form a little impromptu singing society. The Red Army Choir in Exile. What do you say, Fan?"

The Fan remained silent.

"Do you know that he's my best friend?" Rybakov suddenly said of the Fan. "My son's gone, Miss Harosset's running around doing the Devil's work, so who else is there for me? I remember when we first met. I had just landed at Kennedy Airport, my son was being held up in customs—the Interpol fellows wanted to have a little heart-to-heart with him…And then the women from the local Hebrew society came by to give money to the arriving Jews. Well, they took one look at my Christian mug and they gave me a salami instead, and some of that awful American cheese…And then—I guess it was because of the jungle heat that summer—the Hebrews took pity on me and gave me my Fan. He was so spontaneous. Right away, we started chatting like a pair of old shipmates! We haven't been apart since that day."

"I haven't made many friends in this country either," Vladimir mused quietly. "It's hard for us Russians to make friends here. Sometimes I get so lonely—"

"Yes, yes," Mr. Rybakov interrupted, "Very nice, Vladimir, but the day is short, so let us forget our sadness and talk like men." He cleared his throat, then continued magisterially.

3. FATHERS AND SONS

"VLADIMIR, THE FAN WISHES TO RELATE TO YOU A story. A *secret* story."

"Do you like secrets, Volodya?"

"Well, to be truthful—" Vladimir said.

"Sure, everyone likes secrets. Now, our secret story begins with a father and son, both born and raised in the great port city of Odessa. You see, Volodya, a closer father and son there could never be, even though this father, a sailor by profession, was often sailing around the world and had to leave the son in the care of his many lovers. Arrr," Mr. Rybakov growled with evident pleasure. He settled into a nearby recliner and adjusted the pillows.

"Each long separation weighed on the father's heart," he said, closing his eyes. "At sea, he would often conduct imaginary conversations with his son, even if the cook, Akhmetin, that lousy Chechen, would make fun of him mercilessly and undoubtedly would spit in his soup. But then, one day in the late 1980s...guess what happened? Socialism started to collapse! And so, without further thought, the father and son immigrated to Brooklyn.

"Horrible circumstances," Rybakov complained. "A studio apartment. Spanish people everywhere. Oh, the plight of the poor!

Now, the son, Tolya was his name but everyone called him the Groundhog (that's a funny story too, how he got that name)... Anyway, the son was happy to be reunited with his *papatchka,* but he was still a young man. He wanted to bring a girl over, to screw her thoroughly from top to bottom. It wasn't easy on him, believe me. And there was no work around that really took advantage of his natural intelligence. Maybe a few Greeks hired him to blow up their diners for insurance purposes. He was proficient in these matters, so boom boom—" Rybakov took a big slurp of vodka. "Boom boom. He made ten, twenty thousand like that, but still the son was restless. He was a genius, see?" The Fan Man pointed to his head for clarification.

Vladimir touched his own head in agreement. The combination of tea and vodka was making him sweat. He fumbled in his pocket for a tissue, but found only the ten hundred-dollar bills Rybakov had given him. The bills felt crisp, almost starched; for some reason, Vladimir wanted to put them inside his underwear, feel them cosset his privates. "And then the son got a special tip," Mr. Rybakov went on. "He made a connection. He went first to London, then to Cyprus, then to Prava."

Prava? Vladimir perked up. The Paris of the 90s? The stomping ground of America's artistic elite? The SoHo of Eastern Europe?

"Oh, yes," the Fan Man continued, as if he had sensed Vladimir's disbelief. "Eastern Europe. That's where you make the money these days. And sure enough, in a couple of years the son takes over Prava, the cowed natives bending to his will. He runs the taxi racket at the airport, arms contraband from Ukraine to Iran, caviar from the Caspian Sea to Brighton Beach, opium from Afghanistan to the Bronx, prostitutes in the main square, right outside the Kmart. And he sends his lucky father money every week. Now that's a thankful son. Could've put Papa in a nursing home or a psycho farm, which is what children do in these cynical times."

Mr. Rybakov opened his eyes and turned to Vladimir, who was nervously fingering his balding temples.

"So," Rybakov said, "now that the Fan is silent, there's time for us to think the story over. How do we feel about this interesting tale? Are we outraged, in a kind of American way, about the activities of the son? Are we worried about the prostitution and the contraband and the diners blowing up—"

"Well," Vladimir said. "The story does raise some issues." The Rule of Law, that bedrock of Western democracy—that was one issue. "But we do have to remember," Vladimir said, "that we are poor Russians, that we live in difficult times for our homeland, and that we often have to take special measures to feed our families, to survive."

"Yes! An excellent answer!" said the Fan Man. "You're still a *russki muzhik,* not like some of these assimilationist children with their law degrees. The Fan is pleased. Now, Vladimir, I must make a clean breast of it—I baited you up here for more than just herring and vodka and the reminiscences of a tired old man.

"This morning, the Fan and I had a conference call with my son, the Groundhog, in Prava. He, too, is a big fan of your mother. He knows that the son of Yelena Petrovna Girshkin will not disappoint us. Oh, Vladimir, stop with your modesty! I won't hear of it! 'I'm not my mama's son!' he cries. 'I'm a simple man!' You're a little cucumber, that's what you are...

"Well, cucumber, the Fan and I are pleased to offer you the following proposition: Get me my citizenship, and my son will make you an associate director in his organization. The minute I'm naturalized you'll have a first-class ticket to Prava. He'll turn you into a schemer of the first rank. A modern businessman. A...how do you Jews say it...? A *gonif.* Job pays more than eight dollars an hour, that's for certain. Requires knowledge of English and Russian. Candidate should be Soviet and American all at once. Interested?"

Vladimir crossed his legs and brought himself forward; he hugged himself in this position and shuddered a little. But all this physical melodrama was ridiculous. From a logistical standpoint, there was simply nothing there. He was not going to become a mafioso in Eastern Europe. He was the coddled single child of Westchester parents who had once paid twenty-five thousand dollars a year to send him to a progressive Midwestern college. True, Vladimir was not known to traverse a well-defined moral landscape, but trafficking arms to Iran was definitely off his map.

And yet, in the very back of his mind, a window opened and Mother leaned out shouting for all to hear: "Soon my Little Failure will be a Big Success!"

Vladimir shut that window with a bang. "There's really no need for this, Mr. Rybakov," he said. "I will refer your case to my agency's lawyer. He will help you fill out the Freedom of Information Act form. We will find out why your citizenship application was denied."

"Yes, yes. My son and the Fan are of a like mind on this issue as well: You are a Jew, and a Jew isn't stupid; you have to give him something to make it worth his while. I'm sure you're familiar with the old Russian proverb: If there's no water in the sink, then the Yids have had their drink..."

"But Mr. Rybakov—"

"Now, listen to me, Girshkin! Citizenship is everything! A man who doesn't belong to a country is not a man. He is a tramp. And I am too old to be a tramp." There was a moment of silence save for the smacking sounds the old sailor made with his fleshy lips. "Would you be so kind," he whispered, "as to set the Fan to high. He wants to sing a song in celebration of our new understanding."

"Just press the HIGH button?" Vladimir asked, his stomach sounding the requisite music of nervousness. *What new under-*

standing? "My mother says first you must set a fan to medium and then after a while set it to high, because otherwise the motor—"

Mr. Rybakov raised his hand to cut him off. "Service the Fan as you will," he said. "You're a good young man and I trust you with him."

Vladimir felt the heaviness of the word "trust" in Russian, a favorite in the Girshkin household. He rose without ceremony and went over to the fan, pressing the button marked MEDIUM. The apartment was centrally air-conditioned but the new breeze, a fist of cool air punching through the general coldness, was welcome. He hit the button marked HIGH and the blades visibly doubled their effort, their buzz now punctuated by internal creaks and pops.

"I ought to grease him again," whispered Rybakov. "You can hardly hear him with all that creaking."

Vladimir stumbled for a response, but came out with a sort of mooing sound.

"Shh, listen," said his host. "Listen to the song. Do you know this song?" The Fan Man let out a series of raspy creaks himself, and then Vladimir realized that he was singing along:

"Ta-pa-pa-ra-ra-ra-ra Moscow nights.

"Pa-ra-ra-ra-ra-pa-ra-ra

"I won't forget you

"Pa-ra-ra-ra-ra Moscow nights."

"Yes, I know that song!" Vladimir said. "Ta-pa-pa-ra-ra Moscow nights…"

They sang the verse several times, occasionally substituting remembered words for the "pa-ra-ra." Perhaps it was his imagination, but Vladimir could hear the fan keeping tempo with them, if not actually prodding them into the bittersweet ditty.

"Give me your hand," said Mr. Rybakov, opening a creased, vein-ridden palm on the table. "Just put your hand there," he said.

Vladimir looked at his own hand carefully as if he was about to place it inside the fan's grating. Such slender fingers...They said slender fingers would be good for piano, but you had to start early for that. Mozart was—

He placed his hand into the warmth of the Fan Man's palm and felt it close around him like a python over a rabbit. "The Fan is spinning," said Mr. Rybakov and squeezed hard.

Vladimir looked at the spinning fan and thought of his parents and their upcoming weekend barbecue. "Pa-ra-ra-ra-ra Moscow nights." They sang it in Brighton Beach and they sang it in Rego Park, and they sang it on WEVD, New York—"We Speak Your Language"—that the Girshkins had always left the radio tuned to, even when his first American friends from Hebrew school came over to play computer games and they heard the "Pa-ra-ra-ra..." and the two-dollar synthesizer orchestra in the background, and saw his parents at the kitchen table singing along while munching on the verboten pork cutlets, slurping down the mushroom-and-barley soup.

Mr. Rybakov released Vladimir's hand and patted it casually, as one pets a favored dog after it returns with the morning papers. He slumped over the side of his recliner. "Be so kind as to get the bed-pan from my bedroom," he said.

4. WOMEN AND THE VLADIMIR QUESTION

SEVERAL HERRINGS LATER, VLADIMIR BID HIS CLIENT farewell and returned to his humble Alphabet City lodgings. He was due to celebrate his birthday with "little Challah-bread," his lover. But as fate had provided, on this particular day Challah was summoned to the Dungeon, the Chelsea whipping cavern. Four Swiss bankers, recent transplants to New York, had found that in addition to their jobs restructuring Third World debt, they had in common the need to be humiliated by a mother figure, someone a little more substantial than the Dungeon's standard fare. And so Challah's beeper had registered the code $$URGENT$$. Off she went with a little metal box full of dick rings and nipple clamps, to be back by nine, she promised, which left Vladimir with some time alone.

First he took a long cold shower. It was ninety degrees outside that day; inside, a good hundred. Then, naked and washed, he happily roamed around the two-and-a-half rooms of their railroad flat, traversing the narrow path where his urbane belongings and Challah's junk had once gone to war, and were now separated by an unofficial Green Line.

This was already Vladimir's third year of living apart from his parents but the exhilaration of having escaped their tender clutches simply would not cease. He was acquiring a homeowner's mentality. He dreamed of someday cleaning house, of turning the gap between the kitchen and the bedroom, which was now referred to as the "living room" into a personal study.

And what would Vladimir study in his study? Vladimir was partial to short fiction—brief, thoughtful stories where people suffered quickly and acutely. For instance, the Chekhov story where the horse-cab driver tells all his fares that his son has died the other day and nobody cares. Terrible. Vladimir had first read that one in Leningrad, lying as he always did in his sick bed, while Mother and Grandmother fussed in the next room, concocting bizarre Russian folk cures for his bronchial illnesses.

The driver story ("Heartache" its simple name) was shorthand for the young Vladimir's melancholy existence, the growing sense of the bed as his true home. A home away from the sepulchral Leningrad cold, where once he had played hide-and-seek with his father beneath the giant bronze feet of the Lenin statue, its sooty outstretched arm pointing ever upward to the brilliant future. Away from the primary school, where the few times he was deemed well enough to strap on his bright, creaseless uniform and make an appearance, children and teacher alike stared at him as if he was a cosmonaut stricken with the Andromeda Strain, erroneously released from quarantine. And away from Seryozha Klimov, the overfed hooligan—his parents had already given him a crash course in the social sciences—who would come up to him during recess, and gleefully yell, "Jew, Jew, Jew…"

So, you see, young Vladimir had been more than willing to accept the loss of his freedom and formal education, if only he would be left alone with his warm feather bed and his Chekhov and his good friend Yuri the Stuffed Giraffe. But Mother and Grandmother and Father, when he returned from work at the hospital, would not leave him in peace. They fought his bronchial asthma without respite and with the entire *Soviet Medical Encyclopedia* and several less reliable tracts at their disposal. They would roll Vladimir's pale body into hourly rubbing alcohol compresses, hold his face within centimeters of a boiling pot of potatoes, and practice the surreal ritual of "cupping": A set of small glass cups was painfully attached (after a lit match was used to create a vacuum inside each vessel) across the length of Vladimir's back in order to suck out the phlegm that rumbled through the invalid's body. The Stegosaurus Effect, Dr. Girshkin called the wretched rows of glass assembled on his son's back.

NOW THE HEALTHY, older Vladimir paced the length of his imaginary study, in which his childhood volume of Chekhov would share pride of place with newer acquisitions: a martini shaker from the Salvation Army, a biography of William Burroughs, a tiny cigarette lighter cleverly embedded within a hollowed pebble. Yes, the inside of the apartment was becoming too cluttered for Chekhov—there were Challah's batons and whips and jars of K-Y to consider, not to mention the cheap Fourteenth Street spice racks that kept falling off their hooks, and the numerous buckets of cold water Vladimir kept around the kitchen and bedroom so that he could dunk his head when he could no longer stand the temperate status quo. But still, what a pleasure to be alone. To talk to oneself as if to a best friend. His actual best friend, Baobab, was still down in Miami, being venal and unsavory.

AND THEN IT WAS TIME. Challah was at the door fighting the locks. Vladimir closed his mind, worked himself up an erection, and went out to greet her. There she was. But even before he took in her workday face—the lipstick, mascara, and blush melting down in the heat, drawing a second ethereal face a notch below her all-too-real one—she was embracing him and whispering "happy birthday" in his ear, for unlike every other well-wisher of the day, Challah wanted to say it quietly.

Dear Challah with the warm, flat nose, the enormous eyelashes tickling his cheeks, the heavy nasal breathing—queen of everything musky and mammal-like. Soon she noticed what Vladimir had been preparing for her below, the aardvark's tubular snout poking out from within its wiry hedge, and said, "Goodness," in perfect mock surprise. She began unlatching the safety pins that kept together the swatches of black fabric she wore to the Dungeon but Vladimir said, "No, I must do it!"

"Be careful," she said. "Don't rip anything." She made sure he remained erect while he undressed her; the undressing went on for some time. When she was done, only the iron crucifixes remained against her heavy breasts, reminding Vladimir of artillery pieces scattered about a plain. Finally, with her crosses jangling, and his member in hand, Challah took Vladimir into the bedroom.

On the futon, he recalled his mandate: be thorough. He kissed, rubbed his nose against, tugged with his teeth, pinched between thumb and middle finger, poked with what Challah had termed the Girshkin Gherkin, every part of her, even parts that he had grown weary of with the passage of time: the folds that collected on top of her hips, her arms, thick and pink, that pressed him to her not lust-fully but the way he envisioned a mother would grasp her child at the approach of an avalanche.

Finally, when he felt a full gathering of steam between his legs, he went between hers, and for the first time, looked into her face. Dear Challah, dear American friend, with that crimson look of arousal, but also with the restraint to keep Vladimir from biting into her neck or plunging into her mouth, just so she could look into his eyes when they were this close.

So Vladimir closed his eyes. And had a vision.

DRESSED IN LIGHTWEIGHT COTTON CHINOS and tunic, a brown Nat Sherman's cigarette implanted in his mouth, his hair fashionably cut short and continuously waved over to one side by a playful summer wind, Vladimir Borisovich Girshkin issued directives into a cellular phone as he walked along an airstrip. Granted, it was a lousy airstrip. There was not even a plane. But a series of properly spaced white lines etched into the cracked concrete could only mean an airstrip (or else a provincial highway, but, no, that couldn't be).

While in bed, the blind, naked Vladimir was keeping up his *hump hump* with Challah in a desperate bid to orgasm, his fashionable doppelganger in the vision was making progress against the substantial length of the airstrip, beyond which a half-circle of the setting sun, bloated and patchy like rotting fruit, peeked out from the confluence of two gray mountains. Vladimir could clearly see the new Vladimir, his purposeful gait, his agitated face spanning the range of ill humor, but he could not understand precisely what he was saying into the cellular, why the airstrip was isolated by scrub fields on all sides save for the mountains, why he could not daydream himself a plane, fabulous companions, and a set of filled champagne flutes...

And then, just as the coital Vladimir was to reach his elusive target with Challah, the imaginary Vladimir heard a rumble, a boom, a sonic displacement directly above him. A hawk-nosed turbo prop was skirting the runway, headed directly for our hero, flying low enough for him to see the lone figure in the cockpit, or at least the lunatic glimmer in the pilot's eye that could only have belonged to one man. "I'm coming for you, boy!" Mr. Rybakov was shouting into Vladimir's cellular. "Away we go!"

HE OPENED HIS EYES. His face was sandwiched in between Challah's shoulder blades where a constellation of beauty marks formed a soup ladle. The ladle lifted and lowered with her breathing, a lock of her orange hair fell into it.

Vladimir propped himself up on one elbow. In her free time Challah had repainted their bedroom a dentist's-office mauve. She had arranged overlapping retro posters (condensed-milk advertisements and the like) across the ceiling. She had gone out and bought a squash, which now rotted in the corner. "Why did you close your eyes?" she asked.

"What?" He knew what.

"You know what."

"Most people close their eyes. I was overcome."

She burrowed her head into the middle of a pillow, swelling up the sides. "You were not overcome."

"Are you saying I don't love you?"

"You're saying you don't love me."

"This is ridiculous."

She turned around but covered herself with her arms and drew in her legs. "How can you say 'this is ridiculous'? People don't say things like that unless they just don't give a shit. How can you be so flippant? 'This is ridiculous.' How can you be so detached?"

"I'm a foreigner. I speak slowly and choose my words with care, lest I embarrass myself."

"How can you say *that*?"

"Well, what the hell am I allowed to say?"

"I'm fat!" she shouted. She glanced around as if looking for something to throw, then grabbed a roll of her own flesh, the one that collected beneath her breasts before her stomach began. "Say the truth!"

The truth?

"You hate me!"

No, that wasn't the truth exactly. Vladimir didn't hate her. He hated the *idea* of her, but that was different. Still, it was Vladimir who had invited this big woman into his life, and now there was no recourse but to sift through his meager vocabulary of comforting words, to put together the proper blandishments. You're not fat, he thought, you're *fully realized.* But before he could voice those tenuous thoughts, he noticed a large, complicated insect, a sort of roach with wings, hovering directly beneath the canopy of posters. Vladimir moved to defend his crotch.

In the meantime, Challah had let go of her roll of flesh, which fell in luxuriously with its grander compatriot, the stomach. She turned back into her pillow and breathed in so deeply that Vladimir was sure she was going to exhale in tears.

"There's a strange insect coming down on you," Vladimir preempted her.

Challah looked up. "A-a—"

They scampered off the futon as the beast landed between them. "Give me my T-shirt," Challah demanded, once again covering herself with her arms as best she could.

The intruder crawled along the crests and ridges of their bed sheets the way a big-rig truck weaves along a mountain highway, then executed a great leap forward into Vladimir's pillow. It was really something! In Leningrad the roaches were small and lacked initiative.

Challah leaned over and blew at the monster hopefully, but its wings began to stir and she drew back. "God, I just want to go to sleep," she said, putting on her long T-shirt with a childhood character Vladimir was not familiar with, a comical blue imp. "I've been up since six. An assistant DA wanted an entire tea service set up on his back."

"You're not submitting?"

She shook her head.

"If some lawyer touches you —"

"No one's touching me. They know."

He came around the bed and put his arm around her. She pulled away a little. He kissed her shoulder and before he could do otherwise, he started to cry—it happened very easily sometimes, now that his father was not around to object. She held him and he felt himself a very small man in her arms. On the futon, the insect remained in charge, so they went out to the fire escape and smoked cigarettes. She was crying too now with the cigarette in her hand, wiping her nose into her palm so that Vladimir worried her hair would catch fire from the cigarette, and he moved to clean her nose for her.

They drank a cheap Hungarian riesling that spelled "headache" after the third glass. They held hands. The lights were going out at the Garibaldi nursing home across the street, a five-story residence built in the sixties to prove how closely a building could resemble Formica. The Jamaican record store on the first floor, three Bob Marley records and a lot of dope for sale, was gearing up for the night's business, the volume of the reggae constrained by the whims of the sleepy Garibaldi denizens across the street. Along with the cops, they had reached a sort of negotiated settlement, Alphabet City style, with the profitable Rastafarians. Everyone left everyone alone, the music stayed low.

"Hey, in three months I'll be twenty-five," she said.

"It's no big deal, turning twenty-five," Vladimir said. Immediately he felt bad. Maybe it was a big deal to her. "I just got a thousand dollars from a client," Vladimir said. "Maybe we can go to a nice French restaurant for your birthday. The one with that famous *plat de mer*. I read about it in the paper. Four kinds of oysters, a very special crawfish—"

"A client gave you a thousand dollars," Challah said. "What did you have to do to him?"

"Nothing!" Vladimir said. He shuddered at the implication. "It was just a tip. I'm helping him get his citizenship. Anyway, this *plat de mer*..."

"You know I hate those slimy things," Challah said. "Let's just go out for a really good hamburger. Like at that fancy diner. The one we went to for Baobab's birthday."

Hamburger? She wanted to eat a hamburger on her twenty-fifth birthday? Vladimir remembered his parents upcoming barbecue, an event replete with many hamburgers. Could he invite Challah? Could she wear something decent? Could she pretend she was attending medical school where Vladimir had discreetly placed her in the Girshkin family imagination?

"That fancy diner sounds perfect," Vladimir said, kissing Challah's peeling lips. "We'll get Caesar's salads for everyone, gourmet relish, pitchers of sangria, the works..." And the next time they had sex he would keep his eyes open. He would look into her eyes directly. This is what one did to keep a relationship going. These were the desperate measures. Vladimir knew the drill. Preserving his fief, no matter how meager, this is what it meant to be an older, wiser Vladimir.

5. THE HOME FRONT

THE WEEKEND FOUND DR. GIRSHKIN SWEATING BE-neath the midday sun, his bald spot browning like a flapjack on the griddle, as he gestured about with a giant beefsteak tomato. "It is the biggest tomato in New York State," he told Vladimir as he showed it off from every angle possible. "I must write to the Ministry of Agriculture. Maybe they have a prize for someone like me."

"You're a masterful gardener," whispered Vladimir, trying to hustle some encouragement into his faltering voice.

It wasn't easy. Having spent this strange June morning watching oversized radishes bask in the suburban haze, Vladimir had noticed a new and disturbing fact about his father: His father was old. He was a short, bald man, not unlike Vladimir when it came to his slight frame and dark oval face. And although his chest remained firm from the constant fishing and gardening, the black carpet of hair covering it had recently turned gray, his perfect posture had deteriorated, and his long aquiline nose had never looked so frail and thin, the skin around it so sun-wrinkled.

"You know, if the dollar collapses, and we're all reduced to an agrarian lifestyle," Vladimir said, "this one tomato can be an entire entrée."

"Why, sure," the doctor said. "A big vegetable can go a long way.

There were times during the war when one carrot would feed a family for days. For instance, during the siege of Leningrad, your grandma and I, well…if truth be told, we were nowhere near Leningrad. We fled to the Ural Mountains at the start of the war. But there was nothing to eat there either. All we had was Tolik the Hog. A big fellow—we ate him for five years. We even bartered jars of lard for yarn and kerosene. The whole household ran off that hog." He looked sadly at his son as if he wished he had saved a tail-bone or some other memento. Then he had another idea.

"Mother!" he shouted to Vladimir's grandmother, dozing in her wheelchair underneath the giant oaks that delineated the Girshkins' property from that of their supposedly megalomaniac Indian neighbor. "Remember that hog we had? Tolik?"

Grandma lifted the brim of her floppy straw hat with her good hand. "What did you say?"

"Tolik the Hog," shouted Vladimir's father.

Grandma's eyes widened. "So how come that swine never writes me, that's what I want to know," she said, waving a little fist at the doctor and his son. "Boston is close enough, you'd think he'd come down and visit me. I practically raised that bastard after his mother died."

"No, not Cousin Tolik," Dr. Girshkin shouted. "I'm talking about Tolik the Hog. Remember, during the war? In the Urals? He got so big we rode him into town. Remember the hog?"

"Oh," said Grandma. "Oh, yes. I remember a beast. But it wasn't a hog, it was a cow, and her name was Masha."

"Masha was after the war!" shouted Dr. Girshkin. He turned to Vladimir. Father and son briefly looked at each other and shrugged, each in his own way.

"Why would we have a hog?" reasoned Grandma, slowly wheeling herself over from her self-designated post, leaving the oaks defenseless before the Indian and his mythical power saw. "We're

Jewish, aren't we? Sure, your wife eats that pork salami from the Russian store, and I do too sometimes, because that's what's in the refrigerator. But an entire hog?"

She settled her bewildered gaze on the tomato patch.

"She's nearing the sunset, slowly but surely," said Dr. Girshkin. "Sometimes she thinks there's two of me. The good Boris and the evil Boris. If I let her guard the oak trees until she falls asleep, and that can be as late as eight or nine o'clock, then I'm the good Boris. The one that's not married to your mother. If I take her in early, she'll curse at me like a sailor. And you know that in the autumn it gets damn cold no matter how many jackets I put on her."

"That's what awaits us all," Vladimir said, which was the Girshkin family's definitive pronouncement on aging and mortality. It was a perfect time to say it, too, for there they were now, assembled in a perfect row—three generations of Girshkins in sad decline: Grandma getting ready to say good-bye to this world, his father already with one toe in the grave, and Vladimir, the third generation, going through all the motions of a living death.

But the first to go would be Grandma, that devoted country *baba* who had once bought Vladimir his first American cotton windbreaker—the only grown-up to realize that his trendy Hebrew school chums were making fun of his ill-fitting overcoat with its inherent East Bloc smell; the only one to understand the pain in being called a Stinky Russian Bear.

Grandma's first stroke happened five years ago. For some time she had suspected Tselina Petrovna, her clueless neighbor, of a dastardly plan to denounce her to the Social Security Administration and steal her subsidized apartment. One quiet, snowy night it would happen. The Black Marias would roll up to her building, there would be a knock on the door, and the Social Security Police would drag Grandma away.

Grandma begged Vladimir to translate a letter of denouncement against Tselina, citing her for being a British spy. Or was it an East German spy? A Russian, French, or Finnish spy? Everything was topsy-turvy in this country. "Tell me what kind of spy!" Grandma shouted at Vladimir.

Her grandson tried to humor her, but Grandma wept and accused the family of abandoning her. That same night she had the stroke. After the stroke she had a heart attack and then another stroke.

The doctors were astounded by the resiliency of her body, attributing it to her long life in the countryside. Yet even after she was wheelchair-bound and paralyzed on one side, Grandma could not shake her belief that the Social Security men were due any minute. It happened to her cousin Aaron in Kiev in 1949. A pianist by profession, he had had half his fingers amputated in a frozen Kamchatka labor camp. There were lessons to be learned from that.

Finally, Vladimir's father moved Grandma out to the suburbs, where she soon found a new enemy in the face of the "murderous, tree-chopping Hindu" of a neighbor, who had once remarked on the size and beauty of the oak trees straddling the property line. And that's how her heroic vigil in the backyard began.

Vladimir stood behind Grandmother patting her sparse hair. He found a space between two moles atop the warm, wrinkled globe of her forehead and kissed her there, eliciting an astonished look from his father, Grandmother's official keeper. *What's this?* Dr. Girshkin seemed to be saying. *Co-conspirators in my own house?*

"Of course, there's no hog, *babushka*," Vladimir spoke softly. "Who raises hogs in Westchester? It's just not done."

Grandmother grabbed his hand and bit it affectionately with both of her teeth. "My dear one!" she said. "My only one!" And she was right. They were in this together. Mother and Father may have gone ahead and become rich Americans, but Grandma and

Vladimir were still of the same blood, as if a generation had been skipped between them.

After all, she had raised Vladimir, teaching him to write Cyrillic letters when he was four, awarding two grams of cheese for every Slavonic squiggle mastered. She would take him each Sunday to the Piskaryovko mass grave for the defenders of Leningrad—that most instructive of Russia's field trips—where they would leave fresh daisies for his grandfather Moysei, a slight, thoughtful man shyly holding on to Grandma's elbow in wedding photos, who perished in a tank battle on the city's outskirts. And after this simple reckoning in front of a statue of the Motherland, weeping over an eternal flame, Grandma would ceremoniously tie a red handkerchief around Vladimir's neck. Asthma or not, she promised him, he would join the Red Pioneers someday and then the Komsomol Youth League and then, if he behaved himself well, the Communist Party. "To fight for the cause of Lenin and the Soviet people, are you ready!" she would drill him.

"Always ready!" he would shout back.

But, in the end, the Red Pioneers would have to march on without him...In the end, in the late 1970s, to be exact, the gentle, toothy American Jimmy Carter swapped tons of Midwestern grain for tons of Soviet Jews, and suddenly Vladimir and Grandmother found themselves walking out of the International Arrivals Building at JFK. They took one look at the endless America humming her Gershwin tune before them and cried in each other's arms.

And this was Grandma today—wheelchair-bound, imprisoned in one of the world's most expensive backyards, the rustle of stealth station wagons sliding into adjacent driveways, meat burning everywhere, her grandson a grown man with dark circles under his eyes who came to visit his family seasonally, as if they lived in the wilds of Connecticut and not some twenty kilometers beyond the Triborough Bridge.

Yes, Grandma deserved at least one more kiss from Vladimir, but kissing the old woman in front of his father made Vladimir uncomfortable. Grandmother was Dr. Girshkin's life, his burden and domain, just as Mother was Vladimir's. Perhaps after the barbecue, if he still felt this tender and bereft, he could smooch her in private.

"People! Opa!" They looked up. Mother was leaning out of her third-floor study, waving a bottle of rum. "He'll be twenty-six soon. Get out that grill!"

"TODAY I FOUND a new nickname for your father," Mother announced. "I'm calling him Stalin."

"Ha," Vladimir's father said, as he stuffed a flaming weenie into a bun for Grandma. "My wife warms my heart like a second sun."

"Stalin had very nice whiskers," Grandma encouraged her boy. "Now, let's drink, everybody! To Vladimir, our bright American future!"

Plastic cups were raised. "To our American future!"

"To our American future!" Mother toasted. "Well, I had a long talk with Vladimir this week, and I think he's sounding more mature."

"Is that true?" asked Dr. Girshkin of his son. "You told her you would become a lawyer?"

"Don't peg him, Iosef Vissarionovich," said Mother, using Stalin's patronymic. "There are a million mature things Vladimir can become."

"Computer," Grandma grunted. She considered computer programmers as men and women of immense power. The Social Security people were always checking their computer whenever Grandma braved a call to their offices, and they had the power to ruin her life!

"There you go," said Mother. "Grandma is crazy, but wise in her own way. I still say, though, you should be a lawyer. You were such a convincing little liar at the debating society, even with that horrific accent of yours. And I know it's no longer polite to talk about such things, but I must say the money is tremendous."

"I hear Eastern Europe is where you make the money these days," Vladimir said with a knowledgeable air. "This friend of mine, his son owns an import-export business in Prava. A Russian fellow by the name of Groundhog…"

"Groundhog?" Mother shouted. "Did you hear that, Boris? Our son is cavorting with some Russian Groundhog. Vladimir, I expressly forbid you to associate with any Groundhogs from this day forward."

"But he's a businessman," Vladimir said. "His father, Rybakov, lives in a penthouse. Perhaps he can get a job for me! Why, I thought you'd be pleased."

"We all know what kind of businessman calls himself Ground-hog," Mother said. "Where is he from? *Odessa?* An import-export business! A penthouse! If you want to be in real business, Vladimir, you have to listen to your mother. I'll help you get a management consulting job at McKinsey or Arthur Andersen. Then, if you're a good boy, I'll even pay for your MBA. Yes, that's the strategy we should pursue!"

"Prava," Dr. Girshkin mused, brushing stray drops of Coca-Cola from his whiskers. "Isn't that the Paris of the 90s?"

"Are you encouraging him, Stalin?" Mother threw down her hot dog like a gauntlet. "You want him to join the criminal element? Maybe he can be a consultant to your medical practice…Help you defraud our poor government. Why should we have only one crook in the family?"

"Medicare fraud is not really a crime," Dr. Girshkin said, clasping his hands in a professional manner. "What's more, my love, all my new patients are paying for your goddamn *dacha* in Sag Harbor. See, Volodya," he turned to his son, "there's a whole wave of Jewish Uzbeks on the way from Tashkent and Bukhara. Such sweet people. So new to Medicare. But it's just too much work for me. Last week I put in forty hours."

"Too much work!" Mother shouted. "Don't you ever say that in front of Vladimir. That's where his cult of sloth originates, you know. That's why he's keeping company with some Groundhog in his penthouse. He has hardly any role models in this family. I'm the only one who truly works in this house. You just slip your claims into the mailbox. Grandma—you're a pensioner."

Grandma took this to be her cue. "I think he's getting married to a *shiksa*," she said waving an accusative index finger at Vladimir.

"You're being crazy again, Mother," said Dr. Girshkin. "He's dating Challah. Little Challatchka."

"When do we get to meet Challatchka?" asked Vladimir's mother. "It's been how long? Almost a year?"

"How impolite," said Dr. Girshkin. "What are we...savages, that you're ashamed of us?"

"She's in summer school," Vladimir said. He uncovered the dessert plate full of imported Russian candies from his childhood, the chocolaty Clumsy Bear and the caramel-fudgy Little Cow. "All day long, taking classes," he mumbled. "She'll finish medical school in record time."

"She really is inspiring," Mother said. "Women seem more adjusted in this country anyway."

"Well, to women," said Vladimir's father, raising his cup. "And to the mysterious Challah who keeps our son's heart!" They toasted. It was time to set the hamburger meat aflame.

_____

AFTER IT WAS OVER, Mother lay in her mass-produced four-poster bed, nursing a bottle of rum, while Vladimir paced around her enormous berth lecturing on the topic of the day: Sensitivity to African-Americans. One black marketing director was about to be sacked, and Mother wanted to sack him "in the new, sensitive fashion."

In the course of an hour, Vladimir pitted everything he learned during his stint at the progressive Midwestern college against Mother's peerless Russian racism. "So what are you telling me?" Mother said when the lesson was over. "I should bring up the middle passage?"

Vladimir tried again to paint the big picture, but Mother was drunk. He told her as much. "So I'm drunk," said Mother. "You want a drink? Here—wait, no, you might have gotten herpes off that girl. There's a glass on the dresser."

Vladimir accepted a glassful of rum. Mother grabbed a post and hoisted herself up until she was on her knees. "Jesus, our Lord," she said, "please shepherd helpless Vladimir away from his tragic lifestyle, from the legacy his father bequeathed him, from the pauper's flat which he calls home, and from this criminal Groundhog…" She put her hands together but started to tip over.

Vladimir caught her by one shoulder. "That's a pretty prayer, Mother," he said. "But we're, you know…" He lowered his voice out of habit: *"Jewish."*

Mother looked at his face carefully, as if she had forgotten something and it had gone into hiding beneath one of Vladimir's thick brows. "Yes, I know that," she said, "but it's all right to pray to Jesus. Your grandfather was a gentile, you know, and his father was a deacon. And I still pray to the Jewish God, the main God, although, I have to say, he hasn't been helping much lately.

"I mean, what do you think?" she said.

"I don't know," said Vladimir. "I guess it's all right. Do you feel good when you pray like that? To Jesus and to…Isn't there something else? The Holy Something?"

"I'm not sure," said Mother. "I can look it up. I got a little brochure on the subway."

"Well, anyway," Vladimir said, "you can pray to everyone you want, just don't tell Father. With Grandma losing her mind, he's been more into the Jewish God than ever."

"That's what I've been doing!" Mother said. She grabbed Vladimir and held him against her tiny frame. "We're so much alike underneath all your stubbornness!" she said.

Vladimir gently detached himself from his mother and reached for the rum, which he drank from the bottle, herpes be damned. "You look good now," Mother said. "Like a real man. All you have to do is trim that homo ponytail." A teardrop formed in the corner of her left eye. Then one in the right. They overfilled and commenced to flow. "I'm not crying hysterically," Mother assured him.

Vladimir looked over his mother's peroxide-blond curls (no longer was she the *Mongolka* of Leningrad days). He surveyed the running mascara and soaked blush. "You look good, too," he said, shrugging his shoulders.

"Thank you," she sobbed.

He took out a tissue from his pants pocket and handed it to her. "It's clean," he said.

"You're a clean boy," she said, blowing her nose ferociously.

"I'm glad we had this talk," he said. "I think it's time for me to go home now." He walked over to the largest oak door in Scarsdale, New York, beheld its lucent door knob carved from Bohemian crystal, which he had always been too scared to smudge when he was a teenager; come to think of it, was scared still.

"Bye-bye," he said in English.

There was no answer. He turned around to take one last look. Mother was staring at his feet. "*Dosvedanya*," Vladimir said.

Mother continued to appraise his feet. "I'm leaving," Vladimir announced. "I'm going to go kiss Grandmother good-bye, then catch the 4:51 train." The thought of this train cheered him immediately. Express train to Manhattan now departing Scarsdale station. All aboard!

He was almost out of the woods. He was turning the knob, smudging the Bohemian crystal with all five fingers and a soft, sooty palm, when Mother issued a directive: "Vladimir, walk over to the window," she said.

"What's there?"

"Quickly, please. Without your father's trademark hesitation."

Vladimir did as he was told. He looked out the window. "What am I looking for?" he asked. "Grandma's by the oak trees again. She's throwing branches at the Indian."

"Forget your grandma, Vladimir. Walk back to the door. Just as I said, back to the door . . . Left foot, then the right foot . . . Now stop. Turn around. Back to the window once again. Walk naturally, the way you usually walk. Don't try to control your feet, let them fall where they may . . ." She paused. She cocked her head to one side. She got down on one knee and looked at his feet from a new angle. She got up slowly, wordlessly sizing up her son.

"So it is true," she said in a voice of complete exhaustion, a voice Vladimir remembered from their early American days, when she would run home from her English and typing lessons to make him his favorite Salad Olivier—potatoes, canned peas, pickles, and diced ham tossed with a half-jar of mayonnaise. Sometimes she'd fall asleep at the table of their tiny Queens flat, a long knife in one hand, an English-Russian dictionary in the other, a row of pickles lined up on the chopping block, their fate uncertain.

"What do you mean?" Vladimir said presently. "What is true?"

"Vladimir, how can I say this? Please don't be cross with me. I know you'll be cross with me, you're such a soft young man. But if I don't tell you the truth, will I be fulfilling my motherly duties? No, I will not. The truth then..." She sighed deeply, an alarming sigh, the sigh of exhaling the last doubt, the sigh of preparing for battle. "Vladimir," she said, "you walk like a Jew."

"What?"

"*What?* The anger in his voice. *What?* he says. *What?* Walk back to the window now. Just walk back to the window. Look at your feet. Look carefully. Look at how your feet are spread apart. Look at how you walk from side to side. Like an old Jew from the shtetl. Little Rebbe Girshkin. Oh, now he's going to scream at me! Or maybe he's going to cry. Either way, he's going to hurt his mother. That's how he repays his lifelong debt to her, by tearing her to shreds like a wolf.

"Oh, poor, poor Challah. Do you know how sorry I feel for your girlfriend, Vladimir... Think about it, how can a man love a woman when he despises his own mother? It can't be done. And how can a woman love a man who walks like a Jew? I honestly don't see what keeps you two together."

"I think many people walk the way I do," Vladimir whispered.

"Maybe in Amatevka," Mother said. "In the Vilnius ghetto, maybe. You know, I've been keeping an eye on you for years, but it just hit me today, your little Jew-walk. Come here, I'll teach you to walk like a normal person. Come here! No? He's shaking his head like a little three-year-old... You don't want to? Well, just stand there like an idiot, then!"

Vladimir was looking at her drawn and tired face, a residue of anger still pulsing along the upper lip. She was waiting for him, her patience ebbing, a slender laptop perched by the bedside urgently bleating for her attention. He wanted to comfort her. What could he do?

Perhaps, he resolved, perhaps he could improvise his own kind of love for his mother, cobbled together from past memories of an earlier mother—a harassed Leningrad kindergarten teacher and her love for her half-dead boy, the Soviet patriot, the best friend of Yuri the Stuffed Giraffe, the ten-year-old Chekhovian.

He could take her twice-a-day phone calls, pretend to listen dutifully to her screams and sobs, while holding the receiver several centimeters away from his face as if the telephone itself could explode.

He could lie to her, tell her he would do better, because even the invention of the lie meant he knew what was expected of him, knew that he was failing her.

And, undoubtedly, he could do one other thing for her.

It would be the least he could do…

VLADIMIR WALKED OVER to his mother, his feet a pair of Hebraic automatons steadily crossing the crisp parquet, wishing that he could Jew-walk his way back to Manhattan.

"Show me how it's done," Vladimir said.

Mother kissed both his cheeks and rubbed his shoulders, poking with her index finger at his spine. "Straighten up, *sinotchek,*" she said. My little son. He had been out of her good graces too long: that one word made him wheeze with pleasure. "My treasure," she added, knowing he would belong to her for the rest of the day, never mind the 4:51 train to Manhattan. "I'll teach you how it's done. You'll walk like me, an elegant walk, everyone knows who they're dealing with when I walk into a room. Straighten up. I'll teach you…"

And she taught him. He took his first baby steps to her delight. It was all in the posture. *You, too, could walk like a gentile.* You had to keep your chin in the air. The spine straight.

Then the feet would follow.

PART II

GIRSHKIN

IN LOVE

6. THE RETURN OF
BEST FRIEND BAOBAB

SEVEN YEARS AFTER GRADUATING FROM AN ELITE math-and-science high school along with his best friend Vladimir Girshkin, Baobab Gilletti looked very much the same. He was a pale redhead of admirable physique, although the demise of a teenager's metabolism had left him with a new coat of fat, which he constantly tugged at, not without a sense of pride.

Tonight, having returned pink and glowing from his Miami narco-adventures, Baobab was educating Vladimir about his sixteen-year-old girlfriend Roberta. How she was so young and promising. How she wrote avant-garde film scripts and acted in and around them. How she was doing *something*.

The boys were sitting on a broken mohair couch in the living room of Baobab's Yorkville tenement, watching little Roberta squirm into a tight pair of jeans, her bare legs as veined as a newborn's, her mouth full of braces and Wild Bordeaux lipstick. It was too much adolescence for Vladimir, who tried to look away, but Roberta waddled up to him anyway, her jeans around her ankles, and shouted, "Vlad!" kissing his ear and deafening him with her pucker.

Baobab examined his girlfriend's salaciousness through an

empty brandy snifter. "Hey, what's with the jeans?" he said to her. "You're going out? But I thought…"

"You thought?" Roberta said. "Oh, you must tell me all about it, *Liebschen!*" She rubbed Vladimir's grizzly cheek with her own, watching with pleasure as the young man giggled and tried, unconvincingly, to push her away.

"I thought you were staying home tonight," said Baobab. "I thought you were writing a critique of me or a response to my critique."

"Idiot, I told you we're filming tonight. See, if you ever actually listened to me, I wouldn't have to spend half the day banging out critiques and denunciations."

Vladimir smiled. One had to give points to this youth willing to carry on a fight dressed in Baobab's gamy boxers, jeans draped around the ankles.

"Laszlo!" Baobab shouted. "You're filming with Laszlo, am I right?"

"Peasant!" she shouted back, slamming a bathroom door behind her. "Sicilian peasant!"

"What? Come again?" Baobab turned in the direction of the kitchen and the breakables. "My grandfather was a parliamentarian before Mussolini! You Staten Island whore!"

"Okay, okay," Vladimir said, taking hold of one approaching Popeye arm. "Now we go, we have a drink. Come, Garibaldi. Here are your cigarettes and your lighter. We go, we go."

THEY WENT. A cab was hailed to haul them to Baobab's favorite bar in the meat-packing district. A few years hence this tattered part of downtown would catch the eye of the barbarian hordes from Teaneck and Garden City, and later become a bona fide hipster playground, but for now it was all but abandoned at night—a fitting locale for Baobab's favorite bar.

The Carcass had an authentic pool of blood at the entrance, courtesy of a neighboring hog-slaughtering outfit. One could still see the conveyor belts that transported the heifers of yesteryear running along the length of the Carcass's ceiling. Below one could also be as anachronistic as needed: put some Lynyrd Skynyrd on the jukebox, whip out a stick of beef jerky, ruminate out loud on the contours of the waitress, or watch a trio of emaciated graduate students standing around the pool table with their cue sticks at attention, as if waiting for funding to appear. The usual crowd.

"So?" They had both asked the question. Bourbon was on the way.

"This Laszlo person is a problem?"

"Damn Magyar poser's trying to screw my baby girl," Baobab said. "Weren't the Hungarians part of the Great Tatar Horde originally?"

"You're thinking of my mother." *Mongolka!*

"No, I assure you, this Laszlo's quite the barbarian. He has that international odor. And his personal pronouns are a mess…Yes, of course I know how I sound. And if I was a girl aged sixteen and had the opportunity to tango with some putz who had groomed Fellini's dog, or whatever Laszlo's claim to fame is, I'd sign up in a Budapest minute."

"But has he actually made any movies?"

"The Hungarian version of *The Road to Mandalay.* Very allegorical, I hear. Vlad, have I ever told you that all love is socioeconomic?"

"Yes." Actually, no.

"I'll tell you one more time then. All love is socioeconomic. It's the gradients in status that make arousal possible. Roberta is younger than me, I'm more experienced than her, she's smarter

than me, Laszlo's more European than her, you're more educated
than Challah, Challah's...Challah..."

"Challah's a problem," Vladimir said. The waitress was arriving
with the bourbons, and Vladimir looked to her pleasant figure—
pleasant in the Western sense, meaning: impossibly thin, but with
breasts. She was clothed entirely in two large swatches of leather,
the leather fake and shiny in a self-mocking way, absolutely correct
for 1993, the first year when mocking the mainstream had become
the mainstream. Also, the waitress had no hair on her head, an
arrangement Vladimir had warmed to over the years, despite his
fondness for rooting his nose through musty locks and curls. And
finally, the waitress had a face, a fact lost on most of the patrons,
but not on Vladimir who admired the way one overdone eyelash
stuck miserably to the skin below. Pathos! Yes, she was a high-
quality person, this waitress, and it saddened Vladimir that she
wouldn't look at him in the least as she served the bourbons.

"Perhaps these...Oh, I will not succumb to your lingo. Okay,
fine, perhaps these gradients in status between Challah and myself
are no longer enough to arouse me."

"You're saying you've come too close together. Like a marriage."

"That's precisely what I'm *not* saying! There, you see how your
nonsense gets in the way of conversation? I'm saying I don't know
what the hell's going on in her head anymore."

"Not much."

"That's not very nice."

"But it's true. Look, you meet her, you're fresh out of your Midwestern collegiate disaster with that lean, mean Vlad-eater, what was
her name? You're back a confused little eeemigrant in New York, the
little Girshkie-wirshkie, woo-choo-choo, Girshkie-wirshkie..."

"Asshole."

"And then, whoosh! A casualty of the American Dream, par
excellence. She gets whipped for a living! For God's sake, there's not

even the need for symbolism. Enter Girshkie, his compassion, his broken heart, his twenty-thousand-dollar-a-year salary waiting to be shared, and off we go from submission to dominance, and let's not forget hugs, talks, walks—my God, this guy just wants to help. But what's in it for the Good Samaritan, huh? Challah's still Challah. Not terribly interesting. Kinda large there—"

"Now you're resigned to being mean to make yourself feel better."

"Not true. I'm telling you what you already know inside. I'm translating it from the Russian original." But he was being mean to make himself feel better. It was Baobab, after all, who had introduced Challah to Vladimir. The meeting took place at Bao's Righteous Easter Party, an annual event lousy with students from City College, where Baobab was a lifetime scholar and purveyor of Golden Moroccan hashish.

Challah was sitting in a corner of the host's bedroom on a beanbag, staring first at her cigarette and then into her ashtray and then back at her disintegrating conversation piece. Baobab's bedroom being a fairly large (although windowless) affair, the guests had crammed themselves neatly into the corners, leaving plenty of open space for guest appearances.

So, in corner number one there was Challah, alone, smoking, ashing; in corner number two we have a pair of engineering students, a heavyset and demonstrably gay Filipino practicing hypnosis on a very loud and impressionable man half his age ("You *are* Jim Morrison...I *am* Jim Morrison!"); corner number three— Roberta, who had just entered Baobab's life, being purposefully rubbed down by Bao's history professor, a ruddy Canadian hoser; and, finally, corner number four, our hero Vladimir trying to have an intelligent discussion with a Ukrainian exchange student on the topic of disarmament.

The guest appearance was Baobab's. He came in dressed like the

Savior, did a little number with his crown of thorns, some indecent exposure courtesy of his loincloth, got some good laughs out of everyone including Challah who was wrapped into herself in the corner, a huddle of dark cloth and Satanic jewelry. Then he fondled Jim Morrison and, in turn, his hefty hypnotist friend, tried to extricate Roberta from the clutches of the academy, and finally sat down next to Vladimir and the Ukrainian. "Stanislav, they're making toasts out in the kitchen," Bao said to the Ukrainian. "I think they need you."

"That's Challah, a friend of Roberta's," Baobab said after the Ukrainian had left.

"Challah?" Vladimir was thinking, of course, of the sweet, fluffy bread served on the eve of the Jewish Sabbath.

"Her father's a commodities trader, lives in Greenwich, Connecticut, and she works as a submissive."

"She could play Magdalene to your Christ," sneered Vladimir. Nonetheless, he went over to introduce himself.

"Hello," Vladimir said, plunking himself down in her beanbag nest. "Do you know I've been hearing your name all night?"

"No," she said. Only she didn't say it in mock modesty, such as done with a flourish of the arms and a stretch of the word: "Naaaaaawh." Instead, it was just a quiet syllable, perhaps one could even read some plaintiveness into it, which surely Vladimir did. Her "no" meant that no, he hadn't been hearing her name all night. Hers was not a name like that.

Is it possible: Love at first word? And with the first word being "No"? Here one should suspend disbelief and answer affirmatively: Yes, in post–Reagan/Bush Manhattan with its youth pierced, restless, weaned on flashing image and verbally disinclined, it is possible. For with that one word, Vladimir, who had been out of love with himself ever since his ignominious flight from the Midwest, recognized a welcome substitute for self-love. After all, here was a woman who was alone and apart at parties, who worked as a submissive, who, he suspected, allowed herself extravagance only in dress, but otherwise knew that her world had limits.

In other words, he could love *her*.

And even if his suspicions proved wrong, he was still—it is necessary to admit this—aroused by the thought that foreign hands were upon her body, intent on hurting her, while at the same time wondering what kind of sex they could have together, and what he could do to change her life. And she looked cute, baby fat and all, especially in that unholy get-up. "Okay," he said, knowing to tread lightly. "I just wanted to meet you, that's why I came over." Oh, Vladimir, gentle pick-up artist!

But meet her he did. Clearly it had been a while since a man had talked to her at length and with a minimum of intimidation (Vladimir the foreigner was himself intimidated). The next nine hours were spent talking, first in Baobab's bedroom, then in a nearby diner, and finally in Vladimir's bedroom, about their twin escapes— Russia & Connecticut—and within twenty-four hours they were discussing the possibility of further escape, together, into a circumstance where they could at least provide each other with dignity (that exact word was used). By the time Vladimir was ready to kiss her it was already ten in the morning. The kiss was meager yet affectionate, and following the kiss they fell asleep on top of each other, sleeping well into the next day.

BACK AT THE CARCASS, Baobab was still going on about Vladimir's problems in his Baobab way. But Vladimir had just one more thing to say on his own behalf: "Is it true that it could be over with Challah? Can I really end it on my own?" He answered the question himself. Yes, yes. To end it. It had to be done.

"Yes, the break-up," Baobab said. "If you want my expert help, if you want me to write an essay or something, just ask. Or better yet, let Roberta handle it. She can handle anything." He sighed.

"Yes, Roberta," said Vladimir, bent on imitating the cadence of Baobab's speech. "I'm beginning to see, Bao, that just as I must solve my problems by myself, so you must be a man and do something about the Roberta situation."

"Something manly?"

"Within reason."

"Challenge Laszlo to a duel? Like Pushkin?"

"Can you be more successful than Pushkin? Can you see yourself using a side arm, accurately shooting the Tatar, hmm...?"

"Vlad! Are you volunteering to be my second? That's awfully white of you. Come, let's kill that bastard."

"Paff!" Vladimir said. "I won't take part in this insanity. Besides, you said we were going to drink the night away. You promised me early liver failure."

"Your friend is reaching out to you, Vladimir," Baobab said, putting on his crumpled fedora.

"I'm useless in a confrontation. I'll just be an embarrassment to you. In fact—"

But Baobab cut him off by executing a low bow and heading for the door, the ill effects of his battered hat now visibly compounded by his stupid engineer boots. Poor guy. "Hey! Promise me no fisticuffs," Vladimir shouted to him.

Baobab blew him a kiss and was gone.

It took a full minute for Vladimir to register the fact that he had been abandoned, left without a drinking partner on a boozy Sunday night.

Without a drinking partner, Vladimir continued drinking. He knew many Russian songs about drinking alone, but the tragicomic import of their stanzas could not dissuade him from a volley of bourbons and the single gin martini that managed to sneak in, its three crisp olives tinkling in a shapely glass. Tonight we drink, but tomorrow...a long stretch of sobriety in which Vladimir would wake up with a clear head and deal knowingly with immigrants. Such fascinating people. How many of his contemporaries, for instance, got to meet the likes of Mr. Rybakov, the Fan Man? And how many could inspire his confidences?

Resolved: Vladimir's an okay kind of guy. Vladimir toasted to himself with his fifth bourbon, and showed his laminated teeth to the waitress who actually smiled back a little, or at least opened her mouth. "S..." Vladimir began to say (the completed word would have been "So"), but the waitress had already left with a tray of drinks for the graduate students at the billiards table. They drank wild fruity things, the scholars.

Another hour of this, and Vladimir was genuinely debilitated. Nothing could be said in his favor. His image, as seen in a nearby martini decanter, showed a Russian *pyanitsa,* a drunken lout with his thinning hair slicked down by sweat, the buttons of his shirt opened beyond what was desirable. Even his laminated teeth—the pride of the Girshkins—had somehow attracted a gritty element along the bottom row.

The grad students were still shooting pool, maybe he could wave at them, do a drunken wave, that's allowed when you're drunk. He could be a character...

He quaffed the new bourbon down in no time. There was a woman sitting alone at a table no bigger than an ashtray at the end of a row of such tables leading up to the door and the street. How long had she been there? There was something of the *pyanitsa* in her appearance as well—her head was tilted to one side as if her neck muscles had failed her, her mouth was wide open, her dark hair dried and matted. Also noticeable through Vladimir's haze was (starting from the top and working down) paleness, dark eyes, a blank gray sweatshirt, more paleness in the hands, and a book. She was reading. She was drinking. If only Bao had left him one of his books, but what for? So they could read at each other across a bar?

He took out a cigarette and lit it. Smoking made our Vladimir feel dangerous, made him think of running through Central Park at this late hour, sprinting to the sound of urban cicadas, zigzagging left and right like a soccer player, fooling death that lurked in the shadows between the park lights.

It was a plan.

He got up to leave, and the woman looked up at him. As he walked toward the door to outwit death in the park, she was still looking at him. She was right in front of him now and she was still looking at him.

He was sitting in the chair opposite her. Something must have tripped him, or else he just found himself sitting down on the warm plastic. The woman looked about twenty, her forehead developing an interstate of life's first creases.

"I don't know why I sat down," Vladimir said. "I'm going to get up now."

"You scared me," the woman said. Her voice was deeper than his.

"I'm getting up now," he said. He put one hand on the table. The book was *Manhattan Transfer*. "I love that book," he said. "I'm leaving now. I didn't mean to sit down."

Again he was on his feet with the unsteady landscape around him. He saw the doorknob approaching and stuck out an anticipatory hand.

There was a chuckle behind him. "You look like Trotsky," she said.

Good God, thought Vladimir, I'm going to have an affair.

He tasted the bourbon coating his tongue. He tweaked his goatee, pushed up his tortoiseshell glasses, and turned around. He walked back to her, making sure to bend his feet inward so that they wouldn't flop Jewishly to the side, firmly plowing his instep into the American soil ("Stamp the ground with your feet as if you own it!" Mother had instructed him).

"It's only when I'm drunk," he said to the young woman, letting the last word dangle, as if to illustrate. "I look more like Trotsky when I'm drunk." One could do better with introductions perhaps.

He slumped back into the chair. "I can get up and go. You're reading a good book," he said.

The woman put a napkin into her book and closed it. "Where you from, Trotsky?" she said.

"I am Vladimir," said Vladimir in a tone that made him want to add, "and I journey far and wide on behalf of Mother Russia." He restrained himself.

"A Russian Jew," the observant woman said. "What do you drink?"

"Nothing anymore. I'm all drunk and broke."

"And you miss your country," said the woman, trying to match his sadness. "Two whiskey sours," she said to a passing waitress.

"You are so kind," Vladimir said. "You must be from another place. You go to NYU and hail from Cedar Rapids? Your parents work the land. You have three dogs."

"Columbia," the woman corrected him. "Manhattanite by birth, and my parents are professors at City. One cat."

"What can be better?" Vladimir said. "If you like Chekhov and social democracy, we can be friends."

The woman stuck out a long, bony hand which felt surprisingly warm. "Francesca," she said. "So you come to bars alone?"

"I was with a friend, but he left," Vladimir said, and then judging by her name and appearance added: "He was an *Italian* friend."

"I'm flattered," Francesca said.

She then performed a very innocuous gesture—moved an errant twirl of hair upward and over her ear. In doing so, she exposed a ribbon of white skin which the summer sun had been unable to reach. It was the sight of this skin that lifted the drunken, swooning Vladimir up and over the rickety wooden fence beyond which infatuations are kept, grazing off the fat of the heart. Such a thin, translucent membrane, this stretch of skin. How could it ever guard the intellect from the suffocating summer air outside? Not to mention falling objects, perching birds, persons intent on doing harm. He thought he was going to cry. It was all so... But the childhood admonitions of his father were clear: no crying. He tried squinting instead.

"What's wrong?" Francesca said. "You look troubled, dear." Another round of whiskey sours had come out of nowhere. He reached out a trembling hand in the direction of the drink, its maraschino cherry blinking at him like a landing light.

And then a cozy darkness descended, just as a helpful arm was wrapped around his elbow... They were out on the sidewalk and through a blurring of vision he saw a taxi swing past her pale cheek. "Taxi," Vladimir mumbled, trying to stay on his newly christened feet.

"Yes, boy," Fran encouraged him. "Taxi."

"Bed," Vladimir said.

"And where," she asked, "does Trotsky make his bed?"

"Trotsky make no bed. Trotsky rootless cosmopolitan."

"Well, this is your red-letter day, Leon. I know of a nice couch up on Amsterdam and Seventy-second."

"Seductress..." Vladimir whispered to himself.

Before long they were in the cab, headed uptown, past a familiar deli where Vladimir had once gotten something, a roast beef that didn't work out. Next time he looked they had slipped onto the speedy terrace of the West Side Highway, and they were still headed up, uptown.

And to what end? he thought before passing on to the Land of Nod.

7. VLADIMIR DREAMS OF . . .

. . . AN AIRPLANE DRIFTING THROUGH EASTERN EURO-pean clouds rolled together, pierogi-style from the layered exhaust of coal, benzene, and acetate. Mother is yelling to Mr. Rybakov over the roar of propellers: "I remember the semifinals so vividly! Little Failure takes rook, loses queen, scratches his head, check and mate... The only Russian boy not to make it to the state championship."

"Chess," the Fan Man snorts, tapping the altimeter gauge. "A pursuit for idiots and layabouts. Don't even talk to me about chess, Mama."

"I'm just making an example!" Mother yells. "I'm drawing parallels between the arenas of chess and life. Remember, it was *I* who taught him how to walk! Where were you when he was hobbling around like a Jew? Ah, but it's always left to the mother. Who make them their Salad Olivier? Who gets them their first job? Who helps them with their college essays? '*Topic Two: Describe the biggest problem you have ever faced in your life and how you overcame it.*' Biggest problem? I walk like a Yid and I don't love my mother..."

"It would be better if you shut your mouth," Rybakov says. "Mamas are always meddling, always trying to give their boys the teat... Suck! Suck, little one! And then they wonder why their sons turn out cretins. Besides, he's my Vladimir now."

Mother sighs and crosses herself in her new fashion. She turns around to smirk at Vladimir chafing away in the cargo bay, the straps of the parachute kit burning the delicate white meat of his shoulders.

"*Nu*," Rybakov shouts to Vladimir. "Ready to jump, Airman?" Beneath the aircraft, a blue grid of urban light is replacing the void of the countryside. The nascent city is bisected by a dark loop of river, illuminated solely by the lights of barges making their way downstream. The word PRAVA, glowing in neon, is spelled in giant Cyrillic characters on the city's left bank.

"My son is waiting for you... there!" The Fan Man points somewhere between the neon P and the neon R. "You will recognize him right away. He is a substantial man standing by a row of Mercedes. Handsome like his father."

Before Vladimir can object, the doors of the cargo bay open, and the parachutist is engulfed by the cold night air... The nebulous sensation of plummeting in a dream.

I'm falling to earth! thinks Vladimir.

It is not an unpleasant feeling.

8. THE PEOPLE'S VOLVO

VLADIMIR AWOKE AT NOON IN THE UPTOWN STUDIO OF Francesca's friend Frank. This Frank, an evident Slavophile, had decorated his room with a half dozen handmade icons of gold crepe, along with a wall-sized Bulgarian tourist poster showing an onion-domed rural church flanked by a terrifically woolly animal (baa?). Vladimir would never find out exactly what happened on that long journey uptown, how he was wheeled in past the doorman, how the apartment was requisitioned for his use, and the other details lost on the inebriated. Quite a first impression Vladimir must have made—five minutes of conversation followed by a light coma.

But then...! But then...On the Swede-made instant-coffee table...what did he find? A pack of Nat Sherman cigarettes to steal, yes...And next to the cigarettes...Next to the cigarettes there was a note. So far so good. And then on the note...concentrate now...in looped middle-class script, Francesca's last name (Ruocco)... Her Fifth Avenue address and phone number...And, to conclude, a sympathetic invitation to drop by her house at eight and then to a TriBeCa party by eleven.

Success.

With shaky fingers, Vladimir lit a Nat Sherman's cigarette, a long, brown cylinder tasting of honey and ash. He smoked it in the elevator although this was the kind of newish building where smoke detectors abounded. He smoked it past the doorman, out onto the street, all the way into Central Park. Only then did Vladimir remember his original plan, the drunken plan he had formulated before he boldly took the seat opposite Francesca.

Vladimir ran through the park. A happy run interspersed with a hop, a skip, and a jump. What beautiful feet he had! What wonderful Russo-Judeo-Slavo-Hebraio feet... Just right for sprinting down this bike path. Or for a grand entrance at Francesca's Fifth Avenue apartment. Or for setting down on a coffee table at a TriBeCa loft party. Ah, how thoroughly, consistently, delightfully wrong Mother was about everything, about the whole country, about the happy possibilities for young immigrant V. Girshkin. Wrong! wrong! wrong! Vladimir thought as he ran across the Sheep Meadow dotted with unemployed sunbathers on a lazy Monday afternoon, the midtown skyscrapers looking down on them with corporate indifference. Mother, in fact, was serving time in one of those smoked-glass monstrosities built before the last recession: a corner office draped with American flags and a framed photo of the Girshkin Tudor, minus its three inhabitants.

And what a day for a run, too. Cool as early spring, gray and drizzly—the kind of day that felt like playing hooky from school, or, in Vladimir's case, from work. And the kind of day that reminded him of *her*—Francesca—the grayness, the ambivalence, the supposed intelligence that abounded in wet English days; plus the weight of the surrounding dampness brought to mind the way he had been cradled in her neck in the taxi. Yes, here again was a kind person, and, so far, Vladimir had only been involved with kind women. Perhaps to love Vladimir required a certain kindness. In that case, what good luck!

The run, however, ended after one muddy slope as Vladimir's lungs—genuine handiwork of Leningrad—let themselves be known, and the sprinter was forced to seek a rain-soaked bench.

HE MADE IT TO WORK around two. It was Chinese Week at the Emma Lazarus Society and the Chinese lined up behind the China Desk, spilling over into the waiting room where there was tea and a stuffed panda. The few Russians that came out of the wet afternoon giggled at the stream of Asians and tried to emulate the quiet buzz of their conversations with a barrage of "Ching Chang Chong Chung." Fights almost broke out.

Although Vladimir was taught to foster multiculturalism, he looked blankly into the sneering faces of his countrymen, stamping his way through their mountains of documents. Who could think of immigrants on a day like this?

"Baobab, I just met someone. A woman."

There was confusion on the other end of the line. "Sex? What?"

"No sex. But we were in the same bed, I think."

"You're a slave to prophylaxis, Girshkin," Baobab tittered. "All right, tell us everything. What's she like? Thin? Rubenesque?"

"She's worldly."

"And Challah's reaction when she found out?"

Vladimir considered this unhappy scenario. Little Challah Bread. Little Bondage Bear. Ditched once again. Uh-hum. "So how did it go with Laszlo?" Vladimir ventured. "Did you give him the worker's fist?"

"No worker's fist. Actually, I'm enrolled in his new seminar: 'Stanislavsky and You.'"

"Oh, Baobab."

"This way I can keep tabs on Roberta. And meet other actresses.

And Laszlo says he might get us into this new production of *Waiting for Godot* in Prava next spring."

"Prava?" The edges of a strange dream skirted Vladimir's memory; in kaleidoscopic succession he saw Mother, the Fan Man, an empty parachute falling out of the sky. "What nonsense," muttered Vladimir. "I must stop thinking of this Rybakov and think only of my Francesca!" And to Baobab he said, "You mean the Paris of the 90s?"

"The SoHo of Eastern Europe. Exactly. Say, when are you going to introduce me to your new friend?"

"There's a party tonight in TriBeCa. It starts at... Hey! What? You, sir. You in the kaftan... *Put that chair down!*" A small but lively race riot was underway by the fax machine. Vladimir's Haitian colleague was already there, deploying security personnel with gusto, as if she were back on her deposed father's estate in Port-au-Prince. Vladimir was summoned to fetch the agency bullhorn.

"I'M FROM LENINGRAD," he said, bowing his head in gratitude as Francesca's father, Joseph, squeezed a glass of Armagnac into his hand.

"St. Petersburg," said her mother, Vincie, with undue authority and then laughed loudly over her own overbearing nature.

"Yes," Vladimir admitted, although he could never picture the city of his birth—where Lenin's munificent visage peeked out of every kiosk and water closet—going by any other name. He told them the story of how he was born with such a big forehead that the director of the maternity ward personally congratulated his mother on giving birth to the next Vladimir Ilyich.

Her parents cackled up a mixture of genuine laughter and

politeness. With a few more Armagnacs, guessed Vladimir, it would settle on the former.

"That's wonderful," said Joseph, mindlessly layering his industrial-gray hair. "And you *still* have a tremendous forehead!"

Before Vladimir had a chance to blush, Francesca (blushing herself) entered the book-lined living room in a black velvet dress that clung to her like a second skin. "Why, Frannie," Vincie brayed, adjusting her enormous pinkish eyeglasses. "Look at you! Where did you say you were headed tonight, dear?"

"Just to a little party," Francesca smirked at her mother. Vladimir presumed she didn't like being called Frannie, and he loved it—another item for her burgeoning file, along with the contact-lens solution he spotted in the bathroom (and why not glasses?).

"So what do you do, Mr. Girshkin?" Joseph said with exaggerated gravity, as if to suggest that he was not about to take himself seriously, although Vladimir certainly could if he wanted to.

"Leave him alone, Dad," Francesca said, and Vladimir smiled inwardly at this happy American word: Dad. There was something awkward and demeaning, he had always felt, in the Russian *papa*.

"Sometimes your Happy Hegemon act is just a little too convincing," Francesca told her father. "How would you like it if *we* had lost the Cold War and not Vladimir's country?"

Yes, Vladimir liked the Ruoccos, there was no doubt. Both were City College professors, and Vladimir had met his share during his tenure at the math-and-science high school, where professorial offspring herded together to form an intellectual elite. All the welcoming signs were there: a copy of the *New Left Review* on the coffee table; an unlimited supply of booze in the kitchen; their unabashed feeling of pleasant surprise at meeting an intelligent young person after the long days of lecturing to hundreds of sleep-

ing bodies, only to be confronted by overeager Baobab-types during office hours.

"I resettle immigrants," Vladimir said.

"That's right, he speaks Russian," Vincie said, a self-
congratulatory smile on her cracked lips.

"We better go soon," Francesca said.

"Another shot of Armagnac won't hurt anyone," said Joseph,
shaking his head at his daughter and her prudery.

"Oh, you'll get them smashed before the party!" laughed Vincie.
She held out her own glass for a refill.

"And what do your parents do?" Joseph said, overfilling
Vladimir's glass. Vladimir raised his eyebrows and folded his
arms—a gesture performed reflexively whenever his family was
mentioned—until Joseph was visibly worried that he had struck a
sensitive nerve, and Francesca looked ready to disembowel him, or
at least use the word "hegemon" again. But then Vladimir revealed
the Girshkins' exclusive professions, and everyone smiled and
toasted to the foreigners.

WHEN LOOKING BACK at the summer, which Vladimir would
do microscopically in the restless years to come, it could all be said
to have come together in that one evening, although that evening
was not terribly different from the evenings that would follow. It
was simply the first. It set the tone. First the lovely, interested parents. Then the lovely, interested daughter. Then the lovely, interested friends. And then, once again, the lovely, interested daughter
à la carte, off to bed still lovely and interested.

Lovely? Not a catalog beauty: her nose slightly hooked, her
paleness might have been passing for sickly in an era where
everybody seemed to have at least *some* color, and also there was an

inelegance about the gait, the unsteady way in which the foot met the ground, as if one was shorter than the next and she kept forgetting which. That said, she was tall, her hair was long and draped her shoulders like a cape, her eyes were small and as perfectly oval as Fabergé miniatures, their gray the sobering shade of a Petersburg morning above Master Fabergé's workshop; and, from Vladimir's vantage point that first evening, there was that minimalist velvet dress that showed off her small, round shoulders, almost luminous under the sharp Fifth Avenue streetlamps (not to mention the smooth straight white of her back, crossed by two velvet straps).

FINALLY, the lovely and interested friends. They were found that evening amid a spread of black light and loud jazz, the uppermost floor of a TriBeCa loft building. Before it was cleaned the place must have looked like a cattle car traveling cross-country, since now it was all but empty—a couple of couches, a stereo, uncapped bottles of booze that had to be stepped around or picked up and used.

They were a savvy-looking bunch, clothed in the new Glamorous Nerd look that was fast becoming a part of the downtown lexicon. One specimen in a tight, square, wide-collared, polka-dotted shirt was shouting above the rest: "Did you hear? Safi got a European Community grant to study leeks in Prava."

"Fucking Prava again," said another, clad in brown geek pants and penny loafers loaded with actual pennies. "Nothing but a tabula rasa of retarded post-Soviet mutants, if you ask me. I wish the Berlin Wall had never come down."

Vladimir looked on sadly. Not only had he spent his entire life without winning a single European Community grant, but every pathetic piece of clothing he had been trying to shed since he emigrated was now a prêt-à-porter bonanza! Penny loafers! How insufferable. And how old these glam-dorks made him feel, him with nothing but a lousy goatee and the affixed title of Immigrant to temper his protosuburban wardrobe.

He skulked off to another room to meet Francesca's friend Frank the Slavophile. Frank was a man as short as Vladimir, and even thinner. But from this sticklike figure there billowed a head as tumescent as *poori* bread—a Rudolphine red nose, bulbous chin, cheeks so slack the skin above was creased from their weight. "I'm dragooning the whole gang into reading Turgenev's *Sportsman's Sketches* this summer," Frank informed Vladimir while pounding a Dry Sack of sherry into Dixie cups with only partial success. "No man, no woman can claim to be *kulturni* without having read the *Sportsman's Sketches*. Tell me I am wrong! Tell me there is another way!"

"I have read the *Sketches* many times," said Vladimir, hoping his childhood excursions to the Kirov Ballet and the Hermitage had made him *kulturni* enough for his new friend. In truth, the one time Vladimir had skimmed the *Sportsman's Sketches* had been a decade ago, and the one thing he could remember was that they were mostly set outdoors.

"*Molodets!*" said Frank, meaning "good fellow," a term often used by older men to congratulate those younger. How old was this Frank anyway? His closely cropped hair was at stage two of male-pattern baldness, the stage where two hairless half-moons are scalloped out at the temples, as opposed to the little crescents that were indented into Vladimir's hairline. So, twenty-eight, twenty-nine then. And likely a graduate student.

Could it be that they were all graduate students and only Francesca was still in college proper? It could be. The age bracket fit. So did the way they got their jollies—a gaggle of them crowded around a television showing an Indian movie where the romantic principals went through the motions of love but never kissed. And as they touched lightly and coquetted to the sound of sitars and bangles—this dark Romeo and Juliet of the subcontinent—the crowd shouted "more!" and "lip action!" This was in one part of the loft...

In another was Tyson, a Montana Adonis, six feet tall with a leftward-pointing isosceles of blond hair, speaking to a small woman dressed in a sheer sarong and embroidered flip-flops. Speaking in Malay, of course.

The celebrated Tyson quickly took Vladimir aside. "It's a pleasure to finally meet you," he said, lowering his head to Vladimir's level—a most natural motion, like the swing of a boom. He must have had many short friends, such as that ethereal young woman from Kuala Lumpur. "And a pleasure for Frank...We've always been trying to find a nice Russian speaker for Frank."

"It's good to be here," Vladimir said out of gracious instinct.

"Here? *America?*"

"No, no. The party."

"Oh, the party. That. May I speak frankly, Vladimir?"

Vladimir reached up on his toes. Tyson's mouth, a large, jutting affair, was ready to expel something frank. What could it be? "Frank's in a terrible state," Tyson said. "He's nearing nervous collapse." They turned to the Slavicist who was actually looking pretty good there, surrounded by many attractive bespectacled women with lots of laughter and sherry between them.

"Poor man!" said Vladimir, and he meant it. For some reason, this Turgenev business did not seem a good portent.

"He had a disastrous relationship with a Russian woman, a young lawyer from a very predatory family. It went from bad to worse. First, she ended things. Then he was hounding her in a Brighton Beach restaurant where the waiters took him out back and attacked him with skillets."

"Yes, it happens," Vladimir said, and sighed on behalf of his temperamental ilk.

"You know how much all things Russian mean to him?"

"I'm starting to draw a picture for myself. But I should tell you right away that I have no Russian women relatives worth noting." Well, there was Aunt Sonya, that Siberian tigress.

"Then perhaps you can take him out for a walk every once in a while," Tyson said, squeezing both of Vladimir's shoulders, in a way that reminded Vladimir of the friendly, well-bred denizens of his progressive Midwestern college; the long, stoned rides in his Chicagoan ex-girlfriend's People's Volvo; the nights spent drinking himself unconscious with humane scholars who cared. "You could talk in the mother tongue," Tyson continued. "Of course, it would be better if it were winter, then you could both don those nice furry hats... What do you say?"

"Ah!" Vladimir looked away, that's how flattered he was. Half an hour into the party and already they were asking him to help a friend in need. Already he was a friend. "This is possible," Vladimir said. "I mean, I'd love to."

Following those words, those right-felt, inspiring words, Vladimir was crowned with a halo. Why else would the whole party suddenly abandon the far reaches of the loft and crowd around him, asking him questions and at times gently holding on to his arm? The inquisitive wanted to know: What was his prognosis for Russia following the Soviet Union's collapse? ("Not good.") Was he bitter about the new unipolar world? ("Yes, very.") Who was his favorite Communist? ("Bukharin, by a kilometer.") Was there any way to stop creeping capitalism and globalization? ("Not in my experience.") What about Romania and Ceaușescu? ("Mistakes were made.") Was he going out with Francesca, and if so, how far had he gotten?

At that point Vladimir wished he had been drunk already so that he could be charming and giddy with these pretty men and women in their Islamabad University T-shirts. Instead he managed a few shy gurgles. Oh, how he wished he had been in possession of a fur hat, a real Astrakhan *shapka*. For the first time in his life he was aware of the following useful axiom: *It is far better to be patronized than to be ignored.* Before he could act further on that impulse, Francesca summoned him from the kitchen.

Here, the din was glaring; a different caste of people swarmed around a tableful of shrimp cocktail, while Francesca stood beneath rows of corrugated-steel cabinets pleasantly overdressed in her royal velvet, laughing at a drunk Indian man—equally dapper in a tuxedo—pounding at her head with a pair of inflatable antlers.

"Hi," Vladimir said sheepishly to the antlered Indian.

"That's enough now, Rakhiv," Francesca said, reaching out to grasp an antler. A dark tuft of hair looked out at Vladimir from her armpit.

The Indian gentleman turned his long face to scowl at Vladimir, then slunk off past the shrimp eaters. So, Vladimir had competition. How exciting. He was feeling like a very competitive entry tonight, although the Indian had a classical face with that popular sad look.

"A drink!" Francesca said. "I'll make you a Rob Roy. My mother practically birthed me with bitters." She opened the nearest cabinet and took out a cocktail glass etched with the image of a thoughtful-looking egret swooping down over a small crayfish-like creature bubbling out of the wetlands. She turned to another cabinet for limes and a dusty bottle of Glenlivet. "You have to meet the Libber sisters," Francesca was saying.

"Maybe we can go for a walk after this drink," Vladimir suggested.

Her cold fingers smelling of scotch, Francesca patted his cheek, as if to disabuse him of such silly thoughts. "Have you heard of Shmuel Libber, their father?" she said. "He discovered the world's oldest dreidel."

On cue, the Libber sisters emerged from behind a ficus plant— two pale, identical beauties with a slightly Asiatic cast—bearing news of an ancient Jewish spinning top.

"I have heard of your father's work…" Vladimir began, just as Tyson stormed in, ahemed brusquely, and made a show of looking down at his feet.

"Vladimir, some of your friends are here. Could you… please…greet them?"

Vladimir found Baobab in the main room, dressed in his signature colonial khakis, his pith helmet lanced with an ostrich feather, holding on firmly to the little Malaysian student who was bowing politely while pointing with her free hand at an imaginary avenue of escape. "I wear my syphilis like a badge of honor," Baobab was roaring to her over the television's strum of sitars. "I picked it up in Paris, straight from the source. The writings of Nietzsche, if you care to know, are, in essence, syphilitic."

Roberta, resplendent in some kind of Day-Glo leopard nightie and bowler hat, had draped herself over Frank and was squeezing his big cheeks, shouting, "Wubbly, you've got a lot of life in you!"

The silenced crowd was tiptoeing away, the contents of the melting pot sluicing back into the kitchen. But their traffic was slow, their gaze affixed to the cause of their eviction—the fat little man in the pith helmet, the near-naked teenager, and…in the corner.

Challah was sitting in the corner, in the same tired bondage gear that Vladimir had found her in eight months ago, looking down at her drink for companionship as the young intellectuals galloped past her, their inflatable antlers shaking in consternation. She caught sight of Vladimir and waved desperately for him to come over.

By this time Vladimir had taken hold of Baobab who was, in turn, losing his grip on the Malaysian woman. "What is this?" Vladimir whispered. "Why did you bring Challah? Why are you behaving like this?"

"Behaving like what? I'm doing you a favor. Where's the new woman?"

In the kitchen, the deep-timbred sounds of twentysomething commotion were building, with Francesca's voice an indisputable part of the outcry. Meanwhile, in one corner of the living room, Frank was succumbing to the little huntress in braces and negligee; in another corner, Challah was depositing one warm finger into her drink, watching the rusty sherry undulate.

And Vladimir? Vladimir had maybe twenty seconds to live.

9. GENDER AND IMPERIALISM

"PLEASE UNTIE ME NOW," VLADIMIR SAID.

The handkerchief was unfastened. Vladimir removed the blindfold himself. Rich Fifth Avenue light, healthy and dappled, overwhelmed the pale curtains.

"Sorry about the coitus last night," Francesca said. "I was too rough. I was acting out."

"No, it was my fault," Vladimir said, covering his lower quarters with sheets, rubbing his swollen wrists. "Inviting my friends was an act of aggression." With a shaky finger, he traced the teeth marks inscribed on his upper thigh. "By physically acting out against me you became both aggrieved *and* perpetrator. You empowered yourself." These strange yet familiar words, unheard of since his tenure at the progressive Midwestern college, slipped out of his mouth. He knew he was hunting for that notorious animal, subtext. That Bigfoot of the literate world. So what was the subtext here?

He wasn't thinking, in particular, of the painful role-playing, the thoughtful humiliations she had visited upon him (for a time he was completely naked and she dressed in her father's classroom turtleneck and tweeds), but of the entire physical package. Two people just two hundred pounds short of nonexistence burrowing into each other, a dangerous and tenuous situation; the scrape of bone and pubis; the distinct lack of odor that more viable animals regularly produce. Oh, the degenerate joy of the lightweighted.

Fran lowered a T-shirt over her arms, and the two tiny breasts, only slightly larger than Vladimir's soft duo, disappeared into cotton. "Your friends came to that party," she said, "like young imperialists, like little conquerors. They totally failed to see the integrity of our indigenous academic culture and had to frame it in their own atrophied discourse. It might as well have been Leopold's troops traveling up the Congo."

Vladimir felt a pressing need to pull on his underpants; to achieve some kind of parity. (He was starting to feel as if an invisible tennis announcer was constantly shouting off-court: "Advantage: Francesca.") But he had no idea where his underpants had ended up during the drunken melee that preceded their first coupling. And something told him that his nakedness and meek silence were right. That in the face of smarter women it was best to beat a continuous retreat, to slash and burn one's own personal convictions before their sure-footed advance.

Yes, he was convinced now that he had misjudged her, that the easy banter of the nights before was just a beachhead for this confident American woman, and what she really wanted from him, whatever this turned out to be, he couldn't possibly give her.

Because sooner rather than later she would comprehend the limitations of a man who at the ripe age of twenty-five had just been taught how to walk by his mother. What do you do with a man like that? thought Vladimir. You needed the patience of a Challah, or, perhaps, the pathos, and it was rather doubtful that this sleek young woman would have either.

"That fat misogynist fool..." Fran was saying. "Using *syphilis* as a come-on line. Poor Chandra. And that...The large woman with the Weehawken outfit. What the hell was *she* about?"

Vladimir shook his head then buried it in one of Fran's elephantine pillows with their etched scenes of Venetian life. "My friends and I, we're a pretty open-minded bunch," Fran was saying, "but we have our limits. Those people were just inexcusable."

"They grew up watching television," Vladimir mumbled into the comforting pillow. "They looked for prizes in cereal boxes. They're a product of the culture, and American culture in the twentieth century is, by definition, imperialist." But he was apportioning too much blame to his friends, when self-flagellation was the order of the day. He made a note of this.

"And to tell you the truth, it's not really them I'm upset about," Fran said. "They were only there for one night. I'll never see them again. But what does it say about you? About the kind of life you've been living? You're a very smart and unusual man. Well-read, educated, from a different country. How the hell did you end up with that crowd?"

Vladimir sighed. "How do I put it?" he said. He thought of literature. He thought of subtext. In the end his education did not fail him. "You know the Hemingway story 'The Killers'?" he said. "When the killers are coming to get the boxer, what does the boxer say?"

"'I got in wrong.'"

"There you go."

"Now, by quoting Hemingway we're not actually sanctioning the misogyny and racial condescension that defines his body of work."

"Of course not," he said. "Never."

She ruffled the back of his head with its soft bumps and bony ridges. The warm touch was welcome after the night they had had. It bordered on affection, and as much as he did enjoy the roughhousing, he wanted the sweet stuff as well. "So what are you going to do about it?" she said.

"The misogyny?"

"No, the 'getting in wrong' business. Are you just going to settle for this lifestyle?"

"'Life' and 'style' really fail to describe it," Vladimir said.

"I'd say."

She laid down on top of him and put her nose into his neck. Despite its sharp outline, her honker felt sloppy and warm. She whispered into his ear: "Do you know why I like you, Vladimir? Have you figured it out yet? I don't like you because you're sweet or kind-hearted, or because you're somehow going to change my world, since I've already decided that no man is ever going to change my world. I like you because you're a small, embarrassed Jew. I like you because you're a foreigner with an accent. I like you, in other words, because you're my 'signifier.'"

"Ah, thank you," Vladimir said. *Bozhe moi!* he thought to himself. She knows me down to the very last. Small, embarrassed, Jewish, foreigner, accent. What more was there to him? This was what it meant to be Vladimir. He pressed himself to her, thinking he was going to die of happiness. Happiness and the dull pain of being somehow insufficient. Of being half-formed.

"Plus," she continued, "let me say that my friends like you a lot, and my friends mean the world to me. Frank couldn't stop talking about you all night. And even the way you handled your sad friends was impressive. You didn't run away, you stayed and bore the brunt of their poor manners.

"Look, Vlad," she said, "maybe what you need is to get in good for a change. To be around people of your own caliber. I'm not a trained mental-health-care professional, which I think is what you need in the long run, but who knows? Maybe I can help you."

Actually, in her preppy little cotton T-shirt (a subtle mockery of the preppy class, reasoned Vladimir), her great, demonstrative nose supporting a pair of trendy oversized glasses, and the eyes themselves sleep-starved and black-ringed, she did look like a professional of sorts. An older person. A card-carrying adult. She looked a little like Mother, to tell the truth.

"Yes, I agree," Vladimir whispered. "People of my own caliber. Above and beyond, that sort of thing. What's the trick, eh?"

"I'm hungry," she said.

BENEATH A PAIR of rusting golden lions, on the third floor of a midtown tenement, off of dishes decorated with the green-orange emblem of "The Democratic Socialist Republic of Sri Lanka," they ate a brunch of scorching curry and sweet coconut broth.

"Hold my hand," Francesca said after the socialist dishes had been cleared and her pasty visage was blushing from the curry and spice tea. He held her hand.

She took him to the Whitney Museum where Vladimir admired a row of three upright vacuum cleaners beneath Plexiglas. "Ah," Vladimir said uncertainly. "I get it." He brushed his head against her shoulder and in return got his ear pulled gently, in the same way a playful Napoleon once dispensed his good will.

She took him to a gallery where they admired Kiff's painting *The Poet Vladimir Mayakovsky Invites the Sun to Tea,* wherein a smiling sun hops over the horizon to join Mayakovsky for *chai* and rhyme. "Yes," Vladimir said, feeling on more familiar ground. "Perfect," he said, and then declaimed one of the master's verses in Russian, for which he was duly patted on the rump.

Past the yellow July smog, the variegated layers of New York humidity, past these curtains of heat they walked, she in her stern white T-shirt, perspiring visibly under the arms in the European manner, the outlines of her little body carefully drawn. And how did Vladimir look? Vladimir didn't care how Vladimir looked. Good enough to be seen with her, obviously (there she was now by his side).

But on that account he was soon proven wrong. In a cramped East Village store, its interior shrouded with incense, he was forced to buy himself a Cuban guayabera shirt, silky and looped with Art Nouveau–type curlicues. It was the same kind of shirt he had once seen the Fan Man wear, only this one cost an improbable fifty dollars. Brown janitor pants from another salon complemented his new outfit. "Blue jeans . . . What was I thinking?" he said, kicking the dead denim beast on the floor. "Why didn't anyone stop me?" She kissed him on the lips. He tasted the curry and coriander along with her natural acidity; he felt dizzy and withdrew.

They walked across the wider boulevards, the city suddenly alive with meaning now that he was walking with one of its demigoddesses, and he wondered why he could never walk down the street with Challah just so; his hand in hers, two fashionable, modern people, their conversation by turns warm and breezy, by turns analytic and severe . . . She drenched him and his new Panama hat with a just-opened bottle of spring water; and then, in full view of the passersby on Fifth Avenue and Nineteenth Street, on a Saturday afternoon (three P.M.), she ran her hands across his sorry chest, traced the full moon of his navel, and, finally, made a motion around his scared penis. "Look up," she said. "See that? A two-story mansard roof. Atop a cast-iron facade and with marble walls. It's one of a kind. My grandfather built it in 1875. What say you?"

But before he could answer she ran out into the traffic and brought around a cab for him. They were soon in Central Park, in the thickest parts of the Rambles, where the summer trees concealed without fail each towering skyscraper, each loafing tourist. "Take it out again," she said.

"Again?" he said. "Already? Here?"

"Silly you," she said. And when the purple creature was out in the natural light, its single eye blinking, she held it between her thumb and forefinger, and said, "Sure it looks a little small in the daylight, but look how sleek its knob is. Like the hood of a French TGV train."

"Yes," Vladimir said, and blushed, for he had never imagined that his blighted little anteater would be so complimented. "Ach! Easy now. There are people over there... By the gazebo. Ach!"

After five minutes at her hands, this cheap pornography was over and Vladimir was zipping up his new janitor pants, sighing happily, looking over the scruffy little flowerbed, which he had inadvertently pollinated.

It took him several self-involved minutes to notice that Francesca was crying quietly into the crook of her own elbow. Oh, no! What was this? Had he failed her already? He grazed her dry hair with his lips. She wiped her right hand on his shirt. "What's wrong?" he said. "Don't cry," he whispered, almost in the same plaintive tone his father had once used with Mother. ("Oh, why are you crying, little porcupine?" he nearly added.)

She took a square of aluminum foil from her pocket from which were unfolded several pills. These were expertly swallowed without water. "Here, a tissue..." he muttered. Inwardly he was worried that his member's smallness had made her cry, and he pressed her to him all the more violently.

"What's the matter, hm? What's this all about?"

"I'll tell you a little secret," she said, hiding her face in his scruffy guayabera. "A secret which you can never repeat. Promise?"

He promised.

"The secret is... Ah, but don't you know it already? I was afraid you might have guessed it by now. What with the way I was carrying on about those vacuum cleaners at the Whitney..."

The concerned Vladimir was in no mood for frivolity. "Please," he said, waving his arms. "What is the secret?"

"The secret is: I'm really not too bright."

"You're the smartest woman I've ever met!" Vladimir shouted.

"But I'm not," she said. "Why, in some ways I'm worse off than you are. At least you have no tangible ambitions. All I am, on the other hand, is the very obvious product of two hundred thousand dollars spent on Fieldston and Columbia. Even my father says I'm stupid. My mother would confirm it, only she's an idiot herself. It's the curse of the female Ruoccos."

"Your father would never say that," Vladimir said, quickly forgetting the bit about himself having no ambitions. "Look at you. You're only an undergraduate, but already you have such clever academic friends. And they think the world of you."

"It's one thing to be social, Vladimir. Or even to be smarter than average. And, *entre nous,* how frightening what passes for average these days. But to be brilliant like my father! Vladimir, do you know what he's doing at City College?"

"He's teaching history," Vladimir said brightly. "He's a history professor."

"Oh, no, he's so much more than that. He's starting a whole new field. *Evolving* a whole new field, I should say. It's called Humor Studies. It's better than brilliant, it's thoroughly unexpected! And he has New York's two million Jews at his disposal. The perfect population, you guys are both funny and sad. Meanwhile, look at *me.* What am I doing? Attacking Hemingway and Dos Passos from a feminist perspective. It's like hunting cows. I've no originality, Vladimir. I'm washed out at twenty. Even you, with your uncluttered intellectual life, probably have more to say."

"No! No! I don't!" Vladimir assured her. "I have nothing to say. But you... You..." And for the next half hour he comforted her

with all the charm at his disposal: stooping his shoulders in deference of her love of small men; accentuating his accent to seem ever
the foreigner. It was slow going, especially since at the Midwestern
college he had dined solely on meat-and-potatoes Marxism,
whereas she had at her disposal a sexy postmodernism which
would be held in regard for the next six years. But in the end, he
noticed her smiling throughout his litany and absentmindedly
kissing his hand, and he thought: Yes, I will devote my time now to
making sure she feels good about herself and continues her studies
and achieves her dreams. That is my mission. My tangible ambition, as she put it. I shall exist for no other.

Ah, but he was lying to himself. His thinking was hardly that
generous. The immigrant, the Russian, the Stinky Russian Bear to
be precise, was already taking notes. Love was love, it was exciting,
and hormonal, and sometimes even overwhelmed him with the
strange news that Vladimir Girshkin was not entirely alone in the
world. But it was also a chance to steal something native, to score
some insider knowledge, from an unsuspecting *Amerikanka* like
this woman, whose cauliflower ear he was nuzzling with his nose.

Perhaps Vladimir was not so different from his parents. For
them becoming American meant appropriating the country's vast
floating wealth, a dicey process, to be sure, but not nearly as complex and absolute as this surreptitious body-snatching Vladimir
was attempting. For what he really wanted to do, whether he
admitted it or not, was to *become* Manhattanite Francesca Ruocco.
That was his tangible ambition. Well-situated Americans like Frannie and the denizens of his progressive Midwestern college had the
luxury of being unsure of who they were, of shuffling through an
endless catalog of social tendencies and intellectual poses. But
Vladimir Girshkin couldn't waste any more time. He was twenty-
five years old. Assimilate or leave, those were his options.

—————

IN THE MEANTIME, all the kind attention he had lavished upon Fran must have embarrassed her. She gently removed his nose from her ear. "Let's have a drink," she said.

"Yes, yes, a drink," Vladimir said. They took a cab downtown, and, at a Village sake bar, finished a half-magnum of sake and a thumb-sized plate of marinated squid. The total charge for this little indulgence, Vladimir noticed once the buzz of the liquor had subsided, was U.S.$50. This brought the day's total on his part (including the guayabera shirt and janitor pants) to a little over $200—his allowance for two weeks. Oh, what would Challah say...

Challah. The Alphabet City hovel. The cheap spice racks falling off their hooks. The family-sized jars of K-Y lining the hallway. Was she waiting up for him on their sweaty futon, her lubricated baton at the ready? Was it time to go home?

He and Fran were standing outside the sake bar, both reeling a little from the drink and the squid, with Fran somehow steadier on her feet. After a few minutes of silence, she began slapping him playfully about the face and he went to great lengths to pretend he didn't enjoy it. "Ouch," he said in his best Russian accent. "Afch."

"Would you like to sleep over?" she said, as easily as these things could be said. "My parents are making rabbit."

"I'm very fond of game," Vladimir said. And so it was settled.

10. THE FAMILY
RUOCCO

AND SO IT WAS SETTLED FOR THE REST OF THE summer, a summer Vladimir spent at 20 Fifth Avenue, Apartment 8E, the Ruoccos' grand place overlooking Washington Square Park...A park which, if surveyed from the right angle (if you turned your back on the twin slabs of the World Trade Center), would convince you that you were looking at the venerable plaza of a European capital and not the Manhattan of a million opened steam vents and cars backfiring into the night—the grimy and fantastic Manhattan that Challah and Vladimir used to inhabit.

Not to mention the quiet graces of the family that came with this geography: the Ruoccos feasting, constantly feasting from the "gourmet garages" that were taking the town by storm. An avalanche of peppercorns and stuffed grape leaves in handsome containers, resting on real tables (the kind with four legs) on which candles were always lit and above which chandeliers glowed faintly on dimmers.

Within a few weeks, Vladimir was made into an honorary Ruocco. There was not even the hint of an embarrassed smile when the professors found him brushing his teeth in their bathroom at eight in the morning or escorting Francesca to the breakfast table. Yes, clearly the Ruoccos approved of Vladimir for their "developing young daughter" (as Mr. Rybakov would put it). But why? Had the recent fall of the Berlin Wall made Vladimir somehow timely? Did they sniff the swampy air of Petersburg intelligentsia out of his old work shirts? Was that why they begged to dine with his parents, perhaps expecting to break bread with Brodsky and Akhmatova? To their immense consternation, however, Vladimir made sure that this dinner was never to be. Oh, he could imagine it, all right:

MR. RUOCCO: So how do you feel about the new Russian literature, Dr. Girshkin?

DR. GIRSHKIN: Now I am only interested in my wife's hedge fund and Southeast Asian currency splits. *Literatura is kaput!* For dandies like my son only.

MRS. RUOCCO: Have you heard the Kirov Ballet is coming to the Met?

MOTHER: Yes, yes, the pretty dancing. And what kind of a career have you picked out for Francesca, Mrs. Ruocco? She's so tall and beautiful, I somehow see her as an eye surgeon.

MRS. RUOCCO: Actually, Frannie says she wants to follow in our footsteps.

DR. GIRSHKIN: But how is possible? Professorship offer no remuneration. Who will put food on table? Who will contribute to IRA? To Keogh? Plan 401(k)?

MOTHER: Quiet, Stalin. If Francesca will not make money, she will force Vladimir into law school to support family. All will be well, see?

MR. RUOCCO (*laughing*): Oh, I can't quite picture your Vladimir as a lawyer.

MOTHER: Pink-hearted revisionist bastard pig!

Back on the Ruoccos' planet, Vladimir was straining his ear for proof of Joseph Ruocco's reputed disdain toward his daughter along with evidence of his wife Vincie's stupidity. Neither was forthcoming. Vincie was soft-hearted with the displaced Vladimir, shamed and awkward before the cleaning lady, secretly confounded by her daughter's intelligence, and, despite the occasional wise-crack, perfectly obeisant to Fran's father.

As for the Humor Studies savant himself, it was hard to think of Joseph as contemptuous. Sure, he often cut Fran off short by saying "Now, now, have another glass of Armagnac on the house and we'll call it even." But this booze-soaked dismissiveness seemed to Vladimir a distinguished scholar's prerogative, not to mention that older people should be allowed to get away with things at the family table—look at the free rein granted Mother.

Could such small infractions have had repercussions in Fran's mind? Possibly, given that the single currency considered *valuta* at the Ruocco hearth was not the awkward Bellovian potato love that gets passed around at so many American tables, but *respect*. Respect for each other's ideas, respect for their standing in the world—a world the Ruoccos happily left behind in order to bask in each other's company.

So who knew why Francesca was so intimidated by her father; why her psychiatrist had prescribed a battery of pink and yellow pills; why on some nights sex between her and Vladimir could be either the gentle and sympathetic Antioch College–type sex—the sex by committee of two, the insertion of the penis first a quarter of the way, then in gradual increments—and why on other nights the blindfold and her father's tweeds had to come out. Vladimir's mission, as has been previously established, was to comfort and reassure her, while gaining swift entrée into her classy little world. Let these deeper mysteries be solved in their own sweet time. By his young estimation, they would have all of their lives together.

But then, one day, unwittingly, she did it. She managed to hurt him almost irrevocably.

THEY HAD GONE SHOPPING for a toothbrush. At no time was
he happier than when the two of them would embark on these
most mundane of missions. A man and a woman can claim to love
one another, they may even rent real estate in Brooklyn as a sign of
their love, but when they take time out of a busy day to walk
through the air-conditioned aisles of a drug mart to pick out a nail
clipper together, well, this is the kind of a relationship that will per-
petuate itself if only through its banality. Or so Vladimir hoped.

And she was such a thoughtful consumer. The toothbrush, for
instance, had to be organic. A dealership of organic toothbrushes
did exist in SoHo, but it had chosen this particular day to dissolve
into bankruptcy. "Strange," Frannie said, as a person-sized toothbrush was removed from the vitrine by the bickering members of
an Indian family and crammed into a station wagon with Garden
State plates. "They had such a following."

"Oh, what is to be done?" Vladimir moaned on her behalf.
"Where can one find an organic toothbrush in this one-horse
town?" He kissed her on the cheek for no reason.

"Chelsea," she said. "Twenty-eighth and Eighth. I think the place
is called T-Brush. Minimalist, but definitely organic. But you don't
have to go all the way up there with me. Go home and keep my
mother company. She's grilling baby squid in its own ink! You *love*
that shit."

"No, no, no!" Vladimir said. "I promised to go toothbrush-
shopping with you. I'm a man of my word."

"I think I can handle this all by my lonesome," she said. "I'm
sick of dragging you around."

"Please," Vladimir said. "What dragging? There's nothing more
I enjoy than doing these little, um, quotidian things with you."

"*That* I know," she said.

"You know?" he said.

"Vlad, you're too much!" she laughed, poking him in the stomach. "Sometimes," she continued, "sometimes you seem so happy to have a girlfriend. Was this what you dreamed it would be like? Having a New York girlfriend. Shadowing her around town. The devoted boyfriend, so loving, so devoid of any personal interest, just this lovey-dovey, dopey, happy guy. Toothbrush? Don't mind if I do! It's quotidian!"

She said the last word Vladimir-style with its birdlike *kvo*. *Kvo-kvo*, said the Vladimir bird. *Kvotidian*.

"You have a point," Vladimir said. He was unsure of what to say next. Or what she had just said to him. He felt a gurgle in his stomach and tasted something gastric on his tongue. "Very well, then," he said. "No problem." He pecked her farewell. *"Ciao, ciao,"* he croaked. "Good luck with the toothbrush. Remember: medium-soft bristles…"

But as he made his way home, the intestinal ill-feeling, the nervousness tickling his insides continued, as if the tired faces of the shish-kebob-sellers and art-book-hawkers of Lower Broadway, the honored citizens of the midsummer city, were assaying him with open disgust, as if the braggadocio of rap issuing out of boom boxes was actually as threatening as it sounded. What was it, this strange stirring?

Back at the Ruoccos', Fran's bedroom was its usual mess of *samizdat*-like books published by failing presses; heaps of dirty underwear; here and there loose dots of birth control and anxiety medication; the big cat, Kropotkin, prowling about, tasting a little bit of everything, depositing tufts of gray-black fur on panties and literature alike. And the chill in the room…The mausoleum effect…The windows shut, curtains drawn, the air-conditioner always on, a tiny desk lamp the only illumination. Here was the long winter of Oslo or Fairbanks or Murmansk: the New York summer had no business in this twilight place, this temple to Fran's strange ambitions, the desiccation of early-twentieth-century literature, the education and repackaging of one Warsaw Pact immigrant.

His stomach growled once more. Another wave of nausea…

Kvo-kvotidian, said the Vladimir-bird.

Sometimes you seem so happy to have a girlfriend.

Shadowing her around town…

Was this what you dreamed it would be like?

And then he realized what it was, this rumbling in his gullet, this internal displacement: He had been unmasked! She knew! She knew everything! How much he needed her, wanted her, could never have her…All of it. The foreigner. The exchange student. The 1979 Soviet "Grain Jew" poster boy. Good enough for bed, but not for the organic-toothbrush store.

Toothbrush? Don't mind if I do!

Ah, so that's how it was. She had humiliated him on the sly, while he, the diligent note-taker, had failed his mandate once again. And he had tried so hard this time, had gone to such lengths to please all of them under the rubric "Parents & Daughter: How to Love an American Family." He was the dutiful son the Ruoccos never had. Worshiping Dad's Humor Studies. "Yes, sir, the serious novel has no future in this country…We must turn to the comic." Worshiping Mom's *fruits de mer.* "World's best geoduck clam, Miss Vincie. Maybe just a sprinkle more of vinegar." And, God knows, worshiping Daughter. Worshiping, shadowing, soaking up through osmosis.

And still coming up short…

Why?

How?

Because he was all alone in this, this being Vladimir Girshkin business, this being neither here nor there, neither Leningrad nor

SoHo. Sure, his problems might seem minuscule to a contemporary statistician of race, class, and gender in America. And yes, people in this country suffered left and right, were marginalized and disenfranchised the moment they stepped out of the house for coffee and a doughnut. But at least they suffered as part of a unit. They were in this together. They were bound by ties Vladimir could barely comprehend: New Jersey Indians loading a giant toothbrush into a station wagon, Avenue B Dominicans playing stoop-side dominoes, even the native-born Judeo-Americans sharing easy laughs at the office.

Where was Vladimir's social unit? His American friends had always consisted of one man—Baobab—and, upon Fran's unspoken orders, Baobab was completely off limits. He had no Russian friends. For all his years at the Emma Lazarus Society, the Russian community was just a dark, perspiring mass that regularly washed up on his shore, complaining, threatening, cajoling, bribing him with bizarre lacquered tea sets and bottles of Soviet champagne... *What could he do?* Go to Brighton Beach and eat mutton *plov* with some off-the-boat Uzbeks? Call Mr. Rybakov to see if he could attend the baptismal of his youngest fan? Arrange for a date with some Yelena Kupchernovskaya of Rego Park, Queens, soon-to-be graduate of the accounting department at Baruch College, a woman who, if she actually existed, would want to settle down at the fantastic age of twenty-one and bear him two children in quick succession—"Oh, Volodya, my dream is for one boy and one girl."

And what of his parents? Beyond the Maginot Line of the Westchester suburbs, were they faring any better? Dr. and Mrs. Girshkin had arrived in the States in their early forties; their lives had effectively been split into two, leaving only fading memories of the sunny Yalta vacations, the homemade marzipan cookies and condensed milk, the tiny private parties at some artist's flat suffused with moonshine vodka and whispered Brezhnev jokes. They had left their rarefied Petersburg friends, their few relatives, everyone they had ever known, traded it all in for a lifetime of solitary confinement in a Scarsdale mini-mansion.

There they were, driving down to Brighton Beach once a month to pick up contraband caviar and tangy kielbasa, all around them the strange new Russians in cheap leather jackets, women wearing wedding cakes of permed blond hair on their heads, an utterly alien race that just happened to cluck away in the mother tongue and, at least in theory, shared the Girshkins' religion.

Were Vladimir and his parents Petersburg snobs? Perhaps. Bad Russians? Likely. Bad Jews? Most certainly. Normal Americans? Not even close.

ALONE IN THE DARK foreign bedroom, a bedroom he had just recently mistaken for his own, Vladimir picked up Kropotkin, the Ruoccos' beloved family cat, and soon found himself crying into the hypoallergenic designer fur. It was soothing. The mischievous fellow, an anarchist like his Russian namesake, felt incredibly warm and tender amid the climate-controlled hell of Fran's room. Sometimes, when he and Fran were in bed, Vladimir spied Kropotkin looking at them with such feline amazement, as if the cat alone understood the magnitude of what was going on—Vladimir's right hand cupping, squeezing, plying, poking, kneading the pale American flesh of his mistress.

There were nights, after Fran had done her reading for the day, after the desk light had been turned off, when she would end up on top of him, her face contorted into the most difficult grimace, grinding down on him with such force that he was lost in her, that the pejorative term "to screw" came to mind—she was literally screwing Vladimir inside of her, as if otherwise he would somehow manage to fall out, as if this is what held them together. And after she was through with him, after the long tremors of her silent orgasm, she would grab his head and press it into the bony ridge between her little breasts, each nipple alert and pointing to the side, and there they would remain for a long time, locked in a postcoital huddle, rocking back and forth.

This was his favorite part of their intimacy: when she was silent and satiated, when he was blissfully unsure of what had just happened between them, when they were holding on to each other as if letting go would mean for each a quick, dry death. Inside the huddle, he would sniff and lick her; her chest would be covered with sweat, not the gamy Russian sweat Vladimir remembered from his childhood, rather American sweat, sweat denatured by deodorant, sweat that smelled purely metallic, like blood. And only when they woke up the next day, only in the first weak light of the morning, would she actually look his way and mutter "thank you" or "sorry," in either case leaving him to wonder "What for?"

Thank you for putting up with me, Vladimir thought as he wept into the softly mewing Kropotkin. *Sorry* I have to use you and humiliate you. That's *what for.*

THAT NIGHT, after Vincie's lovely squid had been eaten and two bottles of Crozes-Hermitage swilled, Vladimir took Fran into their bedroom and managed to shock both of them by actually speaking his mind. "Fran, you insulted me today," he told her. "You made light of my feelings for you. Then you laughed at my accent, as if I had a choice in where I was born. It was shocking.

You were so unlike yourself, so completely immature. I want..."
He stopped for a moment. "I would like..." he said. "Please, I would like an apology."

Frannie was flushed. Even her lips, purple with wine, were somehow turning red. Against the backdrop of her dark hair and ashen face, they were quite beautiful. "An apology?" she shouted. "Did you just call me immature? What are you, some kind of an idiot?"

"I'm...You...I cannot believe what you say..."

"I do apologize. It wasn't a question. What I meant to say was, and I hope it's not a sign of my immaturity: you *are* some kind of an idiot. Jesus, what did they do to you at that Midwestern college, that finishing school for Westchester's tender sons?"

"Please..." he muttered. "Please don't try to play the class card with me. Your parents are substantially wealthier than mine..."

"Oh, you poor immigrant," she said, a touch of spittle crowning her lower lip. "Someone get this guy a grant. A Guggenheim Fellowship for Soviet Refugees Who Love Too Much. It's a midcareer prize, Vladimir. You have to present a substantial body of love. Should I get you an application?"

Vladimir looked down at his feet, brought them closer together, as if Mother had been hovering over the scene all along. "I think maybe I should go now," he said.

"Well, that's just ridiculous." She shook her head, dismissing the idea. But she also walked over and put her freckled arms around him. He smelled paprika and garlic. He felt his knees buckle under her weight, what little of it there was. "Honey, here, sit down..." she said. "What's happening here? Where are you going? I'm sorry. Please sit down. No, not on my notebook. Over there. Scoot over. Now tell me what's wrong..." She lifted up his downcast chin. She pulled lightly on his goatee.

"You don't love me," he said.

"Love," she said. "What does that even mean? Do you know what that means? I don't know what that means."

"It means you have no regard for my feelings."

"Ah, so *that's* what love means. What a tricky definition. Oh, Vladimir, why are we fighting? You're scaring me to death. Why are you scaring me to death, sweetie? Do I love you? Who cares? We're together. We enjoy one another. I'm twenty-one."

"I know," he said sadly. "I know we're young and we shouldn't throw around words like 'love' or 'relationship' or 'future.' Russians settle down so early, it's absolutely stupid. They're never ready for it, and then they raise these cretinous kids. My mother was twenty-four when she had me. So I don't disagree with you. But, on the other hand, what you said..."

"I'm sorry," she said. "I'm sorry I was so caustic earlier today. I just don't know what to make of you at times. Here is this man, reasonably socialized and sophisticated, who wants to spend a day toothbrush-shopping with me. What does it mean?"

Vladimir sighed. "What does it mean?" he said. "I'm lonely. It means that I'm lonely."

"Well, whatever for? You spend every single evening with me, you've got all these new friends who, by the way, think you're the urban experience nonpareil, and I don't even mean that in a patronizing way... And my parents. Talk about settling down, bub. My parents love you. My father loves you... Lookee here." She jumped on the bed and started banging the wall separating her bedroom from her parents'. "Mom, Dad, get in here! Vladimir's having a crisis!"

"What are you doing?" Vladimir shouted. "Stop! I accept your apology!"

But after a minute of commotion on both sides of the wall, the parents trooped right into Fran's mausoleum, both *professori* dressed in matching silk pajamas, Joseph Ruocco still clutching a bedside tumbler of liquor in his hand. "What is it?" Vincie shrieked, blindly trying to survey the scene through her reading glasses. "What happened?"

"Vladimir thinks I don't care for him," Fran announced, "and that he's all alone in the world."

"What nonsense!" Joseph bellowed. "Who told you that? Here, Vladimir, have a shot of Armagnac. It steadies the nerves. You both look so...agog."

"What did you do to him, Frannie?" Vincie wanted to know. "Are you having a case of the tempers again? She has these little episodes sometimes."

"*A case of the tempers again?*" Frannie said. "Mom, are you becoming *unhinged* again?"

Joseph Ruocco sat down on the bed, on the other side of Vladimir, and put an arm around the mortified fellow. Smelling entirely of alcohol and fermented grape, he nonetheless remained quite steady and assured. "Tell me what happened, Vladimir," he said, "and I will try to adjudicate. Young folks need guidance. Tell me."

"It's nothing," Vladimir whispered. "It's all better now..."

"Tell him you love him, Dad," Fran said.

"Frannie!" Vladimir shouted.

"I love you, Vladimir," said Professor Joseph Ruocco, drunkenly but earnestly elucidating each word.

"I love you, too," Vincie said. She made space for herself on the bed, then reached over to touch Vladimir's cheek, pale, entirely drained of blood. The three of them turned to Frannie.

Fran smiled weakly. She picked up the passing Kropotkin and rubbed his fat stomach. The cat looked up to her expectantly. Indeed, they were all waiting for her to render a verdict. "I care about you a lot," she told Vladimir.

THE RUSSIAN DEBUTANTE'S HANDBOOK

"You see!" Joseph cried. "We all love Vladimir, or care about him a lot as the case may be…Listen, Vlad, you're very important to this family. I got a daughter here, my only daughter, I'm sure your parents must know exactly what that feels like, to have an only daughter…And she's a brilliant daughter…Don't blush, Frannie, don't shoo me away, I know when I speak the truth."

"Daddy, please," she whispered, not entirely in reproach.

"…But brilliance carries a price, I don't have to cite precedent for Vladimir, he's marinated in our culture long enough to know where the American intelligentsia stands on the totem pole. He knows that people marked for greater things are often the least happy of all. And God knows where the hell I'd be today if it wasn't for Vincie. I love you, Vincie. I might as well say it. Before I found Vincie, well…I could be abrasive, let's just say. There weren't many takers. And Frannie…"

"Dad!"

"Let's be truthful, honey. You're not the easiest person to be with. I'm sure whatever you said to Vladimir today was wildly inappropriate."

"Wildly," Vincie said. "That's exactly the right word to use."

"Thank you, Vincie. My point is: There aren't too many people who can handle our Frannie. But you, Vladimir, you're imbued with this patience, this superhuman ability to abide…Maybe it's a Russian trait, queuing for sausages all day long. Ha ha. I'm kidding. But I'm also serious. We know you can live with Frannie's genius, Vladimir, maybe even stoke the embers now and then. I'm not saying get married. I'm saying…What am I saying?"

"We love you," Vincie said. She reached over and kissed him on the lips allowing Vladimir a taste of many things. Medicine. Balm. Squid. Booze.

———

BUT THE RUOCCOS had said it all. The kissing was almost superfluous. They had been honest with him.

He finally understood the dynamic.

It had involved some singular foresight on their part, but after six weeks of living with Vladimir, here's what they had in mind.

They would be a family. Not terribly different from a traditional Russian family, really. Living in the same communal apartment, two generations separated by one flimsy wall, the sound of the young ones' lovemaking reassuring the old ones of their continuity. He would accept his place by Fran's side. Their life would be uneven and strange, but not much stranger, and certainly not as awful, as the life that preceded this one. At least, with the Ruoccos, his lack of ambition was a virtue, not a vice. At least he could Jew-walk to his heart's content. He could spread his feet left and right, he could wear clown's shoes if he so desired, flip-flopping his way to their marital bed, sipping from a glass of nocturnal Armagnac, and nobody would care.

To quote Vincie's kitchen wisdom, they all had bigger fish to fry.

And that would be the compromise, not bad as compromises go. He would never be lonely in America. He would never need turn to the Girshkins for their dubious parental comforts, never have to spend another day as Mother's Little Failure. At the age of twenty-five, he would be born into another family.

He would have reached, all by himself, the final destination of every immigrant's journey: a better home in which to be unhappy.

THAT NIGHT, after the professors had gone back to their bedroom, after calm had been restored, after the organic toothbrush had been removed from its hand-stitched pouch and its gentle fibers brushed against their gums, Fran wrapped him up in a blanket, tucked his favorite extra-fluffed pillow beneath his head, and kissed him good night. "Just relax," she said. "We're going to be okay. Dream of something nice. Dream of our trip to Sardinia next year."

"I will," he said. He hadn't heard of their trip to Sardinia, but that was all right. He had to accept these things on faith.

"Promise?" she said. "Promise you don't hate me."

"I don't," he said. He didn't.

"Promise you won't leave me . . . Just promise."

"I won't," he said.

"And we'll go have a drink with Frank tomorrow. Now there's one person who loves you like crazy."

"Okay," Vladimir whispered. He closed his eyes and lapsed into a dream immediately. They were on a beach in the very south of Sardinia, the skies so cloudless he could almost see the belfries of Caligari in the distance. They were lying naked on a beach blanket and he was erect, *wildly* erect, to use Joseph's parlance, wildly erect and entering Fran discreetly from the back, amazed at how dry she was inside, how she made no sounds of either protest or passion. He spread the dimpled white cheeks of her tiny ass with two hands and slowly, with great difficulty, maneuvered himself inside her brittle womb. As he was doing so, she licked her index finger, turned a page of the nameless journal she was reading, and, yawning, scribbled her lengthy comments at the margins. Flamingos watched them with Sardinian disinterest, while, nearby, beneath a beach umbrella stenciled with the name of their *pensione*, Vincie Ruocco was fellating her husband.

11. VLADIMIR GIRSHKIN'S
DEBUTANTE BALL

IN THE MEANTIME, FRANNIE WAS RIGHT. SLAVOPHILE Frank did love him like crazy. And he wasn't alone.

Beyond the walls of his new family's bastion, its terraced loggia surveying the Gotham plain, Vladimir had attracted a loyal cadre of downtown libertines, louche, mostly white folk with improbable names like Hisham and Banjana, and the occasional expatriate from the working class, some poor Tammi Jones. These round-the-clock hipsters, basting in their own suavity and the heady funk of extreme youth, had such a terrific demand for him that Vladimir soon found that his workday was now only an extension of his sleeping hours; real life began as soon as the last refugee was promptly thrown out of the Emma Lazarus Immigrant Absorption Society at 4:59.

HE REGULARLY SAW Slavophile Frank. They would take walks from Frank's apartment, the house that St. Cyril built, along windswept (even in late summer) Riverside Drive, conversing only in the great and mighty mother tongue. Sometimes they made it as far down as the Algonquin, where Fran awaited them. The Algonquin was a part of the Old New York that Fran so adored, a nostalgia that Vladimir gamely understood, given his own for the sepia-toned Russia of his parents—a sooty and uncomfortable universe, but one with charms of its own. They sat where Dorothy Parker's round table used to be, and Vladimir would buy Frank a seven-dollar martini. "Seven dollars," Frank would cry. "Merciful heavens! People do care about me."

"Seven dollars!" Fran said. "You spoil Frank more than you spoil me. It's... homoerotic."

"Perhaps," Frank said, "but don't forget that Vladimir has an expansive Russian soul. Money is not his concern. Camaraderie and salvation, that's his game."

"He's a Jew," Fran reminded them.

"But a *Russian* Jew," Frank said triumphantly, slurping at his free drink.

"All things to all people," Vladimir whispered. Yet upon sight of the bill his expansive Russian soul shuddered within his body's hairy cage. Truth was that in the thirty-one days of August, Vladimir had expended nearly U.S.$3,000.00, a money trail that blazed across Manhattan as follows:

BAR TABS: $875.00

TRADE PAPERBACKS & ACADEMIC JOURNALS: $450.00

WARDROBE OVERHAUL: $650.00

RETRO LUNCHES, ETHNIC BRUNCHES, SQUID & SAKE SUPPERS: $400.00

TAXI TARIFFS: $350.00

MISCELLANEOUS (Eyebrow waxing fees, aged balsamic vinegar for the Ruoccos, bottles of Calvados brought to parties): $275.00

By August's end, he was broke. A shameful credit card (the first card ever to bear the Girshkin family name) was winging its way north from the usury capital of Wilmington, Delaware. A depressing thought had flitted through Vladimir's mind. Perhaps he could ask Frannie's father for a little handout... Say U.S.$10,000. But then wasn't he already imposing on the Ruoccos for room and board? Not to mention the family's lavish hugs and open-mouthed kisses? To ask for pocket money besides...? What hubris.

Yet it was still a mystery to Vladimir how his new friends— theoretically all were starving students—never worried about picking up a round of drinks at the Monkey Bar or buying a Mobutu-style leopard hat on a whim. The Ruoccos, of course, had inherited a half dozen turn-of-the-century cast-iron fortresses around the city, while Frank's family owned several states tucked away in America's vast interior. And yet they all looked at Vladimir as the rich working man—the grant-toting, philanthropic professional.

But why shouldn't Vladimir spend money for the first time in his life?

Just look at him! There he is at some Williamsburg art opening, sneering, scoffing, sniping, pretending to suffer, subtly insulting the gallery owner (a failed conceptualist), while across the room a radiant Francesca is waving for him to come over, and the drunk Adonis Tyson is urgently bleating his name from beneath a wine cart, trying to confirm Bulgakov's exact patronymic.

It's been thirteen years since the Leningrad sickbed, since that lifetime of reading Tolstoy's descriptions of Winter Palace balls while spitting snot into a handkerchief. Finally, it would seem, Vladimir has found his way out into the world. Finally, our debutant is playing Count Vronsky for the downtown nobility in their checkered bowling pants and burnished nylon finery. The reports from the New World were true: In America the streets are paved with gold lamé.

BUT HE COULDN'T abandon Challah completely. Namely, he couldn't abandon his share of the rent, else Challah would be homeless. It wasn't as if she could crash with friends, after all. She had none. Meanwhile, two months had passed since he had stayed at his legal address on Avenue B. Alphabet City was becoming something of a memory now that its romantic poverty no longer warmed the heart.

The next day Vladimir found himself on Avenue B, sitting at the kitchen table filling out an application for a second credit card. Somewhere outside a piece of chicken was being barbecued, and when he closed his eyes and cleared his ears of the urban cacophony Vladimir could almost imagine that he was nine commuter railstops into Westchester, grilling weenies with the Girshkins.

And then Challah came in.

She might as well have bubbled up from Atlantis, this strange outsized woman with the dark makeup and the exposed midriff showing yet another self-mutilation: a navel piercing, from which a heavy silver crucifix dangled on its way to her crotch. Leave it to Challah not to realize that, while small nasal piercings were sanctioned, a crotch-to-navel crucifix absolutely screamed "Connecticut."

Vladimir was so shocked to see her, he rose automatically from his credit card application, noticing now the full effect of his surroundings: the harness, the leash, the K-Y, the den-o'-vice motif which would have given Dorian Gray a prompt heart attack. So this had been his home! Perhaps Mother had been right about some things.

Challah, on the other hand, did not appear shocked. "Where's the money?" she said. She stepped over a mysterious jumble of faux fur that blocked the way to the kitchen and then turned on the faucet to wash her hands.

"What money?" Vladimir said. Money, money, he was thinking.

"The rent money," came the answer from the kitchen.

That money. "I have two hundred," he said.

Immediately she was back from the kitchen, her arms akimbo. "Where's the other two hundred?" He had never seen this posture (which was such a crucial part of her job) projected at his person before. Who did she think he was? A client?

"Give me a few days," he said. "I'm having a cash-flow problem."

She took a step toward him, and he took a step back to the fire escape, the place he distinctly remembered as their prime cuddling ground, now more plausible as an actual escape route. Fire *escape*. Yes, it made sense.

"No few days," she said. "If I don't pay by the fifth of the month, Ionescu's going to charge an extra thirty dollars."

"That bastard," Vladimir said, hoping for solidarity.

"Bastard?" she said. And then paused as if weighing the heft of that word. Vladimir put his hands out in front of him. He was getting ready to deflect the full force of a comparison between himself and the bastard. Challah spoke instead. "I should be looking for a new roommate, shouldn't I?" she said.

So he had been downgraded to roommate status. When did all this happen? "Sweetheart," he said, rather unexpectedly.

"You bastard," she said finally, but the emotion had clearly been exhausted from that sentiment over the past weeks. Now it was but a statement of fact. "Don't speak to me until you have the rest of the money." She stepped aside to indicate that Vladimir could leave.

As he went past her, he felt a change in temperature; her body was always in deep negotiation with the atmosphere around it, and it made him want to reach out with a comforting arm, the arm he had cultivated for the past month with Francesca. Instead he said: "I'll have the money by tomorrow. I promise you that."

Outside, it was Sunday, the first of September. He was homeless in a certain way, but the heat clothed him in several layers, and, of course, Francesca and his new family were only six avenues to the west. Ah, humiliation. It always left him with a vaguely vinegary taste in his mouth, and, when dispensed by a woman, made him long to see his father, who had a singular appreciation for the ego's lacerations.

Challah had become proficient at her craft.

And he needed money.

PART III

MR. RYBAKOV'S
AMERICAN PAGEANT

PRESENTLY, THE TRUTH BECAME OBVIOUS: STATE-sponsored socialism had been a good thing. Vladimir spent his waking hours daydreaming of the simple life of his parents. A walk along the Neva River with your intended: no charge. Box of stale chocolates and one wilted rose: fifty kopeks. Tickets for two to the Worker's Allegorical Puppet Theater: one ruble, ten kopeks (student rate). Now that was courtship! Empty wallets, empty stores, hearts filled with overflowing... If only he and Frannie could travel back in time, away from the crude avarice of this uncultured metropolis, back to those tender Khrushchev nights.

Vladimir woke up with a start. Oh? And what the hell was this? A daredevil roach was making her way up the death blades of the paper shredder. An enterprising couple in ethnic garb was wrestling with an acculturation facilitator over a set of fingerprints. Dah! He was at work! The Emma Lazarus Immigrant Absorption Society, that nonprofit gulag, was open for business!

Yes, all the signs pointed to his somnolent weekday money-making, every hour bringing with it another U.S.$8.00. He had been asleep from nine to noon. Three hours. Twenty-four dollars. Two dry martinis and a tapa of *jamon serrano*. A Bombay silk handkerchief for Fran.

"Not enough," he said aloud. A recent tête-à-tête with his calculator had pinpointed the need for an additional $32,280 per year to meet Challah's rent and the most basic Fran-based expenditures. With needy eyes he surveyed his little precinct. A junior clerk at the adjacent desk was effortlessly inhaling her homemade noodles and octopus, glancing impatiently at her faux Cartier watch with every breath of food.

"Mmph," the junior clerk said.

This mindless grunt set Vladimir off on a trail of thoughts which brought him, in a roundabout way, back to the money-centered dreams he had been dreaming for the past three hours, and there, in the middle distance, suspended in the air, there floated...an Idea. A turbo-prop flying over a deserted landing strip, its pilot a certain Soviet sailor-invalid.

It took eight rings for Mr. Rybakov to hop over to his phone. "Allo! Allo!" the breathless Fan Man said. There was splashing in the background. The grind of machinery. A kind of improvised yodeling. Well, someone was starting his afternoon on a high note.

"Allo, Mr. Rybakov. Vladimir Girshkin, your resettlement specialist and faithful servant."

"And it's about time," Rybakov shouted. "The Fan and I were wondering..."

"My apologies. Work, work. The business of America is business, as they say. Listen, I was just inquiring about your case in Washington—"

Vladimir stopped. Okay. That was a lie. Not so hard. Just like lying to Mother. Or pretending with Challah. Now what?

"Washington," said the Fan Man. "Columbia District. That's our nation's capital! Oh, you crafty little fuck...Well done!"

Vladimir took a deep breath. He tugged on his polyester tie. It was time for the pitch. It was time for the money. "I was wondering," he said, "if you could reimburse me for the plane fare."

"Of course. Plane fare. Such trifles. How much?"

Vladimir tried on a few sums. "Five hundred dollars," he said.

"Flying first-class, I see. Only the best for my Girshkin. Say, let's meet around five. I'll give you the money and we'll take the SS *Brezhnev* for a harbor run."

"SS *Brezhnev?*" Had Mr. Rybakov peeked into Vladimir's socialist dreams?

"My new speedboat."

"Capital," Vladimir said.

AT THE APPOINTED TIME Vladimir squeezed into an elevator. At ground level he found his own tattered compatriots from the office (their loafers scuffed and unpolished, their dresses acrylic blends from bargain basements) flushed out onto Broadway: a single nonprofit ray amid the gleaming masses of the surrounding law offices and investment firms. He quickly crossed the high-rise graveyard of Battery Park City, and arrived, red-cheeked and winded, at the marina.

The SS *Brezhnev* was a cigarette boat—long, thin, and sleek, a veritable Francesca of the seas—bobbing playfully between two gargantuan yachts, both under the blue flag of Hong Kong, both looking bloated and unwieldy in comparison to their neighbor.

"Ahoy," Mr. Rybakov cried in English, waving his captain's hat.

Vladimir clambered onto the boat and hugged the happy Rybakov. He noticed that both he and his host were wearing vintage trousers, plaid shirts, and shiny ties. Throw in the guyabera and janitor pants, and the two of them could start their own clothing line.

"Welcome aboard, friend," Rybakov said. "A pleasant day for a sail, no? The air is clear, the water placid. And here I have prepared a parcel with your reimbursement and a complimentary sailing cap."

"Thank you, Admiral. Why, it fits just perfectly." Now the look was complete.

"I've had Brezhnev's likeness imprinted on the back. And allow me to introduce you to Vladko, my maritime Serb and first mate. Vladko! Come meet Vladimir Girshkin."

A hatch opened, and from the lower deck there emerged a preternaturally tall, round-chested, pink-eyed, near-naked young man, as substantial as anything Serbian myth ever produced. He blinked repeatedly and covered his eyes. Behind him, a large striped cat (or maybe a small tiger) roamed a devastated landscape of crushed tomato-soup cans, empty gas canisters, deflated soccer balls, and all kinds of time-worn Balkan paraphernalia: coats-of-arms, tricolors, blown-up photographs of fatigue-clad men with guns standing solemnly around makeshift graves.

"Ah, I believe we share practically the same name," Vladimir told Vladko.

"*Ne, ne,*" the Serb protested, his expression still that of a man emerging from a bomb shelter. "I am Vladko." Perhaps his Russian was limited.

"And this," said Rybakov, pointing to a miniature fan mounted on the dashboard, "is the Fan's little niece, Fanya."

"I have had the pleasure of meeting your esteemed uncle," Vladimir started to say.

"But she's too young to talk!" Rybakov laughed. "Oh, you romantic cad." He turned to the Serb: "Vladko, hey there! First mate on the bridge! Start the engines! Away we go!"

With a postindustrial hum like that of a desktop computer powering up, the *Brezhnev*'s engines were engaged. Vladko expertly navigated her past the hefty sloops of the marina, setting course around the southern tip of Manhattan Isle. A boat ride! Vladimir thought with childish glee. It was one of the million things he'd never done. Oh, the stench of the open sea!

"What did you see in Washington?" Mr. Rybakov shouted over the gnashing wind and roiling waters, both easily separated by the *Brezhnev*'s aerodynamic prow.

"Your case remains highly contentious," Vladimir cheerfully lied. Yes, the key was to remain cheerful. Big smile. They were playing Ducking Reality, a delightful little game expressly designed for Russian émigrés. Why, Vladimir's own grandmother was a national champion. "I have met with several members of the House Judiciary Committee..."

"So, I take it, you visited the president at his White House."

"It was closed," Vladimir said. And why was it closed? Easy enough. "The air-conditioning broke."

"And they couldn't turn on a few *fans*?" Rybakov shook his head and his fist in protest to the White House staff. "All these Americans are pigs. Air-conditioning. Hypermalls. Trash, these people. I ought to write another letter to the *Times* on the theme of 'Where Is This Country Going?' Except as a citizen I would have more clout."

"Any day now," Vladimir reassured him. It was good to keep these things open-ended.

"And did you see the president's developing young daughter? That delightful creature!"

"I caught a glimpse of her at the Kennedy Center. She's coming along nicely." Now, this wasn't even lying anymore. This was storytelling for invalids. This was social work. This was outreach to the elderly.

Rybakov rubbed his hands together and winked at Vladimir. Then he sighed and fingered the insignia on his cap. He wiped the water spray off his sunglasses. Leaning against the bow of his speedboat in his sunglasses and cap, this was as close as Mr. Rybakov had ever come to looking like a New World person—rich, American, in control. Vladimir was reminded of his own adolescent daydreams: young Vladimir, the simple-minded son of a local factory owner, running triumphantly down the field of his Hebrew school's opulent Recreation Centrum, the eyes of the local Benetton-clad maidens following intently the brown oblong ball encased in his burly arms as he scored the "home goal" or "home run" or whatever it was he had to score. All in all, Vladimir's American dreams formed a curious arc. During adolescence he dreamed of acceptance. In his brief days at college he dreamed of love. After college, he dreamed of a rather improbable dialectic of both love *and* acceptance. And now, with love and acceptance finally in the bag, he dreamed of money. What fresh tortures would await him next?

"Maybe next time you're in Washington," Mr. Rybakov was saying, "you could introduce me to the first daughter. We could go out for ice cream. A young lady like her could be very interested in my tales of the sea."

Vladimir nodded his assent as the half-moon of southern Manhattan rapidly receded behind them. The skyscrapers, chief among them the World Trade Center towers, appeared as if they were rising directly out of the water (an almost Venetian effect), or as if they were perched on an offering platter.

"There she is!" Rybakov shouted to Vladko. They were fast approaching a cargo ship anchored midharbor, her hull rusted pink, her prow stenciled with the Cyrillic legend: *Sovetskaya Vlast'*, or *Soviet Might*. The vessel flew under the somber red-and-black flag of Armenia, which, as Vladimir remembered from his abbreviated Leningrad schooling, was a land-locked country. "Aha," Vladimir said, his tone full of simulated good nature. "An Armenian flag on a ship. Now here's a curious sight."

Once the *Brezhnev* drew alongside the stern of the *Vlast'*, a rope was thrown overboard by an unseen Armenian sailor and speedily tethered to the *Brezhnev* by the indispensable Vladko. A metallic boat—no, a very uncomplicated raft, like the cover of a shoebox—was soon lowered as well. "I see the Armenians are expecting us,"

Vladimir said. He suddenly thought of Francesca, of her proximity... Why, at this very moment, across the bay and only two kilometers uptown, she was returning from school to the Ruoccos' bright little aerie, dropping her satchel by the bread-maker, washing the heat off her face in the cat's bathroom with its oddly comforting smells. Yes, she was making Vladimir into a human being, an indigenous citizen of this world.

"What Armenians?" Rybakov said. "These are Georgians."

"Georgians," Vladimir said. It was better not to ask questions. But a note of fear sounded in the back of his head, that cramped space where his money dreams were also headquartered. Fear and money. They went well together.

Once the Georgians' lifeboat was aligned with the *Brezhnev*, Vladko rushed over to help Rybakov aboard, but the sporty septuagenarian used his crutches to catapult himself inside. "Look at me!" he cheered. "I can still whack the both of you youngsters!"

"Which gun do I bring?" Vladko mumbled, saddened by his own irrelevance.

Gun? Vladimir's Fear-Money gland coiled around his brain and squeezed gently. "We'll be searched," Rybakov said. "So you might as well bring something impossible to conceal, then turn it in immediately to show compliance. The Kalashnikov, say."

Vladko disappeared below deck.

"Ensign!" the Fan Man said to Vladimir. "Hurry up. The television program about the comical black midget starts promptly at eight o'clock Eastern Standard Time. I cannot miss it."

"You go on," Vladimir said, pretending to play with Fanya, the little fan, as if he couldn't be bothered with Mr. Rybakov's little errands. "I will await your return."

"Oho, what is this?" Rybakov said. "Your presence is both requested and required. We're doing all this for you, you know. You don't want to disappoint the Georgians."

"Yes, clearly not," Vladimir said. "But you must see my concerns. I am from Russia originally, this is true, but I am also from Scarsdale…From Westchester…" This seemed to eloquently sum up his concerns.

"And?"

"And I'm worried about…Well, Georgians, Kalashnikovs, violence. Stalin was a Georgian, you know."

"What a *pizdyuk* you are," Rybakov huffed, alluding to the kind of man who is somehow vagina-like in nature. "The Georgians take time out of their busy schedule to pay tribute to you, they've sailed around the world with duty-free gifts, and you cower like a milksop. Get in here!"

"And I won't have you badmouthing Stalin either," he added.

THE TWO SEAMEN were the largest Georgians Vladimir had ever seen, each about two hundred pounds (the *Vlast'* must have carried some incredible rations), and each with the gloomy oblong face and fertile black moustache common to the men of Caucasus.

"Vladimir Girshkin, these are Daushvili and Pushka, both associates of my son, the Groundhog."

"Hurrah!" the two men said. But quietly.

The swarthier of the two, the one named Pushka, which, Vladimir assumed, was a nickname, for it meant "cannon" in Russian, said in a collegial tone: "And now we will go inside for the *zakuski.* You will have to give us your weapon, blondie."

Vladko bowed and surrendered his immense Kalashnikov, the first weapon Vladimir had ever seen; the Georgians bowed back, and Vladko bowed yet again—a merger between two Japanese banks was now seemingly complete. They walked along the starboard of the *Vlast',* Vladimir eyeing the Statue of Liberty across the harbor, wondering if any crime could be committed directly in her sight.

The color she was painted, Soviet-cafeteria green, did not inspire confidence. Francesca, meanwhile, was likely hunting through the Arts section of the paper, rolling a cigarette over the coffee table, and planning a triumphant evening out for the two of them.

"Watch your little head, friend," Daushvili said. They ducked into a humble room, unexposed pipework serving as roof, the walls decorated with pages of German automobile magazines and the occasional poster of Soviet pop diva Alla Pugacheva parading her strawberry bouffant at the EuroVision Song Contest, crooning her summertime hit "A Million Scarlet Roses." The Georgians were seated around a long foldout table covered in *zakuski*. From afar, Vladimir could already spot the glossy blackness of cheap caviar flanked by plates of rusty herring. He was hoping for skewers of Georgian *shashlik*, preferably lamb, but there was no grill in sight.

The head of the group was not a captain or any kind of sailor. He was, as might be expected, dressed in sunglasses and Versace, as were the two associates to his right and left. All three had classic Indo-European faces: high, sloping foreheads; thin, albeit curved, noses; hazy traces of facial hair around the upper lip. The rest of the coterie was far coarser in appearance—bigger men with bushier mustaches, dressed in track suits. Half looked like Stalin, the other half like Beria. Several of them even wore sailor caps, although the crest of whatever navy they had once belonged to had long been removed.

"I am Valentin Melashvili," the leader announced to Vladimir in a rumbling Bolshoi-grade bass. "The crew of the *Sovetskaya Vlast'* express their admiration for you, Vladimir Borisovich. We have just heard of your rampage through Washington on Mr. Rybakov's behalf. And, of course, we all follow the exploits of your enchanting mother, Yelena Petrovna, in the *New Russian Word* and the *Kommersant Bizness Daily*. Sit, sit . . . No, no, not there. At the head of the table, of course. And who is this gentleman?"

The Serb waved awkwardly, his hair an incongruous yellow mop in a sea of black curls. "Vladko, go outside," Rybakov instructed. "We are with friends now. Go!"

First they disarm the Serb, then they throw him out altogether. "Death!" Vladimir's Fear-Money gland was shouting. "Death is the very opposite of money."

"Well, to begin with," Melashvili said, "a toast to the Ground-hog, our friend, our benefactor, our great mountain eagle circling the steppes...*Za evo zdarovye!*"

"*Za evo zdarovye!*" Vladimir cheered as he plucked a shot glass off the table. Now what the hell was he cheering about? Get a hold of yourself, Volodya.

"*Za evo zdarovye!*" Rybakov shouted.

"*Za evo zdarovye,*" the other Georgians said simply.

"So, here's a question for you, Vladimir," the charming Melashvili said. "I know you've been to university, so you might know the answer to this one. Question: Who on the Lord's earth can match the hospitality and generosity of the Georgian people?"

Obviously a trick question. "No one," Vladimir started to say, but Melashvili interrupted him. "The Groundhog!" he cried. "And to prove it, the Groundhog sends you fifty cartons of Dunhill cigarettes. Pushka, fetch the smokes! Look here. Five hundred packs. Ten thousand cigarettes. Sealed in cellophane to maximize freshness."

Dunhills. Vladimir could easily unload them for two dollars a pack. He could set up a little stand on Broadway. He could call out to the jaded masses in his best immigrant accent, "Dunhill! Dunhill! Top 100 percent number one brand! I give special price! Only just for you!" He could make an even thousand dollars, which, added to the five hundred Mr. Rybakov had given him, would net him $1,500.00 for the day. Now, if he subtracted that amount from the $32,280 he needed for Francesca to love him forever, that would leave him...Let's see, eight minus zero is eight, then carry the one...Ah, math was tricky business. Vladimir never had the patience. "Thank you, Mr. Melashvili, sir," he said, "but, honestly, I do not deserve such favor. Who am I? I am only this young fellow."

Melashvili reached over to ruffle Vladimir's hair, soft and pliable from the application of Frannie's Aboriginal Sunrise shampoo. "What gentle manners," the Georgian said. "Truly, you are a child of St. Petersburg. Please take the Dunhills. Enjoy the European quality in good health. Now, may I ask another question? What do our Golden Youth wear on their wrists these days?"

Vladimir was stumped. "It's a difficult question. Perhaps—"

"Personally," Melashvili said, "I think nothing will do but this genuine Rolex watch. Recently acquired from Singapore. Completely legal. The control number has been removed from the back."

Even better. At least fifteen hundred dollars from some fence on Orchard Street. Together with his previous loot, an even three thousand. "I will accept the Rolex with a heavy heart," Vladimir said, "for how will I ever repay your kindness?" Hey, not bad! he thought. He was getting the hang of this. He executed a little bow, the kind of bow they all seemed to favor—Georgian, Russian, and Serb alike.

He had to admit it was a pleasure dealing with these people. They seemed so much more polite and cultured than the work-obsessed Americans who crowded Vladimir's city. Sure, they likely committed all sorts of unfortunate violence in their off-hours, but then again, look how articuate this Melashvili was! He probably dropped in on Vladimir's uncle Lev whenever he was in Petersburg and they went, together with their wives, to the Hermitage and maybe for some jazz afterward. Bravo! Yes, Vladimir was ready to listen and learn from these people. Maybe he could even introduce them to Fran. He did his little bow again. *How can I repay your kindness?* Indeed.

Melashvili bristled: "No, not our kindness at all," he said. "We are merely travelers of the seas. The Groundhog! The Groundhog is to be thanked. Isn't that so, Aleksander?"

"Yes," Mr. Rybakov said. "Let us all thank my little Hog."

The Georgians whispered their thank yous, but this was hardly enough for Mr. Rybakov. "Let's go around the room," he shouted. "The way they do on that fat *schwartze*'s talk show. Let's talk about what we like most about working for the Groundhog." Rybakov thrust an imaginary microphone at Pushka. "Pushka, you say what?"

"Huh?"

"Pushka!"

"Well," Pushka said. "I guess I'll say that I like working for the Groundhog."

"No, but what specifically," the Fan Man said. "'I like the Groundhog, because…'"

"I like the Groundhog because…" The ensuing two minutes were silent enough for Vladimir to hear the masculine beating of his new Rolex. "I like him because…Because he is merciful," Pushka finally said to everyone's relief.

"Good. Now state an example."

Pushka pulled at his moustache and turned to Melashvili who nodded in encouragement. "An example. State an example. Let me think. Well, I'll give you an example. Back in eighty-nine my brother set up a little black-market currency exchange by the Arbat in Moscow, knowing full well that the Groundhog had already claimed that territory as his own…"

"Oh, no!" several voices said. "God help him!"

"Right, you're expecting the worst," said Pushka, his tone getting stronger as he reached the moral of the story. "But the Groundhog didn't kill him. He could have, but all he did was take his wife. Which was fine, because everyone took his wife. She was that kind of a wife. And so—"

"And so he taught him a lesson without resorting to violence," Melashvili filled in quickly. "You've proved your point: The Groundhog is merciful."

"Yes," the Georgians muttered. "The Groundhog is merciful."

"Very good!" Mr. Rybakov said. "That was a good example and well told. Bravo, Pushka. Now let's continue going around the table. Daushvili, you say what?"

"I'll say..." The big man looked Vladimir over, curling a mangy eyebrow until it reminded Vladimir of a sea horse resting on its side, something he had once seen in an aquarium or perhaps only in a dream.

"I like the Groundhog because..." Rybakov prompted him.

"I like the Groundhog because...Because he holds no prejudice against the southern nationalities," Daushvili said. "Sure, sometimes he'll call me a Georgian black-ass, but only when he needs to put me in my place or when he's in one of his lighter moods. As for persons of the Hebrew race, like our esteemed guest Vladimir Borisovich here, I'd say the Groundhog is positively awed by them. 'Three Yids,' he's always saying. 'All you need is three Yids to rule the world...'"

"Which brings us to the most important point about the Groundhog," Melashvili interrupted. "The Groundhog is a modern businessman. If the marketplace doesn't tolerate prejudice, why should the Groundhog? He needs the best and brightest on his side no matter what shade their ass. And if Vladimir can tame America's immigration police and get Mr. Rybakov his citizenship, well, who can tell how far the Groundhog will take him...Or where eventually he will land."

"Yes," Vladimir said, toying with the clasp of his sparkling Rolex. "Who can tell." He realized that this was one of the first things he had said during the entire interview, or get-to-know-you session, or whatever this was. The others must have noticed this as well, for they looked at Vladimir expectantly. But what more could he say? He had been delighted just to listen to them.

Vladimir finally broke the silence. "Is there any butter?" he asked. "I like a little butter on my caviar sandwich. That's how my mother, the esteemed Yelena Petrovna, used to make it for me when I was just a boy."

A fresh stick of butter was produced. Melashvili gently unwrapped it himself. Several crewmembers helped Vladimir spread it on black bread.

Soon they would toast Mother's health.

13. THE SEARCH FOR MONEY IN WESTCHESTER

DR. GIRSHKIN COUNTED OFF EIGHT HUNDRED DOLLARS in fresh twenties, wetting his fingertips between each and every bill. "It's better that you come to me with your sad money troubles," he said to Vladimir, "than get some damn credit card…"

His fingers shaking with money-lust, Vladimir counted his father's gift. He whispered the mounting dollar amounts in Russian, the language of longing, of homeland and Mother, his money-counting language: *"Vosem'desyat dollarov… Sto dollarov… Sto dvadtsat' dollarov…"* Dr. Girshkin, too, whispered along, so that to Western ears father and son might have been caught in the act of solemn prayer.

Afterward, Vladimir was charmed by how his father neatly arranged a backyard table with napkins and cutlery, as if he was a guru past his prime, receiving one of the few visitors who still bothered to ascend his mountaintop. His father removed a recent Polaroid from the fridge door showing a smiling Dr. Girshkin holding a tremendous glossy-black flounder with the hook still embedded in one fatty lip, and placed it on Vladimir's plate by means of introduction. The fish itself broiled away in the kitchen.

"Now, tell me about this new woman," said his father, taking off his pants, which he did whenever his wife was off the premises. "She's better than Challatchka?"

"One should not even compare," Vladimir said, watching Grandmother wheel herself toward the table then spin around midyard to mind her defenseless oak trees.

"Then will you make a home with her?" his father asked. "No, I think not," he answered the question himself. "It's never too wise to settle down with any one woman so early in life. You know, when I was a young student at Leningrad State, I had my own apartment on the embankment of the River Moika, a prime spot for lechery. And so, at all times of the day, women fellow-students would make their way across the Palace Bridge to spend some time with your father. I was well known, a popular Jew." He looked up to the heavens dimming above, as if his past life continued in some parallel universe.

"But the best, I'll tell you, was when we were sent to work the collective farms during summer breaks. We were all put in freight cars, the women and men in the same cars, mind you! It took three or four days to get to the farms and so the pissing and the shitting was done right out the freight doors. You would be sitting, talking with your chums, when all of a sudden, to your left, a beautiful, round bottom would come out to do the most intimate of business. And some of these women were big and blond, you know, the Slavs! Not that there's anything wrong with our own Jewish types, but, oh, when you found these women all alone in the middle of a hayfield and you'd say, 'Excuse me, I would like to make your acquaintance, comrade so-and-so!' You'd both be sweaty and shitty and drunk, but the fresh young sex out in the fields was sublime."

He jumped up suddenly and said, "Flounder," then rushed off to the kitchen. Vladimir chewed on the heel of the bread loaf and helped himself to vodka. He waved to Grandma, who shouted back something indecipherable and, using both of her frail arms, attempted to return the wave.

His father emerged with a sizzling pan and tossed mangled bits of flounder onto both of their plates; the art of filleting had never found favor with the doctor. "So what's the money for?" asked his father. "You must buy this woman little gifts, the garbage women like?"

"No, it's not that," Vladimir said. "She enjoys having a good time. She doesn't expect me to pay for her, but I have to pay for myself at least." He neglected to mention that he had been adopted by the Ruoccos. One family at a time.

"I don't know about this one," Dr. Girshkin said, stuffing his face with fish and stir-fried cabbage. "Challatchka was so nice and quiet. You could survive on your pauper's salary with her. But maybe this one will make you reconsider your priorities. I'm sure you know you have the smarts to make a lot of money in this country. And through honest work, not like..."

"I consider what you do honest work," said Vladimir, who at one point in Hebrew school had had a long argument with himself concerning the morality of his father's medical enterprise. The argument had been decided in his father's favor, although the reasoning was laced with Talmudisms intricate enough for Vladimir to lose track of in subsequent reenactments. Something about stealing a rich neighbor's cow, then charging him retail for the steaks.

"Honest, well," his father said. "Look what happened to poor Shurik."

"Oh?" Vladimir withdrew a long fish bone embedded between two molars. He remembered Uncle Shurik coarsely reprimanding Vladimir as a child for using the informal address (*ty* as opposed to *vy*) when chatting up Shurik's fat Odessa wife. "What's new with Shurik?"

"I don't know the particulars, and I don't want to know, personally, but they had a search warrant for his offices and everything." His father shuddered visibly, then put his hands together as a calming measure. He poured himself a mug of vodka and took a swig. "They say Shurik specialized in pyramid schemes. Know what those are, Volodya?"

Vladimir shook his head.

"Sometimes it shocks me how little you know about anything. Pyramid schemes, also known as Ponzi schemes, after one Carlo Ponzi. In the 1920s, this guy Ponzi, a little immigrant from Parma, comes to this fat land of ours with some bright ideas. He sets up a little investment club, takes money from greedy idiots, promises them impossibly huge returns, pays them off for a while by stealing from the next round of idiots, and then he screws everybody. Can you imagine it?"

Actually, Vladimir could. A pyramid scheme! Something for nothing. It sounded like a neat idea. How exciting to think his relatives were so gainfully employed. Perhaps they knew Mr. Melashvili and his seafaring Georgians.

"Shurik's going to get some good lawyers, I'm certain. Real American lawyers. But your mother is afraid that some of his files will lead to me, which is really science fiction when you think about it. As it stands, it would take some extraordinary sleuth work and a raft of self-incriminating patients to drag me into jail." His father laughed then coughed fiercely to expel a small bone that had strayed too far into his throat.

Vladimir pretended to busy himself with his flounder. His father had never talked with such candor about his dealings, although nothing was ever hidden from Vladimir. Especially since Mother had always gloated about how she, with only the abysmal education of a Soviet kindergarten teacher, had risen to such corporate prominence legally, while poor, stupid Father had to spend his days defrauding America's paradoxical health care system.

"But as for you, son, my advice is: you do what *you* want to do. That's my final pronouncement. Look at me. I never cared about medicine, about saving or prolonging the lives of my patients, not that I'm such a bad person. I care about other things: fishing, gardening, the opera. The only medical fascination I ever had was on those freight trains with the women. Then your grandmother said to me: become a doctor, you're smart, you'll do well. Well, it certainly turned out to be a lucrative profession in America, the way we practice it here, anyway." He swung his arm around to indicate he meant Fortress Girshkin with the little doctor's shingle blowing in the breeze underneath a fake antique lamp.

Vladimir's father finished off his mug and reached for a vodka refill. "Oh, yes," he said. "Please do what *you* want to do with your life. What do you want to do, anyway?"

"I'm not sure," Vladimir said. "Maybe I want to teach." Teach? Where the hell did that come from?

"Teaching, now that's a strange kind of profession," said his father. "There are some very unexceptional people out there teaching. And what if they send you to teach those kids in Harlem? Or the Bronx? Or Brooklyn? Or Queens? They'd tear you apart, those little animals. I was thinking, are you good with computers at all? Oh, but listen to me. Now I'm telling you what you should do. No, let's drink to your happy but impractical pedagogic dreams."

"And to Grandmother's health," Vladimir said.

"Yes, to that crazy old woman." Dr. Girshkin finished the contents of his mug, then squeezed his mustache for stray drops of the familiar liquid. He sighed, breathing out the firewater. "You know, Vladimir, you and your grandmother are really all I have to live for in the world, well, as far as any man has to live for other people— what is it they say?—no man is an island. Your mother, *nu*, I picture she'll be here with me till the end. We are like one of those many unfortunate corporate mergers they've had in the past decade; we are like Yugoslavia. But if I had to answer the question, who would I die for, if there was, say, a plane hijacking and the hijackers said that one of us had to be killed, well, I'd die for you or Grandmother without thinking twice."

Vladimir wiggled his toes in the tight childhood slippers (made of a resilient moleskin that lent itself to a frisky, animal foot odor) that his parents had saved and forced him to wear during visits. "Why would you die for Grandmother?" he asked. "She's older."

"It's a good question," said Vladimir's father and concentrated on it for a spell while chewing on the flabby underhang of his thumb. It was clear to Vladimir that his father had thought out this hijacking scenario many times. "I would say conclusively that I do not have all that much to live for in my life. I don't mean to sound especially sad but I'm sure many men my age would come to that conclusion. I think the only reason that I would not give up my life in exchange for Grandma's is to be a father to you, but it seems to me that you really haven't needed me as a father for some time now. You have a life that's so far removed from this house, which we worked so hard, your mother and I, to put together, that some-times . . . well, I wonder what the point was."

Vladimir considered his new life with the Ruoccos. How far he had come. Yes. What *was* the point of all that hard work? "Well, I hope we never all get hijacked," he said, moving aside his plate with the fragmented fish skeleton and wiping his dry brow with a napkin.

"I hope so too," Vladimir's father said, although his son remained unconvinced. If not in his professional or family life, then at least by dying at the hands of those reprehensible hijackers with the handlebar mustaches, Dr. Girshkin would be meted out a slice of dignity for all the world to see.

"So remember what we talked about today," said his father. "The most important thing: you do what *you* want to do. And also, don't get married unless you are ready to lose your happy youth. These are the two lessons we've learned today."

Vladimir's father got up, balancing himself against the plastic lawn table. He shook his bad leg (it had fallen asleep during dinner), then looked back to make sure Grandmother was all right as she wheeled herself about the Girshkin gardens. Having satisfied himself of his mother's well-being, Dr. Girshkin limped back into the kitchen to fetch tea and cake, leaving Vladimir to hope that his father had said everything he wanted to say to him.

But he hadn't.

AN HOUR LATER, his cheeks burning from his father's kisses, Vladimir was conveyed from village to city by the 8:12 P.M. Metro-North local train. If his peripheral vision was correct, he could have sworn he saw the flash of Mother's amber brooch, a cheap Baltic treasure, in a train carriage headed in the opposite direction. Soon she would be back in the house, half-asleep on the couch, quietly enumerating for her husband the ignominies suffered during her fourteen-hour work day, the whisperings of American underlings behind her back, the mysterious cabals in the men's room that were surely the signs of a native rebellion, a corporate coup d'etat. They always wanted more, the native-born. More money. Better health coverage. Endless two-week vacations. This is what happened when parents didn't set limits for their children, when one was born into a boundless world.

"Please, porcupine, your troglodyte workers are scared to death of you," the doctor would reassure his wife, as he brought her little dishes of eggplant caviar and whitefish salad, a cup of herbal tea to soothe her nerves. He would prop a pillow under her feet and tune the television to the show they both loved—the one where felonious movie stars were exposed for who they really were.

MEANWHILE, in her upstairs bedroom, Grandmother would be dreaming of a lone oak tree hulking over a garden of milkweed and evening primrose, and in the shade of the oak tree that bow-legged *goy* from the village regiment, a shiny red star on his army cap, would look up from his kasha bowl and smile his abundant country smile for her. Suddenly, they would be dancing a mazurka in some big-city palace of culture, and he would press her against his chest and kiss her lips, first chastely then not...Because here in the hermitage of Grandmother's dreams, among the wispy force fields of desire and history floating over the American suburbs, the kindly Sergeant Yasha finally loved her and there was enough happiness for all.

Downstairs, Dr. Girshkin was still awake. He examined his wife fast asleep on the couch, considered the difficulty of transporting her up to her bedroom, and, shaking his head in regret, retired to his basement abode.

In the basement, surrounded by plaster dust and loose electrical wires, the doctor had tried to recreate for himself the rickety village *izba* where he had spent his childhood: coarse off-white panels lining the walls were supposed to bring to mind the Russian birch; a set of unfinished wooden chairs gathered around a three-legged kitchen table bespoke an admirable poverty. On this table, there was some Pushkin, a little Lermontov, and, for some reason, a wayward copy of the *New England Medical Journal,* which the doctor quickly shunted under his bed. The great warm stove, the centerpiece of his youth, was missing from the ensemble, but what could one do?

The doctor turned on a fan, undressed, ate a conveniently placed piece of cheese, and put himself to bed. I will dream of the well-being of my son, he said to himself. But, alas, the dream would not come. There was something holding him back, an ugly impression from the little dinner party he had had with Vladimir. What was it? He had spoken of the great themes—the futility of love, the ephemeral nature of youth. But he had babbled on about nothing, really! All that verbosity, Russian melancholy, and nostalgia were for naught. As always, he had missed the point. He should have said... Let's see. Well, to start, he should have told Vladimir that he was tired. Just in those words: "Vladimir, I am tired." Yes that's what he should have said. Dr. Girshkin yawned as if to emphasize his tiredness.

And why am I tired, Vladimir? Well, if you must ask, I will answer. I am tired because emigrating to this country, leaving one's hut, one's yurt, one's Soviet-era high-rise requires an ambition, a madness, a stubbornness, a stamina that I have never had.

Ach. Dr. Girshkin rearranged his moist sheets and propped his pillow this way and that. No, that sounded too pathetic, too defeatist. Instead, he should have been more theoretical about the whole matter. "You see, Volodya," he should have said, "the Old World is populated by two breeds of peasants, the alpha peasant and the beta peasant. Now the alpha peasant, she feels the dry soil crack beneath her feet and quickly packs her family's bags for the New World, while the beta peasant, poor fellow with his weak, sentimental heart, stays put and tills the desperate land. Your mother? Well, as you might have guessed, she's the alpha peasant of our family, a force unswerving, impenetrable, inexorable. Do you follow me, Volodya?

"Good! Because let me tell you this: Contrary to your mother's refugee charter, it's all right to be less than your neighbor, to be a beta immigrant here in America where alpha immigrants are the rule. It's all right to let stronger people take responsibility for your life, to let them drag you to a better place, show you how it's done. Because, ultimately, my son, making compromises may be a necessity, but it's the constant weighing and reweighing of these compromises that becomes an illness."

Dr. Girshkin quivered with happiness at his insight. "An illness." Right! Or, perhaps, "a madness." That was better still.

He thought of ways he could share this information with Vladimir—maybe he could tempt him back to Scarsdale with the promise of more money, or they could plan an excursion to the city's famous Metropolitan Museum (their Near Eastern collections were quite impressive). Yes, a museum. The perfect location for imparting important lessons.

Dr. Girshkin finally drifted off to sleep, dreaming of father and son astride a winged Assyrian lion, soaring over the aerials and prickly spires of this unlovely land. The doctor couldn't imagine where the ancient beast was taking them, but, in the end, after a long full day of suffering, it was nice to simply take to the air.

14. THE SEARCH FOR
MONEY DOWNTOWN

THE NEXT MORNING IN MANHATTAN, VLADIMIR SHOOK off the shackles of slumber, vigorously brushed his teeth, took a long cathartic shower, and counted the goods: he had $800.00 from his father plus the $500.00 from Rybakov plus the still unsold Rolex and ten thousand Dunhill cigarettes. "A good start," Vladimir said to Francesca's sleeping form, "but I resolve to do better." And with that Gatsbyesque mantra on his lips, he set off once again for the jolly workaday world of the Emma Lazarus Society. He had barely made it through the reception area when Zbigniew, the Acculturation Czar, leapt out of the processing room and ambushed him. "Girshkin," he said. "It's here."

"Good God! What's here?"

"Your idiot countryman with the fan. Rybakov. His FOIA is here."

"Foh-yah?"

"Freedom of Information Act. *O moi boze!* How long have you been working here, Girshkin?" Zbigniew grabbed his employee's shirtsleeve and dragged him to his lair, the office of the chief acculturator. Here, Lech Wałesa waved to adoring dock workers from one wall, John Paul II smiled weakly from beneath his scepter, and taking center stage was the framed jacket cover of Zbigniew's vanity-press masterpiece *Pole to Pole: A Father & Son's Journey to the Heart of Polonia*.

"He got as far as the citizenship ceremony," Zbigniew rasped happily, waving the government file at him. Vladimir had caught him right after lunch—the most satisfactory, almost postcoital part of the Acculturation Czar's sad little day.

"That far."

"Picture for yourself a little scenario. Rybakov is taking the oath, he is at the part where you have to swear to defend the country against all enemies foreign and domestic, and, well...I suppose he takes this the wrong way or, more likely, he is drunk, because he spontaneously starts beating Mr. Jamal Bin Rashid of Kew Gardens, Queens. Beats him with both his crutches, it says here, while shouting racial no-nos."

"I see."

"Mr. Rashid is talked out of pressing charges, but—"

"The citizenship."

"Yes."

"Well, can't we do something?" said Vladimir. "I mean the man is a documented loon, surely there are exceptions for the mentally ill."

"What can we do for him? We could put him in a home where he won't hurt anybody. We can close down the visa section in Moscow so you Russian bastards stay home."

Yes, of course. "Thank you, *Pan Direktor*," Vladimir said, retreating to the unkempt comfort of his own desk. He rested his head against the desk's cool and unforgiving metal. This wasn't good news at all.

He had wanted Rybakov to get his citizenship.

He had wanted more goods and services out of the Georgians.

He had wanted to visit the Groundhog in Prava to extract some gifts from him personally.

At least there was the nightly dinner with the Ruoccos. Was it bouillabaisse night already? Wait, let's see...Monday—polenta, Tuesday—gnocchi...What came after Tuesday? According to the appointment book, a night with an anachronistic buffoon. A former best friend.

YES, it was Baobab Night. After ignoring Baobab's phone calls for nearly two months, Vladimir felt an ache in his heart, a subtle reminder of his *tonkost*, the Russian word signifying empathy, quiet compassion, a generosity of spirit.

No, that's not true. It was the *money*, of course. Bao had ways of making it, desperate ways.

The Carcass was celebrating its Modern Music Week. On this particular outing, the band and its audience had bridged the gap between artist and patron: both were dressed in accordance with the same flannel-and-boots look that was starting to seep out of the nation's unplugged Northwestern corner. Seattle. Portland, Oregon. Something or someone named Eugene. This was a worrisome development for Vladimir who did not want to wear flannels or boots, certainly not in the summer. He tugged nervously at his ample Cuban shirt. He would have to discuss this with Fran.

Meanwhile, Baobab was giving life to the "grinning from ear to ear" cliché; his entire face, even the thick nose bent at several junctures, was somehow caught up in the act of smiling. The sad thing was that it was Vladimir (just standing there drinking his beer) who provoked all this mirth in lonely Baobab.

Vladimir was reminded of their high school days: Vladimir and Baobab taking the Metro-North Railroad home from the math-and-science high school after a long day of subtle rejections by young women and men alike, discussing better ways to lodge their suburban selves into Manhattan's starry firmament. Wasn't this the same Baobab he once loved?

"Yup, Roberta's still sleeping with Laszlo," Baobab began his update, "but now I think Laszlo wants to sleep with me, too. It'll be a nice way to bring us all together. And I'm drawing up an outline for my own system of thought. Oh, and I think I've finally found a major to call my own: Humor Studies."

"But you're not very funny," Vladimir said.

"Real humor is not supposed to be funny," Baobab said. "It's supposed to be tragic, like the Marx Brothers. And I've found a great professor, Joseph Ruocco. Have you heard of him? He's going to be my advisor. He's both funny and sad. And I'm staying in New York, pal. I'm not joining this whole exodus to Prava, the fucking Paris of the 90s. That shit'll be over in six months, I predict. No, I'm sticking with this Ruocco guy. I'm sticking with reality."

"Baobab, I need money," Vladimir changed the subject.

He gave an overview of his problems in a Baobabian way.

"It certainly sounds like the class struggle to me," Baobab agreed. "Why don't you just tell this Frannie how poor you are? It's not shameful. Look at you...You have the bearing of an emancipated serf. Some women find that sexy."

"Baobab, have you been listening? I'm not going to ask her for a handout."

"All right," Baobab said. "Can I talk simply?"

"Please," Vladimir said. "I'm a face-value kind of guy. I read headlines and weep."

"Okay, simply put, then. Jordi, my boss, is a very nice guy. Do you take my word for it?"

"No drugs."

"He's got a son, twenty years old. An idiot. A nullity. Wants to go to this huge private college near Miami. Yale it's not, but they still have a selection process of sorts. Jordi paid some Indian to take the kid's college boards. The Hindustani did really well, which doesn't really explain how it took the kid six years to finish high school. The college wants to interview the kid. So we've got to send someone down who could talk impressively."

"You?"

"That was our thinking. But, as you can see, I'm white as a sheet. You got that olive-skinned thing going, and with that facial hair you look like a young Yasir Arafat."

"But I'm not quite . . . Jordi's what . . . Spanish?"

"Don't ever call him Spanish. Jordi's *fiercely* Catalan."

"And what happens when the kid shows up next year? Or do I have to go to college for him too?"

"The place is so gargantuan the interviewer will never see this kid again. Trust me, it's foolproof, and I don't even think it's terribly illegal. Impersonating a high school kid: not exactly the crime of the century, just a lame thing do. But for twenty thousand . . ."

"How now?" Vladimir said. Two sets of numbers floated through the stale downtown air. They didn't resolve themselves immediately, but it was clear that $20,000, when subtracted from the needed $32,200, left a fairly workable sum. "How much money?"

Baobab put his wet palms on Vladimir's little shoulders and shook him. He pulled down Vladimir's snap-brim until it was tight enough to hurt. He breathed his sour breath all over Vladimir and smacked his face, only half good-naturedly. His nose was getting even fleshier and he was looking and perspiring like a man twice his age and with a heart condition too. "You better start valuing our friendship," he said. And then he added something straight out of Girshkinland, or perhaps straight out of any familial relationship: "You fall in love with a woman, you fall out of love with a woman,

but your best friend Baobab is always there, even if he's not always
the most attractive guy to have around. You just never know when
you're going to need old Baobab."

"Thank you," Vladimir said. "Thank you for that."

15. THE SEARCH FOR
MONEY IN FLORIDA

A PEACH CADILLAC.

Vladimir had never seen one before, but he knew these vehicles once played an important part in the cultural development of the United States. This particular peach Caddy was idling by the curb of the Miami International Airport and belonged to a man who, along with most Mongolians and Indonesians, went by only one name; in this case, Jordi.

Jordi had amiably carried Vladimir's enormous duffel bag stuffed with collegiate attire through the airport maze and was remarking on how Vladimir had had the good sense to come prepared, though he would have gladly taken Vladimir shopping for a tweed jacket and rep tie. "That's what I like about you immigruns," he was saying. "You're not spoiled. You work hard. You sweat rivers. My father was an immigrun, you know? He built up our family's business with his own hands."

Built up his business? With his own hands? No, Jordi neither sounded nor resembled the drug dealer out of central casting, which Vladimir was expecting with some dread. He wasn't even Picasso-looking, which, Vladimir imagined, was the semblance to which all Catalan people aspired. He looked like a middle-aged Jew with a textile business. Middle-aged but closer to retirement than the glory days: his wide face burrowed with the wrinkles of over-tanning; his gait was brisk and yet he took the time to swagger in his glowing ostrich-skin loafers like a man with accomplishments behind him. "I have often dreamed of visiting Spain," Vladimir told him.

"*Si ma mare fos Espanya jo seria un fill de puta,*" Jordi said. "Do you know what that means? 'If my mother was Spain I'd be a son of a bitch.' That's what I think of the Spanish. White spics, that's all."

"I would only visit Barcelona," Vladimir assured the Catalonian.

"Eh, the rest of Catalunya ain't bad either. I fucked some little lady in Tartosa once. She was like some kind of dwarf."

"Small women can be nice," Vladimir said. He wasn't thinking of anyone in particular.

"We'll have to take off the goatee," Jordi said, once they were in the chilled car. "You look too old with the goatee. We're sending the kid to college, not to law school. Law school comes later."

What a coincidence: Jordi and Mother had similar plans for their progeny. Perhaps an introduction was in order. But how terrible that Vladimir would lose his prized goatee, which made him look five years older and ten years wiser. Fortunately, the very same hormones that were skimming off the top of his head were already sprouting hair efficiently most places below. And then there was the matter of the twenty thousand dollars. "I'll shave right away," Vladimir said.

"Good boy," Jordi said, reaching over to squeeze Vladimir's shoulder. His hands smelled like baby powder; the rest of his smell, as circulated by the gale-force air-conditioning, consisted of nine parts citrus-based cologne, one part male. "There's some soda in the cooler if you want," he said. He had that quaint working-class Queens pronunciation which turned "soda" into "soder," "tuna" into "tuner," and the U.S. into a mythopoetic land called "Ameriker."

Around them swirled the blightscape of motels with German

and Canadian flags, crappy chain restaurants with electrified cows and lobster tails, and, of course, the ubiquitous palms, those dear old friends of the temperate Northeasterner. "This is a nice car," Vladimir said, by way of conversation.

"It's a little too niggered up, don't you think? Tinted windows, oversized tires…"

Ah, a little racism before lunch. Time to put your progressive instincts to work, Vladimir. The Girshkins spent a hundred thousand dollars a year on your four-year socialist powwow in the Midwest. Don't let the alma mater down. "Mr. Jordi, why do you think people of color prefer tinted windows and the like? I mean, if that really is the case."

"Because they're monkeys."

"I see."

"But take a peach Caddy without the tinted windows and the fat tires, and you got yourself a classy car, correct? I'll tell you something: I rent four hundred of these a year. Everyone who works for me—New York, Miami, Côte d'Azur—everyone's got a peach Caddy. Don't like my style, work for someone else, *barrada. Pendejo.* Subject closed."

Meanwhile, the trashy motels of the north were giving way to the dignified Art-Deco facades of South Beach, and Jordi told Vladimir to keep a lookout for the New Eden Hotel & Cabana, which Vladimir remembered from his past journeys through South Beach as a tall, somewhat crumbling resort next to the modernistic loop of the Fountainebleau Hilton, the flagship of the mink stole era.

The New Eden's vertical, once-opulent lobby was built around a meticulously scrubbed chandelier careening several stories down to a circular arrangement of fraying velvet recliners. "Elegance never goes out of style," Jordi said. "Hey, look at all these good folks!" He waved to a gaggle of retirees with such gusto that Vladimir assumed they had all come from the old country together. But, to Jordi's disappointment, there was hardly a stir from the New Eden gang, its members enjoying a splendid afternoon's torpor. For those awake, Bunny Berrigan was playing over the speakers, vegetarian liver was being served in the Green Room—too many distractions to notice the arrival of Jordi and Vladimir, an unusual duo by anyone's standards.

Jordi returned from the reservations desk with some further bad news: "My secretary screwed up our reservations, the cow," he said. "Would you mind splitting a room with me, Vladimir?"

"Not at all," Vladimir said. "It'll be like a slumber party."

"Slumber party. I like that. That's a good way to put it. Why do little girls get to have all the fun?" Why? There was a very good reason why little girls, and only little girls, got to have all the fun at slumber parties. But Vladimir was going to have to find out for himself.

VLADIMIR PUT DOWN Jordi's grimy little electric shaver and looked at various angles of his scrubbed and itching face in the bathroom's three-sectional mirror. What a disaster. The sickly Vladimir of Leningrad looked back at him, then the scared Vladimir of Hebrew school, and finally the confused Vladimir of the math-and-science high school: a triptych of his entire lusterless career as a youngster. What a difference a little merkin-like hair made around his thick lips.

"Well?" Vladimir stepped out into the sunlit bedroom smothered in an endless assortment of floral patterns and wood, a New England bed-and-breakfast motif strayed way past the Mason-Dixon Line. Jordi looked up from his paper. He had sprawled out on one of the matching beds, dressed only in his swimming trunks. His body was loosely organized like a booming sunbelt city, suburban rivulets of fat spilling out in all directions.

"All of a sudden an attractive young man appears before me," he said. "What a difference a little shave makes."

"Is the interview tomorrow?"

"Hm?" Jordi was still appraising Vladimir's virgin face. "That's right. We'll go over what you have to say. But later. Now go out and play in the sun, tan your chin so that it don't stick out. And help yourself to some of this expensive champagne. You won't believe how much it costs."

Vladimir took the elevator down to the exit marked "cabana and pool." Outside, one could see why the deck chairs were empty and the beefy cabana boys loafing: Florida off-season in three-digit temperatures was a scary proposition.

Despite the misery, Vladimir toasted this stretch of coast with his champagne flute. He said, *"Vashe zdorovye,"* to the seagulls screeching above. The whole setup felt like home to Vladimir. In his youth, the Girshkins used to descend on the pebbly beaches of Yalta each summer. Dr. Girshkin had prescribed a daily dose of sun for the ailing Vladimir. Mother would park him for hours beneath that blinding yellow orb to sweat and cough up phlegm.

He was not allowed to play with other children (his grand-mother had branded them spies and informants), nor was he allowed a dip in the Black Sea, as Mother feared that a ravenous dolphin would eat him (several bottlenosed specimens could be seen disporting along the coast).

Instead, she had devised a game for them to play. It was called Hard Currency. Each morning Mother would have tea with an old friend of hers who happened to be a clerk at the Intourist Hotel for Foreigners and would brief Mother on the latest exchange rates. Then she and Vladimir would memorize the figures. They would start: "Seven British pound sterling equals..."

"Thirteen dollars American," cried Vladimir.

"Twenty-five Dutch guilders."

"Forty-three Swiss francs!"

"Thirty-nine Finnish markka."

"Twenty-five Deutsche marks!"

"Thirty-one Swedish krona."

"Sixty...Sixty-three...Norwegian..."

"Wrong, my little dope..."

The penalty for failure (and the reward for success) was a paltry Soviet kopek, but one day Vladimir managed to rack up an entire five-kopek coin, which Mother sadly fished out of her purse. "Now you can afford a Metro ride," she said. "Now you will get on the Metro and leave me forever."

Vladimir was so shocked by this pronouncement that he started to cry. "How can I leave you, *Mamatchka?*" he whimpered. "Where will I take the Metro all by myself? No, I will never ride the Metro again!" He cried all afternoon, suntan lotion dribbling down his cheeks. Not even a masterly display of acrobatics on the part of the man-eating dolphins could cheer him.

Ah, childhood and its discontents. Feeling much older and happier, Vladimir decided to mail Fran a postcard. The New Eden gift shop had an impressive selection of naked rumps dusted with sand, the manatee begging to be saved from extinction, and close-ups of plastic pink flamingoes roosting in Floridian front yards. Vladimir settled on the last of these as being perfectly representative. "My dear," he wrote on the back. "The immigrant-resettlement conference bores me to no end. How I hate my work sometimes." The conference had been a stroke of genius on his part. He even told Fran he was presenting a lecture based on his mother: "The Pierogi Prerogative: Soviet Jews and the Co-optation of the American Marketplace."

"I practice shuffleboard and mah-jongg whenever I can," he wrote to Fran, "just to get a leg up on you in time for our golden years. But before you don your babushka and I slip into a nice pair of bright-white slacks, let us, sometime soon, travel across this entire nation, and you can fill me in on your life from day one. We could be like tourists (i.e., bring a camera, look a certain way). I don't know how to drive, but am willing to learn. Can't wait to see you in three days and four hours."

He posted the card, then paid a visit to the Eden Roc bar, where he was duly interrogated about his age before the barkeep finally caved in on account of his receding hairline and gave him a lousy beer. That hairless chin of his, jutting out like a little boiled egg, was already becoming a liability. Two beers later, he decided to face up to his one other New York responsibility, this one a matter of duty not pleasure.

An irritated Mr. Rybakov came on the line immediately: "Who? Devil confound it. Which hemisphere is this?"

"Rybakov, it's Girshkin. Did I wake you?"

"I don't need sleep, commandant."

"You never told me you hit Mr. Rashid during the naturalization ceremony."

"What? Oh, but I'm in the clear on that one. My God, he was a foreigner! My English is not so good, but I know what the judge told me: 'To protecting country...against foreigner and domestic enemy...I am swearing...' Then I look to my left and what do I see? An Egyptian like the one at the newsstand who always overcharges me five cents for the Russian paper. Another foreigner trying to defraud the workers and the peasant masses and convert us to his Islam, that lousy Turk! So I did what the judge told to do: I defended my country. You don't give an order to a soldier and expect him to disobey. That's mutiny!"

"Well, you've certainly put me in an awkward position," Vladimir said. "I'm down here in Florida right now, playing tennis with the director of the Immigration and Naturalization Service, begging him to reconsider your case. It's forty degrees Celsius here and I'm about to have a myocardial infarction. Do you hear me, Rybakov? An infarction."

"Oi, Volodechka, please, please get me into that hall for the ceremonies again. I'll behave this time. Tell the director to forgive me that one incident. Tell him that I'm not all well up here." Nine hundred miles up the coast, Rybakov was surely tapping away at his forehead.

Vladimir sighed the deep sigh of a father coming to terms with his offspring's limitations. "Fine, I'll call you once I get into the city. Practice being civil in front of the mirror."

"Captain, I am following your directives without question! All power to the Immigration and Naturalization Service!"

JORDI LAY on his stomach, watching a show about a modeling agency, grunting along as the feeble bon mots flew and negligees slithered to the ground. The remains of his early dinner and two empty champagne bottles were lined up on a little table intended for card games or the like; an additional champagne bottle was afloat in a bucket of melted ice. It was possible to imagine a silver tray from the *Lusitania* bearing a hastily scribbled champagne bill floating in to join this hedonism in disrepair.

"I like the brunettes," said Vladimir, sitting down on his bed, shaking sand out of his sneakers.

"Brunettes are tighter than blondes," Jordi posited. "Do you have a girlfriend?"

"Yes," Vladimir said, beaming with pride at this admission and feeling even younger than his clean-shaven face.

"What color hair?"

For some reason Vladimir thought of Challah's reddish curls, but then he caught himself and answered correctly: "Dark, very dark."

"And how does she take it?" Jordi wanted to know. With sugar or with milk, was that the question?

"She takes it well," he said.

"I mean how does she...Oh, just drink, boy. You have to be as drunk as me to be my friend!"

Vladimir did as he was told, then asked about Jordi's son, that big imbecile.

"Ah, little Jaume." The proud papa sat up and slapped his haunches, businesslike. He turned down the volume on the television, until the models' squealing was down to the whisper of the waves brushing against the sand outside. "He's a bright kid, he just can't do well in a school environment. So maybe you shouldn't talk like you're too book-smart, but mention a couple of books if you can. Now, he's into football although they kicked him off the team last year." This uninspiring fact seemed to bring about a little reverie on Jordi's part. "But I blame the coach, the school, and the Board of Ed for not understanding my boy's needs," he said at last. "So here's to my little Jaume, attorney-at-law. With God's help, of course." He gulped down most of a champagne bottle in ten incredibly well-spaced swallows, as if a coxswain was coaching him along.

"This is important information," Vladimir said. "I don't know much about sports. For instance, what's the name of the team here?"

"Oh, boy. You Manhattan kids can be a bunch of queers sometimes. Here they're called the Dolphins, and back home we've got two teams: the Giants and the Jets."

"I've heard of those," Vladimir said. Could those teams have had any more insipid names? If Vladimir were ever to own a franchise he'd call it something like the New York Yiddels. The Brighton Beach Refu-Jews.

Jordi dictated additional trivia about the Super Bowl, the Dallas Cowboys, and the mythical cow-women who attended to them, while room service brought up a swordfish, unbearably bland despite the hail of black pepper beneath which it suffocated. Vladimir munched on this mediocrity as Jordi began enumerating his son's finer points: for instance, he never hit his girlfriend even when circumstances demanded it; and he knew, beyond the shadow of a doubt, that money didn't grow on trees, that hard work never killed anybody, that without pain there was no gain. Vladimir worked with these commendable attributes, then suggested some more tangible activities for little Jaume: the boy spent his free time running the Catalan Culture Club at school; he helped old Polish ladies get to their weekly deviled ham at the Church of Saints Peter and Paul; he wrote letters to his local congressperson demanding better lighting for the local softball field (see interest in sports above).

"Here's to little Jaume looking out for old Polack broads," Jordi said. "And why aren't you drinking, sweetheart?"

Vladimir pointed to his bladder then went to the rosy bathroom to relieve himself. When he came out, two representatives of room service—young, pimpled Adam and Eve of the South— were waiting to present him with another bow-tied bottle. "On the house, sir."

The sun had long since disappeared when Vladimir felt the full giddy nausea of champagne drunkenness and ordered himself to stop. He sat down hard on his bed near the balcony and felt it sway a little in all four directions. Something was askew, and it wasn't just the physical universe reeling from booze. The idea of appearing in front of a college admissions officer, of impersonating a dullard's son, suddenly seemed as easy as hunting cows. Yes, an entire alternate moral universe was opening up before Vladimir, an alternate Americana populated with fellow beta immigrants living easy and drinking hard, concocting pyramid schemes like Uncle Shurik, while the other country continued to grind out leather

THE RUSSIAN DEBUTANTE'S HANDBOOK

sofas and Daisy Duck place mats in places as stupid as Erie and
Birmingham, as remote as Fairbanks and Duluth. He turned to
Jordi, half expecting confirmation of his silent discovery, to find
the latter studying Vladimir's lower half through his champagne
goblet, misty with breath. Jordi looked up, his heavy eyelids grown
narrow with concentration; he let out three seconds worth of bullshit laughter then said, "Don't get scared."

Vladimir felt very scared, as if the Finnish doorlock to the Girshkin fortress was suddenly snapped open by an experienced hand,
while the alarm system ceased its wail and the neighbor's fierce
suburban dog turned in for the night. The Fear-Money gland
wasn't even active yet, but the rest of him knew. "Hey, correct me if
I'm wrong," Jordi said, swinging his feet between their two beds, his
trunks tight with the outline of his shaft, twisted and constrained
by the elastic, "but you fooled around with Baobab before, right? I
mean, you've been with other boys."

Vladimir followed the single horrific spot of wetness along the
inseam of Jordi's trunks. "Who, us?" he said, jumping off the bed,
so unsure of the fact that he had spoken that he repeated himself.
"Who, us?"

"You're so much like Baobab that way," Jordi said, smiling and
shrugging as if he understood this was something the boys just
couldn't do anything about. "It doesn't mean you've got the homosexual feelings or anything, *coco*, though you could learn up on
football a little. It's just in your constitution. Look, I understand,
and you're not going to read about it in the *Post* tomorrow."

"No, no, I believe there's been a misunderstanding," Vladimir
began, working off the erroneous middle-class premise that when
in trouble it was best to sound educated. "I have mentioned earlier
my girlfriend—"

"Yes, good, okay," Jordi said. "This discussion is over, prince."
Then, in one move, the technicalities of which were lost on

Vladimir, he had sprung to his feet and snapped off his shorts, his penis swinging upward then falling into position. Vladimir averted his gaze from it, watching instead the bulbous shadow it cast upon the neatly made-up bed that separated them. Without warning, there was a flurry of motion: Jordi had struck his own head and cried out, "Wait! K-Y!" Vladimir's instant recall was of the cabinet that contained Challah's lubricant; quickly that image was discarded as irrelevant. He retreated in the direction of the balcony and the four-story drop, already calculating between the probable death behind him and what was in front of him.

But as Jordi reached down into the suitcase beneath him, Vladimir's eyes made contact with the oak door to his rear—the kind of respectable door you would find gracing the better homes of Erie and Birmingham, Fairbanks and Duluth. There it was, the barrier that separated him from the outside world of hotel staff and sun-drenched retirees and acceptable person-to-person relations. In the single instant that it took to establish the association between himself and the door, he bolted.

A fist grabbed the tail of his billowing T-shirt, pulled, then slammed Vladimir, shoulder-first, into the wall. After the initial pain there was Jordi, or, more precisely, fragments of his sweating body—an armpit here, a nipple there—pressing against Vladimir's face, until he found himself nose-to-nose with his tormentor. *"Au va!"* Jordi screamed, spitting into both his eyes, sinking his nails. "Fucking *fogo!* Twenty grand isn't enough for you, bitch?"

Vladimir closed his eyes tightly, seeing the sting of the foreign saliva swirl into circle-eight figures of pain. "I didn't—" he started to say but instantly forgot what it was that he didn't. What came to mind instead was an image of Fran, her raised clavicle, her sideward-pointing breasts bunched together in a sports bra, her honest smile when she entered a room full of friends. She was going to make him into a human being, an indigenous citizen of this world.

And then Vladimir punched him.

He had never hit a person before in his life, or heard the crunch of knuckle bone ramming cartilage; once, enraged at the pool-keeper's stupid collie at the upstate *dacha*, he had swatted its fluffy hind with a badminton racket: that was the extent of his violence.

Vladimir had hit the nose or near the nose, yet there was not a hint of blood between the two perfectly round and fur-lined nostrils; there was only Jordi's measured nasal breathing and the wide-eyed look of a confused toddler whose xylophone had just been taken away, and for no apparent reason.

There was a momentary lapse in the pressure of Jordi's nails buried in his shoulders, not that the weight of his hands had been altogether lifted, but there was, as Jordi's absent expression suggested—a moment.

Vladimir ran. The door opened then slammed behind him, the carpet was arrow-red and seemed to point his way to the elevator, but he couldn't afford to wait for the elevator to appear. Next to the elevator—stairs. He burst upon the humid staircase and began looping his way down, his feet at times heroic facilitators of his escape, at other times two dead objects over which the rest of his body threatened to trip, smashing his head into the concrete below.

The sound of pursuit was thankfully missing, but all that meant was that Jordi was on his way down in the elevator. Vladimir would bolt into the lobby right into Jordi's arms. "There you are, boy," Jordi would say, grinning unbearably as he explained to the hotel staff about their lovers' spat. Yes, Vladimir had read about that happening once before and in a case involving a convicted cannibal, no less.

He landed hard on the last stair, a thigh tendon seemingly snapping beneath the weight of the rest of him. Vladimir limped into the velvet-and-glitter lobby where his face, distorted by lack of oxygen and sporting a ghastly hue, received a comprehensive round of looks from the geriatric crew manning the recliners. Not to mention his T-shirt torn at the shoulders.

Vladimir caught sight of the row of elevator banks, one assertively registering descent: "Three.......Two......."

He had stood there transfixed by the numbers long enough to hear an elderly voice articulate a prolonged: "Vaat?"

Then he was out the palatial doors, past the circular driveway, and running with no heed for objects moving or stationary. Running quite literally, as they say, into the night, and the Floridian night, stinking of car exhaust, fast-food onions, and maybe a little something of the sea, accepted him and shrouded him in its boiling darkness.

EVERYTHING HAD CHANGED. HIS BODY HAD BEEN EAS-
ily handled by a man whose intent was to hurt. And the man had
done it, had smashed his shoulder and spit into both his eyes. How
meager the insults of his childhood by comparison to what had just
happened. All the miserable years of adolescence, the daily drub-
bing at the hands of parents and peers, had been no more than a
dress rehearsal; all those years, it turned out, young Vladimir had
only been *preparing* himself for victimhood.

He massaged and pressed his cheek against his damaged shoulder. It had been some time since he had had to provide tenderness
for himself, and the self-pity felt unfamiliar, as if from another lifetime. He was resting, half-naked, against a squat little palm tree in
what might have been a national forest but was actually the front
garden of a vast condominium complex. And he was still having
trouble breathing: the throaty tingle of an approaching hacking
cough was upon him and he tried hard to ignore it. As a respected
Park Avenue pediatrician had once told him, half of an asthma
attack was psychological. One had to divert one's attention with
other matters.

The other matter, aside from the asthma, consisted of leaving
Miami, of finding a cab and getting to the airport. Of course, Jordi

was probably already on his way there, off to meet his estranged lover at Gate X departing for La Guardia. But this boundless Miami metroplex had more than one egress. There was, Vladimir remembered, another airport out of which his parents would fly on discounted carriers with names like SkyElegance and Royal American Air. It was Fort Lauderdale's airport, up the coast.

Now what? He put on the remains of his T-shirt and coughed up a chunk of mucus thick as a sponge and traced with rills of blood. In his wallet Vladimir found the remnants of his take from his father and Mr. Rybakov: $1,200.00 in denominations large and small. Bonanza number two was a lone taxi circling the condo's driveway, waiting for the crowd with smart shoes and breathing linen to come out and play. Vladimir scrambled past the shrubbery, then took his time strolling over to the cab, a millionaire enjoying the freedom of a torn shirt on a Sunday night. The cabdriver, some kind of Middle Eastern pituitary giant, nevertheless checked out his attire thoroughly in the rearview mirror and asked if Vladimir's girlfriend had kicked his ass. His nameplate read Ben-Ari, or Son of a Lion, as Vladimir remembered from Hebrew school where many of these huge lion cubs were in evidence.

"And I'm leaving the bitch for good," Vladimir said (given the events of the last hour, it was oddly comforting to appropriate that word—"bitch"). "To the Fort Lauderdale airport!" he commanded.

He waited till they were way past the Eden and into the North Beach section to pull into a phone booth under the swaggering shadow of O'Malley's Blarney Leprechaun, with his three-for-one Guinness special. "Please wait for me," Vladimir told the driver.

"No, I will drive off without the fare," said the Son of a Lion, a friendly Israeli growl substituting for laughter.

He dialed Royal American Air and found out that it had gone out of business last Tuesday. SkyElegance now operated only between Miami and Medellín, although they were working on a nonstop to Zurich. Finally, a mainstream airline sold him a ticket on the next flight to New York for the equivalent of two weeks' salary.

Vladimir didn't blink at the price—he was still alive and possibly things would soon return to normal. Return to Fran, that is (the days measured out by cigarettes, chocolate, and coffee; the mornings with Frank talking shit about Kerensky's provisional government over the breakfast table; the joys of opening one of Vincie's packed lunch boxes at the Absorption Society: carpaccio-and-endive on toasted seven-grain, a generous sprig of balcony-grown mint, plus two tickets to a lunchtime concert at Trinity Church featuring a visiting Prava quartet—yes, he would need to spend forty days and nights just snuggling in bed with all three Ruoccos to cleanse himself of the last two hours).

In the interim, his recent maneuvers with the airline had empowered him, and now he was ready to dispense some authority Baobab's way. He dialed the bastard collect, and after the familiar, bumbling voice hesitantly accepted the charges, Vladimir began without restraint: "So, I just spent some time looking over Jordi's prick, and I meant to ask you, to borrow Jordi's words, how do *you* take it?"

On the opposite end of the eastern seaboard there was silence. "And he still hasn't given you the Brooklyn College franchise?" Vladimir said. "I think for all your hard work you might at least demand Brooklyn. Don't sell yourself short, Thumper."

"He didn't, did he?" Baobab said.

"No, he didn't, you living proof of social Darwinism. I'm standing by the road to the airport, my shoulder's bashed in, I can hardly walk, but my asshole's still intact, thanks for asking."

"Listen." Baobab paused as if he himself was listening. "I really didn't...He would grope me sometimes or squeeze my ass, but I thought—"

"You thought?" Vladimir said. "Are you sure? Remember how you always had extra time on tests in school because you had the doctor's note saying you were dyslexic? You faked that note, didn't you? Come clean now. You're not dyslexic, you're just a fucking idiot, am I right?"

"Now—"

"Now let's take stock, why don't we? You're twenty-five years of age, majoring in Humor Studies, your girlfriend can't go to the movies without a legal guardian, and your boss is keen on banging your bum for kicks. And you wonder why you don't get together with Fran and her friends more often? Believe me, that would be the last I'd ever see of Fran. Her anthropological curiosity only goes so far."

"Okay," Baobab said. "I heard you. Okay. Where are you, exactly?"

"Are you going to make everything all right, sweetheart?"

Baobab remained calm. "Where are you, Vladimir?"

"I told you, on the way to the airport. My meter's running."

"And where is Jordi?"

"Gee, I would think he's trying to find me, unrequited love and all."

"Cut it, cut it," Baobab said. "So he tried to . . . And you ran away?"

"Well, I hit him first," Vladimir said. "I socked him a nice one!" Socked him a nice one? When would this night end already?

"Jesus Christ. You really are fucked beyond anything. Listen, don't take a plane to New York. Go to Wichita, go to Peoria—"

"Oh, for fuck's sake!" shouted Vladimir, a pinch of apprehension already registering on his uncharted Fear-Money gland, uncharted save for when it ran against his bladder. "What, he's going to track me down in New York and kill me?"

"I doubt that *he* is the one that's going track you down, but, yes, he might very well take the time out to kill you, and maybe

fuck you one last time for good measure. Vlad, listen to me! He's
got a hundred people working for him in the Bronx alone. Last
year my friend Ernest, this crazy spic who used to run the
LaGuardia College franchise, he called Jordi a *maricón,* as a joke,
you understand…"

"And?"

"'And?' you say? *And?* Who do you think these people are?"
Baobab shouted. "The Catalan cartel! My God, the way they kill,
the flair with which they commit violence…It's *modernismo!* Even
you Russians can learn a thing or two. And then there's the fact that
he tried to…That you know that he's—"

"I see what you're saying, now. You're saying that although you
were fully aware that this man is a killer and a pederast, you
nonetheless encouraged me to go down to Florida with him. To
stay in the same hotel with him."

"How the hell was I supposed to know? I knew he liked that
waif look, but you've got all that hair on your face."

"Not anymore, you dolt!"

"Look, you needed the money!" Baobab said. "I thought this
was a way to win back your respect. You're the only friend I have,
and you've been spending all your time—"

"Oh, so it's my fault now. You are one deluded monkey, Baobab.
I'm trying to stay mad at you, but it's not easy considering…Con-
sidering this is just a night for me, but you're going to spend an
entire lifetime in this condition. Fare thee well, my poor sod."

"Wait a second! He's probably tapped my line. He's probably
going to have the Miami airport surrounded."

"Well, he's in for a surprise because I'm going to the Fort Lauderdale airport."

"Jesus Christ! Don't tell me that! The phone's bugged."

"Yes, and I'm sure all of Lauderdale is surrounded by angry
Catalonians with semiautomatics and glossy headshots of me. Is

there free therapy at City College? Why don't you look into that after your humor class?"

"Wait! Forget the bus terminals and the train stations! And don't rent a car! He can trace…"

Vladimir hung up and ran to his impatient Israeli.

"Onward!" he shouted.

"YOU'RE IN BIG TROUBLE, nachon meod?" the Lion said. He laughed and laughed, upsetting the rearview mirror with his happy hands.

Vladimir looked up. He had actually been asleep for a minute or two. This is what extreme fear did to him after its initial effects petered out: it put him to sleep. A thoroughly fear-inducing, but somehow dreamless sleep, its sole background—a bottomless void.

A look out the window proved that all of Florida looked exactly the same from a moving vehicle. The sign on the opposite side of the highway read: BAL HARBOUR 20. Bal Harbour was to the immediate north of Miami Beach. That was good. They were headed in the right direction and the highway was empty.

Now what the hell was that Lion saying? Vladimir recognized the last two words from Hebrew school. "*Nachon meod,*" Vladimir repeated.

"So I was right!" the Israeli said. "You *are* a Russian Jew. No wonder you're in trouble. You people are always in trouble. You make the Spanish look good."

Hey, what did everyone have against the impoverished, yet always-yearning Russian people? "Aw, come on, *hever,*" Vladimir said, remembering the Hebrew word for "friend." "You're hurting my feelings."

"I'm not your *hever,* asshole. So what did you do back there? Kill your girlfriend?"

Vladimir ignored his comment. He was on his way. Soon his long Floridian nightmare would be over. He would never have to look at a palm tree again, or deal with another coarse, gaudy, overweight peasant.

"Hey, doesn't that sign say 'airport?'"

The Lion hit his horn to warn a moped of impending disaster, then swerved right. They drove in silence for a while, the overhead roar of jet engines providing a soothing accompaniment for Vladimir, reminding him that in less than an hour it would be his turn to take to the air. Every sign they passed said "airport" now, or else "motel" or "lobster." Eat, screw, and leave: that was the narrative of this particular highway.

Gradually, the traffic worsened, and the Lion began moaning familiar Hebrew curses, which constituted the bulk of Vladimir's knowledge of that language. Whoredom was a big theme with the Israelites. 'Go fuck your mother and bring me a receipt,' that was a popular one. Sex, family, commerce—it pushed all the right buttons.

They were creeping along, now. The moon, low and pink, looked perfect for this setting (why was New York's moon always so lofty and gray?).

There were two peach Cadillacs in front of them and one on the left. He must have booked a seat on some kind of senior citizens' special. He looked at the flight info scribbled on his hand. He checked his still-unsold Rolex. Flight 320, depart Fort Lauderdale 8:20, arrive New York La Guardia 10:35. The official dénouement of his peripatetic little southern tragedy would soon be printed out on card stock and placed in a paper folder with the airline's logo.

And then, a thought. Actually, more than a thought. Four thoughts. Coming together as one.

Depart Fort Lauderdale;

peach Cadillac;

two in front, one on the left;

Jordi's trunks tight with the outline of his shaft, a single horrific spot of wetness spreading along the inseam.

HE SLIPPED TO THE FLOOR. Half of an asthma attack was purely psychological. You had to think straight. You had to say to yourself: I'm going to keep breathing.

"What is this?" the Lion shouted. He adjusted his rearview to get the full view of the cowering Vladimir. He turned his hundred-pound head around. "What are you doing? What shit is this?"

Inhale, exhale, one, two, three. With a wobbly wrist, Vladimir threw two hundred-dollar bills at the Lion. "Take the next exit back," he whispered. "There's been a mistake...I don't want to go to the airport...They're going to kill me." The Lion kept looking at him. The outline of his droopy chest stared at Vladimir from the partition of his floral shirt, reminding Vladimir, for some reason, of a heart attack. Vladimir threw another hundred-dollar bill. And then another.

"Damn!" the Lion shouted. He hit the wheel in masculine fashion. "Damn, whore, fuck," he said. He inched forward. He put on his turning light. Vladimir crept up and looked at the car on the left. The window was down; a young man with a mustache of no more than three hairs, sweating visibly in a silk jacket and buttoned-up shirt, was screaming something into his cell phone. His companion, a twin by the looks of him, was clicking something between his legs. He heard a language not unlike Spanish. No, French. He heard both Spanish and French. Vladimir crawled back down. He reemerged for a glimpse of the rear window. There was a peach Caddy directly behind them. And another one. And another one. There was a peach Cadillac in every lane. They were in a traffic jam of peach Cadillacs.

The Lion kept repositioning their car rightward. "I drive a cab," he chanted. "I know nothing. Livery driver. Dual citizenship. Eight years here and I love it."

Vladimir covered himself with a handy map of Georgia that was lying on the floor. He must have spent an hour like that: bathed in his own sweat, smelling the blood on his upper lip, cocooned within the furry hold of the Lion's Crown Victoria. Each second he thought he head the clicking sound or the mention of "Girshkin" amid the international conversation next door. He found himself too exhausted to think about it. The dreamy void loomed ahead, but he could hardly permit himself to fall asleep. Stay awake! Breathe! Think of the turbo-prop skirting the runway, so close, too close . . . and yet copilot Rybakov knew exactly what he was doing, the fearless grin on that pumpkin face spoke of a history of near-misses.

Meanwhile, back on the ground, the Lion kept turning on the right signal, which emitted a comforting mechanical chime, the belltone of American civilization as far as Vladimir was concerned. The car drifted into the rightmost lane, then inched its way onto a service road. "Agaa!" the Lion shouted.

"What's wrong?" Vladimir screamed.

But it must have been a war cry, a release of tension, because at that point the Lion stepped on the gas, and the car squealed past the following: a self-proclaimed "pancake palace"; a New Souls Rising Millennial Temple & Spa; an unidentified store shaped like an igloo; two minor country roads; fifty hectares of arable land; a grove of palm trees; the vast parking lot of something called Strud's.

It was at Strud's that the Lion came to a full and complete stop. The car's suspension let out an ominous creak, which Vladimir immediately matched with a bloody exhale. "Get out!" the Lion said.

"What?" Vladimir wheezed. "I just gave you four hundred dollars."

"Get out! Get out! Get out! Get out!" the Lion screamed, the first two times in Hebrew, the final two in his new language.

"But look!" Vladimir shouted, indignity overcoming asthma. "We're in the middle of..." It was hard to say where. "What am I supposed to do? At least drive me to the bus station. Or Amtrak, or, no...Let me think. Just drive north somewhere."

The Lion spun around to face the back seat and grabbed Vladimir by his shirt. His face—stubby double-jointed nose, gray bags under the eyes glistening with sweat—reminded Vladimir of Jordi's miserable physiognomy. And this was a fellow tribesman! They spoke the same language, had the same god, and the same-shade ass. There was a moment of silence in the car, save for the sound of Vladimir's shirt tearing further in the Israeli's hands and the heavy breathing of the Lion, who was clearly looking for words to elucidate the finality of their driver-passenger relationship. "Okay," Vladimir preempted him. "I know where I'm going. I have nine hundred dollars left. Take me to New York."

The Lion brought him closer, breathing onion and tahini all over his sweating passenger. "You," he said. The next word could have been "little," but the Lion chose to leave his harangue at the level of a pronoun.

He let go of Vladimir and turned around, crossing his arms on top of the steering wheel. He snorted. He uncrossed his arms and tapped the steering wheel. He pulled a golden Star of David from the confluence of his hairy cleavage and held it between thumb and index finger. This little ritual must have given him focus. "Ten thousand," he said. "Plus the cost of an auto-train back."

"But all I have is nine hundred," Vladimir said, even as he caught his wrist sparkling in the sunlight. Success! He threw his Rolex over the Lion's shoulder, where it made a rich and hopeful sound against his meaty lap.

The Lion gave the watch a healthy shake then held it against his ear. "No serial number on back," he mused. "Automatic chronograph." He consulted his Star of David once again. "Nine hundred dollars plus the Rolex plus five thousand more you get from a cash machine."

"My credit limit is three thousand," Vladimir said.

"Oofa," the Lion said and shook his head. He opened his door and started moving his bulk outside.

"Wait! Where are you going?"

"I have to call my wife and explain things," the Lion said. "She thinks I have a girlfriend." And then, with shoulders hunched and both hands jammed into the pockets of his silk trousers, the Lion set off for the bleak discount wasteland of Strud's.

VLADIMIR SLEPT through the eastern seaboard.

It wasn't as if the drive was uneventful. The conked-out Vladimir, mumbling comforting childhood words in his sleep (kasha, Masha, baba), managed to miss a flat tire, a half-hearted chase by some inept South Carolina patrolmen, and the Lion screaming and flailing wildly as a friendly Southern critter, perhaps a chipmunk, rubbed up against him at a Virginia rest stop.

Twenty-five hours of uninterrupted sleep, that was the legacy of Vladimir's northward journey.

He woke up in the Lincoln Tunnel, somehow knowing immediately where he was. "Good morning, criminal," the Israeli grumbled up front. "Good morning and good-bye. Soon as we're out of the tunnel, I will say *shalom* to you."

"I think for five thousand dollars you can drop me off at my home," Vladimir said.

"Ai! Listen to this *gonif!* And where is home? Riker's Island?"

Where was home? Vladimir actually had to think about it for a second. But when it came to him, he couldn't help but smile. It was three P.M. according to the dashboard clock and Francesca would likely be at home, in her bedroom mausoleum, surrounded by text and counter-text. He hoped that his twenty-four-hour absence, the missing humidity of his breath against her neck at night, the lacuna in his constant considerate companionship, in his "superhuman ability to abide," to quote Joseph Ruocco, was already taking a toll on her; that when he walked through the door, her face would register something perfectly out of character—the unalloyed happiness of dating Vladimir Girshkin.

They turned down Fifth Avenue and Vladimir squirmed in his seat. Just a minute more. Come on, Lion! The Israeli nimbly cut through the traffic of yellow cabs, leaving raised fists and honking in his wake (just look at that upstart with the Crown Victoria and the Florida license plates). The names on the storefronts were now as familiar as family—Matsuda, Mesa Grill...In a previous lifetime, Vladimir had left a small fortune at each of them.

"*Gonif* comes home," the Lion said, pulling up to the beige Art Deco of the Ruoccos' building. "Don't forget to tip," he said.

Half-dazed and half-civil, Vladimir fished a final fifty-dollar bill out of the torn pocket of his torn shirt and passed it to his driver.

"Keep it," said the Lion, suddenly avuncular. "And try to live a clean life if you can, that's my advice to you. You're very young. You've got a Jewish brain. There's still hope."

"*Shalom*," Vladimir said. His strange adventures with the big Israeli were coming to an end. Closure was an elevator ride away. And there, ambling into the lobby with his unique dinosaur-like gait, was Joseph Ruocco, surviving the heat in his too-colonial-for-comfort khaki ensemble ("Conradian," Fran had called it). Vladimir was about to surprise him with a shout of "*Privyet!*," a familiar Russian greeting he had taught the Ruoccos, when he saw that the professor was accompanied by—

———

WELL, that wouldn't be accurate. First he heard the voice. No, first he heard the laughter. They were laughing. No, that's not true either. First he heard the professor's voice then he heard the bullshit laughter, then he heard the other voice, and *then* he saw.

A giant hand, gold-cuffed, Florida-brown, and smelling of baby powder was slapping the professor manfully about the shoulders.

A peach car of a familiar make was parked along the sidewalk of 20 Fifth Avenue, its blinkers blinking.

Jordi was making a new friend. One both funny and sad.

"What happened to your shirt?" the young Brazilian doorman started to ask Vladimir, almost loud enough for the professor and Jordi to hear at the opposite end of the lobby.

But before he could finish, the beat-up man before him, this little guy who accompanied the Ruoccos' daughter every day, and who always seemed to the doorman either too sheeplike or too haughty for his own good…this trembling, barefaced Lothario was out the door, across the avenue, around the corner, gone from sight. He was *history,* thought the doorman, smiling at the phrase he had picked up from a headline in the *Post.*

"I'M NOT GOING TO WICHITA," Vladimir said, the word "Wichita" rendered by his accent as the most foreign word imaginable in the English language. "I'm going to live with Fran and it's going to be all right. You're going to make it all right." But even as he was laying down the law, his hands were shaking to the point where it was hard to keep the shabby pay-phone receiver properly positioned between his mouth and ear. Teardrops were blurring the corners of his eyes and he felt the need to have Baobab hear him burst out in a series of long, convulsive sobs, Roberta-style. All he had wanted was twenty thousand lousy dollars. It wasn't a million. It was how much Dr. Girshkin made on average from two of his nervous gold-toothed patients.

"Okay," Baobab said. "Here's how we're going to do it. These are the new rules. Memorize them or write them down. Do you have a pen? Hello? Okay, Rule One: you can't visit anyone—friends, relatives, work, nothing. You can only call me from a pay phone and we can't talk for more than three minutes." He paused. Vladimir imagined him reading this from a little scrap of paper. Suddenly Baobab said, under his breath: "Tree, nine-thirty, tomorrow."

"The two of us can never meet in person," he was saying loudly now. "We will keep in touch only by phone. If you check into a hotel, make sure you pay cash. Never pay by credit card. Once more: Tree, nine-thirty, tomorrow."

Tree. Their Tree? *The* Tree? And nine-thirty? Did he mean in the morning? It was hard to imagine Baobab up at that unholy hour.

"Rule Five: I want you to keep moving at all times, or at least try to keep moving. Which brings us to…" But just as Rule Six was about to come over the transom, there was a tussle for the phone and Roberta came on the line in her favorite Bowery harlot voice, the kind that smelled like gin nine hundred miles away. "Vladimir, dear, hi!" Well, at least someone was enjoying Vladimir's downfall. "Say, I was thinking, do you have any ties with the Russian underworld, honey?"

Vladimir thought of hanging up, but the way things were going even Roberta's voice was a distinctly human one. He thought of Mr. Rybakov's son, the Groundhog. "Prava," he muttered, unable to articulate any further. An uptown train rumbled beneath him to underscore the underlying shakiness of his life. Two blocks downtown, a screaming professional was being tossed back and forth between two joyful muggers.

"Prava, how very now!" Roberta said. "Laszlo's thinking of opening up an Academy of Acting and the Plastic Arts there. Did you know that there are thirty thousand Americans in Prava? At least a half dozen certified Hemingways among them, wouldn't you agree?"

"Thank you for your concern, Roberta. It's touching. But right now I have other...There are problems. Besides, getting to Prava...What can I do?...There's an old Russian sailor...An old lunatic...He needs to be naturalized."

There was a long pause at this point and Vladimir realized that in his haste he wasn't making much sense. "It's a long story..." he began, "but essentially...I need to...Oh God, what's wrong with me?"

"Talk to me, you big bear!" Roberta encouraged him.

"Essentially, if I get this old lunatic his citizenship, he'll set me up with his son in Prava."

"Okay, then," Roberta said. "I *definitely* can't get him his citizenship."

"No," Vladimir concurred. "No, you can't." What was he doing talking to a sixteen-year-old?

"But," Roberta said, "I can get him the next best thing..."

17. THE AMERICAN PAGEANT

THE TREE WAS A RATHER FRAIL AND TRAMPLED-UPON oak, its gnarly branches shadowing its equally beat-up cousin, the Bench. Tree and Bench existed together, now and forever, in the little park in back of the math-and-science high school where Vladimir and Baobab were issued an academic challenge and where, subsequently, they had failed to meet that challenge, and, instead, had retired to the Bench beneath the Tree. During a particularly upsetting acid trip, Baobab had carved his initials and those of Michel Foucault into the Bench, beneath which, in the style of lower-school girls, he had written, "BFF." Best Friends Forever.

Vladimir, pining for the simplicity of those wasted days, bent down and traced the initials with one nostalgic finger, then held himself in check: Such nonsense!

A car horn went off behind him.

Roberta was peeking out of a cab door, waving her big yellow boater. "Get in!" she shouted. "They're trailing Baobab uptown. Move!"

THEY HAD PULLED UP TO an old warehouse by the Holland Tunnel. The place was a low-ceilinged affair, its torn parapet floors patched up with strips of linoleum, a sign for Arrow Moving and Storage, the previous tenant, incompletely scraped off the front door. Vladimir was seated with Roberta in the rear section, which was roped off for "Guests of Naturalization Candidates." The other "guests," all marvelous actors and dear friends of Roberta, as was explained to Vladimir, looked dressed for a wedding, an Islamabad or Calcutta wedding—the number of turbans and saris among the attendees had reached critical mass. At any rate, gone was the dark-T-shirt-and-tight-trouser uniform germane to the ranks of young unemployed thespians.

It was a festive atmosphere: the handsome men and women milled about, playing with the balloons, arguing over coffee brands and whether moving to Queens was a viable alternative to a social life.

"What each of them wouldn't do to get into Laszlo's bunk," Roberta said, while keeping one clammy hand upon Vladimir's. She wore a manly herringbone suit and a transparent white shirt over a black bra of elaborate construction which brought out and augmented her meager bosom. Her hair had been tied back with little ribbons of silk, and her gaunt cheeks rouged. There was no mistaking her for a sixteen-year-old unless she opened her mouth and exposed her ironwork. "I," she announced to Vladimir, pointing at her name tag, "am Katerina Nieholtz-Praga, scion of an old Austrian family, and wife of the Italian industrialist Alberto Praga. Al is getting his citizenship today, but purely for business purposes, you understand. His heart is still in Tuscany, with his olive farm, his two Arabians, and his mamma."

"God help us all," Vladimir said. He sat, stooped and unshaven, in a huge sports jacket Roberta had brought for the occasion. He had tried shaving in the bathroom of his room in the squalid Astoria motor lodge, which he had procured with his remaining fifty dollars, but found that he couldn't keep his hands steady or his face still.

Laszlo walked out from the dressing room. He was a spindly gentleman, wearing a judge's robe that barely reached down to his thighs, a sort of judicial miniskirt. Wisps of uncombed gray hair jutted out from his head in the shape of a lopsided crown. "Are you the client?" he asked Vladimir in remarkably clear English. He must have spent years scouring his Hungarian accent with steel wool. He probably couldn't pronounce "paprika" at this point.

"That's me," Vladimir said. "How's our man doing?"

"He's real good, one hundred percent okay. Right now he's in the dressing room, getting to know the other, you know, the citizens." Laszlo folded his frame down to Vladimir's level and put both hands on his shoulders; Vladimir flinched from recent experience.

"So," Laszlo said, "this is our standard False Naturalization Ceremony Event, or FNCE, as we say in our industry. We do maybe a couple such events per year, and also a couple deluxe packages, which is the same thing but on a boat and with hookers." And here Laszlo blinked, curling one tremendous brow. Roberta winked, too, and Vladimir, feeling the pressure, followed suit with a series of rapid blinking.

"Roberta said I can wire you the three thousand from Prava," Vladimir spoke up.

"Yes, plus the FNCE standard package specialized one hundred percent lateness handling charge of an additional U.S. three thousand dollars. As per agreement!"

"I see," Vladimir said. "Six thousand dollars." The Hungarians were adapting to the free market quite nicely. He woud have to borrow some cash from Mr. Rybakov's son. Still, it was nice of Roberta to fix this up on such short notice.

"Right," Laszlo said. "Guests, assume your positions!"

The crowd of faux Zimbabweans, Ecuadorians, and the like scrambled over their folding chairs, brushing against one another and giggling. Laszlo climbed up the makeshift stage to his lectern, which was actually composed of several cardboard boxes expertly covered by an American flag and outfitted with a portable microphone. A colorful seal reading "Department of Justis" hung in the background, another excellent approximation, except for that slight misspelling and the somewhat frightened expression in the eye of the American eagle. "And now let us welcome the candidates for na-tu-ra-li-zation!" Laszlo boomed.

Applause from the guest sector as the candidates filed in one by one: Jewish and Anglo women in dark makeup and bizarrely overdone headdresses of grapes and mint leaves; men with wavy, blond hair and perfectly suburban physiognomies dressed as if they had just escaped from the set of *The Man of La Mancha,* and other such apparitions.

Mr. Rybakov hobbled in. He wore a dark blue suit, doublebreasted and carefully tailored to minimize his paunch. Rows of redand-yellow Soviet medals covered a great portion of his breasts, yet his tie sported the Stars and Stripes to accentuate his change of allegiance. He smiled inwardly, looking at the floor, trying to follow the footsteps of the kimono-clad woman in front of him.

Vladimir couldn't help himself. Upon seeing the Fan Man he sprang to his feet and clapped the loudest, shouting with a Russian cheer, *"Ura! Ura, Aleksander!"* Roberta pulled on his jacket, reminding him that the point was not to get Rybakov riled up, but all the sailor did was smile meekly to acknowledge his friend, then took his seat beneath a giant crepe banner that read CONGRATULATIONS, NEW AMERICANS. They had parked him between the Italian industrialist Alberto Praga and another Caucasian-looking individual in order to avoid the previous incident with the Arab. However, in front of him sat a "Ghanaian" woman bearing a giant straw basket of fruits on her head, likely obscuring part of his view. That had been an oversight.

They sang the anthem, then Judge Laszlo rose and brushed his hand against his eyes, deeply affected by this particular rendition. "America!" Laszlo said and nodded with understanding.

"America!" Rybakov shouted from his seat, nodding similarly. He turned around to give Vladimir an upturned thumb.

Laszlo smiled at the Fan Man and pressed one finger to his mouth for quiet. "America!" he repeated. "As you can tell from my accent, I too once sat where now you sit. I came as a small child to this country, learned the language, the customs, worked my way through, ah, judge school, and now am most privileged to help you complete your long journey to American citizenship."

There was spontaneous applause during which the Fan Man got up and shouted: "I come to Vienna first, then I go to America!"

Laszlo waved at him to sit down. He put his finger to his lips once again. "What is America?" he resumed, spreading his shoulders, looking up to the stained ceiling in wonderment. "Is it a hamburger? Is it a hot dog? Is it a shiny new Cadillac with a pretty young woman underneath a palm tree…?"

The guests shrugged and looked at each other. So many choices.

"Yes, America is all this," Laszlo explained. "But it is more, much more."

"I collect Social Security," announced Mr. Rybakov, waving a hand for recognition.

Laszlo ignored him this time. "America," he continued, both robed arms swinging through the air, "is a land where you can live a very long life and when it is time to die, when you look at yourself, you can say definitely: all the mistakes, all the triumphs I have had, all the Cadillacs and the pretty women, and the children that hate me so much they call me by my first name and not 'daddy' and not even 'father,' this is all because of me. Me!"

Laszlo's students agreed, vigorously doffing their sombreros and waving around their kente cloth, repeating among themselves, "Me! Me!"

"This part of the Stanislavsky Method I don't quite recognize," Vladimir said.

"Ignoramus," Roberta said.

The oath of allegiance was administered, the Fan Man mumbling right along, careful not to turn on his fellow candidates during the "all enemies, foreign and domestic" bit. Finally, they were called upon to get their certificates: "Efrat Elonsky...Jenny Woo... Abdul Kamus...Ruhalla Khomeni...Phuong Min...Aleksander Rybakov..."

Rybakov went up to the podium, dropped his crutches, and draped his arms around Laszlo who nearly buckled under the weight. "Thank you, Mister," he whispered in his ear. He turned to Vladimir and waved his certificate through the air, his eyes streaming. "Ura!" he shouted. "Ura to America! I am America!" Vladimir waved back and took a snapshot with the Fan Man's Polaroid. Despite the Ghanaian woman distributing ceremonial fruits from the basket on her head, despite Roberta loudly smooching the dapper Alberto Praga, yes, despite it all, Vladimir found himself moved. He blew his nose into the coarse, acrylic handkerchief that came with Roberta's sports jacket and waved his little American flag made of a similar fabric.

THEY DIPPED PRETZELS into the baked salmon salad which Laszlo's crew had spread out over the time-worn aluminum desks left over from the moving company. "This is not very much," Mr. Rybakov said to Vladimir. "We can go home. I have herring."

"Oh, I've eaten enough of your fish," Vladimir said.

"Shut your mouth," Rybakov said. "All the fish in the Caspian

Sea would not be tribute enough for you, young King Solomon. Do you know what it has been like for me all these years? Do you know what it is like, to be a man without a country?"

Vladimir reached far across a table for another container of salmon, determined not to show his betrayal. And, yes, he knew what it was like.

"What if there is a war?" asked Mr. Rybakov. "How will you defend your motherland if you don't have one?"

"That's right, you can't," Vladimir said.

"Look at me, for example. I'm all alone in this country, I've got no family, no friends to speak of. You—you're going to Prava. The Fan—all I had was the Fan, but now I have this!" He took the certificate out of his jacket pocket. "Now, I am a citizen of the greatest country in the world, if you discount Japan. Listen, I'm not young anymore, I've seen just about everything a man can see, so I know how it is: you're born, you die, there's nothing to it. You have to belong somehow, to be a part of a unit. Otherwise, what are you? You're nothing."

"Nothing," repeated Vladimir. Laszlo was pointing to a clock. The show was almost over.

"But you, Vladimir, my dear young man, in Prava you will be part of something so big, so tight, you will never again have to wonder what unit you belong to. My son will take care of you like his own. And after I finish those business dealings with Miss Harosset and these damn Kandunsky paintings, may they all go to the devil, I will come and visit you and my Tolya. How about that?"

"We will have a great time, the three of us," Vladimir said, picturing them rowing down a river with a basket of fried chicken and a jar of herring.

"And I will walk through the streets of Prava, with my chest stuck out proudly..." He stuck out his chest. "I will walk as a big, beautiful American."

Vladimir put his arm around Mr. Rybakov's lumpy back and pressed the old sailor to him. His smell reminded him of his step-grandfather's who died in America after a prolonged bout with cirrhosis of the liver, kidney stones, and, if one could trust Dr. Girshkin's diagnosis, an imploded lung. There it was—the vodka breath; the musky aftershave; and that certain brisk industrial scent, which brought to Vladimir's mind the image of machine oil sprinkled liberally across the gears of a rusted Soviet metal press, the kind at which Vladimir's step-grandfather once pretended to toil. It pleased Vladimir that the Fan Man smelled the same. "And now, Comrade Rybakov," he said, "or, as we say in this country, Mister Rybakov, you will permit me to buy you several drinks."

"O-ho," Rybakov said and squeezed Vladimir's nose with his many-flavored fingers. "Well, let's go find a bottle then!" They helped each other out into the oddly silent street where the afternoon sun bore down on the cast-iron facades and on a string of idled moving vans.

HIS LAST FEW HOURS in Manhattan were spent in a cab with tinted windows; Roberta had been kind enough to advance him a thousand dollars from her considerable savings, and advised him to stay mobile and not to call anyone (especially "the woman"). As for Baobab, according to Roberta, he was holed up with relatives in Howard Beach, while his uncle Tommy tried to broker a cease-fire with Jordi.

Meanwhile, Vladimir spent two hundred dollars going around the limestone curve of the Flatiron building, down Fifth Avenue past the Ruoccos' apartment house, then through the smaller Village tributaries that lead to the Sheridan Square subway station. It was from this station that Fran would daily disembark on her way back from Columbia, and Vladimir was entertaining the odd hope of seeing her, just one more glimpse, for memory's sake. He made fifty of these trips, all of them in vain. It was remarkable the cabby didn't drive him straight to Bellevue.

Fifth Avenue, the first Friday of September, the heat and business of a late afternoon, the shish-kebab stands closing down for the day, women with suggestive crescents of calf departing work at furious clips, another grand evening in the making here in the documented epicenter of the precise navel of the universe, the first New York evening that would pass without Vladimir in attendance. Yes, good-bye to all that. Good-bye to Vladimir Girshkin's America, its lofty landmarks and sour smells, good-bye to Mother and Doctor Girshkin and their tomato patch, to the several strange-duck friends that were cultivated, to the flimsy goods and meager services that gave sustenance, and, finally, to his last hope of conquering the New World, to Fran and the Ruocco Family, good-bye.

And good-bye to Grandma. To think of America, he had to start with her, the only one who had consistently tried to better his stay here, she who had chased him over the hills and dales of the Girshkins' upstate *dacha* trying to force-feed him wedges of cantaloupe, deep bowls of farmer cheese…How simple life would be if it began and ended with food-for-love and an old woman's sloppy kiss.

And what of Fran? On his final Village circuit he thought he saw her, a straw hat, a bag of peppers for the Ruoccos' nightly feast, a leisurely wave to an acquaintance passing by. He was mistaken. It was not her. But while he was under false impressions, his instinct was to lunge out of the slow-moving cab, press his lips to one studded ear, and say…what? "Nearly raped by a drug lord. Marked for death. Gotta run." Even in contemporary circumstances, where just about everything is possible, this was not possible. Or perhaps he could have said it in terms she would appreciate, the words of the doomed Swede boxer in the Hemingway story:

"Fran, I got in wrong."

But after this nonencounter with Fran, he ordered the driver to the airport. There was nothing more to be done. America, it seemed, was not entirely defenseless against the likes of Vladimir Girshkin. There was a sorting mechanism at work by which the beta immigrant was discovered, branded by an invisible ß on his forehead, and eventually rounded up and put on the next plane back to some dank Anatevka. The events of the last few days were no mere coincidence, they were the natural culmination of Vladimir's thirteen years as an unlikely Yankee Doodle, a sad mark on his Assimilation Facilitator's record.

Well, fuck America; or, in poetic Russian parlance, *na khui, na khui.* He was almost glad that he didn't see Fran, that the past, which only yesterday was the present, was over. He had failed once again, but this time he had come away all the wiser. The boundaries, the contours of victimization at the hands of Mother, Girlfriend, and this dough-bellied adopted land of his, were all too clear. He would never suffer like that again. In fact, he would never be an *immigrant* again, nevermore a man who couldn't measure up to the natives. From this day forward, he was Vladimir the Expatriate, a title that signified luxury, choice, decadence, frou-frou colonialism. Or, rather, Vladimir the *Re*patriate, in this case signifying a homecoming, a foreknowledge, a making of amends with history. Either way...Back on that plane, Volodya! Back to the part of the world where the Girshkins were first called Girshkins!

HE DUG HIS NAILS into his palms and watched tangible Manhattan become a cardboard skyline behind him. Soon enough he would remember precisely what he was leaving (everything; her) and have his little crying jag on the plane.

But a few hours later he would already be on the other side, the low-rent side of the planet, recovering, reconnoitering, thinking of pyramid schemes and rich Americans scarfing down pork and cabbage beneath a topcoat of Mittel Europa mist...

Thinking of getting in good.

PART IV

PRAVA, REPUBLIKA STOLOVAYA, 1993

18. THE REPATRIATION OF
VLADIMIR GIRSHKIN

THIRTEEN YEARS BEFORE, ON THE WAY FROM ONE jerry-built life to another, from the grim, disorganized airport in Leningrad with its faintly fecal odor and the toxic-sweet stench of Soviet detergent on the ground to the grim, organized one in New York where PanAm jumbo jets sat by departure gates like patient whales, Vladimir Girshkin had done the unthinkable and wept. It was the kind of outburst his father had prohibited at the conclusion of toilet training, on the grounds that there were few things left in the world that separated the sexes, but tears and sniffling certainly headlined the list. On that pug-nosed Aeroflot liner, trapped between rows of American tourists playing tea time with their hard-currency samovars and discovering the pleasant reductive logic of the Russian nesting doll, a livid Dr. Girshkin, surely comical-looking to the Westerners around him in his torn leather parka and ruined horn-rimmed glasses (both victims of last-minute violence at the hands of his wife), grabbed his son by the collar and ordered him to the lavatory to complete his whimpering.

As the older Vladimir now sat in a similar aluminum loo thousands of meters above Germany, his jeans around his ankles, his flowing nose in a towelette, his thoughts easily came around to his earlier bout of transatlantic despair: the customs hall in Pulkovo Airport, Leningrad, the spring of 1980.

It was only on the night before the Girshkins' departure that the strange truth had finally been revealed to Vladimir: The family would not be taking the train down to their hutlike *dacha* in Yalta as had been promised; instead, they were to fly to a secret place, its very name unmentionable. A secret place! An unmentionable name! A-a! Small Vladimir was soon hopping about the apartment, jumping from suitcase to suitcase, making a fort out of the closet using his heavy galoshes as battlements, nearly precipitating an asthma attack through his adolescent rampage. Mother restricted him to the living-room couch, which smelled of childhood sweat and served as his bed come ten o'clock, but Vladimir would not be so easily restrained. He grabbed Yuri the Giraffe, the stuffed war hero whose spotted chest was pinned down with Grandfather's Great Patriotic War medals, and threw the rattling creature up against the ceiling until the perennially unhappy Georgians in the flat above began stomping for quiet. "Where are we going, Mama?" Vladimir shouted (back then she was still known to him informally as Mama). "I'll find it on the map for you!"

And Mother, paranoid that her easily excitable son might spill their destination to the neighbors, only said, "Far."

And Vladimir, jumping through the air, said, "Moscow?"

And Mother said, "Farther."

And Vladimir, jumping still higher, said, "Tashkent?"

And she said, "Farther."

And Vladimir, now reaching nearly the same height as his flying giraffe, said, "Siberia?" Because that's as far as it got, and Mother said that no, it was even farther than that. Vladimir spread out his beloved maps and traced his finger farther than Siberia, but it wasn't even the Soviet Union out there. It was something else. Another country! But *nobody* ever went to another country. And so

Vladimir spent the night running around the flat with volumes of the *Great Soviet Encyclopedia* under his arm, screaming in alphabetical order, "Afghanistan, Albania, Algeria, Argentina, Austria, Bermuda…"

It was the next day at customs, however, that the Girshkins' departure took a turn for the worse. The well-fed men of the Interior Ministry in their tight polyester uniforms, now completely without reason for concealing their hatred for the soon-to-be ex-Soviet family before them, obliterated their luggage, tearing apart the wide-collared Finnish shirts and the few passable business suits smuggled through the Baltics, clothes which Vladimir's parents had hoped would last them through their first interviews in New York. This was done ostensibly to find any hidden gold or diamonds that exceeded the minuscule amount allowed to leave the country. As they tore through Mother's address book, shredding anything with an American address, including her Newark cousin's instructions on how to get to Macy's, a particularly large gentleman, whom Vladimir would never forget as having had a mouth frighteningly empty of teeth (even the silver kind that were standard issue to middle-aged Warsaw Pact citizens) and a strong smell of sturgeon on his breath, said to her: "You'll be back, Yid."

The agent had proved to be rather prescient, for after the Soviet Union collapsed Mother did return on several occasions to buy up a few choice pieces of the former empire for her corporation, but at the time all that occurred to Vladimir was that Mother—the bulwark against the storm outside the window, the woman whose word was the law of the household, from whose hands could come either a mustard compress that would torture through the night or a glossy volume on the Battle of Stalingrad that would be moored by his bedside for a year—was a Yid. Granted he had been called a Yid before; in fact, he had been called that every time his health allowed him a foray into the gray world of Soviet education. Yet he had always thought of himself as being the most thorough of Yids—small, stooped, sickly, and with a book regularly by his side. But how could anyone say that of Mother who not only read to Vladimir about the Battle of Stalingrad but looked ready to wage it all by herself.

And to Vladimir's surprise, as the pages of her address book scattered about her and as the customs agents roared in appreciation of Comrade Sturgeon-Breath, Mother did nothing but twist the strings of her little leather purse around her whitened hand, while Dr. Girshkin, avoiding the frightened gaze of his son, made slight and ambiguous gestures toward the departure gate and their escape.

Then, before he knew it, they were buckled in, snow-covered, gas-streaked Russia rolling beneath the airplane's wings, and only then did Vladimir allow himself the luxury, the necessity, of crying.

Now, thirteen years hence, with the jet headed in the opposite direction, Vladimir felt the intervening years effortlessly collapsing into a meaningless interlude. He was the same little Volodechka with the Yid last name, with the eyes puffed from crying and the nose wet from running. Only this time destiny wasn't a Hebrew school carefully landscaped into a sylvan Scarsdale lot followed by a progressive Midwestern college. This time around, destiny was a gangster named after a fuzzy marmot.

And this time there would be no room for those silly mistakes—those slips of the amateur assimilationist—that had nearly cost him his life a week ago in a fading Floridian hotel room with that loose-fleshed naked old man; those brief bouts of idiocy and self-victimization that had put him on this Lufthansa flight fleeing New York and his imperious Francesca in disgrace. They belonged to an earlier Vladimir, a sweet and transparent one for whom the world had little use.

There was a knock on the bathroom door. Vladimir wiped his

face, stuffed his pockets full of emergency tissue, and headed out past the rows of grumbling retired Virginians on a group tour waiting for the facilities, some with their cameras slung around their necks as if in preparation for that wayward Kodak moment en route to the crapper. He resumed his seat next to the window. The plane was riding over a patched carpet of thin, feathery clouds, a sign, his father had taught him over one country breakfast at the *dacha*, of an impending change in weather.

VLADIMIR STOOD on the ramp breathing European air, his shirtsleeves rolled down against the autumn wind. The Virginians were gasping at the lack of modern connecting gates between the plane and the tired-looking green terminal, which Vladimir nostalgically pegged as late-socialist architecture, the kind built after local architects had long given up on constructivism and just said: "Hey, here's some greenish glass and something not unlike cement. Let's make a terminal." Above the building, in large white letters: PRAVA, REPUBLIKA STOLOVAYA. Oddly enough, in Russian "Republika Stolovaya" meant "the Cafeteria Republic." Vladimir smiled. He was a big fan of the meaty Slavic languages: Polish, Slovak, and now this.

Then the passport check, where his first Stolovan native appeared, light-haired and beefy, with a beautiful golden mustache. "No," he said to Vladimir, pointing first to the passport photo of the college-era Vladimir with his goatee in full bloom and his dark, wispy hair extended to his behind, and then to the newly shaved, short-haired Vladimir before him. "No."

"Yes," Vladimir said. He tried to assume the same tired smile as in the passport, then pulled on his emerging chin hairs to indicate the forest to come.

"No," the passport agent said meekly, but stamped Vladimir's passport anyway. Clearly, socialism had fallen.

He picked up his valise at the luggage carousel and was ushered along with the Americans into the arrival lounge where a gleaming American Express cash machine lay in wait for them. The visiting moms and dads were picking their offspring out of a line-up of slick, young urban types, dressed as if they had just burgled New York's famed Screaming Mimi's boutique. Vladimir made his way through the maternal hugs and paternal shoulder-slapping to the doors, which, through a cryptic red arrow, promised escape. But he also took note of the situation: young Americans being visited by their moneyed elders. Moneyed? At least middle-class, these fiftysomethings in rumpled cords and goofy oversized sweaters. And nowadays the upper class looked down to the middle for tips on casual dressing, so anything was possible.

And then, as instantaneously as a plane falling out of the sky, the scene was russified.

Small-arms fire exploded outside.

A dozen car alarms engaged.

A detachment of men, each with a small Kalashnikov at hip level, swiftly parted the Americans into two screaming herds.

The requisite red carpet was rolled out between them.

A convoy of BMWs and armor-plated Range Rovers was assembled in protective formation.

A crepe banner bearing the curious legend PRAVAINVEST #1 FINANCIAL CONCERN WELCOME THE GIRSHKIN was unfurled.

And only then did our man finally catch sight of his new benefactor.

Flanked by three associates, all aglow in their nylon sports jackets and matching space-age trousers made out of alpaca or maybe silicon, the Groundhog solemnly approached. He was a burly, pocked little man with his eyes slightly crossed and his hair parted to make the least of a disappearing hairline.

The Groundhog placed one paw on Vladimir's shoulder, hold-

ing him in place (as if he would dare move), then stuck out his other
hand and, in his best Ukrainian accent, said rhetorically: "You are
Girshkin."

Yes, Girshkin he was.

"So, then," the Groundhog said, "I am Tolya Rybakov, the president of PravaInvest, also called..." He looked around to his two
immediate associates—one Groundhog-sized, the other closer to
Vladimir's physique—both too busy staring closely at Vladimir to
pay their boss any mind. "As my father might have told you, I am
also called...the Groundhog."

Vladimir continued to shake his hand, trying to make up for his
own hand's small size with vigor and motion, while muttering, "Yes,
yes, I have heard. Very pleased to meet you, Mister Groundhog."

"Just Groundhog," the Groundhog said tersely. "We don't use
titles in this company. Everyone knows who they are. This—" he
pointed to the enormous man with small Tatar eyes and a bald
dome encircled by rings of wrinkles like the cross-section of a
sequoia, "This is our chief operations officer, Misha Gusev."

"Are you called the Goose?" Vladimir asked, seizing on the
name's Russian meaning and the Groundhog's penchant for animal names.

"No," Gusev said. "Are you called the Jew?"

The Groundhog laughed and waved an accusatory finger at
Gusev, while the third man—small but solid, with blond hair as
fine as a baby's, his eyes cobalt blue the way Lake Baikal's waters
had been some centuries ago—shook his head and said, "Forgive
Gusev, he is a serious anti-Semite."

"Yes, right," Vladimir said. "We all have our..."

"Konstantin Bakutin," the third man said, offering his hand.
"Call me Kostya. I am the Chief Financial Officer. Congratulations
on your exploits with the Immigration and Naturalization Service.
That's a tough nut to crack, and it's not like we haven't tried."

Vladimir began to thank his conational in his most weighty, elaborate Russian, but the Groundhog pulled them outside, where between clusters of tour buses and forlorn Polish-made taxis stood a caravan of BMWs, each sporting a yellow "PravaInvest" logo across the bow, each surrounded by tall men in purple jackets of an unusual cut, loosely bridging the gap between business suit and smoking jacket. "These are mostly Stolovans," explained the Groundhog. "We hire a lot of local labor." He waved to his people as Gusev stuck two thumbs into his mouth and whistled.

In an impressive piece of postmodern choreography, twelve car doors were opened simultaneously by twelve lanky Stolovans. An associate relieved Vladimir of his luggage. Inside, the sober German interiors were violated beyond comprehension with Jersey-style zebra-striped seats and woolly cupholders.

"Very pleasant decor," Vladimir said. "Very, as they say in American computer circles, user-friendly."

"Oh, Esterhazy does these for us," the Groundhog said, whistling to a hairy little man sulking about in the shadows of a Range Rover. Esterhazy, bare-chested in his black leather jacket, his leather pants capped off by suede Capezios, waved a pack of Camel cigarettes at Vladimir and gave the Hog a thumbs-up. "Yes, the Hungarians have always been ahead of the times," said the Groundhog, almost sighing with jealousy.

With this international discussion at an end, the procession took off for the highway, Vladimir watching out for the first telltale signs—the flora and fauna, the brick and mortar—of his new country. Within minutes, the brick and mortar appeared on both sides of the road, like a signpost signaling VLADIMIR'S CHILDHOOD, NEXT HUNDRED EXITS: an endless stretch of rickety plaster Soviet-era apartment houses, each edifice peeling and waterlogged so that the inadvertent shapes of animals and constellations could be recognized by an imaginative child. And in the spaces between these

behemoths were the tiny grazing spaces where Vladimir sometimes
played, spaces adorned with a fistful of sand and some rusty
swings. True, this was Prava and not Leningrad, but then these
houses formed one long demented line from Tajikistan to Berlin.
There was no stopping them.

"First lesson in the Stolovan language," Kostya said. "These
housing complexes the Stolovans call *panelak*s. It is evident why,
no?" When nobody answered, Kostya said, "Because they look like
they're made out of panels."

"But we don't bother learning Stolovan," the Groundhog said.
"The bastards can all speak Russian."

"If they give you any problems," Gusev said, "give me a ring,
and we'll run them over like we did in '69. I was there, you know."

The blocks of flats continued for at least another ten minutes,
interrupted occasionally by the grimy sarcophagus of an overused
power station or the Orwellian skyline of factory smokestacks
barely visible from within the billowing clouds of their own emis-
sions. At times, Vladimir would point to a rising office tower
marked as the future site of an Austrian bank, or an old warehouse
being spruced up to accommodate a German car dealership, at
which point his hosts would say as a chorus: "Everywhere you turn,
money for the taking."

Just as the *panelaks* seemed ready to run out and the Prava of
travel brochures about to redeem her promise of cobblestone streets
bisected by the silver indentations of tram lines, the procession
lurched to the right along a winding sandy path that on occasion
would break out into asphalt, as if to show the motorcade just how
civilized life could sometimes be. In the distance, perched against
the bluff of an eroded hill, the Groundhog's own *panelak* compound
awaited, its balconies like the parapets of a vast socialist fortress.
"Four buildings, two constructed in '81, two in '83," the Groundhog
rattled off.

"We got the whole thing in '89 for less than 300,000 dollars U.S.," added Kostya, and Vladimir wondered whether he should commit these figures to memory in the event of a quiz. Instantly, he felt tired.

They pulled into the compound's quadrangle where several American jeeps stood at attention alongside a tank with a gaping hole for a barrel. "Very good," said the well-disposed Groundhog. "Gusev and I have to take off for town, so Kostya will show you your apartment. Tomorrow we have what I call the *biznesmenski* lunch. That's a weekly event, by the way, so bring some ideas, write something down."

Gusev sneered good-bye and the motorcade began the complicated task of making their way around the tank and heading onward to golden Prava, while Kostya, whistling a Russian folk tune concerning boysenberries, waved Vladimir toward the entrance of a building unceremoniously labeled #2.

The lobby was cramped with two dozen men and their rifles, sweating away beneath a bare light bulb; loose playing cards and empty liquor bottles covered the floor, and several flies, thick and dazed with overfulfillment, lethargically scuttled about the landscape. "This is Vladimir, an important young man," Kostya announced.

Vladimir bowed slightly in the manner of an important young man. He turned around to make sure he wasn't leaving anybody out. "*Dobry den,*" he said.

A man of indeterminate age, his face covered with red beard and glow-in-the-dark children's Band-Aids, lifted his Kalashnikov and mumbled back the greeting. Evidently he was speaking for everyone.

"Gusev's top men," Kostya said as they turned into a corridor. "All former Soviet Interior Ministry troops, so I wouldn't step on their toes. Don't ask me what exactly we need them for. Certainly don't ask Gusev."

The corridor ended with a door slightly ajar, the word KASINO written upon it with industrial grease, and Dire Straits' "Money for Nothing" audible within. "In need of renovation," said Kostya as a forewarning, "but still a money-maker."

The Kasino was the size of Vladimir's math-and-science high school gymnasium, and seemed to have as much to do with gambling as the other facility did with sports. Clusters of folding tables and chairs were filled with young blond women smoking and trying to look dangerous in the brief light of several halogen lamps.

"*Dobry den*," the gentlemanly Vladimir said, although by then the *den*' might have very well turned into evening outside the Kasino's windowless gloom. A frontal mass of unfiltered smoke floated his way from the lungs of a woman whose skin was the greenish color of raw onion, and whose tiny body was seemingly held in place by the weight of her shoulder pads.

"This is Vladimir," Kostya said. "He's here to do things with the Americans."

The trance was broken: the women pulled themselves up and crossed their legs. There was giggling and the word "*Amerikanets*" was said many times. The vixen with the shoulder pads struggled to her feet, leaning against her folding table for support, and said in English, "I am Lydia. I am driving Ford Escort."

The others thought that tremendously witty and applauded. Vladimir was about to say a few encouraging words on their behalf, but Kostya took his arm and escorted him out of the Kasino, saying, "Ah, but you must be tired from travel."

They went up two flights, the staircase redolent of beef stew and the starchy smells of Russian family life, and emerged onto a brightly lit corridor of flats. "Number twenty-three," said Kostya, swinging about a key chain like a bed-and-breakfast proprietor.

They went in. "Main room," Kostya said with an epic sweep of the arm. The space was filled entirely by an olive-colored Swedish couch, a bulky television set, and Vladimir's opened and searched-through valise. The magazine articles he had photocopied on Prava's expatriate scene were scattered about; his punctured shampoo bottle was gurgling under the couch, a river of green trailing away from it. Ah, those curious Russians. It was nice to be back in a land of transparency.

"Next stop, bedroom with a nice big bed," Kostya said. There was also a simple oakwood dresser and a window overlooking the smokestacks defining the horizon. "Here is a kitchen with good equipment, and there is a small room for working and thinking important thoughts." Vladimir peeked into a walk-in closet occupied by a school-sized desk and a Cyrillic typewriter on top of it. He nodded.

"In Moscow this apartment would be for two families," Kostya said. "Hungry?"

"No, thank you," Vladimir said. "On the plane, I—"

"A drink, maybe?"

"No, I feel rather—"

"Then to bed." Kostya put his hands on Vladimir's shoulders and guided him into the bedroom, reminding Vladimir of how freely Russians touched one another; such a change from his adopted homeland across the ocean, where even his father, the once-earthy friend of the collective farmer, had been keeping a proper American distance as of late. "This is my card," Kostya said. "Call at any time. I am here to protect you."

Protect? "But aren't we all comrades together?" said travel-weary, sleepy-eyed Vladimir, as if he were auditioning for Soviet *Sesame Street*.

No answer to that question was forthcoming. "After the *biznesmenski* lunch," Kostya said, "the two of us will go see Prava. I have a feeling you will have an appreciation for the city's beauty, which the rest of our cadre… Well, what can I say? I'll get you tomorrow."

AFTER HE LEFT, Vladimir went through his luggage looking for a bottle of minoxidil. Per Francesca's admonitions against premature baldness, he was becoming something of a hair-tonic addict. He went into the toilet, which was a drab affair, distinguished by a shower curtain with a larger-than-life peacock, its plumage blazing, its drooling beak ready to make love to anything remotely feathered and egg-bearing.

Vladimir moved the hair aside from his temples, found the areas in need, and rubbed down a prolific amount of the minoxidil to make up for the round missed on the plane. He watched his eyes narrow in the bathroom mirror while a single wayward drop of the drug descended his forehead to pollinate his goatee.

In the bedroom, he felt the thick down comforter, its outer casing embroidered with flowers just the way they had made them in Leningrad. Vladimir was ready to crawl under it, but something happened—his knees must have weakened and he found himself on the carpet, which was as scraggly as his chin. Several things occurred to him. Fran, Challah, Mother, home. He was trying to keep his eyes open and focused on the perfectly white ceiling above him, yet, in the end, even the promise of the comforter and its mothering qualities failed to keep him awake, and he fell asleep on the floor.

19. MAKING
NEW FRIENDS

THE *BIZNESMENSKI* LUNCH WAS IN FULL ROAR. A RED-
nosed, pot-bellied cretin who had been introduced to Vladimir as
the junior deputy assistant to the associate director for financial
oversight had said some questionable things about the Groundhog's Ukrainian girlfriend and was in the process of being ejected
by a pair of enormous men in purple jackets. His screams grew
even louder after the doors were closed behind him, but Vladimir's
tablemates hardly seemed to care—additional cartons of Jack
Daniel's were being wheeled into the dining room by the Kasino
crew, undressed to the hilt for the occasion.

Across the table a dozen chicken Kievs had been laid waste to,
and now formed a poultry Borodino of twisted bones and splat-
tered butter. There was much argument about whether the
sausages in the center of town were best inside American-style
buns or on a traditional piece of rye bread, and every statement
was punctuated by the sharp exhale of cigarette smoke and a
leisurely reach for the bottle.

Vladimir coughed and wiped his eyes. At one end of the table
Kostya was quietly putting away a side of mutton; at the other end,
an elk of a Slav—one of the several that formed the heavily boozed

cortege around Gusev—shouted praise of rye bread and vodka, and cucumbers so fresh from his garden, they still smelled like shit.

Then the Groundhog's fist came down on the table hard and there was silence. "Okay," said the Groundhog. "*Bizness.*"

The silence continued. The bushy-browed gentleman next to Vladimir turned to face him for the first time throughout the meal, eyeing him like a second helping of chicken. Eventually the others followed suit, until Vladimir poured himself a shot with shaking hands. He had been abstaining from food and drink all afternoon out of nervousness, but now that seemed less than a good idea. "Hi," Vladimir said to the assembled. He looked down to his whiskey as if to a TelePrompTer, but the clear liquid had nothing to impart except courage. He drank. *Oofa!* On an empty stomach it was quite a depth charge.

"Don't be scared, have some more," the Groundhog said. There was polite laughter led by Kostya who was trying to put a friendly spin on the hilarity.

"Yes," Vladimir said, and drank again. The second whiskey made such an impression on his empty gullet that Vladimir jumped to his feet. The Russians leaned back; there was the rustle of hands locating holsters underneath the table.

He looked to his notes, which were written in huge block letters and littered with exclamation points, like agit-prop slogans in a May Day parade. "Gentlemen," Vladimir announced. But then he paused just as quickly as he had started... He had to take a breath. It was happening! This nebulous plan he had patched together during his last days in New York was coalescing into something as tangible as an Austrian bank or a German car dealership. "They say Uncle Shurik specialized in pyramid schemes," his father had told him, standing in the fertile backyard of the Girshkin estate, feeding his son flounder. "Know what those are, Volodya...?"

Aha. He knew. Pyramid schemes. Also known as Ponzi schemes, after one Carlo Ponzi, Vladimir's new patron saint, the alpha immigrant from Parma, the little *gonif* that could.

Vladimir looked to the Russians sitting before him. Those dear elks. They smoked too much, drank too much, killed too much. They spoke a dying language and, to be honest, were themselves not too long for this world. *They were his people.* Yes, after thirteen years in the American desert, Vladimir Girshkin had stumbled upon a different kind of tragedy. A better place to be unhappy. He had finally found his way home.

"Gentlemen," Vladmir said once again. "I want to do a pyramid scheme!"

"Oh, I like pyramid schemes, brothers," said one of the more amiable elks who wore the airbrushed image of his bloated, mangy-haired toddler on his lapel. But in other quarters the grumbling and eye-rolling had already started. Pyramid scheme? Not again.

"Perhaps it doesn't sound like the most original idea," Vladimir continued. "But I've done some research and discovered the perfect population for just this sort of thing. Right here in Prava."

Gasps and muttered confusion around the table. The *biznesmeni* looked to one another as if this mysterious population might be somehow personified by Grisha the Kasino manager, or Fedya the director of sales and promotions. Whom else did they know in this town?

"Are you speaking of the Stolovans?" the Groundhog said. "Because we've already taken the Stolovans for a ride. We're under investigation by the ministries of finance and public health, and by the department of fishing and hatcheries, too."

"Yes, no more Stolovans," his associates muttered.

"Gentlemen, how many Americans do you know?" Vladimir said.

The muttering stopped, and all eyes turned to a thin, shaky young man named Mishka who had spent much of the meal in the bathroom. "Hey, Mishka, how about that little girl of yours?" Gusev said. There was laughter and enough male horsing around for Vladimir to get a few friendly kicks in the shins and an elbow to the ribs.

Mishka was trying to sink his great big head into his tiny shoulders. "Stop it. Shut up," he said. "I didn't know it was that kind of bar. Groundhog, please tell them..."

"Mishka met an American girl with a penis," several people eagerly explained to Vladimir. More bottles were uncorked and toasts made to the hapless Mishka who scurried out of the room.

"No, no, I don't mean that segment of the population," Vladimir said. "I mean the whole English-speaking expatriate community in Prava. We're talking roughly fifty thousand people here." Well, give or take thirty thousand.

"And do you know how much money they have on average?" He looked each man in the eye before answering, although, truthfully, he had no idea. "Ten times as much as the average Stolovan. This is roughly speaking again. Now, the beauty of this project is essentially this: turnover. Americans come, Americans go. They stay for a few years, then they go back to Detroit and get lousy jobs in the service industry or at their father's firm. While they're here, we milk them for all they're worth. We promise to send them dividends across the ocean. And when we don't, what are they going to do? Come back and prosecute? Meanwhile, we've got fresh blood arriving by the planeload."

The men twirled their drinks and tapped their chicken bones against the china in contemplation. "All right. My question is this," Gusev said. He stabbed out his cigarette with one brusque jab—a nice statement of purpose in itself. "How do we get the Americans to invest in the first place? These are, to my knowledge, mostly

young people and so they're gullible, but they're not exactly
everyday investors."

"A good question," Vladimir said. His eyes traveled the room as
if he were a substitute teacher trying to conquer a new domain.
"Did everyone hear the question? How do we get the Americans to
invest in the first place? Here is the answer: self-esteem. Most of
these young men and women are trying desperately to justify their
presence in Prava and the interruption of their education, their
careers, and so on...We make them feel like they're taking part in
the resurgence of Eastern Europe. There's an American saying, spoken by a famous black man: 'If you're not part of the solution,
you're part of the problem.' This saying has deep resonance in the
American psyche, particularly among the liberal kind of American
this city attracts. Now, we've got them not only becoming part of
the solution but making money in the process. Or so they'll think."

"And you believe this can actually be accomplished?" the
Groundhog said quietly but directly.

"Yes, and I'll tell you what it takes!" Vladimir cried to his disci-
ples, throwing his arms in the air with Pentecostal fervor, the zeal of
the born-again. "It takes glossy brochures. We'll have to have them
professionally made, not here, perhaps in Vienna. Oh, and we'll
need artists' renderings of the five-star resort on Lake Boloto that
we're never going to build, and then an annual report featuring the
smoky factories knocked down to make way for pleasant little corporate parks with recycling bins for glass and newspapers...Sure,
plenty of environmental stuff. That will sell. I see holistic centers
and Reiki clinics, too."

He was on a roll. There was no more grumbling. Gusev was
scribbling on his napkin. Kostya was whispering to the Groundhog. The Groundhog first seemed agreeable to Kostya's counsel,
but a minute later the mercurial Hog slammed the table once

again. "Wait one minute," the Groundhog said. "We don't know any Americans." Kostya had set him up well.

"That, friends," Vladimir said, "is why I'm here with you today. I propose that I single-handedly infiltrate the American community in Prava. Despite my fluent Russian and my tolerance of drink, I can easily double as a first-rate American. My credentials are impeccable. I have attended one of the premier liberal-minded colleges in the States and have a profound appreciation for the dress, manners, and outlook of the disaffected young American set. I have lived many years in New York, the capital of the disaffected movement, have had many angry, disenfranchised friends of the artistic persuasion, and have just completed a romantic liaison with a woman who in both looks and temperament personifies the vanguard of this unique social group. Gentlemen, with no intention of conceit, I assure you—I am the best there is. And that's that."

Kostya, that dear man, began to applaud. This was a lonely sound at first, but then the Groundhog picked up one hand, looked it over as if instructions were written on the back, sighed, picked up the other hand, sighed again, and finally brought his hands together. Immediately, dozens of fat, sweaty palms began smacking one another, there were shouts of *"Ura!"* and Vladimir turned crimson.

This time it was Gusev who put his fist down and silenced the table. "What do you want?" he said. "For yourself, that is."

"Not much, actually," Vladimir said. "I need a certain amount per week for drinks, drugs, taxis, whatever it takes to ingratiate myself in the community. Based on experience, I know that it is best to be seen in as many clubs, bars, cafés as possible, thereby creating a self-perpetuating aura of notoriety. What this costs in Prava, I don't know. In New York, with housing taken care of, I would wager three, four thousand dollars a week. Here, I believe, two thousand would suffice. Plus an initial six, seven thousand in relocation costs." That would take care of his little debt to Laszlo and Roberta.

"I think Gusev means what do you want in terms of profit-sharing," said the Groundhog, looking to Gusev for confirmation.

Vladimir held his breath. Did they mean *on top* of his ludicrous two-thousand-a-week request? Did they have any idea... But, wait a second, could he have betrayed his ignorance of *bizness* etiquette by not asking for profit sharing... There seemed enough money to go around; the dining hall looked like a Versace showroom. There was nothing left to do but shrug and declare nonchalantly: "Whatever you think reasonable. Ten percent?"

There was consensus throughout the room. It certainly seemed reasonable. When these men thought percentages it was usually in increments of fifty. "Comrades," Vladimir said. "Fellow *biznesmeni*, I want you to be convinced—I'm not out to fleece you. I am what in America is called a 'team player.' So..."

So? He tried to come up with an appropriate segue. "So let's drink to success!"

After this there were many toasts in favor of the team player. A queue was forming to shake his hand. Several boisterous entrepreneurs had to be ejected from the room after stepping out of turn.

THEY PULLED AWAY from the compound. It was a breezy, beautiful day; even the chemical haze seemed agreeable to Vladimir: its job was to correct the eternally smiling, self-satisfied sun with a measure of historical accuracy. Kostya sat in front, playing with the fuzzy dice. Their driver, a Chechen resplendent in the mammoth-woolly Chechen national hat, had eyes the color of tomato puree and looked ready to mash the tail end of any cardboard Polish Fiat that was traveling at less than the speed of sound. "Look," Kostya said.

A series of broad, neoclassical facades, seamlessly attached one to the next, stretched to the right, cream-colored and placid despite a belligerent pair of watchtowers peeking out from behind. And in the center of the mélange, flying buttresses and spires spanned a sooty Gothic church that quite easily eclipsed the surrounding complex in presence and scale. "Jesus," Vladimir said, his face pressed to the window. "What a beautiful mess."

"Prava Castle," said Kostya modestly.

To celebrate this unabashedly tourist moment, Vladimir lit one of the moldy local cigarettes that were presented to him by the Groundhog at the conclusion of lunch. He rolled down a window just as a pair of smiling M&M's waved their white-gloved hands at him—the personable candies were welded to the side of a streetcar. "Ah!" Vladimir said as the old beast rumbled by. He looked back to the castle still scrolling on the right then back to the waving M&M's disappearing on the left. He felt unconditionally happy. "Driver, play some music!" he said.

"ABBA's greatest hits?" the fellow asked. It was a rhetorical question.

"Play 'Super Trooper,'" Kostya said.

"Oh yes. I like that one," Vladimir said. A sycamore-scented breeze blew through the car, as the Nordic cuties crooned off the tape deck and the three ex-Soviets bopped along in accents of varying quality. They began to descend, looping around the hill upon which the castle was perched, just as a tram swung the other way, missing them by centimeters. "Fucking Stolovans!" shouted the Chechen.

And then Vladimir looked down. He had picked up the expression "sea of spires" from some travel brochure back at the airport's

tourist office, and while there were certainly golden spires reflect-
ing the late-summer sun in the architectural stew below, it seemed
rather partial of the pamphlet to fail to mention the sloping red
roofs landsliding down the hill and into the gray bend of water that
Kostya pointed out as the Tavlata River. Or the enormous pale-
green domes on both sides of the river capping massive Baroque
churches. Or the tremendous Gothic powder towers, strategically
spread out along the cityscape, like dark medieval guards protecting the town from the usual nonsense that had managed to con-
sume so many European skylines throughout the years.

There was only one incongruous structure, giant and brooding
in the background, but it single-handedly managed to cast a
shadow over half the city. At first, Vladimir suspected it was an
oversized powder tower blackened from years of use...Only...
Well...No, one could no longer deny the painful truth. The structure was a kind of giant shoe, a galosh, to be exact. "What is it?"
Vladimir shouted to Kostya over ABBA.

"What? You've never heard of the Foot?" Kostya shouted back.
"It's quite a funny story, Vladimir Borisovich. Should I tell it?"

"Please, Konstantin Ivanovich," Vladimir said. He had forgotten
how he knew Kostya's patronymic, but this salt-of-the-earth man
was surely the son of an Ivan.

"Well, as soon as the war ended, you see, the Soviets built the
world's tallest statue of Stalin over Prava. It was really something.
The entire Old Town was just sandwiched between Stalin's two feet;
it's amazing he didn't step on it." Kostya rewarded his own joke
with a little laughter. How he relished speaking to Vladimir! It was
obvious to the latter that had Kostya been born in a saner time, a
different country, he could easily have been a beloved school-
teacher in some gentle, slow-witted province.

"Then, after the Great One passed on," Kostya continued,
regaining his official didactic tone, "the Stolovans were allowed to

blow off his head and replace it with Khrushchev's, which, I'm sure was a great consolation. *Finally,* two years after the Gabardine Revolution, the Stolovans managed to dynamite most of Nikita, but... Well, don't ask me exactly what happened... Suffice to say, the fellows who won the Left Foot contract were last seen in St. Bart's with Trata Poshlaya. Remember her? She was in *Come Home, Rifleman Misha,* and, oh, what was the one set in Yalta? *My Albatross.*"

"PravaInvest could dynamite the Foot," Vladimir volunteered, momentarily forgetting his corporation's unbearable lightness of being.

"It's very costly," Kostya cautioned him. "The Foot is right at the base of the Old Town. If you don't use the explosives just right, you'll blow half the city into the Tavlata."

If PravaInvest couldn't do it, then Vladimir vowed to mentally erase the Foot from his line of sight, even as it imposed its galosh-like shadow over the architectural grace of the cityscape.

Yes, giant foot aside, Prava continued to do its golden act beneath him, and then it dawned on Vladimir that this Prava was not without its charm; that while it was no *Weltstadt* like, say, Berlin, it was no shitty Bucharest either. Consequently, what if the Americans here were more the sophisticated Fran-and-Tyson variety than the deluded Baobab kind? Vladimir's stomach grumbled with worry. Kostya, as if he had sensed Vladimir's concerns, said: "A pretty town, yes? But New York must be still more beautiful."

"Are you joking?" Vladimir said. They skipped a series of red lights and careened onto the tram rails of a bridge connecting the two parts of the city. Sparks flew and their driver cursed the Stolovans once more for their bloody infrastructure.

"Well," said Kostya, ever the diplomat, "but New York must be bigger."

"That's right," Vladimir said. "It's the biggest." But he was not reassured.

They swerved off the embankment and into a street lined with stately Baroque dwellings in various stages of disrepair yet still wearing their ornamentation, their gables and coats of arms standing out like the flounces on a worn Hapsburg gown.

"Stop here," Kostya said. The driver slammed into the nearest stretch of sidewalk.

Outside, Vladimir did a little dance of happiness, a sort of cross between the jitterbug and the *kazachok*, feeling he could trust Kostya with this momentary lapse of reason. The Russian smiled sympathetically and said, "Yes, it's a beautiful day."

They found a café, one of the many from which white plastic tables reached out to the sidewalk, the tables covered with pork, dumplings, beer, and surrounded by Germans. Indeed, there were tourists everywhere. The Germans formed entire phalanxes of cheerful, drunk Swabians and purposefully striding Frankfurters. Teams of dazed Munich grandmothers on church trips staggered out of pubs to trample the yapping dachshunds being walked by their angry Stolovan counterparts: the *babushka*s. Upon first sight of them, Vladimir felt a kinship with these wizened survivors of both fascism and communism, whose city was clearly no longer their own, and who stared contemptuously from inside their meager headscarves at their bejeweled neighbors from across the border. He could easily picture his own grandmother in their place, except she would never consent to owning a hungry dog, preferring instead to feed her son extra portions.

But the Germans, although ubiquitous, were not alone. Clusters of stylish young Italians glided down the boulevard, trailing Dunhill smoke in their wake. A knot of Frenchwomen with identical buzz-cuts stood before a café menu, eyeing it skeptically. And finally Vladimir heard the sing-along of an American family, large and solid, arguing over whose turn it was to carry the goddamn video camera. "But where are the *young* Americans?" he said to Kostya.

"The young ones don't take the tourist route too often. Although you do see them on the Emanuel Bridge, singing and begging for money."

"We don't want the basket cases," Vladimir said.

"Well, I do know of a popular expatriate café for you," Kostya said, "but first we should celebrate your arrival with a drink. Yes?"

Yes. They picked up the drinks menu. "My God," Vladimir said, "fifteen crowns for a cognac."

Kostya explained to him how that amounted to fifty cents.

A dollar was thirty crowns? Two drinks for a dollar? "Yes, of course," said Vladimir Girshkin, the all-knowing international businessman. "Allow me to treat you," he added magnanimously. And he took it further, thinking: at an allowance of two thousand dollars a week, he could budget four thousand drinks for himself. Of course, he couldn't get too greedy, he would have to buy a lot of people a lot of booze, and then there were taxis and dinners and whatnot, but still, five hundred drinks a week was not such an unreasonable figure.

A waiter, his face as droopy as a dachshund's, wearing the familiar oversized purple jacket and a Prussian mustache, dragged himself over to their table. "*Dobry den*," he said. It was the same greeting as in Russian, Vladimir noted cheerfully. But then Kostya said a mouthful of words that only vaguely resembled the Russian version of "Can we have two cognacs, please."

They drank. A group of Italian schoolgirls marched down the street, waving some sort of crowing-rooster puppets at them. A pair of the bronze nymphs took their time passing by Kostya and Vladimir's table, looking at each of them in turn with their great round eyes two shades darker than the cognac. The embarrassed

Russians quickly turned away to face each other, then snuck furtive glances as the Italian girls rounded the corner. "So you said you had a relationship with an extraordinary American woman in New York," Kostya said, his voice atremble.

"Several women," Vladimir said nonchalantly. "But one was better than the others, as I suppose is always the case."

"True," said Kostya. "It has always been my dream to go to New York and find the nicest woman there and to live with her in a big house on the outskirts of town."

"It's always best to live in the center," Vladimir corrected him, "and the nicest woman is hardly the most interesting. It's a question of balance, don't you think?"

"Yes," Kostya said, "but for children it's best to find someone nice, and to hell with the rest."

"Children?" Vladimir said and laughed.

"Sure, I'll be twenty-eight next spring," Kostya said. "Look," he bent his head forward and pulled at the gray hairs clumped together at the center of his crown. "Now, of course, I would like a woman who will go with me to the symphony and the museum, and, if she insists, to the ballet. And she should be well-read, too, and like children, of course. And be able to keep house, for I'd like a big house, as I've said. But this is not too much to expect from a beautiful American woman such as the one you described, I don't think."

Vladimir smiled politely. He raised two fingers to the passing waiter and pointed at their empty glasses. "So have you anyone in Petersburg?" he said.

"My mother. She's all alone. My father's dead. She's dying slowly. Cirrhosis. Emphysema. Dementia. Her pension comes out to thirteen dollars a month. I send her half my paycheck, but I still worry. Maybe I should move her out here someday." And here Kostya sighed the familiar sigh of Vladimir's Russian clients at the

Emma Lazarus Society; the lung-emptying sigh that comes with a lead weight attached to the neck. The flaxen-haired gangster had gone quite soft on his mama.

"Do you ever think of going back to Russia?" Vladimir said, wishing instantly he could retract those words because the last thing he wanted was for Kostya to leave.

"Every day," Kostya said. "But I could never find anything in Petersburg or Moscow that pays quite so much. The *mafiya* is certainly over there..." Kostya paused, as they both reflected upon that single, unmentionable word. "But it's much more dangerous. Everyone's ready to reach for their guns. Here, things are calmer, the Stolovans are better at keeping order."

"Yes, the Groundhog certainly seems like a pleasant individual," Vladimir said. "I doubt that there's anyone bent on causing him harm. Or his associates."

Kostya laughed, twisting his tie around his fingers like a little boy given his first clip-on. "Are you trying to ask me something?" he said. A second, uninvited round of cognacs had arrived. "Truthfully, there are some Bulgarians who aren't terribly happy about how he's cornered the high end of the strippers' market, but these are just little grudges that can be solved with a few bottles of this..." He lifted his glass. "No need for the bullets."

"None," Vladimir said.

Kostya looked to his watch. "I must go to a meeting," he said. "But we should do this regularly. Oh, and also, do you run?"

"Run?" Vladimir said. "Like to catch a bus?"

"No, to build physical endurance."

"I don't have any physical endurance," Vladimir said.

"Well, it's settled then. Next week we'll go running. There's a nice little trail in back of the compound." They shook hands, and Kostya wrote down directions to the expatriate place on a napkin. It was called Eudora Welty's. Then, true to form, the energetic young man got up and ran down the street, rounding the corner in no time.

Vladimir yawned spectacularly, finished off his cognac, then waved the waiter over for the bill, which came out to a little over three dollars. It was time to meet the Gringos.

20. THE WRITER COHEN

BY THE TIME HE FOUND THE SUBTERRANEAN EUDORA'S, Vladimir was already lost in the vast gastronomical abyss between lunch and dinner. Six souls remained in the restaurant's cavernous digs, which suggested the place was once something other than the Cajun expat emporium it had become—perhaps a torture chamber where Catholics and Hussites hanged each other by the nose hairs from the barrel-vaulted ceiling. Now the only sign of tortured religiosity was the one advertising seared monkfish on a bed of fennel.

A waitress came to meet Vladimir. She was young, nervous, American, with a short, grizzly haircut, and dressed in some kind of kilt. She had the bad manners to call Vladimir "hon," as in "Have a seat, hon." She was Southern, too.

Vladimir perused the menu and his compatriots in late dining. To his immediate left was a table of four women and a dozen empty beer bottles. The women were dressed for the seventy-degree weather in engineer boots, corduroys, and T-shirts of various gloomy hues: hospital dun, narcolepsy gray, the black of the void. They talked so softly that Vladimir was unable to catch a single word despite their proximity, and they all looked terribly familiar, as if they had gone to Vladimir's Midwestern college. He felt the urge to sneeze out the school's name to see if he would get a response.

The remaining customer was a beautiful fellow: slender and pale, broad-shouldered and leonine with a bell-curve mane of heavy light-brown hair that was surely the sign of a healthy organism. If scholars of beautiful people could raise any objections to this gentleman it might be the slightly aquiline nose—what does the lion need of the eagle?—and also the awkward fuzz covering his chin that made it possible to imagine his physiognomy with either a real beard or no beard, but certainly not with this sad moss.

The fellow was scribbling away in a notepad, the requisite empty beers were lined up on the table, his cigarette was on autopilot, smoking away in the grooves of the ashtray, and now and again his gaze would travel the restaurant, casually brushing past the table populated by the opposite sex.

Vladimir ordered a dish of pit-barbecued pork and a mint julep. "And what's the beer everyone's drinking here?" he asked the waitress.

"Unesko," she said and smiled. He had betrayed himself as a newcomer.

"Yes, one of those too."

He rummaged his satchel for his thick, shaggy notebook, a holdover from college: a poem here, a stab at fiction there. He threw it down so that its spine would ring against the table, then did his best to seem impervious to the stares of the women's table and the young Hemingway across the room. He took out his marble Parker, embossed with the logo of Mother's corporation, and he smiled at it. Or rather, to it.

To those who have observed Vladimir throughout the years, it would have appeared his standard smile, the weight of it sunk into his jutting lower lip and the hazy, peaceful green eyes. But Vladimir (through reading too many bad novels, perhaps) believed that a smile could convey an entire story if only he sighed and shook his head with good humor at the right moments. In the instant case, Vladimir hoped this smile would say, "Yes, we have been through a lot together, this pen and I. We have kept each other from falling apart through all the strange, self-inflicted years. Portland, Oregon; Chapel Hill, North Carolina; Austin, Texas; then, of course, Sedona, Arizona. Maybe Key West. Hard to remember. Lots of barely functioning cars, women who didn't care, bands that fell apart because the personalities involved were just too strong. And through it all: the pen. Writing. I am a writer. No, a poet." He had heard that poetry had cachet here. Everybody was rhyming, jazz clubs were branching out into poetry slams. But then he had to distinguish himself... "I am a writer-poet. No, a novelist-poet. But for a living I make investments. A novelist-poet-investor. Plus I do dance improv."

Vladimir was smiling at his pen for too long now. Enough with the pen already. He lowered himself into a poem. It was a poem about Mother; it came easy, Mother lent herself well to verse. His two drinks arrived and the waitress smiled at his efforts. Yes, they were all in this together.

He was making good time, describing how his mother looked in a Chinese restaurant, using such imagery as "a small string of pearls from her birthland," which had scored good marks from a comparative literature professor back at the Midwestern college. Then tragedy struck. His globetrotting pen ran out. Vladimir shook it as gracefully as he could, then started aheming to the Eudora Welty's other artist-in-dining. The fellow would not respond, lost (or pretending to be lost) in work, he narrowed his eyes and shook his head at the words before him as if they were his undoing. He bunched up his mane with both hands then let it unravel—it unraveled very elegantly, like a Chinese fan. He sighed and shook his head with good humor.

The women's collective, however, responded by hushing their already subsonic conversation. They looked at Vladimir and his pen with great mystery and worry as if they were lost tourists confronted with a spontaneous native dance on a street far from the safety of their Hilton. Vladimir picked up his beer, his sole credential, and walked over to the women. "Pen?" he said.

One woman had a purse; she opened it and tore through a ream of facial tissues, new and used. She stole frightened glances at her compatriots until one of them—the blond spikes of her porcupine-cut bristling with authority—spoke up for her: "She doesn't have a pen." The others nodded.

"You need a pen?" It was the writer. He had pressed his lager against his cheek, which Vladimir took to be an international symbol of good will by way of mild inebriation.

"I need a pen," Vladimir said, feeling the drama was about to come to a head. He crossed over to the writer mumbling thanks to the women for their effort (no response), and accepted a ballpoint. "Damn thing ran out," Vladimir said.

"A writer carries two!" the writer barked. "Always." He put the beer down and, with his round and cratered chin held high, appraised Vladimir as would a grade school principal his most bumbling charge.

"That one ran out too," Vladimir said, although his strained voice pronounced him guilty—guilty of packing only one pen. "I've been writing too much today."

Too much writing? Too much was never enough. Now it seemed for certain his idiocy would do him in, but instead the writer said: "Write anything good?"

"This poem about my Russian mother in Chinatown," Vladimir said, trying to exoticize himself with as many ethnic references as possible. "But I'm just not getting it right. I came here, came to Prava, to get enough distance and I'm still lost."

"How'd you get a Russian mother?" the writer asked.

"I am Russian."

"Shhh." They looked around. "The barmaid is Stolovan," the writer explained.

A pair of uneven saloon doors separated the bar area from the rest of the joint; the Russophobic Stolovan was somewhere behind those doors. Vladimir looked down to his feet in embarrassment and took a swig of his beer in lieu of something to say. Yes, he was definitely starting to lose ground with all the fits and starts afflicting his attempts at conversation with the literary god. He decided, against his best instincts, to take a stab at honesty, that mortal enemy of the pyramid schemer. "I just got here," he said. "I'm still a little out of it as far as the locals go."

"Forget about them," the writer said. "This is an American town. Why don't you sit down? Come on, take a break from your Russian mommy poem for a second. Oh, don't look so sore. Hell, I remember my mother-as-muse stage. Trust me, the maternal teat will still be there tomorrow morning."

And then Vladimir knew he was going to like this guy. The helpful instructions about always having two pens, the worldly attitude toward the Stolovans, and now the learned appraisal of the maternal teat, all confirmed that the writer was what the uninitiated would call an asshole. But Vladimir knew these pretty castoffs of well-to-do America, cruising along on their five-year plan of alcoholic self-discovery, then trolling desperately for a five-year renewal option. *Hell, I remember my mother-as-muse stage.* What disarming aggression. It was Midwestern progressive college redux, confirmation that this Adonis was definitely in Vladimir's cards, his "Patient Zero."

Vladimir took a seat just as a second mint julep was brought out by the waitress, smiling soberly at her countrymen's meeting of the minds. Vladimir polished off his first beer and placed it on the outgoing tray. "Another?" she said.

"Please."

"Nuts?"

"No nuts."

"Lemon?"

"*Sans* lemon."

"On me," said the writer, impressed by the brevity, the honesty of the exchange. Now they were in Raymond Carver territory. "Drinking up a storm?" he said to Vladimir as the latter reached for the julep.

"Jet lag. I'm out of it," Vladimir said. Think. Carver dialogue. Deceptively simple yet profound. "I haven't got it all together yet," Vladimir said, as he looked away mysteriously.

"You find a place to live?"

"My boss gave me a flat in the suburbs."

"Boss?" The writer's mouth came open revealing Yankee orthodontia at its best. He shook his head, his mane rippling; it felt very natural to just reach out and touch the silky thing. "You mean you got a job? With whom?"

The iconoclast scribbler seemed to perk up nicely at this mention of the material world. Vladimir imagined a background of worried parents, angry transatlantic phone calls, pouches full of law-school applications being dragged through the streets of Prava by exhausted Stolovan postmen. "A development firm," Vladimir said.

"Development firm? What are you developing? My name's Perry, by the way." He stuck out a hand. "Perry Cohen. Yes, it's a surprising name. I'll have you know that I'm the only Iowa Jew ever."

Vladimir smiled, thinking: what happens if there's another Iowa Jew in the room when he introduces himself as the sole specimen? The embarrassment! He filed that one away for future leverage. "How'd you Jews get all the way out to Iowa?" he asked. ("I'm a Jew, too," he added for reassurance.)

"My father's the Jew," Perry explained. "My mother's the mayor's daughter."

"And the mayor let her marry a Jew. How nice." There. He was catching the vibe. The expat, in-your-face vibe. "Your father must be blond like you. And assimilated, too."

"He's Hitler with a circumcision," Cohen said. And as he said it, something uncalled for, perhaps even unscripted, took place: his head bent forward so that his mane naturally covered his face, and beneath the mane Vladimir noticed—what? A quick nasal exhalation to forestall a whimper? A rapid blinking of the eyes to shoo away the moisture? Teeth biting hard into a quivering lip to bring it back in line? But before Vladimir had a chance to ponder the question of whether this was a true display of emotion or a performance for his benefit, Cohen brushed his hair back, ahemed loudly, and regained his composure.

"Hitler, yes," Vladimir said, eager to appear blithely unconcerned. "Do tell."

And so Cohen told Vladimir the story of his father. The two men had known each other for two minutes now; a pen had been transferred from one to the other; ethnic backgrounds had been established; a few sallies had been launched. Was that all it took—the equivalent of two dogs sniffing out each other's rear—to get the writer Cohen to tell the story of his father?

Could this story have been Cohen's trademark then? His theme? One thing Vladimir had learned from his years of wandering and self-invention was that it was important to have a theme. A coherent story you could riff off when the opportunity presented itself. A chance to more firmly establish yourself in other people's minds. Cohen's story, ironically enough, wasn't even his own; it was his father's. But Cohen was desperately trying to make it his own.

He even had visual aids to help him along! A Polaroid of his father, an especially pink and heavy American Jew, tiny eyes partly covered by an enormous brow drenched in sweat, the rest of him stuffed into a green checkered suit, his arm around Richard Nixon in front of a sign reading, "Des Moines Business Caucus— 1974." Both men smiling at each other as if this was not 1974 but just another undistinguished year in the course of the American presidency.

"Da-ddy," Cohen said, rubbing his thumb on his father's bald dome, aping the voice of a three-year-old. And quite a papa he was. On Perry's thirteenth birthday, when, according to Hebrew scripture, Perry was supposed to be saddled with the dubious responsibilities of manhood, his father presented him with a gift. "I'm changing your name," his father declared. "You shouldn't have to go through life as a Cohen." He gave his son a ream of paperwork to sign. His name would now be Perry Caldwell.

Now, Cohen had had intimations of this self-hate business before. He was named *Perry,* after all. On high holy days, the only times when his father would take Perry into faraway St. Louis for services, he would make a habit of referring to the rabbi as Reverend Lubofsky. "Hope the Reverend lays off the Gipper this year," he'd say, crumpling his big, sad, fleshy-lipped face in frightened anticipation of any Iowa local seeing them pull into the little synagogue's parking lot.

And so Cohen found himself at the progressive Midwestern liberal arts college (a sister institution to the one Vladimir attended), a college where communal father-hatred was the norm, and where Cohen excelled particularly. In the early nineties the school also served as a kind of way station for hundreds of unhappy Midwestern young men and women on their way to the redemptive land of Prava. Cohen, angry and confused, took the cue by junior year. And here he was.

SO THAT WAS HIS STORY! That was Cohen's theme! His father was a rich asshole. How shocking. Vladimir was ready to attack Cohen with his own background, from the Jew-baiting of Leningrad to his years as a Stinky Russian Bear in Westchester. Assimilation, my ass. What do *you* know of assimilation, spoiled American pig? Why, I'll show you...I'll show you all!

Oh, and the way Cohen had told the story. Lowering his voice during the bit about the Gipper, trying to sound hurt but brave when recalling his father's transgressions. Crocodile tears, my suburban friend. Your father could be a deforester of forests and a murderer of Hutus, but in the end what determines your fate is the size of your trust fund, the slope of your nose, the quality of your accent. At least his daddy wasn't accusing him of *walking* like a Jew. God damn it! Vladimir could just kill this Cohen! But instead he shook his head mournfully and said, "My God. It's hard to believe such things can still happen in this day and age."

"I can't believe it either," said Cohen. "I hope you don't mind me sharing it with you." *My* sharing it with you, Vladimir mentally corrected him (idiot Americans didn't even know their own language). And no, as long as there was hard currency down the road, he did not mind.

"My relationship with my father is something that really informs my work," Cohen continued. "And I thought you're the kind of person..."

Oh? What kind of person was he?

"You seem very wise and world-weary."

"Ah," Vladimir said. Wise and world-weary. Well he got *that* right, the son of a bitch. But then the supercilious Girshkin softened a little. Come to think of it, wise and world-weary was possibly the kindest thing you can say to a twenty-five-year-old. And then the Iowan *was,* as we have said, a big, attractive fella, a grungy lion (if only Vladimir could look more like him), confident enough of himself to share his intimacies over the course of a single beer. Plus, he had nice, heavy rural hands, the hands of a man, and had probably slept with all kinds of women. Vladimir, too, had designs on manhood, and to that end, Vladimir wanted to be Cohen's friend. The need for friendship and closeness was not something Vladimir imagined would rekindle so soon after his ignominious flight from the States, but it was certainly there; Vladimir was still a social animal with the need to rub up against fellow creatures. And he had before him this lion. This goofy wandering beast.

Cohen finished by asking Vladimir if he could see his mother poem. "It's not ready yet," Vladimir said. "I'm sorry."

A long silence followed his apology. Cohen may have felt rebuffed after his own fifteen minutes of candor. But soon the pit-barbecued pork arrived and the waitress cleared her throat to remind them that they had a waitress.

"Oh, you never told me what your company develops," Cohen said finally.

"Talent," Vladimir said. "We develop talent."

VLADIMIR AND COHEN walked off the pork as the sun pre-pared for its bedtime swoon into the river. Over the Emanuel Bridge they went to the tune of buskers playing saxophones behind Bata shoe boxes lined with velvet; a blind accordion player and his wife belting out German beer-hall songs with great aplomb and to the jingle of the largest coins; a rendition of *Hamlet* by a pair of peppy young California blondes drawing stares and whistles from young Stolovan men but little coinage from

THE RUSSIAN DEBUTANTE'S HANDBOOK

their embarrassed conationals. With all this low-tech commerce and entertainment, the bridge felt to Vladimir like the oldest crossing imaginable, a stone carpet unfurled from the castle over-hanging the scene like a one-piece skyline. It was lined on both sides with statues of saints, grimy with coal dust and contorted into heroic positions. "Look," Cohen said, pointing out three indistinct figures lost in the robes of two of the grander saints. "That's the devil, that's a Turk, and that's a Jew."

Ah, so we were back to Cohen's grand theme again. Vladimir tried to put together a smile. He was feeling happy and pleased with himself after their lunch, but knew that his mood was mal-leable under the depressant weight of alcohol and didn't want the tragic curve of history to put him in a state. "Why are they under-neath the saints?" he asked out of obligation.

"They're supporting them," Cohen said. "They're the support team."

Vladimir didn't want to press it further. It was some sort of medieval humor, but what did those stalwarts of Christendom know, with their earth flat and reason always falling off the edges? This was 1993, after all, and with the exception of the nascent slaughter in the Balkans, the African Horn, the ex-Soviet periphery, and of course the usual carnage in Afghanistan, Burma, Guatemala, the West Bank, Belfast, and Monrovia, the world was a sensible place.

"Now I'm going to take you to my favorite place in this city," Cohen said. And then, without warning, the restless man broke into a power walk, so that momentarily they quit the Emanuel Bridge and gained the embankment. Navigating past the churches, the mansions, and the singular powder tower that had chosen to decamp on this side of the Tavlata, they ran into a cozy lane, which ascended the city's heights alongside the castle. Here, squat mer-chant's mansions were marked by mosaics of ancient occupations and family quirks: three tiny violins, a goose fat from centuries of inertia, an unhappy-looking frog. Vladimir was on the lookout for a gherkin; perhaps his family had had a Prava past as well.

It was a struggle maintaining his pace up the hill. The pollution was deadly; life itself seemed to reek of coal. Cohen, however, was making good time, although now that his friend wasn't seated, Vladimir noticed that he carried a heavier-than-average load at the bottom, and his thighs, too, had benefited from the city's pork masterpieces.

Cohen ducked into a lane even more narrow than the last, which soon exhausted itself into what could no longer be termed a lane, rather a confluence of the pastel backsides of four buildings. He seated himself on one of a series of steps leading to a phantom doorway that had long become a wall, and told Vladimir that this particular skylit cubicle was the most special corner of Perry Cohen's Personal Prava. This was where he came to write his columns and poems for one of the town's English papers, the woefully misnamed *Prava-dence.*

So this was Cohen's special place? They had run up and down the four hills of Prava for this? While the rest of the city (minus the Foot) was an endless stretch of panoramic vistas, Cohen had chosen the tightest, most prosaic corner of Eastern Europe...Why, Vladimir's *panelak* had more character. Wait a second. Vladimir took another look. He must learn to think like Cohen. This was the key. A century ago he had taught himself to think like Francesca and her urban-god friends. Now he must adapt once more. What makes this place special to Cohen? Look closely. Think like Cohen. He likes this place because...

Got it! It's special because it's not special, and hence it makes Cohen feel special for choosing it. Special and different. He was different for coming to Prava and now he had validated his difference once more by choosing this place. Vladimir was ready to proceed. "Perry, I want you to make me a writer," he said.

Cohen was instantly on his feet again, towering over Vladimir with his hands raised expectantly, as if any moment now they were going to hug over some declaration, ruffle each other's hair over a mutual understanding. "A writer or a poet?" he asked, his breathing now as rapid as that of an older, corpulent man.

Vladimir thought about it. Poetry would probably take less time per unit. Surely that was why Cohen had chosen it. "A poet."

"Have you read much?"

"Well..." Vladimir entertained a poetic list that would have made Baobab proud: "Akhmatova, Wolcott, Milosz..."

No, no. Cohen didn't want to hear about them.

"Brodsky? Simic?"

"Stop right there," Cohen said. "See, like too many poets start-ing out, you've already read too much. Don't look at me like that. It's true. You're overread. The whole point of coming to the Old World is to chuck the baggage of the new."

"Oh," Vladimir said.

"Reading has nothing to do with writing. The two are diametri-cally opposed, they cancel each other out. Look, I need to know, Vladimir, do you really want me to be your mentor? Because if you do, you should be aware that it will involve some risk-taking."

"Art without risk is stasis," Vladimir said. "I told you that I wanted to be a poet, so I shall place myself in your hands, Perry."

"Thank you," Cohen said. "That's very kind of you to say. And very brave. May I...?" They had the hug for which Cohen had been preparing, Vladimir hugging back with all his might, pleased that the day had already netted him two good friends (Kostya being the first). Indeed, caught in the fine-smelling Cohen's embrace, Vladimir decided to put the Iowan Jew in the basement of his pyra-mid scheme's pyramid, down where the dollars and Deutsche marks were to be stacked beneath the promissory notes.

"Perry," he said. "It is obvious we will be friends. You've taken me into your world, now I must reciprocate. As it happens to be, I am a fairly rich man and not without some influence. I wasn't kidding when I said my company was developing talent."

The next two cryptic lines had come to him during the *biznesmenski* lunch. He had had the good sense to jot them down inside his palm. "Talent, Perry, may be an ocean liner with only a few staterooms, but I can't let people like you spend your life in steerage. Will you allow me to make you wealthy?"

Cohen was moving closer in preparation for another hug. My God, another one! So this was Cohen when he wasn't sitting around Eudora's, deriding *arrivistes* for having less than two pens and suckling off the maternal teat—Cohen the gentle literary lion, the sweet-tempered dawdler of Stolovaya. Vladimir was suddenly happy to have submitted to his mentoring. Was that all it took to turn Cohen into an affectionate sap? Had Vladimir just single-handedly validated the young man's place here in a tight, banal corner of Prava? Did he just make a friend for life?

At this point, the writer nearly had his arms around him, but when it was clear that no hug was forthcoming (Vladimir had his limits, after all), Cohen patted his shoulder instead, and said: "All right then, my financial Sherpa. Let's go downtown and I'll introduce you to my crowd."

THEY TOOK A TRAM down the hill, so that the castle loomed above them once again. Now its palace facades were floodlit in artificial yellow while the cathedral extended its spires and crosses in a spectral green—two lovers that didn't speak the same language.

Vladimir asked for a geography lesson as the tram rocked them back and forth on its journey across the Tavlata, heaving them into the neatly groomed old-timers who were entitled to their tram seats by law and derived a great, silent pleasure from watching the two standing foreigners tumble to their knees.

Cohen, like Kostya, was glad to play tour guide. He pointed at the passing landmarks, his fingers leaving nicotine smudges on the tram windows. There, on the hill, to the left of the castle, where they just talked "the talk" as it would later be known, where the roofs were tiled red and where the most important embassies and wine bars were clustered, that was called Malenka Kvartalka. "The Lesser Quarter!" Vladimir said, pleasantly surprised whenever his birth language intersected with Stolovan. But why this demeaning name for such a magnificent neighborhood? Cohen had no answer to that.

And where they were going—the "sea of spires" as seen from the morning's first descent into the city, that was the Old Town. And to the south of the Old Town, the part of the city where the spires thinned out a bit and the roofs glimmered with more restraint, and the giant galosh of the Foot lorded over the proceedings like a phantom rubber commissar, was the New Town—which wasn't so new, Cohen explained, dating back merely to the fourteenth century or so. "So what's in the New Town?" Vladimir asked.

"The Kmart," Cohen whispered with mock reverence.

AFTER CROSSING into the Old Town, they drank many coffees in the plush if worn interior of the Café Nouveau, which ran amok with all the excesses of its namesake period: gilded mirrors, seats and carpets smothered in red velvet, the indispensable nymph of white marble. It was a long evening of listening to the ramblings of the young American on the subject of present-day poetry and art, the total of which left Vladimir feeling fortunate that he himself had no literary proclivities, harbored no bone-headed artistic intentions, else his meandering life would truly come to a bad end.

After all, look where the delusional Cohen now found himself, and Cohen was a rich dandy, not some dismal Russian whose life chances were pretty lousy from the get-go.

AS VLADIMIR WAS THINKING these thoughts and nodding along to Cohen's discourse, their environment began to improve. A Dixieland jazz ensemble (composed entirely of Stolovans) took to the stage, the joint began to swing, the pretty marble tables soon filled up with pretty boys and girls, and Cohen's corner emerged as a popular destination.

Subsequently, it became hard for Vladimir to remember how many of America's finest sons and daughters he met that particular night. Throughout the evening, he remembered being especially cold and aloof while lots of hands were given for him to shake as Cohen presented Vladimir Girshkin, international magnate, talent scout, and soon-to-be poet laureate.

Few knew what to make of him; Vladimir accepted this. And what did Vladimir make of them? Well, to start with, they were a fairly homogenous group—white middle Americans with a fashionable grudge, that was the lowest common denominator. Native-born folks who never had to struggle with the dilemmas of an alpha peasant or a beta immigrant because five generations down the road every affluent young American was entitled to the luxury of being second-rate. And here in fairyland Prava, bonded by the glue of their mediocrity, they stuck together as if they had all been born in the same Fairfax County pod, had all suckled the same baby-boomer she-wolf like so many Romuluses and Remuses. The rules were only different for obvious outsiders like Vladimir who had to perform some grand gesture—conduct the Bolshoi, write a novel, launch a pyramid scheme—to gain a modicum of acceptance.

He noted their clothes. Some were dressed in the flannels,

which, Vladimir had noticed, were spreading by way of Seattle during his last month in the States. But the glam-nerd look, Francesca's
most tangible gift to Vladimir, was in evidence as well. The shirts
way too tight, the sweaters too fluffy, the glasses too horn-rimmed,
the hair coiffed either with seventies' extravagance or fifties'
restraint. But look how much younger than Vladimir these specimens were! Twenty-one, twenty-two, maximum. Some probably
couldn't get served in American bars. He was old enough to be
their teaching assistant.

Nevertheless, he would persevere. Wisdom came with age.
Already, Vladimir could see himself declared an elder statesman.
Another way to look at it: Despite their relative youth, the
nouveau-nerds were hobbled by their unremarkable suburban
demographics, while Vladimir, as a former New Yorker, was a freak
by nature. But he was not the only freak. Others who tried particularly hard to stand out included Plank, a thin and nervous man
who carried a yapping bite-sized dog—some kind of cross between
a Chihuahua and a mosquito—in a little homemade pouch that
was wrapped with silver lace. Women passing by took turns telling
him how cute his dog was, its grimy, sorry little head constantly
peeking out from its mobile home like a furry earflap with two
eyes. But Plank, true to the game, wouldn't smile or acknowledge
them beyond a nod, knowing how out-of-season such sentiments
could be. Cohen told Vladimir that Plank bred these customized
minidogs in his *panelak* for the old Stolovan ladies, but Plank did
not warm to Vladimir, stating: "There's not much money in it, you
know." Oof, was that an antibusinessman slur? Did he not realize
that Vladimir's true love was the muse?

Vladimir did better with Alexandra: tall, slender, dark-haired,
with a round, full Mediterranean face and a small, intelligent curve
of bosom. In fact, she was (dare Vladimir think it) not unlike
Francesca except her face was too conventionally pretty with its

high cheekbones and long natural lashes stretching upward in two parabolas. With Fran you had to find the beauty and fall in love with the blemishes, while Alexandra's ready-made good looks seemed the perfect physical match for Cohen. The way Cohen's eyes were firmly fixed on the silhouette of her body, sheathed in nothing but a tight-fitting black turtleneck extending into matching hose (no glam-nerd threads for her, thank you), certainly confirmed as much on his part.

Before Vladimir could be formally introduced, Alexandra grabbed his head and pressed the furry thing into the soft, bare crux of her neck. "Hi, honey!" she said. "I've heard all about you!" She had? But how? Vladimir had only met Cohen three hours ago.

"Come! Come with me!" She draped her arm around his and was leading him toward a kind of Art Nouveau tapestry hanging from a velvet wall—long swirls of multicolored swan feathers encircling what seemed to be a stylized *Pietà*. Yes, dear old Art Nouveau, thought Vladimir. Thank heavens, Abstract Expressionism and Co. had slain that gaudy beast. "Look! Look at this!" Alexandra shouted in her throaty, smoky voice. "A Pstrucha!"

A what? Oh, who cares...She was heavenly. That collarbone. You could see it through the turtleneck. She was like a swan herself. Red lipstick, black turtleneck. A haiku right there.

"Are you familiar with Adolf Pstrucha? I've got Pstrucha on the mind. Look at my book bag. Look at it!" It was, indeed, crammed with a dozen or so colorful books on the P-fellow. "Now Pstrucha wasn't really Stolovan. He belonged to Slovene Moderna. Are you familiar with Slovene art? Oh, my dear boy, we must take a trip to Ljubljana. You mustn't deprive yourself any further. Anyway, our man Pstrucha was practically laughed out of Prava. It was such a reactionary place in the early 1900s, the shithole of the Austro-Hungarian Empire. But..."

She lowered her head conspiratorially and brushed her collarbone against Vladimir's shoulder, so he could feel the immense weight of it, her body armor, her naturally occurring breastplate. "But personally I think the Stolovans were laughing at his name. Pstruch. It means 'trout' in Stolovan. Adolf Trout! It's too much! Don't you agree? Say, have you ever been trout-fishing? I know you Russians love to fish. I went fishing in the Carpathians with this French guy who knows Jitomir Melnik, the prime minister, and I just *know* the frog would be interested in your PravaInvest. Would you like me to introduce you? Would you like to have dinner? Or we could do lunch if you're busy. Or, nowadays, I'm trying to wake up in time for breakfast."

Yes, yes, yes. Yes on three counts, Vladimir thought. Breakfast, lunch, and dinner. And then maybe we can take a nap together. No, best to keep her awake and talking. Her words, so soft, so light, the consistency of a flan... Vladimir wanted to reach over and eat her conversation. Follow it right into her little mouth. But, horror of horrors, Alexandra had a boyfriend, or what passed for one—a chubby Yorkshire fellow named Marcus who looked like he could have been a rugby player before all this Eastern Bloc a-go-go stuff happened. While Alexandra pleasantly queried Vladimir on his writing ("About your mother? Oh, how interesting!"), her boyfriend loudly attacked the café's other patrons with his hip Briton-on-the-edge routine (*Wot? Wot* did you say? C'mere y'cunt!), eliciting forced laughter from Cohen and Plank. It was clear that everybody looked up to this Marcus runt; they looked up to him because he was dating Alexandra, the crown jewel of Prava.

Then there was Maxine, introduced as a student of American culture, dressed entirely in polyester and sweating accordingly in the warm caffeine haze of the Nouveau. Her short hair had been gelled into one blond upward-pointing clump that seemed ready to take off for the stars, and she had moist blue eyes that looked at everything, including Vladimir, with amazement. She was also a diplomatic conversationalist, talking to everyone in turn, first Cohen, then Plank, then Marcus, then Alexandra, then finally Vladimir. "I'm writing a treatise on the mythopoetics of Southern interstates," she said to him. "Have you ever been?"

Vladimir liked her expressiveness and the warmth of her hand. He told her of his experiences with Midwestern interstates. How driving behind the wheel of his Chicagoan girlfriend's Volvo in college he had nearly killed a family of chipmunks. It was a safe and pointless conversation, certainly safer than Vladimir's driving, until gutsy Vladimir dared ask her why, as a self-proclaimed student of American culture, she was living in Prava. She lifted her latte to cover her mouth, and mumbled something about needing distance. Ah, good old distance.

Overall, Vladimir felt he scored well at the café portion of the popularity contest, despite Marcus and Plank's uniting to grumble about rich little pissers, meaning, well, Vladimir. But Vladimir would not succumb. His mental reflexes, sharpened by the afternoon's initial sparring with Cohen, saved the day once more as he announced what he planned to do with his riches. Why, of course, he was going to start a literary magazine. Cohen at first seemed offended at not being told of the endeavor beforehand, but soon the whispers of "lit mag" suffused the room and, before they knew it, the regulars at Cohen's corner were doing their condescending best to shoo away the literary hopefuls at the gates.

Vladimir, still amazed at his own idea, played it down. How the hell was he going to sell this one to the Groundhog? But then he remembered that the students at his Midwestern college used to have not one but two literary magazines, so how hard would it be to start up a little press in Prava? Besides, they were already doing glossy brochures for the "company." It wouldn't take too much more to print up a few hundred copies of something half-decent on the side. "Does anyone have editorial experience?" he asked his new crowd. Of course they all did.

AFTER THEY HAD DRUNK ENOUGH COFFEE to keep them floating at an arm's length from the ceiling for a week, the crew retired downstairs where a primitive-looking disco was pounding out something not entirely avant-garde. "How Cleveland," sneered Plank at last year's music, yet no one turned their backs on the scene (was there any alternative?), venturing instead to their own rickety side table, one of many bracketing the amorphously shaped dance floor. "Beer!" cried Maxine. And soon bottles of Unesko lined the table—an additional line of defense against the bodies moving without grace or surety in the revolving police-car beams and the lethargically thumping strobe lights. "This is all we have," Plank said to Vladimir, Vladimir having clearly grown on him since the announcement of the literary magazine. "I hope you weren't expecting New York on the Tavlata."

"Well, we'll see what we can do about *that*," said the emboldened Vladimir. "Yes, we shall see."

Alexandra was tugging on his ear, anxious to give him a census of the place. "Look at the backpackers! Look how big they are! Oh, that frat-hog with the Ohio State T-shirt! Oh, he's priceless!"

"What's their function?" Vladimir said.

"None," Cohen said, wiping beer off his chin. "They are our mortal enemies. They must be destroyed, torn apart by the *babushka*s like a ham on Christmas, dragged by the trams through the twelve bridges of Prava, hung from the highest spire of St. Stanislaus."

"And where are our people?" Vladimir shouted to Alexandra above the din.

She pointed around to the back tables, which, Vladimir now realized, were reserved for their fellow artists, slopping beer calmly amid the suburban feeding-frenzy.

An ambassador from one of those tables, a tall young buck in a Warhol T-shirt, brought a sleek blue water pipe filled with hashish. Vladimir was now introduced as "magnate, talent scout, poet laureate, *and* publisher." They smoked the sweet and peppery hash, refilling the pipe enough times for their fingers to become brown and sticky, for this was the moist and lethal kind of hash that could only result from Turkey's proximity. The fellow offered it to Vladimir for six hundred crowns a gram, but Vladimir was too tweaked to deal with both crowns and the metric system. He bought two thousand dollars' worth anyway and made another lifelong friend in the process.

There was little he would remember after the hashish entered the picture. There was the dancing with Maxine and Alexandra and possibly the boys. A wide swath of floor was cleared of backpackers by brown-shirted disco personnel, and Vladimir's crowd was invited to get up and boogie. At this point a serious fracas broke out. A sorority sister crying foul jumped on Vladimir, of all people. Stoned beyond capacity, Vladimir thought he was being romanced, what with all that sweet-smelling American flesh around him and a pair of manicured claws dug into his sides. Only when Alexandra started to drag the sister off by the hair did Vladimir realize that he was at the center of some kind of class antagonism.

She did this hair-pulling with aplomb and Vladimir, free of his burden, must have thanked her profusely because he remembered her saying "Aww" in the purple-gray-green haze of disco lights and hash smoke, and kissing him on both cheeks. Then he felt good about the whole clumsy incident since it had further polarized the crowd into "us" versus "them" and in the space of one short evening he had placed himself squarely in the "us" column of the register.

Then, sometime during the taxi ride up to his compound, he remembered poking the dozing Cohen and trying to point out the city below, its floodlights put out, but the yellow moon still traveling along the bend of the Tavlata, the airplane warning lights blinking off the cuff of the Foot, a lone Fiat huffing its way past the silent embankment. "Perry, look at how beautiful," Vladimir said.

"Yes, good," said Cohen and fell back asleep.

Finally, he was looking up at the walls of his *panelak* castle, remembering how imposing Casa Girshkin had seemed during the high school days of returning from Manhattan late at night, intoxicated, incoherent, and unresponsive to his ever-vigilant mother's queries in both Russian and English. He walked into the lobby where Gusev's men had fallen asleep, some with their playing cards still in their hands. Empowered by the smell of the lobby, he crawled upstairs in search of his bed, missing his floor twice. At last he found his room, then his bed.

She was a pretty one—Alexandra, he thought, before sprinkling himself with minoxidil and quietly passing out.

21. PHYSICAL CULTURE
AND HER ADHERENTS

NOBODY WOKE HIM UP. EVER. NOT ONLY HAD VLADIMIR forgotten to pack his alarm clock but the Groundhog and the human tentacles of his vast apparatus were apparently still nice and cozy in bed with their girlfriends and rifles till well into the afternoon. Kostya, it turned out, spent his mornings in church.

Vladimir found out this ecclesiastical tidbit on his fifth Prava day. He woke up late to what might have been an explosion at one of the Paleolithic-era factories lying low against the velvet horizon, but it could have very well been an explosion within Vladimir himself—last evening's *pivo* and vodka and schnapps had arranged themselves as unfortunate bedmates in his stomach and Vladimir was forced to heave all over the sterility of his prefab bathroom, the lecherous peacock grinning knowingly from the shower curtain. Vladimir noticed the fowl had on a tight pair of boxer shorts in the hues of the Stolovan tricolor and had an avian bulge to boot.

The previous night, the third installment of the Café Nouveau saga, had left Vladimir gripping for the side of his body where he imagined his liver lived out its troubled existence, and so he put on a New York Sports Club T-shirt (they had canvassed the Emma Lazarus Society for membership—as if anyone had the money!) with the vain hope that he could be made fit by the power of suggestion. He walked down to the empty Kasino, hoping Marusya, the perpetually drunk old lady behind the counter, was dispensing cigarettes and her special hangover brew. She was not.

Kostya, however, was there, wearing a jogging suit fluorescent enough to put the peacock to shame, and a heavy gold chain with cross and anatomically correct Jesus weighing down nearly to his stomach. "Vladimir! What a beautiful day! Have you been outside?"

"Have you seen Marusya?"

"You don't need her on a day like today," Kostya said, tugging at his Christ. "Give your lungs a break, I say." He looked closely at Vladimir's T-shirt, until it appeared to Vladimir that his scrawny self was under examination and he hunched forward his shoulders in defense. "Sports club," read Kostya out of sequence. "New York."

"It was a gift."

"No, you're very lean, you must jog."

"I'm just naturally a very healthy man."

"Come with me," Kostya said. "There's space behind the houses. We'll jog. You'll build lower-body strength."

Lower body? Meaning what—below his mouth? What kind of talk was this? Of course, his Chicagoan girlfriend back in the Midwestern college had made him run around a very sophisticated, computer-monitored field—their school's concession to its athletic fringe-element. "You'll thank me for this someday," his former girlfriend used to say. Aha. Thank you, darling. Thank you for the gift of pain and sweat.

But then Kostya placed one of his beautiful paws, fingernails carefully trimmed, on Vladimir's shoulder and led him out like a rebellious cow that had taken too much to the dank, moldy confines of her barn, into the hazy sunshine and sickly grass of early-autumn Prava.

Here it was very *dacha*-like: weeping willows wept under the weight of the tetra-hydro-petra-carbo whatever-the-hell-it-was being belched out of the smokestacks; postcommunist rabbits bounced about lethargically as if fulfilling some demented party directive nobody had bothered to rescind; and Kostya beamed like a farmer glad to be back after selling grain in the city. He unzipped his jogging suit to reveal a chest bereft of hair, and said things like "oooh," "*bozhe moi,*" and "we're in God's country now."

There was a clearing. An oval path of sand had been splashed about, probably by the jogging enthusiast himself, and the sun, free of the willows, burnt down upon the scene mercilessly. *If there is a hell on this earth*... thought Vladimir to himself, covering his burning head with his palm in an effort to prevent the minoxidil from burning off, if such a thing was possible. Now what?

"To stand around is pointless!" shouted Kostya, negating centuries of Russian peasant wisdom, and then began to run like a madman around the sandy path. "Onward! Onward!"

Vladimir lamely broke into a trot. There was something one had to do with the arms; he looked to Kostya who was raising dust across the field and tried to purposefully strike the air, left, right, left, right. Christ. Perhaps he should have finished college just to avoid this madness. But then college graduates were often conscripted to play racquetball in Wall Street gyms. Although there was always social work... for quiet people who liked the shade.

He went around, three years added to his life per every lap completed. He grasped for the thin Stolovan air. He felt sweat as thick as shampoo separating his skin-'n'-rib body from his flimsy cotton tee. He felt globs of mucus coagulate in his defective lungs while he hobbled from one foot to the next like one of those awkward Floridian birds.

Kostya slowed down to keep pace with him. "So? Do you feel it?"

"*D...Da,*" Vladimir affirmed.

"You feeling good?"

"*D...Da.*"

"Better than ever?"

Vladimir cringed and waved his arms to indicate his inability to talk. "A healthy mind in a healthy body," hollered his tormentor. "Now, which Greek said that?"

Vladimir shrugged. Zorba? Couldn't be. "Socrates, I think," shouted Kostya. He sped ahead of Vladimir as if to show him how it could be done. Soon he disappeared completely. Vladimir panted. His eyes were clouded over with tears, his pulse was going faster than the Fan Man's fan set to HIGH. Then the sandy path disappeared also. It got dark, maybe there was a cloud overhead. There was the crunch of grass and twigs. There was a shout of "Hey." He hit something hard with his head.

VLADIMIR'S THROAT passed a ball of phlegm the size of a frog. He looked at it lying next to him in the grass. Kostya was dabbing his forehead with a handkerchief. "So you ran into a tree," he said. "No big deal. The tree's all right. You just got a dash of blood here. We have American Band-Aids in the house. Gusev's men go through them like vodka."

Vladimir blinked a couple of times then tried to flip himself over. This resting-under-a-tree part was nice, much better than running around in the sun. Did he feel stupid? Not at all—varsity sports weren't on his résumé. Maybe now the idiot Kostya would leave him alone to his asthma and his alcohol. "Okay, so we'll start out slow next time," Kostya said. "I see we have some limitations."

We? Vladimir tried to beam disgust into the madman's face, but it was too busy looking all sweet and puffy, while the hands carefully worked his wound as if Vladimir were Kostya's best buddy brought down at Stalingrad. Vladimir pictured this scene on a recruiting poster entitled: "You're in the *mafiya* now!"

"Right," Vladimir said. "Start out slow next time. Maybe we'll do some…" He could think of no Russian equivalent to power-walking. "We'll lift some light weights or something."

"I got those," Kostya said. "Light and heavy, however you like them. But my guess is you need to develop your cardiovascular system."

"No, I think I need to lift some very light weights," Vladimir said, but there was no arguing with Kostya. They would run slowly around the track while bearing light weights every noon on Monday, Tuesday, Thursday, and Saturday. "The other days I'm in church," explained Kostya.

"Of course you are," Vladimir said, staring blankly at his own blood flowing dark and somber against the outrageous pinks and violets of Kostya's jumpsuit. Fuck him. But he had one thought: "Isn't church only on Sunday?"

"I help out in the mornings on Wednesday and Friday," explained the cherub. "They have a very small Russian Orthodox community here and they really need a lot of help. My family, you see, has very strong religious roots going back to before the revolution. We've had priests, deacons, monks…"

"Oh, my grandfather was a deacon," said the absentminded Vladimir.

And that was how he got himself invited to church.

ON THE AMERICAN FRONT, things were moving. When the afternoons of loafing around the compound, pretending to develop a business strategy and learn the local language exhausted themselves, Vladimir, along with Jan, the youngest, least mustached of all the Stolovan drivers, flew past the castle down to the golden city. The BMW assigned to him, Vladimir learned, was not of the top class such as the ones requisitioned by Gusev and some of his direct subordinates and, of course, the Groundhog who had two

Beamers, one with a fixed roof, the other a convertible. Vladimir learned a lot about cars from Jan, on whom he would also practice his Stolovan. While his new friend derailed trams and scared the living crap out of dachshunds and *babushka*s alike, Vladimir learned to say: "This car is bad. There's no five-disc CD changer." And, alternatively: "You have a face that is attractive to me. Come inside my nice car."

His web expanded from Eudora Welty's and the Nouveau to the Air Raid Shelter, the Boom Boom Room, Jim's Bar, and even, after one mistaken foray, Club Man. There were whispers:

"That's the publisher, the new one."

"He's the talent scout. For that multinational. PravaInvest."

"The novelist, you must have heard of him...Sure, he's published all over the place."

"I've seen him with Alexandra! She asked me to light her cigarette at the Nouveau once..."

"We should buy him a Unesko."

"My God, he's sneering our way."

In the course of it all, Vladimir had developed a solid, workmanlike crush on Alexandra. He looked all over her undeniably accomplished body, whenever her eyes scanned the menu, the beer list, the wine list, or were somehow otherwise engaged, then brought the little slips of memory back to his *panelak* where by night they fueled his dreams, by day provided contemplation: her lips, soft and maraschino-red against the gray-brick backdrop of the Old Town Hall; breast seen from above, overhanging a square marble table; long tanned arms reaching out constantly to embrace some local celebrity, press him into her signature raised clavicle. It was nothing heavy, like it had been with Francesca. Just a refreshingly honest (albeit pathetic) and sexually-affirming thing to do, and he went about doing it methodically. He asked her to lunch, but to allay any suspicion of his romantic intentions he had to ask all of them in turn, and frequently Marcus accompanied her. These were business lunches where nothing got accomplished, ideas for the magazine were pushed around like mah-jongg tiles, but ultimately it was the gossip and who-bedded-who crap that was published breathlessly in the sweet and smoky café air. Alexandra, sadly, bedded only Marcus, the rugby runt, who Vladimir learned was an asshole par excellence, but one that nipped and tugged at his own ass daily for the coveted spot of editor-in-chief.

"Oi, these fucks," Marcus would say in a Cockney adopted from years of being physically big and artistically small in London's West End, as he scanned the sourpussed patrons of the café/bar/disco/restaurant. "The next Hemingway they think they are." And there was Marcus's problem: he didn't write. He acted, and, in an effort to bridge the gap between what he could do and what Prava wanted him to do, he had taken up painting and what Alexandra hopefully termed "the graphic arts." Vladimir figured he'd slot him in for art editor, which would theoretically mean that Marcus would "edit" however many of his own pieces he wished, stick them into the damn thing, and call it a day.

For editor-in-chief Vladimir's system of patronage telegraphed Cohen in both italics and bold print. Also for best friend, pal, buddy, that sort of thing. Cohen was indispensable. The nabobs liked him, Vladimir learned, because he stumbled and said absolutely wrong things like "faggot" and "gosh," and he looked the part, too—this thick rural Iowan. At the same time, he was an angry and disdainful Jewish fellow, suspicious that the Midwestern mohel, short on practice, had taken a little too much of his wiener on the eighth day of his life, a crisis commensurate with being the supposedly sole Iowan Jew (not to mention one who had Hitler for a father), which proved once and for all that the world was out to get him, and so here he was in Prava, the edge of the known world.

He also was well connected up in Amsterdam and down in

Istanbul, producing tiny packets *par avion* that were the finest in hydroponic science and Turkish know-how and led to many placid, indebted expressions on both sides of the Tavlata. Vladimir's old friend Baobab, of course, was similarly occupied, but the fool across the ocean carried out his enterprise not out of social concern, but for crude, selfish profit (his stuff was notoriously full of seeds and twigs, too).

And let's not forget that Cohen was Vladimir's mentor, a position Cohen never failed to mention, as in "I'm mentoring Vladimir tomorrow," and "We have a very satisfying mentorship." It took place in the cramped Lesser Quarter alley where Cohen and Vladimir had first reached their literary understanding. Vladimir's attempts to change the venue in favor of the gorgeous park that curved upward off the Lesser Quarter and apparently overlooked the castle itself, not to mention the Old and New Towns across the river, were futile. Too obvious for Cohen. "Creativity flourishes only in small, blighted spaces—janitor's closets, cold-water flats, rabbit hutches…"

Why argue? They went over Cohen's singular work ("And from the bedroom there's the sound / of two lovers reading Ezra Pound") as if they were rabbinical scholars finally granted access to the kabala, until one day Cohen said: "Vladimir, you're in for a treat. There's going to be a reading."

In for a treat? Could one still say that in 1993? Vladimir, for one, wouldn't gamble on it. "But I'm not ready to read yet," he said.

"I know you're not," Cohen laughed. "I'm the one who's reading. Oh, don't look so sad, Grasshopper. Your time will come."

"I see," Vladimir said. But it was strangely disheartening to hear that he wasn't ready to read, even though the arbiter of his worth was this mangy lion from the American interior. Vladimir knew he was no poet, but surely he wasn't *that* bad.

"Three o'clock, tomorrow. Café Joy in the New Town, it's a

block from the Foot. Or we could just meet by the left toe. And Vlad…." Cohen put his arm around him, an action that frightened bashful Vladimir to this day. "There's no dress code, of course, but I always make sure I wear something beautiful when I present myself to Joy society."

THE JOY. Vladimir lay on his stomach in his little blond-wood boudoir, meditating on this fabled venue and his chance to impress the crowd with his *own* verse, to stamp his artistry onto the mass of wealthy English speakers, potential investors all, and to begin (finally!) Phase Two of the master plan.

Phase One had gone off without a hitch. He had introduced himself, nay, *insinuated* himself into this unpolished mass of Westerners on the cultural make. But now he had to clinch the deal. To prove to the likes of the dog-breeder Plank and the rugby runt Marcus, that he was not just a businessman out to buy some bohemian friends with a lit mag and a thousand free drinks. And if he could pull off a reading at the Joy, well then… On to Phase Three! The actual "take the donkeys for a ride" phase. (Hey, maybe he could even steal Alexandra from Marcus, somewhere around Phase Two-and-a-Half, say.)

In the meantime, PravaInvest stocks—engraved with all the flourishes and pomp of karate green-belt certificates for suburban tykes—had just been printed and were ready for sale at only U.S.$960 a pop. Discerning investors everywhere, take note.

And so, to work. He took out his notebook filled unimpressively with notes from Cohen's tutelage and turned to the "Mother in Chinatown" poem that he had started that fateful day at Eudora Welty's.

He read the first few lines of the Mother poem to himself. *A small string of pearls from her birth land*... Ludicrous, yes. But definitely of the moment.

On the other hand, what if...? What if Cohen and the whole Crowd saw right through him? What if they were baiting Vladimir to the Joy only to expose the international-magnate-talent-scout-poet-laureate-publisher for the shameless operator he really was? Vladimir sniffed the air around him, worried he was giving off a fraudulent odor. Sniff-sniff... Nothing but the smell of wet dust and the dizzying tang of an electrical fire next door. Furthermore, what if Cohen took umbrage at being upstaged at the reading? What if he united his minions—Marcus, Plank, that other emaciated guy, whatever his name was—and outflanked Vladimir for good? Whom could Vladimir summon on his own behalf? True, Alexandra might defend him, that nutty dear. Plus Alexandra had complete discretion over Marcus and was thoroughly worshipped by Maxine and that other blonde, the one who always wore hipwaders and carried a Chinese parasol... But that would only split the Crowd in half. What was he going to do with just half a Crowd?

If only someone competent could advise him.

If only Mother were here.

Vladimir sighed. There was no getting around it. He missed her. This was the first time that mother and son were separated by five thousand miles and the loss was palpable. For better or worse, Mother had run Vladimir like her own five-and-a-half-foot fief up to this point. Now that Vladimir had abandoned her, he was entirely on his own. Put differently, if you subtracted Mother from Vladimir, what had you? A negative number, by Vladimir's calculations.

She had been with him from the bitter start. He remembered Mother the twenty-nine-year-old xylophone teacher dutifully preparing her asthmatic son for kindergarten, five months after school had started for the healthier children. The first day of class was a time of immeasurable anxiety for any Soviet toddler, but for half-dead Vladimir it was accompanied by the fear that his boisterous new chums would chase him around the schoolyard, push him down, sit on him, knock the last breath out of his battered chest. "Now, Seryozha Klimov is the hooligan," Mother educated Vladimir. "He's the tall one with the red hair. You will avoid him. He won't sit on you, but he likes to pinch. If he tries to pinch you, tell Maria Ivanovna or Ludmila Antonovna or any other teacher, and I will run over and defend you. Your best friend will be Lionya Abramov. I think you played with him once in Yalta. He has a wind-up rooster. You can play with the rooster, but don't get your shirtcuffs caught in the gears. You'll ruin your shirt and the other children will think you're a cretin."

The next day, per Mother's instructions, Vladimir found Lionya Abramov sitting in a corner, pale, trembling, a great green vein pulsing along his monumental Jewish forehead; in other words, a fellow sufferer. They shook hands like adults. "I have a book," Lionya wheezed, "in which Lenin is in hiding and he builds a camouflaged tent out of nothing but grass and a horse's tail."

"I have one like that, too," Vladimir said. "Let's see yours."

Lionya produced this particular volume. It was pretty, indeed, but, with its miniscule text, clearly meant for someone twice their age. Still Vladimir found it hard to resist coloring Lenin's bald dome a proper shade of red. "You have to watch out for Seryozha Klimov," Lionya informed him. "He might pinch you so hard you'll bleed."

"I know," Vladimir said. "My mama told me."

"Your mama's very nice," Lionya confessed shyly. "She's the only one that makes sure they don't hit me. She says we're going to be best friends."

A few hours later, lying on a mat during rest time, Vladimir embraced the tiny curled-up creature beside him, his first best buddy, just as Mother had promised. Maybe tomorrow they could go to the Piskaryovka mass grave together with their grandmothers and lay flowers for their dead. Maybe they would even be inducted into the Red Pioneers side by side. What good fortune that he and Lionya were so alike and that neither of them had siblings . . . Now they would have each other! It was as if Mother had created someone just for him, as if she had guessed how lonely he had been in his sick bed with his stuffed giraffe, the months spinning away in twilight gloom until it was June again, time to go down to sunny Yalta to watch the Black Sea dolphins jump for joy.

Wheezing along with his new pal, Vladimir hardly noticed that Mother had slipped into the room and was leaning over their prone bodies. "Ah, *druzhki*," she whispered to them, a word meaning, roughly, "little friends," a word Vladimir to this day considered one of the most tender of his youth. "Has anyone assaulted you yet?" she asked them.

"No one has touched us," they whispered back.

"Good . . . Then get some rest," she said, pretending they were battle-hardened comrades returning from the front. She gave them each a Little Red Riding Hood chocolate candy, as tasty a candy as one could hope for, and rolled them into a blanket. "I like your mama's hair, the way it's so black you can almost see yourself in it," Lionya said thoughtfully.

"She is beautiful," Vladimir agreed. His mouth coated with chocolate, he went to sleep and dreamt that the three of them—Mother, Lionya, and he—were hiding along with Lenin in his horse-tail tent. It was cramped. There wasn't much room for bravery or anything else. All they could do was huddle together and await an uncertain future. To pass the time, they took turns braiding Mother's lustrous hair, making sure it framed her delicate temples just so. Even V. I. Lenin had to admit to his young friends that "it is always a great honor to braid the hair of Yelena Petrovna Girshkin of Leningrad."

BACK IN HIS PRAVA *panelak,* Vladimir got up from his bed. He tried walking the way Mother had shown him a few months ago in Westchester. He straightened his posture until his back hurt. He put his feet together gentile-style, nearly scuffing his shiny new loafers, a parting gift from SoHo. But in the end he found the whole exercise pointless. If he could survive Soviet kindergarten hobbling Jewishly from humiliation to humiliation, then surely he could survive the scrutiny of some Midwestern clown named Plank.

And yet, even at a distance of half the globe, he could still feel Mother's fingers poking his spine, her eyes moistening, the lyrical hysteria well on its way…How she had loved him once! How she had doted on her only child! How she had set an absolute standard for herself: I will do anything in the world for him, throw myself in front of the likes of Seryozha Klimov, enlist five-year-old playmates to his cause, leave my dying mother behind to emigrate to the States, force my ne'er-do-well husband into a life of illicit profit, just to make sure little Vladimir continues to breathe each shallow breath in safety and comfort.

How does one person sign over an entire lifetime to another? Selfish Vladimir could hardly begin to imagine it. And yet generations of Jewish-Russian women had done the same for their sons. Vladimir was part of a grand tradition of ultimate sacrifice and unbounded insanity. Only he had somehow managed to break free of this filial bondage and now found himself motherless and alone, punished and chastened.

What do I do now? Vladimir asked the woman across the ocean. *Help me, Mama…*

Amid the ghostly warble of old Soviet satellites circling over Prava, Mother gave her answer. *Proceed, my little treasure!* she said. *Take those uncultured bastards for all they're worth!*

What? He looked up to the cardboard ceiling above him. He had not expected such criminal candor. *But how can you be sure? What about the wrath of Cohen...*

Cohen's an ignoramus, came the reply. *He's no Lionya Abramov. Just another American, like that smiling hippopotamus-girl at my office who tried to screw me over last week. Who's smiling now, fat suka?... No, the time for Phase Two has come, my son. Take your little poem to the reading. Do not be afraid...*

Grateful for the imprimatur, Vladimir lifted his hands up to the sky, as if he could reach out across the ether of uncertain space and false memory and once again braid Mother's hair on the long train ride to Yalta, massage the white scalp between her parted locks. *If I succeed tomorrow,* Vladimir told her, *it will be because of you. You are the mistress of daring and perseverance. No matter how I may place my feet, I am endowed with everything you have taught me. Please do not worry for me...*

My whole life is worry for you, Mother replied, but at this juncture, with a great declarative thump, the living-room door nearly collapsed under the force of two rifle butts.

22. IN THE STEAM ROOM

"VLADIMIR BORISOVICH!" A DUO OF THROATY RUSSIAN voices shouted from the hallway, interrupting Vladimir's transatlantic séance. "Hey, you! Opa! Wake up in there!"

Vladimir quickly waddled over to the door, losing both slippers in his haste, his ears still ringing with Mother's godlike intonation. "What is the meaning?" he shouted. "I am an associate of the Groundhog!"

"The Groundhog wants you, pussycat," one of the louts shouted back. "It's *banya* time!"

Vladimir opened the door. "What *banya?*" he said to the two big peasants, their faces completely yellowed by a lifetime of drinking, so that in the pale glow of the hallway they appeared perfectly green. "I have already bathed this morning."

"The Groundhog said take Vladimir Borisovich to the *banya,* so put on a towel and let's go," they said in unison.

"What nonsense."

"Do you dispute the Groundhog?"

"I follow the Groundhog's imperatives blindly," Vladimir told his intruders, who both looked like adult versions of Seryozha Klimov, the hooligan from kindergarten. What if they tried to pinch him to death à la Seryozha? Mother was certainly not here to protect him, and Lionya Abramov, his former best buddy, was probably running some sleazy night club in Haifa. "Where is this *banya*?" Vladimir demanded.

"Building three. There is no changing room, so put on your towel now."

"You expect me to walk over to building three in nothing but a towel."

"That is the procedure."

"Do you know who you're talking to?"

"Yes," the two men answered without hesitation. "We answer to Gusev!" one of them added, as if that alone explained their impertinence.

AS TOWEL-CLAD VLADIMIR walked across the courtyard to the third *panelak* flanked by his two armed escorts, a group of Kasino whores peeked out of their gloomy hole to whistle at the near-naked young man, who instinctively covered his breasts with both hands the way he had seen buxom girls do it in pornographic literature. So it had been a setup! Gusev angling to humiliate him, that turd. Perhaps he had forgotten that Vladimir was the son of Yelena Petrovna Girshkin, the ruthless czarina of Scarsdale and Soviet kindergarten both ... Well, thought Vladimir, we shall see who will fuck whom, or, as they say in Russian in two simple, elegant syllables—*kto kovo*.

The *banya* wasn't a true Russian bathhouse with its peeling walls and charcoal-stained stoves, but rather a tiny prefab Swedish sauna (as dull and wooden as Vladimir's furniture), which had been attached to the *panelak* in a makeshift manner, like a space module to the Mir. Here, the Groundhog and Gusev were slowly cooking themselves alongside a platter of dried fish and a small barrel of Unesko.

"The King of the Americans has deigned to bathe with us," Gusev announced upon Vladimir's arrival, fanning himself with a large salt-encrusted perch. Without clothes, Gusev's body matched the Groundhog's curve for curve, a preview of what Vladimir would look like ten years hence unless he succumbed to Kostya's exercise regimen. "And have we been sleeping 'till this late hour?" Gusev asked. "My men tell me your car and driver have been idle all day."

"And what business is this of yours?" Vladimir said carelessly as he picked up the traditional bundle of birch twigs with which the Russian bather flogs himself, supposedly to improve circulation. He flicked the birch through the air in what was meant to be a menacing gesture, but the wet twigs only said, "Shoo," in a sad and lethargic way.

"What business?" Gusev bellowed. "According to our money man, in the past two weeks alone you've spent five hundred U.S. dollars for drinks, a thousand for dinners, and two thousand for hashish. For hashish, mind you! And this when Marusya has her own little opium garden right here on the premises. Or perhaps our opium's not good enough for you, eh, *Volodechka?* Some thrifty Jew we've found ourselves, Groundhog. He thinks he's the party boss of Odessa."

"Groundhog—" began Vladimir.

"Enough, the two of you!" the Groundhog shouted. "I come to the *banya* for relaxation, not to hear this pettiness." He spread himself out on a bench, his stomach overhanging both sides, sweat running down the pocked immensity of his dorsal plane. "Two thousand for hashish, ten thousand for whores...Who cares? Melashvili just phoned from the *Sovetskaya Vlast'*, they're leaving Hong Kong with nine hundred thousand worth of crap. Everything's fine."

"Yes, everything's fine," Gusev sneered, biting off the perch's head and spitting it onto the steaming logs in the corner. "Melashvili, that nice Georgian black-ass has to toil the world over to keep our Girshkin happy—"

Vladimir leapt up in anger, nearly dropping the towel that covered his small manhood, a weakness he did not want exposed. "Not one more word from you!" he shouted. "In the past two weeks I've befriended nearly every American in Prava, I've started work on a new literary magazine which will take the Western element by storm, my name has appeared twice in *Prava-dence,* the expatriate's journal of record, and tomorrow I will be an honored guest at an important reading of rich English-speakers. And after all the work I've done, most of it stupid and degrading, you dare accuse me…"

"Aha! Do you hear that, Goose?" the Groundhog said. "He's publishing magazines, making rich friends, going to readings. Good boy! Keep at it, and you'll make me proud. Say, Gusev, remember those readings we used to go to as kids? Those poetry contests… Write a poem on the theme 'The Oft-Tested Manliness of the Red Tractor Brigade.' Such fun! I fucked a girl at one of those, I surely did. She was dark like an Armenian. Oh, yes."

"I do not question your authority," Gusev began, "but I do—"

"Oh, shut up already, Misha," the Groundhog said. "Save your whining for the *biznesmenski* lunch." He reached over to the fish platter and shoved a small specimen into his mouth. "Vladimir, my friend, come here and strike me with the twigs. Got to keep my blood going, or I'll melt on the spot."

"I beg—" Vladimir started to say.

"Hey, hey, fellow!" Gusev shouted as he leapt to his feet. "What's the meaning? Hey! Only I am permitted to whip the Groundhog. That's practically *diktat* around here. Just ask anyone in the organization. Put down those twigs, I say, or it won't be cheerful for you."

"You're being petty again, Mikhail Nikolaevich," the Groundhog warned. "Why shouldn't Vladimir give me a whipping? He's a strong young buck. He's worked hard. He's earned it."

"Just look at him!" shouted Gusev. "He's flabby and weak-wristed. He's half my age and already his breasts are distended like a cow's. Oh, he'll whip you like a little pederast, that's for certain! And you deserve so much better, Groundhog."

Any discomfort Vladimir may have had at the prospect of whipping his employer faded with Gusev's words. Before he even knew it, his hand had made an angry gesture through the air and there was a clap of thunder at the Groundhog's back. "Mwwwaaarff!" cried the Groundhog. "Uga. Hey, there. That's the stuff!"

"Is this the whipping of a pederast?" shouted Vladimir, shockingly unconcerned over the illogic of that sentence, as he flagellated the Hog once again.

"*Bozhe moi,* that's pain, all right," the Groundhog grunted with pleasure. "But a little higher up next time. I've got to sit on that thing."

"To the devil with both of you!" Gusev whispered loudly. He stepped up to Vladimir on his way out, ostensibly to give him the look of a lifetime, but Vladimir, knowing better, busied his eyes with the red topography of the Groundhog's back, a challenge for any budding cartographer. Still, he couldn't avoid a glimpse of Gusev's neck, a thick and corded piece of anatomy, despite the corpulent disorder below.

Only after Gusev had slammed the door behind him did Vladimir remember his childhood fear of saunas, the paranoid feeling that someone was going to lock the door and let him steam to death inside. He thought of himself and the Groundhog trapped together, their skin as translucent as that of a steamed dumpling, nothing inside but boiled meat: it seemed like the worst death imaginable.

"Oh, but why have you stopped," moaned the Groundhog.

"No, I shall prevail over that fat-necked bastard," Vladimir muttered to himself, and he set to task with such ferocity that upon his first strike a purple-black pimple exploded, and the Hog's heavy blood made its way through the sauna's fishy air, which was as thick and inviolable as Gusev himself.

"Yes, yes," the Groundhog shouted. "That's the way! How quickly you learn, Vladimir Borisovich."

PART V

THE KING
OF PRAVA

23. THE UNBEARABLE
WHITENESS OF BEING

THE JOY WAS A VEGETARIAN RESTAURANT BUT BENEATH it lay a meat market of a disco where the perennially hard-up regulars lured unsuspecting backpackers, many still sporting their Phi Zeta Mu T-shirts, into nights of forgetfulness and mornings of waking up on a futon in the nether reaches of Prava's suburbs, trying to connect with an authority figure back in the States on an antiquated telephone that could barely reach out across the Tavlata. On Sundays they had readings.

Vladimir went down the threadbare stairs, where the small pink-and-mauve dance floor was lit up by a series of overly bright halogen lights, giving the place the look of a rather impersonal womb. Presently, this arena accommodated three rings of plastic chairs and weathered couches and recliners; randomly placed coffee tables were home to bright, shapely drinks from the bar; and the artists and spectators themselves wore their Sunday best—jackets all around and hair tied or slicked back. Earrings and piercings gleamed peacefully from within their thoroughly scrubbed fleshy enclosures, gusts of rolled American Spirit tobacco emerged from fresh-colored lips, lingered in newly trimmed goatees.

The young men and women cast to populate this postmodern Belle Epoque turned to face the new entrant and kept their gazes fixed as he walked into the inner circle of seating where a space was reserved for him between Cohen and Maxine, the mythologizer of Southern interstates.

Vladimir walked in with his legs atremble. He had made a terrible mistake immediately upon his arrival by instructing Jan to deposit him at the front door to the Joy, where the entering hordes were treated to the spectacle of an artist alighting from a chauffeured BMW. True, he was supposed to be a *wealthy* artist, but this arrogant spectacle was undoubtedly a mistake, the kind of faux pas that within minutes would be circulated to Budapest and back by Marcus and his Marxish fiends.

To Vladimir's further chagrin, it appeared that the few readers in the group were distinguished by a spiral notebook much like his own, a fact not lost on Cohen who stared at Vladimir's tome, mouth agape, then turned to its owner, his eyelids at half-mast with contempt.

It was, thus far, a silent gathering. Plank was asleep on an enormous imported La-Z-Boy recliner, dreaming of last night's bacchanal. Cohen was too angry to make a peep. Even Alexandra was uncharacteristically silent. She was too busy looking over Vladimir and Maxine, probably trying them on as a couple; the blond and sprightly Maxine had just been picked out as Vladimir's mate by the Crowd's informal council on dating. But, of course, it was long, trim Alexandra that Vladimir wanted. Her beauty, her unreserved enthusiasm contributed heavily to his infatuation, and yet there was more: He had found out recently that she was born of a lower-class family! Semiliterate Portuguese dock workers from a place called Elizabeth, New Jersey. The idea that she had come to Prava from this noisy, poorly lit, deeply Catholic household with its abusive men and pregnant women (what else could it have been like?) restored much of Vladimir's lapsed faith in the world. Yes, it could be done. People could change their life chances with a few elegant strokes yet remain beautiful and at ease and kind and solicitous, too. Alexandra's world, despite its artistic pretensions, was a world of possibilities; there was so much she could teach him, she with a stocking ripped exactly at the point where one world-class thigh began to curve into shape.

Meanwhile, the silence continued, save for the last-minute scribbling of some of the artists. Vladimir was frightened. Were they still thinking about his BMW? Any minute now, it seemed, a Stalinist denunciation was to begin, with him the purgee.

Artist 1, a tall dirty-haired boy in Coke-bottle glasses: "Citizen V. Girshkin is charged with antisocial activity, the promulgation of an odious persona and nonexistent literary magazine, and possession of an Automobile of the Enemy as defined in the USSR Criminal Codex 112/43.2."

Girshkin: "But I'm a businessman..."

Artist 2, a big-eared redhead with cracked lips: "Enough said. Ten years hard labor in the People's Limestone Extraction Facility in Phzichtcht, Slovakia. Don't start with the 'Russian Jew' crap, Girshkin!"

Instead, a sinewy, older gentleman emerged from the shadows. He had no hair save for two sets of overgrown curls rising above his head like devil's horns, and sagging corduroys that could have accommodated a matching tail. "Hi, I'm Harold Green," he said.

"Hi, Harry!" This was Alexandra, of course.

"Hi, Alex. Hi, Perry. Wake up, Plank." Harry Green's eyes—kind and avuncular, but also with the requisite expatriate glaze that plagued every English speaker in Prava—settled on Vladimir, where they blinked slowly and repeatedly like a skyscraper's warning lights.

"He owns this place," Maxine whispered in Vladimir's ear. "He's the son of very rich Canadians."

Harold instantaneously ceased to be a mystery, one less variable in Vladimir's co-optation formula. He imagined patting the dear fellow's naked crown, suggesting minoxidil, a new interior decorator for his club, a new worldview for his cocktail hour, a sizable investment in Groundhog, Inc....

"So, we've got here a list." Harold picked up a clipboard. "Anyone not penned their John Hancock, or Jan Hancock for those of you of the Stolovan persuasion?"

Vladimir saw his hand rise, a small, pale creature.

"VLADIMIR," Harold read off the clipboard. "A Stolovan name, no? Bulgarian, no? Romanian, no? No? So who do we have to start? Lawrence Litvak. Paging Mr. Litvak. Please step right up, Larry."

Mr. Litvak tucked in his Warhol T-shirt; checked his zipper momentarily; brushed back a tendril of blond, dreadlocked hair, and took to the magic spot from which Harold had spoken. Vladimir recognized him from the Nouveau and likeminded places, where he always had as his sidekick an enormous blue bong, and where he was happiest when regaling passers-by with war stories culled from his brief, standard-issue life.

"This is a story," Larry said, "called 'Yuri Gagarin.' Yuri Gagarin was a Soviet astronaut who was the first man in space. Later he died in a plane crash." He cleared his throat, a little too thoroughly, and gulped back the fruits of his besieged lung.

Poor, dead Yuri Gagarin was conscripted into a tale about Larry's Stolovan girlfriend, a veritable Rapunzel whose untrimmed hair and penchant for Tony Bennett played at fantastic decibels made her an outcast in her own *panelak.* That is, until Prince Larry came along, fresh from his proving grounds at the University of Maryland, College Park: "'Prava will be good for you,' my writing professor POSITED. 'Just don't fall in love,' he said EVINCING what would happen if I did to the contrary, as had happened to him in 1945, a young G.I.," etc.

The narrator installs our heroine Tavlatka—a water nymph as her name suggests, and as the long and graphic scene in the communal swimming pool amply illustrated—in his apartment conveniently located in the Old Town. (How did Larry get the money to live in the Old Town? Vladimir made a mental note for PravaInvest purposes.) They smoke a lot of hash and have sex, "in the manner of the Stolovans." Meaning what? Under a blanket of ham?

Ultimately, the relationship hits a snag. At some point in the middle of the sex a conversation on the space race is launched and Tavlatka, soiled by a decade of agit-prop, insists that Yuri Gagarin was the first man on the moon. Our narrator, a leftist softy, to be sure, is still an American. And an American knows his rights: "'It was Neil Armstrong,' I hissed into the small of her back. 'And he was no *cosmo*naut.' My Tavlatka spun around, her nipples no longer erect, a tear welling in both eyes. 'Get you out of here,' she said, in that funny yet tragic way of hers."

After that things really fall apart. Tavlatka boots our hero out of his own apartment and he, with no place to go, starts sleeping on a little tatami mat by the New Town Kmart, selling nudes of himself to old German ladies on the Emanuel Bridge (go, Larry!), making just enough money for the occasional knockwurst and a Kmart pullover. There's no mention of what Tavlatka does, but one remains hopeful that she makes good use of Larry's Old Town pad.

Here, Vladimir lost the narrative thread for a while, his eyes doing a Baedeker's tour of Alexandra's ankle, but he did manage to catch the scene where Tavlatka and the narrator seek the truth in an old Stolovan library smelling "sourly of books," and then the grand finale in bed where both Tavlatka and Larry emerge with their bodies "drenched, satiated . . . understanding that which the mind cannot."

FIN and BRAVO! BRAVO! The circle congregated around Litvak to pay their dues. Cohen had a turn at the wunderkind with a full frontal hug and hair ruffle, but Larry had bigger fish to fry: He was looking for pan-seared Girshkin on a bed of shallots in red wine sauce. "Remember me?" he croaked to Vladimir from within Cohen's anaconda grip. He half-closed his eyes, managed to loosen the top button of his shirt, and rolled his head about to demonstrate his usual late-night demeanor.

"Right," said Vladimir, "Air Raid Shelter, Reprè, Martini Bar..."

"You never told me you were starting a literary mag," Larry said, maneuvering out of Cohen's arms, nearly throwing the jilted Iowan off balance.

"Well, you never told me you were a writer," Vladimir said. "I'm a little hurt, actually. Your talent is shocking."

"How strange," Larry said. "That's the first thing I usually mention."

"No matter," Vladimir said. "That story definitely belongs in..." They never had settled on a name for the magazine. Something Latin, French, Mediterranean—yes, Mediterranean cuisine was gaining in global popularity, surely its literature would follow. Now what was the name of that famous Sicilian alchemist and charlatan? *"Cagliostro."*

"Dig the name."

Indeed. "Only I can't really make that kind of editorial decision," Vladimir said. "You need to talk to my editor-in-chief Perry Cohen over there. Me, I'm just the publisher." But before Vladimir could redeem his plummeting stock with Editor & Friend Cohen, Harry Green was lowing for them all to sit and pipe down in his purposeful Canadian Prairie way. "Vladimir Girshkin," he called out. "Who is Vladimir Girshkin?"

Who indeed?

Vladimir Girshkin was a man who once instinctively moved in the wrong direction and invariably got knocked down every time he saw a person running his way. Vladimir Girshkin once said "thank you" and "sorry" when there was absolutely no need, and often employed a bow so deep it would have been excessive at Emperor Hirohito's court. Once upon a time Vladimir Girshkin held Challah in his reed-thin arms and prayed that she would never be hurt again, and, to that end, vowed to be her protector and benefactor.

But presently he held a single sheet of paper in front of him, his right arm unfolding predictably like an architect's swivel lamp... Steady as she goes...

He read:

This is how I see my mother—
In a dirty Formica restaurant,
simple pearls from her birthland
around her tiny freckled neck.
Sweat-dappled,
she is buying me a three-dollar dish of lo mein,
gleaming over the gold watch
we found for a bargain,
four hours of a heatstroke Chinatown afternoon
behind us. Blushing as she says,
"I'll just have water, please."

There it was. A poem with little to impart but with clean lines like the room at a good bed-and-breakfast: simple wooden furniture, a tasteful framed print hanging above the couch of some sylvan scene—moose-in-brook, cabin-lost-in-trees, whatever. In other words, thought Vladimir, it was absolutely nothing. The kind of garbage that finds its own void and soundlessly disappears into same.

Pandemonium! Standing ovation! A regular riot! The Bolsheviks were storming the Winter Palace, the Viet Cong were massing around the American embassy, Elvis had entered the building. Apparently nobody in the Joy crowd had yet thought of writing a small poem that wasn't entirely self-conscious or self-referential. NATO planes had not yet been called in to carpet-bomb the city with William Carlos Williams's collected work. It was quite a coup for Vladimir.

Amid the blare of applause and the trumpet of Maxine delivering her lip-to-lip kiss for the public record, Vladimir made a note of another promising phenomenon: a woman of deeply American appearance (although she was not blond), a clear-skinned, full-faced, brown-haired young woman dressed in mail-order outdoorsy pants and linen blouse, who probably smelled like an environmentally correct shampoo of apples and citrus with an undercurrent of rain-forest soap, was clapping away, her ruddy face made all the more so with simple, unabashed adulation for Vladimir Girshkin. Our man in Prava.

UPSTAIRS, at the vegetarian portion of the Joy, a round metal table of Stolovan unsturdiness was rolled out for the conquering heroes; it tipped back and forth beneath portions of black hummus the consistency of loam and the tureens of beet-red minestrone top-heavy with actual beets. Vladimir got placed in a little male semicircle of Cohen (who refused to look at Vladimir), Larry Litvak (who wouldn't bother looking at anyone else), and Plank (unconscious). Vladimir glanced about nervously, feeling a heterosexual opportunity being squandered. To wit, the clean and comely American woman he had branded with his verse had also made the trek upstairs. She was sitting at the "Carrot Bar" with the rest of the peons, chatting up a tourist boy. At measured intervals she looked over to Vladimir's table and smiled with her ointment-shiny lips and milk-white teeth, as if to quash the rumor that she wasn't enjoying herself.

King Vladimir waved her over—it was something new he was learning to do with his hand. And he was getting good at it, for instantly she picked her purse off the bar and left the tourist boy with his beer and his crew cut and his stories of what the governor did at his sister's wedding.

"Scoot over," Vladimir said to the boys and the seats were shuffled, water spilled, complaints voiced.

She was awkward, navigating to her seat ("sorry, sorry, sorry") and Vladimir didn't help matters by moving closer to sniff at her linen blouse. Yes, rain-forest soap. Correct. But what to make of the rest of her? She had what in the Girshkin family would be considered the beginnings of a nose, an outcropping really, a small belvedere overlooking the long, thin lips, circular chin, and beneath that the full breasts that bespoke a successful American adolescence. Vladimir had but one thought: Why was her hair past shoulder-length, given the present-day urban conventions that demanded shortness, brevity? Was she, perhaps, a stranger to hipness? Questions, questions.

But like most pretty people she made a positive impression on the Crowd. "Hi," Alexandra said to her, and by the sparkling expression on her face it might as well have been a cry of *"Landsman!"*

"Hi," the newcomer said.

"I'm Alexandra."

"I'm Morgan."

"Nice to meet you, Alexandra."

"Nice to meet you, Morgan."

And then the niceness ended and was replaced by a universal uproar over the talentless Harry the Canadian and how everything would be so much better, so much more dignified, if they (the

Crowd) owned the Joy and its literary legacy. Here all eyes turned to Vladimir. Vladimir sighed. The Joy? Wasn't the goddamn literary magazine enough for them? What next, a Gertrude Stein theme park? "Listen," Vladimir said, "we've got to get the ball rolling on *Cagliostro*."

"Ca— what?" Cohen said.

"The magazine," Larry Litvak said with a roll of the eyes. When not stoned out of his gourd he apparently found ignorance quite shocking.

"We're calling it *what*?" Cohen said, turning on Vladimir.

"Remember you were reading that obscure Milanese metahistorical journal about that Sicilian charlatan and alchemist, Cagliostro, and you said, 'Hey, aren't we all just a little like him, staking out our claim in this postsocialist wilderness?' Remember?"

"Cag-li-ostro!" Alexandra said with flair. "Oh, I like that."

There were murmurs of approbation.

"Right," Cohen said. "Actually I was thinking of a couple of names, like maybe *Beef Stew*, but… You're right. Whatever. Let's just run with my first thought."

"So this is not going to be a mainstream journal," Morgan said. She looked very sober there, with her hands in her lap, her eyes open wide, her well-plucked eyebrows raised as she tried to put in her two cents among the loud and fractious Crowd. It was bewildering for Vladimir to see a beautiful person who didn't make herself the center of attention in one way or another (Alexandra always pulled it off so well!), and he didn't make things any easier by saying: "Main*stream*? We're not even treading the same brook as the others."

But before she could be embarrassed, the conversation instantly shifted toward the topic of the lead piece, and L. Litvak brazenly put forth his Yuri Gagarin space odyssey, when Cohen turned to him and said, "But how can we even consider passing up Vladimir's poem for the top spot?"

Everyone hushed. Vladimir searched Cohen's face for sarcasm, but it looked tempered, not so much resigned as perspicacious, understanding. With the empty beer bottles in front of him and a smudge of hummus in the fluff of his pseudobeard, Vladimir took a mental snapshot of Cohen as he had pretended to have taken a picture of Mother in the nonexistent Chinese restaurant. Friend Cohen getting wisdom, catching on.

"Yes, of course, Vladimir's poem," said the awakened Plank.

"Of course," Maxine said. "It's the most redeeming piece I've heard since I've come here."

"By all means, Vladimir's poem!" shouted Alexandra. "And Marcus can decorate it. You can draw something, honey."

"Then you can put my story right after it," Larry said. "It'll act as counterbalance."

Vladimir picked up a glass of absinthe. "Thank you, everyone," he said. "I would like to take the credit for this work myself, but, sadly, I can't. Without Perry's mentorship, I could have never cut to the heart of the matter. I'd still be writing the adolescent crap, the shaggy-dog poems. So, please, a toast!"

"To me!" Cohen smiled his "Sunrise, Sunset" elderly papa smile. He reached over to pat Vladimir's head.

"You know..." Morgan was saying after the ripples of the toast had subsided and no one had anything else to say. "You people. This reading. This is all so new to me. Where I come from... Nobody... This is sort of how I pictured Prava. This is kind of why I came here."

Vladimir's jaw dropped at the sound of this unsolicited honesty. What the hell was she doing? You don't just admit these things, no matter how true they are. Did Young Beauty (with the long brown hair) need an introductory course in poseurdom? Self-invention 101?

But the Crowd soaked it right in, punching each other's shoulders in jest. Yes, they sort of kind of knew what she was talking about, this sweet, dazzling newcomer in their midst.

They took Morgan with them after they left the Joy. Later, when Alexandra got the chance to be alone and personal with her in a decaying Lesser Quarter ladies' room, she found out that Morgan had found Vladimir's poetry "brilliant" and Vladimir himself "exotic." So maybe there was hope for her, after all.

BUT VLADIMIR PUT HER OUT of his mind. There was serious work to do. Phase Two had gone off without a hitch; bad poetry had carried the day; the checkbooks were out and ready. He looked to Harold Green, generously making his way past the supplicants at the Carrot Bar, each begging for one of the Joy's hefty artist-in-residence grants. By the looks of him, Harold was on the most important mission of his life. Destination: Girshkin.

No doubt about it, Phase Three's time had come.

The suckling phase.

24. COLE PORTER
AND GOD

WAKE UP, SHOWER, AND GET TO CHURCH. VLADIMIR did as his pebble-sized Judeo-Christian conscience told him. He swallowed vitamins and drank glasses of water. His new alarm clock was still howling. He put on his one and only suit bought on a whim from the new German department store for tens of thousands of crowns and realized that it was meant for a person twice his size. "*Dobry* fucking *den*," he said to himself in the mirror.

In the side lot by the opium garden, his car was idling along with Jan. The sky was a desolate bleached-out blue with patches of russet clouds as thick as bark on which, it seemed, advertisements could be placed and sailed above the city. Kostya was doing some nature stuff with a rose bush, pruning it, perhaps; the gardening lessons imparted by Vladimir's father had long lost their relevance.

"Good morning, Tsarevitch Vladimir," Kostya said upon seeing him. He looked more dignified than ever today—no nylon, just khakis, brogues, and white cotton shirt.

"Tsarevitch?" Vladimir said.

Kostya ambled over and snapped the shearlike things at Vladimir, missing him by centimeters. He seemed all too happy at the prospect of a Russian Orthodox Sunday. "The check cleared from the Canadian!" he shouted. "What's his name? Harold Green. The club owner."

"The full quarter million? You mean...Heavenly God...Are you saying that...?" Was he saying that U.S.$250,000.00, the equivalent of fifty years of wages for the average Stolovan, had gushed into the Groundhog's kitty like the Neva River melting in the spring? And all through Vladimir's free-market treachery? No, it could not be. The world rested on sounder poles: north and south; the Dow Jones and the Nikkei; the wages of sin and the minimum wage. But to sell two hundred and sixty shares of PravaInvest at U.S.$960.00 a pop...That was out there in Loop-de-Loop Land where Jim Jones, Timothy Leary, and Friedrich Engels rode their unicorns up and away into the pink-purple sky.

True, Vladimir did recall Harry drunk and delusional at the Nouveau's Martini Bar, his head in his hands, his pate, bald and moist, gleaming like the martini decanters arrayed above the bar. Slobbering, weeping: "I have no talent, my young Russian friend. Only off-shore accounts."

"Get out of here!" Vladimir barked without warning, surprising even himself. This was the tone of Mother addressing one of her native-born underlings, some poor accountant with a state school education. Was Vladimir drunk? Or was he more sober than ever? It felt like a little bit of both.

"What?" Harry said.

"Get out of this country! Nobody wants you here."

Harry pressed his drink to his chest and shook his head without comprehending.

"Look at you," Vladimir continued bellowing. "You're a little white boy in a big white man's body. Your father and his capitalist cronies destroyed my nation. Yes, they fucked the peace-loving Soviet people right and proper."

"But, Vladimir!" Harry cried. "What are you saying? What nation? It was the Soviets who invaded the Stolovan Republic in 1969—"

"Don't start with your cozy little facts. *We do not bow to your facts.*" Vladimir suspended his diatribe for a minute and took a deep breath. *We do not bow to facts?* Hadn't he seen that slogan once, in his youth, on a communist propaganda poster in Leningrad? Just what the hell was he becoming? Vladimir the Heartless Apparatchik?

"But you're wealthy yourself," Harry protested through his tears. "You have a chauffeur, a BMW, that nice felt hat."

"But that is my right!" Vladimir bellowed, ignoring the kindly impulses his better organ—his heart—was pumping through the left ventricle along with the liters of frothy type-O blood. There would be time to indulge Mr. Heart later... This was war! "Have you not heard of identity politics?" Vladimir shouted. "Are you daft, man? To be rich in my own milieu, to partake in the economic rebirth of my own part of the world, why, if that's not part of my narrative, what the hell is?" At this point, Vladimir himself almost became misty-eyed as he pictured Francesca, the woman at whose feet he had learned the ways of the world, walking in through the gilded doors of the Nouveau's Martini Bar, smiling wanly as Vladimir beheaded this sorry creature in the same way she used to castrate the politically challenged masses in New York. Oh, Frannie. This is for you, honey! Let greatness and beauty prevail over baldness and nullity...

"My narrative!" Vladimir resumed screaming. "It's about me, not about you, you imperialist American swine."

"I'm Canadian," Harry whispered.

"Oh, no, you don't," Vladimir shouted, grabbing him by the folds of his oversized rugby sweater. "Don't even go there, pal."

AND LATER, in the rank Nouveau bathroom, where the piss of the English-speaking world mingled on the chipped marble, Vladimir personally applied minoxidil around the Arctic outposts of Harry's remaining hair, while a lone, smashed New Zealand tourist looked on, one hand poised to reach for the door in case things went too far.

By this point, Vladimir was rocked from side to side by waves of pity. Oh, that poor Harry Green! Oh, why was embezzlement so cruel? Why couldn't rich people just spontaneously give money away like that nice Soros fellow? Vladimir even leaned over to kiss Harry's wet brow like a concerned parent. "There, there," he said.

"What do you want me to do?" Harry said, wiping his scarlet eyes, blowing his tiny twisted nose, trying to regain the quiet dignity that, before this wretched evening, had been his signature. "Even if I do grow back my hair, that's only half the battle. I'll still be old. I'll still be a . . . What did you call me?"

"An interloper."

"Oh, God."

"Harry, my sweet man," Vladimir said, recapping the minoxidil bottle, his portable fountain of youth. "What am I going to do with you, huh?"

"What? What?" Vladimir looked at Harry's reflection in the mirror. Those huge red eyes, the freckled chin, the receding gums. It was almost too much. "What are you going to do with me, Vladimir?"

AND TWENTY MINUTES LATER, winding through the darkened streets around the walls of the castle, the parapets coming in and out of the corners of vision, Beethoven's Seventh blaring off the CD player, Vladimir held the checkbook steady on the crying Canadian's lap. To be honest, Vladimir was shaking a little, too. It was hard to come to terms with what he had done. But this wasn't really *the worst* kind of crime, now was it? They were going to print a literary journal! A journal with Harry's name prominently displayed. It was all part of the familiar cultural Ponzi scheme practiced the world over—from third-rate dance collectives to those idiotic creative-writing programs. The participants put in their time and money, dutifully attended each other's kazoo recitals and poetry readings, and by the end of the day the only ingredient missing from their enterprise was the actual talent (much as a regular Ponzi scheme lacks the actual cash). Still, was it so terribly wrong to give people a little hope...?

"PravaInvest will do for you what cultural relativism did for me," Vladimir said, patting the soft head resting warmly on his shoulder. "Now, two hundred sixty shares is not a lot. I've got a couple of Swiss going in for three thousand. But it's an introduction to the global continuum. It's a start."

"Ooh, if only my father knew where his lousy money was going!" Harry laughed. "I can't wait to fax him that *Cagliostro* journal. And pictures of that hospital in Sarajevo! And the Reiki clinic, too!"

"Now, now," Vladimir said, as the car's headlights illuminated an archway carved into a castle wall, beyond which the Lower City was repositioning itself so that its spires would lie directly at Vladimir's feet. "Let's not be spiteful, Harry." And he gave his new investor a pleasant squeeze, then ordered Jan to set a course for Harry's villa, where his gurgling friend, reeking of minoxidil and self-love, could be deposited for the night.

And that was that. The cash register opened, the digits turned, the sun rose once again over Prava.

————

"YES, THE FULL QUARTER-MILLION," Kostya said, confirming yesterday's wondrous news, as he fell on his knees before the young tsar and kissed his hand with his dry, chapped lips.

"And ten percent of it is mine," Vladimir said. He had not intended to say it out loud, but to stifle a sentiment like that was not possible.

"The Groundhog said he will give you twenty percent as an incentive," Kostya said. "Can you lunch with him after church?"

"Of course!" Vladimir said. "Let's hurry then! Jan, start the car!"

"No expensive car, please," Kostya said.

"Pardon?"

"We show our piety on the way to church by taking public transportation like the rest of the congregants."

"Oh my God! Are you serious?" This was a little much. "Couldn't we just take a Fiat or something?"

Jan smiled and twirled the car keys around his meaty forefinger. "I'll drive you gentlemen as far as the metro station," he said. "Now be good Christians and kindly open your own doors."

THE METRO WAS DESIGNED in the Lenin's Starship motif: the walls chrome-plated in futuristic shades of that socialist-friendly color, ecru; the cameras at the edge of the platform recording the reactionary tendencies of the passengers; the Soviet-built trains that inspired many an Ode to Moving Metal from besotted Slavs around the bloc; the recorded voice of some sturdy, no-nonsense Heroine of Socialist Labor over the public address system: "Desist in entering and exiting! The doors are about to close."

And close they did, as fast as lightning cranked out of some totalitarian power-station out in the woods. Look! Everywhere

Vladimir turned—Stolovans, Stolovans, Stolovans! Stolovans in Prava, of all places! *Dobry den'*, Milan! Howdy do, Teresa? Did you get a haircut, Bouhumil? Panko, stop climbing on the seats!

The wagonful of these "Stolovans on the Move" rumbled toward the Tavlata. At the Castle station they picked up some British grade-schoolers in uniform who swiftly moved to one corner and behaved themselves like good little gentlemen. They were disgorged at the Old Town station, the last outpost of Tourist Prava, and were replaced by teenage locals with out-of-control acne, polyester leisure suits, and high-tops.

On and on they went. The distances between the stations got progressively longer. The bored teenage boys were now making slurping sounds to one of their girlfriends, a tall pimpled beauty in a Lycra skirt who took out a book and busied herself flipping through the pages, while a *babushka* waved a fist the size of a beefsteak tomato at the boys and shouted something about their "unsocialist upbringing."

"Hooligans!" Kostya said. "And on a Sunday, too." Vladimir nodded and pretended to doze off. At his present rate of ascension he could foresee a time when it would be possible to tell Kostya the Angel to bugger off, and to let his debauchery and projected lechery assume the sum total of his waking hours. But he had to have a friend in the Russian circuit, a shield from Gusev and the merry men with the Kalashnikovs out in the lobby. Everyone held Kostya in high regard, this Vladimir knew. When Kostya went to church, it was as if he went to church for all of them. Plus he knew something about computers—you could never underestimate that.

And then, while Vladimir never enjoyed the huffing and puffing sessions beneath the sun, and the craziness with the ten-pound dumbbells, he was aware of a new physical vitality that went along nicely with his new big-man-on-campus image. For instance, he was straighter, and, as a consequence, taller. His breasts, the objects

of Gusev's merriment, which had at one point reached such a state
of disrepair that even Vladimir himself had started to find them
mildly arousing, were slowly being shaped into two hard little
mounds suitable for flexing. His lungs were in better order, too—
he didn't leave a trail of mucus behind after each lap; when smoking hashish he could keep the smoke in longer and let it percolate
among the nooks and crannies of his asthma-scarred villus.

But still he wanted freedom from the Lord's man in Prava, or at
least a lighter schedule. More time to splash water on his face and
get his bearings in the morning.

BY THE TIME they disembarked they were the only ones left on
the train. At ground level the main smokestack of a factory rose
dramatically above them like a NASA rocket with a serious fire in
the capsule. In one direction a distant huddle of *panelak*s shimmered in the translucent chemical haze. In another direction there
appeared to be a vast stretch of nothing. Kostya looked toward the
nothing, using his hand as a visor against the late morning sun.
Vladimir looked to the cherub and smiled, trying to appear both
enthusiastic and confused. He made a few epic sweeps of the hand
as if to indicate that the "nothing" was not a good thing and the
powder towers and jazz clubs of the Golden City were really more
his cup of grog.

Kostya remained unmoved. He found a bus schedule tacked on
to an enormous electrified fence that enclosed the factory. "There,"
he said. "There should be one now."

And by the dictate of God, Kostya's coconspirator, an entirely
empty double-jointed bus, its two tremendous halves bound
together by a thick oval of rubber, rounded the corner, raising dust
in its wake. The bus stopped, let out a long sigh as if overcome by
its loneliness for passengers, and opened its many doors.

THEY RUMBLED THROUGH the fields of emptiness, the giant factory growing distant in the dirty rectangle of the back window. The empty fields looked to Vladimir as if they had been tortured by Romania's dreaded Securitate, the soil randomly upturned and heaped into mounds or depleted into mini-canyons.

Kostya sat pensively, his hands cupped together as if he was praying already, which might have been the case. "You know, my mother's very sick," he said without the customary preamble.

"How terrible," Vladimir quickly replied.

"Yes. I don't know how it will turn out. I'm going to pray for her."

"Of course." Vladimir fidgeted quietly. "I'll pray for her too."

Kostya gave his thanks and turned to the window and the empty view. "If you want," Vladimir said, "I can give you the money to fly her to Austria for better medical treatment. That is, if you need the money."

"I thought about that. Of doing it with my own money. But I want her in Russia in case she . . . I want her to be surrounded by her own people." Vladimir nodded as if he could appreciate the sentiment, but somehow the phrase "her own people" reminded him of the fact that these concerned and helpful (and mythical) Russians of the medical profession were a far cry from *his* own people, whom Kostya's mother would probably not appreciate milling about her deathbed with their legendary big noses and dirty hands. But then again, that was just an assumption. There were some Russians who weren't like that. Kostya, for one, knew of Vladimir's missing foreskin and never said anything derogatory. On the other hand, he was taking him to church.

Amid the empty fields they came across "The International Technological Joint Venture—FutureTek 2000," announced by a freshly painted billboard on the side of the road. It resembled something of a Victorian-era factory mated to a grain silo, really just a collection of thick, rusted pipes and bulbous metal containers joined together at odd angles. To think that somewhere within this pastiche of industrial decay a new fax modem was waiting to be born was to invest too much hope in the resilience of the human spirit.

Now, thought Vladimir, you take some white plaster walls, throw them up around the factory, perforate a mock-tinted window along one of the sides, stick a couple of recycling bins out front, and presto! Why sell worthless shares to Stolovans at ten crowns a pop, when you can unload them to Americans at ten *dollars?* He made a note.

THE CHURCH was hiding behind the factory, with a small field of failing carrots separating the two. It looked rather Appalachian, the church did—a little corrugated tin shack with a metal Orthodox cross that gleamed amid the empty surroundings like a television antenna bringing news of civilization beyond. "Please," said Kostya and opened the door for him.

You couldn't mistake the parishioners for anything but Russians. Tired, stern faces that even in the meditative act of prayer looked ready to kick some ass for their fair share of beets, sugar, and a parking space for the beat-up Lada microsedan. Broad, heavy bodies bursting with thick veins and copious sweat, looking as if they had been somehow blown out of proportion by a diet of meat and butter—par for the course in a world where one had to appear as formidable as a tank to start the wheels of distribution turning.

Kostya bowed to a few of them and pointed at Vladimir, eliciting several difficult smiles and the tiniest of whispers. Vladimir hoped he looked more like Jesus than Trotsky to them, but an icon above the altar showed the prototype of the one whose second coming was awaited—a very gentile Christ indeed, with light brown hair verging on dirty blond, the traditional soft-focus physiognomy, and, of course, a look of supreme transcendence that Vladimir didn't even want to begin to fathom. Yup, he was in church.

But it wasn't too shabby, the service. There was a certain uncertainty to the message, the way the priest, as bearded and robed and wizened as could be (you knew you were getting your piety's worth with this guy), would belt out, singsong-like: "Je-sus has risen!" and the crowd would reply in unison, "Verily, He has risen." Nice the way this central fact had to be constantly affirmed. But *of course,* He has risen. What would it all mean if He hadn't risen, eh, Vanya?

And crossing yourself was great too, kneeling and crossing endlessly. It felt good—swift and powerful. The *goys* were good with the swift-and-powerful shtick. Columbus and his wooden armada sweeping into the New World on an Atlantic breeze and a prayer; the medieval English galloping through hot, dusty Palestine bedecked in a ton of steel. Crossing, always crossing themselves. Before the Hebrew God you could only bow repeatedly and feel sorry about your place beneath Him, but with Christ there it was, with your hand—up, then down, then right, then left. Christ has risen? Why, yes, verily.

Vladimir must have crossed himself impressively because several of the *babushkas,* their blue eyes glowing within their shawls, were clearly taking note of his vigorous motions and loud proclamations. Kostya gave him a smile so wide it could have been redeemed for a place in Heaven. This went on for a while, the tiny room suffused with the brightness of candles and a pair of oversized, out-of-place halogen torchieres like the floor samples Vladimir had seen at the German department store. The smell of sweat and the incense swung about by the priest was getting a bit heady and just as Vladimir was making sure the back door was still present and accessible, Christ was resurrected one last time and it was all over.

They lined up before the priest who kissed them in turn and said something brief to each congregant. Waiting on line, Kostya introduced Vladimir to a couple of nice old ladies whose doubts about "the dark one" had dissipated over the course of the services like the whoosh of stale air released over the empty horizon upon the opening of the front door. The priest kissed Vladimir on the left cheek and the right, his breath smelling surprisingly of dill pickles, and said, "Welcome, my dear young one. Christ has risen."

"Yes, um," said Vladimir, although there was, of course, a better way of saying it; they had, in fact, just said it three hundred times. But His Holiness, broad-shouldered and erect despite his considerable age, with his booming voice and pungent kisses, would make even the most godless members of the Spartacist League quiver in their ankle-high Doc Martens. "You must be Greek," the priest said.

"Half-Greek, half-Russian," Vladimir said. It just came out that way.

"Delightful. Will you join us for a little meal now?"

"Sadly, I can't. I'm expected with my family in Thessalonica. I was just off to the airport. But next week, definitely."

"Delightful," the priest said again, and then he had his turn with Kostya, who whispered something into his ear which made the priest laugh uproariously, his beard, as grand and white as his person, taking on a hairy life of its own. It was a mirth Vladimir could not understand, since God's business was, by all means, a serious one, especially when one of your flock proved to be a Jew in Greek's clothing.

He bowed his way past the congregants and out the door, where a steady autumn rain was gathering force and the sky appeared a tablecloth of unrelenting gray.

WELL, that was all over with, thank God, and off he was in his marvel of Bavarian tinkering, speeding away on the Tavlata's eastern embankment, thinking Faster! Faster, Jan! for the Groundhog and the most expensive restaurant in Prava awaited. Oh, he had been duplicitous with the Angel, as always, getting off at a suburban metro station to "briefly visit an American friend, a pious man of Serbian lineage..." And there, by prior arrangement, Jan and the unholy Beamer awaited their master. Taking the metro to lunch—a little too déclassé for an upscale *gonif* like Vladimir.

The restaurant was situated opposite the castle, with full view of the river growing full under the autumn rain, tourists galloping across the Emanuel Bridge, their umbrellas torn apart by a wind strong enough to have breathed life into a hundred Golems. It was a restaurant popular with rich Germans and American mommies and daddies visiting their drifting progeny, and, yes, a certain Russian "entrepreneur."

The Groundhog kissed Vladimir on both cheeks and then presented his own pock-marked ones. Vladimir closed his eyes and uttered a ridiculous "Mwa!" with each kiss.

With the male Eastern European love overture complete, Vladimir was allowed to take his seat; across the table, the Groundhog squirmed like a happy little papoose in its swaddling clothes, only he was a large, corpulent mafioso in an unflatteringly tight brown suit. "Look," he said, "your appetizer's already here!"

True enough, there was a circle of fatty rings of squid lying atop, of all things, butternut squash, with some sort of powder dusted in the middle that smelled vaguely of parmesan and garlic. At twenty dollars a plate, the restaurant promised to serve no carp, its wine list was purged of the sickly-sweet Moravian vintages that made Prava's head spin, and the proprietors had airlifted an actual old guy from Paris to tickle their Steinway's ivories beneath a huge Art Nouveau spread of frolicking nymphs. *Bon appétit!*

The Groundhog munched, both cheeks bulging. "Beautiful job with that Canadian donkey," he said once his squid was finally dispatched. "That's right, why not start out big? Why not a quarter million?"

"This money is good," Vladimir said. "The world owes us for the last seventy years. This money is very good."

They drank bottles of Chardonnay, beaming at each other in the unspoken argot of success. By the fourth bottle, and with the braised hare in pimiento reduction well on his way, the Groundhog got sappy. "You're the best," he said. "I don't care who you are, what tribe you came from. You're just the greatest."

"Stop it."

"It's true," the Groundhog said, working fast on the complimentary bread and horseradish paste. "You're the only one I don't have to worry about. You're an adult, a businessman. Do you know what trouble I have with Gusev's men?" He flipped the Russian bird—the thumb stuck between the index and middle fingers—to a table by the kitchen where members of his bouffant-haired, pinstriped security team were slumped over their empty Jim Beam bottles.

"Oy, tell me," Vladimir said, shaking his head.

"I'll tell you," the Groundhog said. "You know I got problems with the Bulgarians, right? With the whole stripping and prostitution racket on Stanislaus Square? So these men of Gusev's, these fucking cretins, they go to the Bulgarians' bar and the usual nonsense starts about the girlfriends, the questions of who fucked who first, and who sucked who where. And when it's all over they got this one guy, Vladik the Dumpling, that's the Bulgarians' number two, actually… They got him strung up by his feet over the bar, and they cut off his dick and his balls, and they bleed him to death! That's fucking Gusev's men for you! No brains, no skills, nothing. They cut off a man's dick and his balls. I said to them, 'Where do you idiots think you are—Moscow?' This is Prava, the waiting room to the West, and they're going around cutting—"

"Right," Vladimir said.

"They're cutting—"

"Yes, the mutilation of genitals. I hear you," Vladimir said. "Where's the bathroom?" he asked.

After assuring himself of the wholeness of his scrotum and padding it with a layer of crispy Stolovan toilet paper (as if that would stop the revenge-minded Bulgarians!) Vladimir felt the return of good cheer swell up across his nether region. By the time he staggered back to the table he was nearly ebullient. "You've got to have a talk with Gusev!" he shouted across the table. "We're businessmen!"

"You have a talk with him," the Groundhog said, throwing up his hands. "You tell him, 'This is how we do business in America, and this is how we *do not* do business in America.' A line has to be drawn for those simpletons."

"Correct, correct, Groundhog," Vladimir said, quickly toasting with a glass of schnapps. "Only, trust me, you should be the one telling them. They're not scared of me."

"They will be scared of you," the Groundhog said. "As scared as they are of God. Which reminds me, here's a toast to Kostya and his mother's health."

"To a speedy recovery."

The Groundhog suddenly looked serious. "Volodya, let me speak from the heart. You and Kostya are the future of this organization. I see that now. Before it was fun, sure, run around, blow up a few diners, cut off some dicks, but we got to get serious. This is the nineties. We're in this . . . 'informational age' . . . we need 'Americanisms' and 'globalisms.' Do you know where I'm coming from?"

"Oh, yes," Vladimir said. "I say we call a meeting, the whole organization."

"Whores and all," said the Groundhog.

"We're going to teach them America."

"*You're* going to teach them America."

"Me?" Vladimir said, swallowing a cognac.

"You," the Groundhog said.

"Me?" Vladimir feigned surprise yet again.

"You're the best."

"No, you're the best."

"No, you."

What happened next was as good an argument for temperance as any. "You're the top," Vladimir sang, squeezing in a shot of pear brandy between the lyrics. "You're the Colosseum."

He must have been louder than he thought, for the pianist instantly shifted out of his Dr. Zhivago repertoire and struck up Vladimir's tune. The pianist was, like nearly everyone in Prava, open to suggestions.

"You're the top," Vladimir continued even louder, with the Germans around him smiling appreciatively, thrilled, as always, at the prospect of free foreign entertainment at tableside. "You're the Louvre Museum."

"Get up and sing, *Tovarisch* Girshkin!" The Groundhog kicked him hard under the table for encouragement.

Vladimir staggered to his feet, then fell over. A further prod from his employer brought him up again. "You're the melody from a symphony by Strauss! You're a Bendel bonnet, a Shakespeare sonnet, you're Mickey Mouse!"

The Groundhog leaned in, his expression quizzical, and pointed to himself. "No, no, you're the Groundhog," Vladimir whispered reassuringly in Russian. The Groundhog pretended to sigh with relief. Hey, the Hog was a fun fella!

"You're the top," Vladimir crackled. "You're a Waldorf salad. You're the top. You're a Berlin ballad..." The waitstaff was trying hard to position a microphone in his direction.

"You're the purple light of a summer night in Spain...You're the National Gallery, you're Garbo's salary, you're cellophane." He wished he could translate one of the lines into German to get an extra kick from the red-faced *deutsches Volk,* maybe hit them up for a tip or a date. "I'm a lazy lout who's just about to stop..."

Oh, what a ham you are, Vladimir Borisovich.

"But if baby...I'm the bottom...You-ou-ou're the top."

There was a standing ovation greater than at the Joy on poetry night. The Groundhog's security detail regarded their master uncertainly, as if waiting for the secret code to spring into action and spray the whole room with bullets so that no witnesses to this little musical number would remain. There was cause for alarm, as the Groundhog, doubled over with laughter, slipped under the table like a surfer caught in the undertow, and remained there for some time laughing and hitting his head against the table's bottom. Vladimir had to coax him out with the lobster claws which, true to the menu, really did sit atop a lime-green spread of kiwi puree.

25. THE HAPPIEST
MAN ALIVE

HE DECIDED TO DATE MORGAN, THE NICE GIRL THE crowd had picked up at the Joy.

It wasn't a political decision and not so much an erotic one, although he was attracted to her form and pallor, and, maybe, just maybe, she would make a good Eva to his Juan Perón. But his romantic stirrings extended even beyond public relations. He was lonely for a woman's company. When he arose from an empty bed, his mornings seemed strange and disjointed; at night, passing out into the comforter, as soft and licentious as it was, was somehow not enough. It was hard to understand. After all the complications that American women had put him through (and would he even be here in Prava if it weren't for his Frannie?) he still depended on their company to make him feel like a young mammal—so vital, affectionate, and full of sperm. But this time around *he* would take charge of the relationship. He was beyond the "appendage" stage of following Fran around and swooning at the mere mention of semiotics. It was time for someone innocent and pliable like this Morgan, whoever the hell she turned out to be.

There were several courtship options for him. A great deal of them involved various permutations of chance meetings in clubs, poetry readings, strolls across the Emanuel Bridge, or during the hours spent queuing up at the town's only laundromat—a hub of expatriate activity. At each of these venues, he, Vladimir, would prove himself superior in intellect, grace, conviviality, and name-dropping, thereby accumulating enough social points to be later cashed in for a date.

Or he could do things the old-fashioned, proactive way and call her up. He decided (since, according to Alexandra, his social coordinator, everything was set for the Eagle to land) to try the latter and rang her from the car phone. But the Stalin-era telephone exchange would not connect the two lovers-to-be; instead of Morgan he kept getting a venerable *babushka* who by the fifth call rasped that he was a "foreign penis" and should "fuck off back to Germany."

And so Vladimir buzzed Alexandra instead. She and Morgan had twice done the "girls night out" thing and were becoming fast friends. From Alexandra, yawning and likely in Marcus's arms, he got Morgan's address out in the boonies and a few bon mots concerning a young girl's virtue. He longed to orient his car's compass in the direction of Alexandra's suburbs, and to ask *her* to the movies or wherever it was people went on dates. But he pressed forward, way beyond the river and the preliminary factoryscape, to a quiet stretch of asphalt and a lone and lonely apartment house which seemed as if it had been blown several klicks downwind from its *panelak* brethren by some bureaucratic storm.

Morgan lived on the seventh floor.

He took an elevator smelling comfortably of kielbasa, whose iron door required his whole being to open and shut (the exercises with Kostya were already proving useful), and knocked on the door of apartment 714-21G.

There was stirring within, a slight creak of springs set against the quiet jabber of television, and Vladimir was instantly afraid that he had been preceded by some large American boy, which would explain both the creaking springs and the television being on on a Friday night.

Morgan opened the door without asking who it was (the way non–New Yorkers have an appalling tendency to do) and she was, to Vladimir's welcome surprise, alone. In fact, she was extremely alone, with two dumpy television anchors doing the news round-up in Stolovan; on the coffee table a small pizza from the New Town shop where they piled up such daring combinations as apples, melted Edam cheese, and sausage gravy; and on the win-dowsill a bored cat, a hefty Russian blue, mewing and scratching at the freedom beyond.

Morgan was sporting a pink starfish-shaped rash on her fore-head (a distant cousin of the wine-dark splotch on Gorbachev's head), which she had slathered with a thick layer of cream, and was wrapped up in a lavender terry-cloth robe several sizes too small, the kind one expects to receive upon being consigned to a cut-rate nursing home. "Hey, it's you!" she said, her round American face smiling perfectly. "What are you doing all the way out here? Nobody ever comes to visit me."

Vladimir was caught short. Seeing her as she was, he was expecting several minutes of embarrassment from her over the state of her wardrobe and forehead. Embarrassment which, he hoped, would make him look good by comparison and help him press the case for why she should go out with him and fall in love with him too. But here she was, happy to see him, actually willing to admit that she didn't get many visitors. Vladimir remembered her unsolicited honesty at the Joy when she had first met the Crowd. Now she was coming through with several more heapings of the stuff. *What fresh pathology was this?*

"Sorry to barge in unannounced," Vladimir said. "I was in the neighborhood on some business, and so I thought…"

"That's all right," she said. "I'm so glad you're here. Please, *entrez.*

What a mess. You'll have to excuse me." She made her way to the couch, and, with the benefit of the snug bathrobe, Vladimir now noticed that her thighs and backside, while not particularly large in and of themselves, were somewhat larger than the rest of her.

Now, why wasn't she rushing to change out of that ridiculous bathrobe? Didn't she want to impress her guest? Hadn't she told Alexandra that she found Vladimir exotic? Of course, Ravi Shankar was exotic, and how many women of Vladimir's generation would sleep with *him?* Vladimir briefly entertained the thought that Morgan was comfortable being who she was in her own house, but then dismissed such outlandishness. No, something else was going on.

She closed the pizza box, then dropped a magazine on top of it. As if that would conceal the damning proof of her solitude, thought Vladimir. "Here," she said. "Make yourself at home. Sit. Sit down."

"We're modernizing a factory near here," Vladimir said, pointing vaguely to the window where he assumed another factory in need of a tune-up lay in wait. "It's very dull work, as you can imagine. Every couple of weeks I have to come in and argue with the foreman about cost overruns. Still, they're good workers, the Stolovans."

"I wasn't doing much myself," she shouted from what must have been the kitchen, for Vladimir heard water running. She was likely dealing with the creamy buildup on her forehead. "I live so far from the center. Leaving this place is such a bother."

Such a bother. An older person's phrase. But said with a young person's carelessness. Vladimir recalled this kind of paradox from the young Middle American natives he encountered during his college year, and the recollection relaxed him. After they were both settled on the couch and she had brought out a sad little local wine and a paper cup for Vladimir to drink from (the splotch on her forehead remained!), a question-and-answer period followed, one which Vladimir found as familiar as the words to the "Internationale."

"Where's your accent from?"

"I am Russian," Vladimir said, in the grave voice which that admission called for.

"That's right, Alexandra told me something about that. I studied a little Russian in college, you know."

"Where did you go?"

"OSU," she said. "Ohio State." It sounded perfectly reasonable coming out of her mouth, but it made Vladimir think of the "frathog" at the Café Nouveau whose Ohio State T-shirt had made Alexandra laugh.

"So Russian was your major?"

"No, psychology."

"Ahh..."

"But I took a lot of humanities classes."

"Ohh..."

Silence.

"Do you remember any Russian?"

She smiled and straightened out a growing partition in her robe, which Vladimir had been watching carefully, feeling piglike and uncouth in his voyeurism. "I just remember a few words..."

Vladimir already knew what those few words were. For some reason, Americans undertaking his impossible language were compelled to say "I love you." Perhaps this was a legacy of the Cold War. All that suspicion and lack of cultural exchange fueling the desires of young, well-wishing American men and women to bridge the gap, to dismantle those nukes by falling into the arms of some soulful, enigmatic Russian sailor, or his counterpart, the warm and sweet-tasting Ukrainian farmer girl. The fact that, in reality, the soulful Russian sailor was smashed out of his mind half the time and held to a rather loose definition of date rape, while the sweet-tasting Ukrainian farmer girl was covered in pigshit six days out of the week, was fortunately concealed by that gray and nonporous entity, the Iron Curtain.

"*Ya vas loobloo,*" she said on cue.

"Why, thank you," Vladimir said.

They laughed and blushed and Vladimir felt himself naturally moving across the couch to be closer to her, although a very safe distance remained. The way her unfashionably long brown hair was coiled limply around her neck, the way it ended in tangles across the faded lavender of the bathrobe made Vladimir feel sorry for her; it aroused him too. She could be so beautiful if she wanted to. Why wasn't she then?

"So, what are you doing tonight?" he said. "Feel like taking in a movie?"

A movie. That sacred rite of dating which he had never performed. Not with his college girlfriend, the Chicagoan (straight to bed); or Frannie (straight to bar); or even Challah (straight to nervous tears and hiccuping).

And how about "taking one in"? You couldn't go wrong with a boy who used language like that and probably waved earnestly and said, "Take care, now, hear," when Uncle Trent took off for the Rotary Club. Accent be damned, you were safe with Vladimir Girshkin.

She squinted at her tiny watch and tapped it purposefully, as if she was on a tight schedule which Vladimir had rudely thrown off-kilter with his dreams of cinema and maybe one of his skinny arms around her shoulders. "I haven't seen a movie since I got here," she said.

She scooped up the latest *Prava-dence*, and leaned toward Vladimir to hold the paper aloft for them both. Despite her being disheveled and marooned on a Friday night, a clean smell emerged from the crux of her uplifted arms. Was there ever a time when American women weren't so extraterrestrially clean? He really wanted to kiss her.

According to the paper, Prava was awash with Hollywood movies, each stupider than the next. They finally settled on a drama about a gay lawyer with AIDS, which was apparently a big hit in the States and was approved by many of that nation's sensitive people.

Morgan excused herself to the bathroom to change (finally!) while Vladimir took in her room, lovingly filled with mass-manufactured knickknacks from both the New World and the Old, which lined several plywood "instant" shelves: a fading charcoal drawing of Prava's castle, a tiny moss-green mermaid statue from Copenhagen, a cracked beer stein from some place called the Great Lakes Brewing Company, a blown-up photo of a fat, disembodied hand dangling a striped bass (Dad?), a framed flyer advertising an industrial noise band named "Marty and the Fungus" (old boy-friend?), and a copy of Dr. Seuss's *Cat in the Hat.* The only incongruous item was a large poster illustrating the Foot in all its Stalinist glory leaning precariously over the Old Town Hall. Beneath it, a Stolovan slogan: *"Graždanku! Otporim vsyechi Stalinski çudoviši!"* Vladimir could never be sure of the funny Stolovan language, but translated into normal Russian this could be an exhortation along the lines of "Citizens! Let us take the ax to all of Stalin's monstrosities!" Hm. That was a little unexpected.

He closed his eyes and tried to take all of her in—the warm round face, the serious gaze, the awkward little mouth, the soft body bundled in terry cloth, the harmless errata on her shelf. Yes, there were probably quirks and inconsistencies in her personality with which Vladimir would eventually have to contend, but, at present, she certainly made for a wonderful demographic. Vladimir, too, could make himself into a pretty good demo: his recent income ranked him in the upper ten percent of U.S. households, and he believed in monogamy with a sad kind of romantic fierceness that would certainly put him ahead of most men in the polls. Yes, the numbers were right; now the magical American love thing had to happen, which it usually did when the numbers were right.

And then he noticed that she was out of the bathroom and talking to him about something... What was it? The Foot? He had been looking at the Foot poster. What was she saying? Down with Stalin? Up with the people? She was definitely saying something about the Foot and the long-put-upon Stolovan nation. But despite her insistent tone, Vladimir was too busy thinking about a strategy to make her love him to hear the particulars of what she was saying. Yes, it was time for the love thing to happen.

WELL, she did look good after her makeover! She was dressed in a little silk blouse which, she must have been aware, defined her contours closely, and had her hair completely up, save for a few stray wisps that fell out of the bun adorably, after a fashion he had seen in contemporary New York subway ads. Perhaps later he could take her to Larry Litvak's cocktail party—to which he had been invited by phone, postcard, and several gooey encounters with the man himself—and, once there, show her exactly where Vladimir Girshkin was lodged in Prava's social firmament.

The theater was in the Lesser Quarter, meters from the Emanuel Bridge and close enough to the castle to be in audible range of the bells of its cathedral. Like all real estate of its caliber the theater was crammed with young foreigners, the bulk of them wearing black-and-orange down jackets and baseball caps with logos of American sports teams worn backward. This was the year's fall fashion-statement for that hideously sterile human mass expanding via satellite from Laguna Beach to Guangdong Province—*the international middle class*—and it made Vladimir yearn for winter and heavy overcoats and the end of the tourist season, as if there would ever be an end.

On the plus side, the global men all stared at Vladimir's date as if she was the living embodiment of the reason they slaved away night and day at their engineering textbooks and accounting software, and the looks they reserved for *him*, that goateed shrimp of a poet, were enough to demonstrate for those of a Catholic disposition envy's place among the seven deadly ones.

As for the women, bah! all those jangling gold bracelets and tight V-neck sweaters were for naught—no one, not the Bengali heiress nor the lawyer from Hong Kong wore her finery with such confidence and familiar grace as the candidate from Shaker Heights, Ohio. (During the anxious ride into the center, he had learned the name of the particular Cleveland suburb where Morgan grew tall and fair.)

Right! No matter which gender he encountered that night it certainly seemed that this whole enterprise, this date, had gotten off on the right foot, and to celebrate Vladimir bought at the concession stand a minibottle of Becherovka, the hideous Czech liqueur that tasted of burnt pumpkin. And for the lady, a little flask of the Hungarian booze called Unicom, which, despite its lingual similarity to a United Nations relief agency, was the source of innumerable atrocities to the stomach and its sensitive lining.

"Cheers!" They clinked their drinks and, predictably, Morgan gagged and coughed as would any mortal this side of the Danube, while Vladimir comforted her with improvised manliness, even touched her sweaty hand a little, out of concern, and wanted for a brief second to live forever in such circumstances (i.e., being manly; being envied; touching her, if only at the extremities). But then the lights went down and the mating ritual, such as it was, became a bit murky for Vladimir since there was little opportunity for him to try out his witticisms and even less occasion to put on the moves. How could he, after all, with half the audience sniffling and bawling as the attractive hero on the screen became more and more emaciated with the progression of the awful disease, eventually to lose his hair then pass away by the closing credits?

What a scene there was then! By the time the curtains went down noses were trumpeting throughout the theater as if the castle walls outside belonged to ancient Jericho. But Morgan's face was placid, if a little glazed over, and they stumbled wordlessly to the exit sign and into the street. They stood, still silent, watching the Fiat taxis being commissioned by departing moviegoers while the first drunken processions of Italian university students loudly made their way past the ominous shadow of an adjacent powder tower to some disco wonderland beyond.

Vladimir couldn't wait to vent. "I hated it!" he shouted. "Hated it! Hated it!" He did a little dance in the shadows of the flickering street lamps, as if to demonstrate the primordial force of his hatred. But it was time for some kind of intellectual breakdown, so he said: "How trite. How revoltingly simple-minded. To turn AIDS into yet another courtroom drama. As if the only way Americans can express anything anymore is through legal proceedings. I'm so utterly underwhelmed."

"I don't know," she said. "I think just making this movie was a good thing. So many people have issues. Especially where I come from. My little brother and his friends can be such homophobes. They just don't know any better. At least, this movie talks about AIDS. Don't you think that's important?"

What? What the hell was she quacking about? Who gave a fuck what her brother thought about queers. The point was the movie failed as a work of art! Art! Art! Weren't the Americans here in Prava for art? Why the hell was *she* here? A little reasoned rebellion before grad school? A chance to show off to the suburban losers in

Shaker Heights: "That's me and my Russian ex-boyfriend in front
of the hotel where Kafka took an important crap in 1921. See that
plaque by the door? Pretty nifty, huh?" He hadn't even bothered to
ask Morgan what she was doing here in Prava, but the sad alterna-
tives—teaching American English to local businessmen or wait-
ressing the breakfast shift at Eudora's—were all too obvious. Oh,
there was so much he needed to show her. So much she needed to
know about the society in which she had landed. Yes, he would go
the extra kilometer for this sweet Cleveland cutie. Those hale little
cheeks. That nose.

"Well," he said after a little while had passed and a weak-willed
burst of rain had made them a little wet. "I certainly need a drink
after that turkey."

"How about Larry Litvak's cocktail party?" she said.

So she had been invited, damn it! Now the burning question of
our times was: Why, earlier, had she been by herself in her *panelak*
watching television with the cat? Perhaps she was getting ready—
the shower, the bathrobe, the ointment on the forehead. Or, worse
yet, she didn't even care about Larry Litvak's party. *Devil confound
it all!* thought Vladimir to himself in Russian, a phrase that floated
in angry and unannounced whenever his worldly disequilibrium
mounted to truly Dostoyevskian proportions.

"I also know of a little out-of-the-way club," he ventured. "No
one's ever heard of it, and there's plenty of actual Stolovans." But
she insisted on the cocktail party, and now there was nothing to do
but go. As if to underscore the situation, Jan and the Beamer pulled
up stealthily behind them and started flashing their headlights for
attention. The evening was set.

BUT ALL WAS NOT LOST, not by a long shot. When they
opened the door to Larry's pad, the multitudes did let loose with a

tumbler-shaking "VLAAAAD!" and, of course, cried out nothing to the barely known Morgan, although surely she was admired in a silent way.

Larry Litvak lived, per his astronaut story, in the Old Town, actually on the outskirts of the Town, bordering Prava's sprawling bus terminal, which, like all bus terminals, exuded nothing but rankness and ill-health, and was populated by a cast of characters fit for a television exposé.

The lights were down, way down, reminding Vladimir of college parties where the less one could discern of one's companions, the more distant beds would rumble by the early morning's light. Still, Vladimir could see that this was a spacious flat, built in the booming interwar period when Stolovans were still expected to live in apartments larger than their dachshunds' quarters. In fact, the ceilings were so high, the place could have been mistaken for a SoHo loft, but reality abounded in the scary, socialist furniture— the squat, utilitarian divans and easy chairs outfitted in the kind of furry, worsted material that the *babushka*s enjoyed wearing on cold days. As if to accentuate his furniture's prickly quality, Larry had installed three bergamots in the center of the main room and had placed miniature floodlights beneath them so that their craggy branches spread unsettling shadows against the ceiling and walls.

"It's quite a place," Vladimir shouted to Morgan over the din, with the implied knowledge of having been there many times before. Morgan looked to him in incomprehension. Things were happening too fast: there were hands being thrust at Vladimir from left and right, some already wet and reeking of gin, not to mention the frequent hugs and mouth-to-mouth kisses Vladimir received from impassioned well-wishers. Clearly, the young lady wasn't used to a Girshkin-sized social persona. Did she have any choice now other than to love him?

They were carried by the crush of people into a kitchen

smoothly lit with candles where Larry was situated, his bong working overtime, and several of Prava's more hippielike denizens swaying to Jerry Garcia, their expressions blank, their bodies loose and loafy like palm trees caught in the wind. "Hey, man," said Larry, dressed in a transparent black kimono, which revealed in its entirety his sinewy but muscular frame—the show-off. He hugged Vladimir tightly until the latter could feel every part of him.

"Hey, man," he kept repeating, and Vladimir fondly recalled his high school days when he and Baobab and the rest of them were always stoned and would spend the day mumbling: "Hey, man... don't eat that *thing*, man...that *thing* is for later, man..." Oh, the innocence of those days, that brief period in the Reagan/Bush era when the sixties had returned to American high schools in force. The stooped posture, the half-closed eyes, the hundred-word vocabulary. Oh.

The hippies were introduced, their names sliding in and out of memory. The pièce de résistance, the bong almost a meter in length, was wheeled around for the guest of honor. Larry bent down to light it while Vladimir sucked on the rancid mouthpiece, then passed it to Morgan who tackled it like a good sport.

SATISFIED, Vladimir took her arm and they floated back into the main room, scarcely remembering to tell the "we'll be right back" party lie to Larry Litvak and company. Here, there was another crush around Vladimir and his date, this one consisting entirely of tall, elegant men in chinos, wire-rims, and nose rings plying Vladimir with drinks, mentioning by name *Cagliostro* and (surprisingly) PravaInvest, then cheerfully prodding their women friends into the foreground for brief introductions. This whole setup was reminiscent of a nineteenth-century ball in the Russian provinces, when the local society men had spotted the general arrived fresh from Petersburg and then closed in on him full of platitudes and talk of business, toting their beautiful wives behind them as a sign of their own rank and good breeding.

The year 1993? Well, such anachronisms could have been a sign of the much-discussed Victorian revival. And while it was shocking for Vladimir to meet these non-Bohemians who wore their nose rings out of fashion and not rebellion, it struck an old, aristocratic chord in him (for in the early twentieth century the Girshkins had owned three hotels in the Ukraine) and he responded with a mounting sense of noblesse oblige: "Yes, pleased to meet you...Of course, I've heard of you...We ran into each other at the Martini Bar at the Nouveau...Such pleasant circumstances...This is Morgan, yes...And you are?...And this is?..."

Of course, being under the liberating influence of a meter's worth of dope quickly added hilarity to the proceedings, setting Vladimir's mind at ease as he floated above the masses and their babbling and screeching and clucking. Soon his Russian accent emerged in force, lending Count Girshkin an aura of authenticity, which left the fair representatives of Houston and Boulder and Cincinnati twice enamored of the small poet and businessman around whom all of Prava's expatriate world would now seem to revolve.

He felt Morgan tugging at his sleeve, no longer amused at being marginalized. "Let's find Alexandra," she whispered and, whether she meant it or not, touched Vladimir's ear with her balmy nose.

"Let's," Vladimir said, and he put his arm around her and squeezed the broad Ohioan shoulders, so healthy and amenable to squeezing.

They broke through the cordon of well-wishers and arrived at the bergamots which, swaying from the winds of a distant fan, scratched at Vladimir's face until he stopped to look stupidly at his arboreal assailants as if to say: "Don't you know who I am?"

Behind the little trees they saw a long, satin couch flanked by similar recliners on which the Crowd had decamped along with several martini decanters and entire carafes of curaçao. They sat laughing and passing judgment without stop at those around them like some hastily assembled Style Council. Occasionally they entertained outsiders who approached with little bundles of paper bearing words or drawings, and sometimes with little computer disks. It seemed that the upcoming first issue of *Cagliostro* had swelled their heads nicely; a frontal assault by Mexican bees would have proved superfluous.

Cohen spotted them amid the shrubbery: "There he is! Vladimir!"

"Morgan!" Alexandra shouted with something like awe, determined to raise the standing of her newfound friend.

The couple approached and a glittering sky-blue divan was rolled out for them as if by the Devil's command. Alexandra kissed Morgan on both cheeks, while Vladimir shook hands with the boys and sweetly kissed Alexandra on one cheek, and was kissed, in turn, on both.

The boys had outdone themselves, channeling the glam-nerd look into a formal direction: ash-brown sports jackets and shirts of mourning hues with morose little ties snaking down to their bellies. Alexandra wore a new taupe riding jacket, evidently from one of Prava's more accomplished antique shops, beneath which was her customary black turtleneck and matching tights.

But one was missing from the group. "And where is Maxine?" Vladimir said, biting his tongue as he remembered that the Expat Dating Committee had already slated the Girshkin-Maxine nuptials for early next spring, and here he was, playing the field with Morgan.

Sure enough, as soon as he mentioned Maxine, a look passed over Morgan's face, the look of a child lost in a crowded train station, and Larry's party was, of course, infinitely stranger than any of the world's train stations and just as crowded. "Maxine's taken ill," Alexandra said. "Nothing serious. She'll be up on her feet tomorrow."

The "up on her feet" business was evidently meant to discourage Vladimir from attempting any change in the woman's verticality. Clearly, Alexandra had told Morgan everything she needed to know about Vladimir's steamy nonaffair with Maxine.

The situation was unwittingly defused by the excited Cohen who hadn't seen Vladimir in a couple of days and all but jumped on him. "My friend needs to step to the bar," he shouted, roaring drunk. "You girls talk among yourselves." Vladimir looked back at Morgan, worried about leaving her behind. Fortunately, the sight of two attractive women, Morgan and Alexandra, chatting with gusto had the effect of keeping potential suitors at bay. The predatory young men of Prava were easily confounded by the phenomenon of women making do without them.

At the bar, a tiny affair jutting out of an oak bookshelf filled with the collected works of Papa Hemingway, the patron saint of the expatriate scene, the irrepressible Cohen attempted to fix Vladimir a gin and tonic by spilling vodka all over his new imported loafers. When informed by the laughing Vladimir that *gin* not vodka went into a gin and tonic, Cohen spilled that on him too.

"So, you've been tying one on," Vladimir said.

"I've been tying one on for the past five years," Cohen said. "I'm what in the liquor industry is called an alcoholic."

"Me too," Vladimir said. He had never given the matter much thought, but the words certainly rang true.

"Well, let's drink to that!" cried Vladimir in an effort to shoo away the approaching discomfort, and they clinked their glasses.

"Speaking of tying one on," Cohen said, "Plank and I are ready for a major bout with the bottle tomorrow. To the finish!" He winked in the direction of the bar.

"I see," Vladimir said. He saw Cohen and Plank as two pugilists duking it out, slow-motion, with a sweating bottle of Stoli in some sort of performance-art piece.

"You care to join us? None of this shit. Just the three of us. The men." Then, without warning—and when did he ever give warning?—Cohen threw his arms around Vladimir and squeezed hard. By this time the lights had been dimmed to the degree where the two of them looked like yet another couple on the express checkout lane to bed. The frightened Vladimir peeked out from within his friend's grasp and tried to maneuver an arm free to signal to the crowd and Morgan that this was not his idea of a good time, but he was hard-pressed to think of the appropriate signal. Anyway, Cohen soon let go and Vladimir saw to his welcome relief that a critical mass had been reached in the room and nobody gave much of a damn about anyone else, really. Even unabashed homosexual sex with the accompanying grunts broadcast over the stereo system would probably go unnoticed for several minutes.

"Aww, we miss you, man," Cohen said. "You're so busy with work and…." He stopped, tired of sounding like a jilted lover.

Across the room Vladimir saw Plank looking disgustedly into his drink as if he had been slipped a diuretic, while on the couch next to him Alexandra and Morgan gestured up a storm of conversation. What was it with these disconsolate young men? Was being the cornerstone of Prava's elite not enough for them? Did they expect to lead meaningful lives as well? "All right," Vladimir said. "We'll go out by ourselves. We'll have a good time. We'll drink. We'll get drunk. All right?"

"All right!" shouted Cohen. Brightening, he reached for a bottle, even as Vladimir saw Morgan glancing his way, pointing discreetly at her watch. Did she want to leave already? With Vladimir in tow?

Was she not having a good time? No one eloped from a Larry Litvak party before the clock struck three in the morning. It was simply good manners.

"So how's your writing?" Vladimir asked Cohen.

"Pitiful," said Cohen, his big lips quivering characteristically. "I'm too in love with Alexandra to even write about her anymore..."

And there was the crux of the problem—love had come to town and Plank and Cohen had bought time shares in that ever-expanding development. Judging by Cohen's trembling lips and wet eyes, he was already in Phase III, by the lapping pool and the Jack Nicklaus–designed golf course.

"So don't write about her," came a stern, gravelly voice, which Vladimir first imagined might belong to Cohen's grandfather on his Jewish side, arrived in Prava for the approaching high holy days. He looked about for the source until Cohen pointed downward and said, "I'd like you to meet the poet Fish, also from New York."

The poet Fish was not a midget but he brushed by that category with little room to spare. He looked like an unwashed twelve-year-old, and his hair was thick and matted, an overturned bowl of ramen noodles; despite all this he had the voice of Milton Berle. "Charmed," the poet said offering Vladimir his hand as if he expected it to be kissed. "Everyone's talking about Vladimir Girshkin," he said. "It was the first thing I heard at the baggage carousel."

"Stop it!" Vladimir said. To himself he thought: *And what do they say?*

"Fish is staying with Plank for a couple of days," Cohen said. "He's been published by an Alaskan literary journal." And then Cohen turned instantly pale as if he had just seen someone across the room, someone who tugged at his memory in a most inopportune way. Vladimir even followed the dim light of his eyes to see who it might be, but then Cohen simply said: "I've got to go and retch," and the mystery was solved.

"So," Vladimir said, now that Cohen had left the dwarf on his hands (he hoped the little guy at least looked exotic to others). "A poet, huh?"

"Listen here," the poet said, rising on his tippy-toes to breathe into Vladimir's chin. "I heard you got a little something going here, this PravaInvest shit."

"Little?" Vladimir fanned out like a peacock upon sighting his mate-to-be. "We're capitalized with over thirty-five billion U.S. dollars..."

"Yeah, yeah, yeah," said the poet Fish. "I've got a business proposition for you. Ever snorted horse tranquilizer?"

"I beg?"

"Horse tranquilizer. Just how long exactly have you been out of The City?"

Vladimir presumed he meant New York City and was shocked to remember that no matter what they did out here in Prava and Budapest and Cracow, The City—that long grid of blasted streets and no apologies—still remained the bull's-eye of the galaxy. "Two months," he said.

"It's everywhere," Fish said. "In all the clubs. You can't be an artist in New York and not snort the horse. Trust me, I know."

"How's that?"

"It's like a frontal lobotomy. It clears your head out when there's gridlock. You think of nothing. And here's the best part—it lasts only fifteen minutes per snort. After that you're back to doing your thing. Some even report having a renewed sense of self. Of course, that's mainly the prose writers. They'll say anything."

"Are there any side effects?" Vladimir asked.

"None. Let's go out on the balcony. I'll show you."

"Let me think—"

"That's precisely what you don't want to do. Look, I've got this veterinarian near Lyon, he's on the board of a major pharmaceutical there. We can corner the Eastern European market with your Pra-vaInvest. And what's a more likely distribution point than Prava?"

"Yes, well," Vladimir said. "But is it legal?"

"Sure," Fish said.

"Why not?" he added, seeing that the matter was not yet put to rest.

"Well, it helps if you own a horse," he said finally. "I just bought a couple of sickly ones down in Kentucky. Come on already." And he led him out of the room, as Morgan and Alexandra stared from their couch, alarmed at the strange spectacle of PravaInvest's executive vice president following intently on the heels of a leprechaun.

The balcony overlooked the bus terminal, which, despite the majestic glint of the full moon, remained a tortured patchwork of cement and corrugated metal.

And then there were the buses:

From the West came the two-story, deluxe models with television screens flickering and air-conditioners tracing their green exhaust against the asphalt. These would disgorge streams of clean, young backpackers from Frankfurt, Brussels, and Turin, who immediately set to celebrating their newfound East Bloc freedom by showering each other with roadside Uneskos, flashing peace signs to the waiting cabbies.

From the East came the appropriately named IKARUS buses: terminally ill, their low, gray frames shuddering to the finish line; the doors opening slowly and obstinately to let out the tired families from Bratislava and Kosice, or the aging professionals from Sofia and Kishinev who held their briefcases close to their sparkling polyester suits as they made their way to the nearby metro station. And Vladimir could almost smell these briefcases, which, like his father's, likely contained the leftovers of a meaty lunch packed for the road, leftovers that might now serve as dinner—Golden Prava was getting expensive for the average Bulgarian.

But Vladimir's examination of this unhappy dichotomy, a
dichotomy which was in some ways the story of his life, which
brought on feelings of both elation and remorse—the elation of
having a special, privileged knowledge of both East and West, the
remorse of fitting finally into neither—was interrupted by the
stinging, crystal-edged horse powder which the poet Fish administered to him nasally and then

not

much

happened.

Perhaps that's an exaggeration. Something, of course, happened, even while Vladimir withdrew into the upper stories of his
brain where the thin mountain air was not conducive to the cogni-
tive process. The buses kept arriving and departing but now they
were just buses (buses, you know, transport, point A to point B)
and Fish rolling up and down the balcony naked, howling, and
waving his tiny purple penis at the moon was just a young man
with his purple penis, howling. *Nothing much was happening in a
big way.* In fact, nonexistence was no longer so unfathomable (and
how many times had he, as a morose child, shut his eyes and
plugged his ears with cotton, trying to imagine The Void), but
rather a fairly natural progression of this goofy happiness. The
floating, bottomless joy of anesthesia.

And then the fifteen minutes were up and, like clockwork,
Vladimir was noiselessly airlifted into his body; Fish was putting
on his clothes.

Vladimir stood up. He sat down. He got up again. Anything for
sensory experience. He sliced at his fingers with his business card

for a bit, before presenting it to the poet. Very enjoyable. He was ready to plunge into the Tavlata.

"I'll send you a starter kit with instructions," Fish was saying. "And also some of my poetry."

"I have fallen under the influence of John Donne," he added, buttoning up his funky elfin tunic.

"SO, ARE YOU A GOOD PERSON?" MORGAN ASKED.

It was five in the morning. After the party. An island in the middle of the Tavlata, connected to the Lesser Quarter by a single footbridge of uncertain origin; an isle that seemed all but abandoned by Prava's vague municipal services; an overgrown jumble of mammoth trees and the little shrubs that clung to them the way baby elephants rub up against the feet of their mothers. They were sitting on the grass behind a tremendous oak with its boughs fully leafed despite the advance of autumn; this redoubtable old-timer welcomed in the passing seasons at his own discretion. On the other side of the footbridge, high above them, moonlight fell on the spindly buttresses of the castle's cathedral, giving St. Stanislaus the appearance of a giant spider which had somehow scampered over the castle walls and settled in for the night.

The question was whether or not he was a good person.

"I have to preface this by saying I'm drunk," he said.

"I'm drunk, too. Just tell the truth."

The truth. How did it come to this? Just a minute ago he was kissing her alcohol-soaked mouth, feeling under her armpits for the wetness he loved, rubbing himself against her thigh, getting a voyeuristic excitement from the passing beam of his car's headlights—devoted Jan was keeping an eye on them from the embankment.

"Speaking comparatively, I'm a better person than most I know." This was a lie. He had only to think of Cohen to know he was lying. "All right, I'm not a great person per se, but I want to be a good person to you. I've been good to others in the past."

What the hell kind of conversation was this? She was leaning against a rotting log next to some kind of sacrificial heap of used Fanta cans and condom wrappers; her hair was tangled with weeds; there was a lipstick smudge on the tiny, retroussé tip of her nose; and Vladimir's dribble was hanging from her chin.

Was Vladimir a good person? No. But he mistreated others only because the world had mistreated him. Modern justice for the postmorality set.

"You want to be good to me," she was saying, her voice surprisingly steady, even as she drunkenly tipped back and forth from the slightest breeze.

"Yes," Vladimir said. "And I'd like to know you better. Unquestionably."

"You really want to hear about what it was like to grow up in Cleveland? In a suburb? My family? Being the oldest child? The only girl? Um...Basketball camp? Can you fathom a girls' basketball camp, Vladimir? In Medina County, Ohio? What's more, do you even care? Do you want to know why sometimes I'd rather be out camping than in a café? How I hate reading other people's poems just because I have to? And how I hate listening to people all the time like your friend Cohen when he starts going on about his damn Paris in the twenties?"

"Yes," Vladimir said. "I want to know all of it. Absolutely."

"Why?"

It wasn't an easy question. There were no tangible answers. He would have to make something up.

While he was thinking, a brisk wind started and the clouds rolled northward, so that when he lifted his head straight up and ignored the fact that he was at the very epicenter of the city, it was possible to imagine the island afloat and traveling south, navigating the twists and bends of the Tavlata until it finally emerged in the Adriatic Sea. A little more sailing then and they could beach their island ship on the shores of Corfu; frolic amid the rustle of tiny olive trees, the harmonies of the goldfinches. Anything to survive this interrogation.

"Look," Vladimir said. "You hate it when Cohen starts talking Paris and the whole cult of the expatriate. But I have to say: There is something to it. The most beautiful three lines in literature that I've ever read are the very last lines of *Tropic of Cancer*. Now let me lay down the caveats first: By saying what I'm saying, I'm not sanctioning the misogynist, race-baiting Henry Miller as a human being, and continue to cast grave doubts on his abilities as a writer. I am only expressing my admiration for the last few lines of this particular novel... Anyway, Henry Miller is standing by the banks of the Seine, he's been through just about every kind of poverty and humiliation possible. And he writes something like (and excuse me if I'm misquoting): 'The sun is setting. I can feel this river flowing through me—its soil, its changing climate, its ancient past. The hills gently girdle it about: its course is fixed.'"

He wiggled his hand in between her two warm palms. "I don't know if I'm a good person or a bad person," Vladimir said. "Perhaps it's not possible to know. But right now I am the happiest man alive. This river—its soil, its climate, its ancient past—being with you at five in the morning in the middle of this river, in the middle of this city. It makes me feel—"

She pressed his own hand to his mouth. "Stop it," she said. "If you don't want to answer my question, then don't. But it's something I want you to think about. Oh, Vladimir! Listen to you! Not *sanctioning* some poor Henry Miller as a *human being*. I'm not even sure what you mean, but I know it's not pretty..." She turned away from him, and he was left to stare into the stern little bun of her hair.

"Look, I like you," she said suddenly. "I really do. You're smart and sweet and clever, and I think you want to do right by people. You've really brought the community together with *Cagliostro,* you know. You've given a lot of people their first chance. But I feel that...in the long run...that you'll never really let me into your life. I feel that after spending just one day with you. And I wonder if it's because you think I'm just this idiot from Shaker Heights, or whether there's something terrible you don't want me to know."

"I see," Vladimir said. His mind was racing for an answer but there was little he could say that would make her believe him. Maybe, for the first time in a long time, it was best not to say anything.

On the bank opposite the castle, the first touches of dawn were setting light to the gold dome of the National Theater that flared above the black toes of Stalin's Foot like a holy bunion; a tram full of early workers was crossing a nearby bridge with enough rumble to send tremors through their little isle. And just then the wind turned ugly, conspiring with Vladimir's plan to wrap his arms around her. Her silk blouse provided poor traction for his embrace, but he could feel her, infinitely warm and solid and smelling of sweat and spent kisses. "Shh," she whispered, guessing correctly that he was about to speak.

Why couldn't she make this easy for him? Weren't his lies and evasions valid enough? And yet, here she was, Morgan Jenson, a tender but unsettling prospect, reminding Vladimir of someone he used to be before Mr. Rybakov stumbled into his life with news of a world beyond Challah's desperate grasp. A soft and unsurefooted Vladimir, whose mornings were crowned with a double-cured-spicy-soppressata-and-avocado sandwich. Mother's Little Failure. The man on the run.

PART VI

THE TROUBLE
WITH MORGAN

HE HAD NEVER SEEN SUCH STRONG LEGS.

A month had passed since Larry Litvak's party, but those legs—firm white flesh mottled by young blue veins, each thigh a stanza of socialist realism—continued to thrill and beguile young Vladimir. Waking up in Morgan's *panelak* apartment at an ungodly seven in the morning, Vladimir saw the aforementioned legs, thick, muscular, perhaps a bit unfeminine to his unenlightened eyes, and, what was the word, springy? She sprang out of bed on those legs, rushed to the bathroom where she scrubbed and rinsed and prepared herself for a long day's work. These were legs that had been put to the toughest use from early age, and each day of basketball camp had only added to their agility and muscular heft. And now these legs, if the occasion ever warranted, could easily have piggybacked Vladimir across Mount Elbrus.

But instead of Mount Elbrus, the legs we have spoken of, firm like eggplants in a pair of denims and hiking boots, were soon put to use at a Stolovan national park, a basin of green between two rocky cliffs two hundred kilometers to the north of Prava. Surprisingly, the home-loving Vladimir was called upon to accompany her through this wilderness. He had had Jan drop them off at the mouth of the park, and then, with Morgan's sturdy legs supporting a foldup tent tethered to her back, they crossed an interminable vista of underbrush-clogged forest, rills expanding into proper streams capped off with foamy waterfalls, a meadow, which served as the home to an unpredictable deerlike animal that peeked out of the tall grass with its dark liquid eyes. Finally, the sweating, grunting Vladimir, holding onto a walking stick with one hand and carrying a little sack of Chinese apples in the other, found himself on a granite ledge overlooking a minilake where fish, frogs, and dragonflies commuted to and from the various mossy shores. Vladimir breathed in the clean air, felt Kostya's spirit smile approvingly from a nearby tree, and watched Morgan take off her tent-pack and begin to assemble the damn thing.

"Hello, creation!" he shouted, spitting onto a lily pad that bobbed along indifferently. Despite nature's dictatorial regime, its cult of greenness, he had found himself enjoying their two-hour hike, the way the landscape trembled before him, animals scampering, tree branches giving way, and now came the real payoff—a rare chance to be completely alone with his new friend in a queer and beautiful place.

It was about time. They had barely spent one daylight hour together in the weeks following Larry's fête. Just as Vladimir had suspected, Morgan worked as an English teacher. She held a ten-hour-a-day job imparting the language to a mostly proletarian audience in the suburbs, aspirants to Prava's burgeoning service industry who wanted to say, "Here is a clean bath towel," and "Would you like me to call the police now, sir?"

Teaching English was the standard job for those Americans in Prava who didn't have full parental backing, and Morgan went about it in her own methodic way—responsibility *über alles*—ignoring all of Vladimir's attempts to get her to play hooky and spend the day running around with him. Vladimir was sure that all of her male students were in love with her and had asked her out many times for coffee and drinks in the quick-fire, automatic way of European men trying to seduce American women. He was also sure that she would immediately turn red enough to make all but the most incorrigible lotharios reconsider their attack and would say in her slow, tutorial way: "I have boy friend."

HE WATCHED HER DIG her heels into the dry autumn soil and then start to hoist the tent canvas over a pair of sticks. Her legs were never as beautiful to Vladimir as when they were folded over her great big bottom, the way they were at present. He felt the stirrings of excitement and pressed a palm against his groin, when he was distracted by that thing with feathers: bird.

"Hawk!" Vladimir cried as the predator circled overhead, its terrifying beak pointed at his person.

Morgan was banging another stick into the ground with a rock. She wiped her forehead and breathed hot breath down her shirt. "A partridge," she said. "Why don't you help me set this up? You don't like to exert yourself very much, do you? You're sort of a...I don't know how to describe you...A chewer of cud."

"I'm a capital loss," Vladimir confirmed. *A chewer of cud.* That was clever! She was catching on. The Crowd was working its magic.

He held the tent's canvas in place, while she worked the rocks and sticks. He watched over her with quiet admiration, trying to picture a brown-haired girl, pretty but not the prettiest in her sixth grade, squashing mosquitoes against her forehead on a back porch; at her feet, a partly deflated rubber toy lying on its side, a dinosaur from a television cartoon; waterlogged cards on the patio table, slimy to the touch, their reds and yellows running together, a diamond knave without a head; upstairs in the master bedroom the last tremors of an inconsequential fight between Mother and Father about some instance of jealousy, a petty humiliation, or per-

haps just the boredom of this particular life with its summer hot
dogs, pennant championships, lake effect winds, November
democracy, the raising of three children with strong springy legs
and big hands that reached out to touch and comfort, that hoisted
fat little bodies up elm trees to frighten squirrels out of nests,
offered up basketballs to the permanently gray skies, pitched tent
stakes into the ground...

Here Vladimir stopped. What did he know? What could he
know of her childhood? It was poor luck, a sun-blinded stork that
had plucked him down at the Birthing House on Tchaikovsky
Prospekt and not the famed Cleveland Clinic. Ach, the old questions of the beta immigrant: How did one go about changing one's
warbling tongue, one's half-destroyed parents, the very stink of
one's body? Or, more personally: how did *he,* Vladimir, end up
here, a third-rate criminal in the middle of a crisp European forest, watching a tent going up lakeside, a tough, handsome, and yet
entirely unremarkable woman silently building a temporary home
for the both of them?

"Are you getting tired?" he asked her with what he thought was
real affection, holding on to the canvas with one hand and reaching
down to pat her damp hair with the other. She was fussing with a
tent pole, a hook, and another implement, and he was touched by
the sight of a body more plausible than his, the body of a woman
who approached the earth on equal terms; all of her—feet, biceps,
kneecaps, spinal column—all of her serving a purpose, whether
hopping three trams to the far reaches of Prava, miming down the
price of a root vegetable at the Gypsy market, or hacking her way
through straw-colored foliage.

Fran, Challah, Mother, Dr. Girshkin, Mr. Rybakov, Vladimir
Girshkin, each had invested a lifetime into building a refuge from
the world, be it a bed of money, a talking fan, a cordon of books, a
rickety basement *izba,* a shelf of half-empty K-Y jars, a shaky pyra-

mid scheme...But this woman, seen here wielding an awl-type thing over a difficult stake, had nothing in particular to run from. *She was on vacation.* She could have been puffing grass in Thailand, biking through Ghana, or snorkeling above that infernal Barrier Reef, but she happened to be here, bopping along to the cultural beat of a failed empire with her powerful legs and good disposition. And at some point her vacation would be over and she would go home. He would be waving her good-bye from the tarmac.

"I'm almost finished," she said.

She was almost finished, which made Vladimir feel sad, prematurely abandoned, angry, in awe, in love, at a loss—many things that somehow came together and expressed themselves as arousal. Those thick legs again. Denim covered in soil. It was a strange feeling, but oddly natural, elemental. "Good," he said, reaching down to barely touch a warm shoulder. "That's good."

She looked at him. It took her a few seconds to gauge the way he was moving from foot to foot, the frisky eyes, the labored breathing, but then she was instantly embarrassed, a young kind of embarrassment "Oh, boy," she said and looked away, smiling.

They climbed into the perfect little tent and he quickly pressed himself against her, his hands sunk into her natural roundness and he squeezed and he squeezed, gasping for joy, praying he was going to make good with all this squeezing. And then it occurred to him...One word.

Normalcy. What they were doing was inherently normal and right. The tent was a special zone in which desire existed as a normal urge. Here you took off your clothes and your partner did likewise and there would be, hopefully, a great deal of arousal mixed with tenderness. This idea, as clear as the lake glistening outside their tent, scared Vladimir almost to the point of impotence. He squeezed Morgan all the harder and felt dryness in his throat, a sudden need to urinate.

"Hi there," he said awkwardly. This was becoming a favorite phrase. It made him feel romantic in an informal kind of way, like they were already best friends as well as near-strangers about to get naked.

"Hi there," she replied in kind. He mechanically pawed at her chest for a few minutes, while she stroked his neck and quivering throat, lifted up his shiny nylon shirt and squeezed his pale stomach, all the while looking him over with an expression that was, if anything, tolerant, attentive, engaged in the problem of Vladimir Girshkin. In the shallow light of the Stolovan sun suffusing the tent with a tawny yellow, she looked older to him, the flesh on her face raw and kneaded, her eyes narrowing gradually in what could have been a flash of tiredness passing for arousal (Vladimir was keen to interpret it as kindness, even a state of grace). There was a jolt of static when he touched her forehead and she smiled sadly for him, at the way her body was electrically charged against his and whispered "ouch" on his behalf.

The repetitive stroking motion was making her listless. She propped her head up on one hand, brushed some thistles off of Vladimir, assayed the situation, realized she had to take charge, unzipped and removed Vladimir's janitor pants, squeezed out of her own jeans, her freckled, soft skin coloring the air with the earthy aroma of the hiker, and helped Vladimir climb atop of her.

"Hi there," Vladimir said.

She touched his face absentmindedly and looked away. What was she thinking? Only yesterday she had seen Vladimir and Cohen practically horsewhipping that poor Canadian club owner, that unfortunate Harry Green, over some aspect of the nascent Yugoslav war, and now here he was, Vladimir the conqueror, shivering in the tent's autumnal chill, rubbing up against her stomach as if he didn't know quite how to conjoin with a woman, this man who could not put up a tent, who by his own admission could not do much of anything, really, other than talk and laugh and wave his tiny hands and try to be liked by others. She took hold of him and tweaked him with a familiar up-and-down motion, a little rough twist now and again that he seemed to enjoy. He closed his eyes, coughed dramatically, the deep rumble of phlegm echoing through the tent, then issued a kind of moan: "Ma-hum," Vladimir said. "Aaf," he concluded.

"Hi there, strange fellow," she said. It just came out that way, and by her awkward smile Vladimir knew that she immediately wanted to retract it, for she must have felt pity, a halo of sympathy that could also have been a long ray of the voyeuristic sun worming its way between them; but, no, definitely it had been sympathy...Ah, if only he could tell her...Dear Morgan...She had been asking the wrong questions that night in the middle of the Tavlata. He was neither a good or a bad person. The man lying on top of her, goose bumps dotting his chest, little brambles of facial hair pointing in the four major directions, eyes pleading for some sort of release, wet trembling hands cupping her shoulders—this was a wrecked person. How else could someone be so clever and yet so stumped? How else could someone shudder so terribly, so earnestly before an unassuming woman like herself?

He was preparing to address her at length, but just then she lifted him up, took his member off her stomach, guided it where it needed to go. He opened his mouth, and she must have seen bubbles forming at the back of his throat, as if he was struggling to breathe underwater. He stared at her with incredulity. He looked ready to mouth the words "Hi there" one more time. Perhaps to forestall this eventuality, she took hold of his ass and plunged him onward, filling the tent with his happy roar.

27. WHAT IF
TOLSTOY WAS WRONG?

THEY WERE DOING WELL.

Alexandra had taken charge of their relationship from the outset. A kind of free-floating modern yenta, she would call both Vladimir and Morgan every day to make sure everyone's emotional passport was in order. "The situation looks positive," she wrote to Cohen in a confidential communiqué. "Vladimir is increasing Morgan's range of reference, her cynicism is slowly peaking, she no longer looks at the world from a position of middle-American privilege, but at least partly through the eyes of Vladimir, an oppressed immigrant facing systemic barriers to access.

"V, for his part, is learning to appreciate the need for a hands-on dialogue with the physical world. Whether spotted making out with M on the Emanuel Bridge early morning or discreetly patting her down at the premiere of Plank's cinema-verité extravaganza, this is a side of Vladimir we're more than happy to acknowledge! What's next for them, Cohey? Living in sin?"

Morgan's flat certainly had plenty of space for cohabitation, two tiny bedrooms of a sort and one mysterious room, which was sealed up with duct tape and barricaded by a sofa. A picture of Jan Zhopka, the first Stolovan "working-class president" under the communists, hung over the door to the banned room. Zhopka's face, a big purple beet with several functional holes for sniffing out bourgeois sentiment and singing agit-prop ditties, was further insulted by a crudely drawn Hitler-cropped mustache.

Vladimir had always wanted to ask about Morgan's views on the strange times they lived in, the collapse of communism after Reagan's sucker punch in the mid-80s, but he worried her response would be too typical, reactionary, Midwestern. Why put up an anti-Zhopka poster when all the cool kids were going after the World Bank? He decided to ask her about the sealed room instead.

"The roof is leaking something terrible in there," Morgan explained the situation in her informal English. They were on the living-room couch, Morgan sitting on top of him, henlike, trying to keep him warm (like most Russians of a certain class, Vladimir had an unnatural fear of drafts). "The landlord sends this guy over every few weeks to patch things up," she said, "but that room is still a no-go."

"Europa, Europa," Vladimir muttered, shifting Morgan from thigh to thigh to keep her warmth circulating. "Half the continent's under repair. Speaking of, there was some Stolovan guy, a Tomash, I believe, buzzing up yesterday. He kept yelling 'To-mash is here! To-mash is here!' I told him I wasn't interested in any Tomashes, thank you. This neighborhood is full of freaks, by the way. You shouldn't be out here alone. Why don't I get Jan to drive you around?"

"Vlad, listen to me!" Morgan turned around and grabbed him by the ears. "Don't ever let anyone in the apartment! And don't go near that room!"

"Ai, please, not the ears!" Vladimir squealed. "They'll be red for hours. I have to officiate at the Vegan Olympics tonight. What's wrong with you?"

"Promise me!"

"Ai, let go . . . Yes, of course, I won't, I swear. Oh, you big corn-fed animal!"

"Stop calling me that."

"I'm being affectionate. And you *are* bigger than me. And more corn-fed. It's identity—"

"Yes, identity politics," Morgan said. "Anyway, asshole, you told me we'd finally go to your place this weekend. You said you'd finally introduce me to your Russian friends. That guy who called yesterday was so cute and scared. And I've never heard of such an exotic name: *Surok*. Sounds kind of Indian. I looked it up in the dictionary, and I think in Stolovan it means 'mole' or 'marmot' or something. What does it mean in Russian? And when am I going to meet him? And when are you going to take me to your place? Huh, asshole?" She pulled on his nose, but gently.

Vladimir imagined Morgan and the Groundhog breaking bread at the weekly *biznesmenski* lunch, with its customary postprandial discharge of weapons, deflowered Kasino girls going down on the Hog to the tune of ABBA's 'Take a Chance on Me,' Gusev drunkenly railing against the Yid-Masonic global conspiracy.

"It's out of the question," Vladimir said. "There's no hot water in the entire *panelak* until December, the boiler's leaking sulfites, there's airborne hepatitis in the elevator..."

And the whole place is the preserve of armed thieves and bandits mostly drawn from the ranks of the former USSR's toe-crushing, electric shock–happy security organs. "You know, I've got to get out of that place," Vladimir said. "Maybe I should just move in here? We'll save on rent. What do you pay? Fifty dollars a month? We could split it. Twenty-five each. What do you think?"

"Well," Morgan said. "That would be fine, I guess." She plucked a piece of fluff from Vladimir's chest hair, examined it closely, then set it down in her lap where it floated dreamily along the inseam of her jeans. "Except."

Minutes passed. Vladimir prodded her stomach. Theirs was a relationship more silent than most he had known, and it suited him well—a lack of words implying a lack of conflict, the sleepy embraces and mutual gargling in the morning articulating a simpler, working-class kind of love. And yet, there were times when her silence seemed misplaced, when she would stare at Vladimir with the same uncertainty she reserved for her cat, an abused local stray who under Morgan's care had grown to Western proportions and now lived a somber, secret life by the windowsill.

"Except," Vladimir said.

"I'm sorry..." she said. "I—"

"You don't want me to move in with you?" She didn't want Vladimir Girshkin on a dusk-to-dusk basis? She didn't want to teach him how to scrape mold off the shower curtain? She didn't want to grow slow and fat with him, the way other couples did in their *panelaks*? "I'm practically living here as it is," Vladimir whispered, scaring himself with the sadness of his voice.

She rose from her nesting place, exposing Vladimir to the killer drafts. "I've got to go to work," she said.

"It's Saturday," Vladimir protested.

"I've got to tutor that rich guy on the Brezhnevska Embankment."

"What's his name?" Vladimir said. "Another To-mash?"

"I suppose so," she said. "Half the men in this country are named Tomaš. It's kind of an ugly name, don't you think?"

"Yes," Vladimir said, drawing an enormous goosefeather comforter over himself. "Yes, it is. In any language." He watched her change into long underwear. He tried to stay angry at her, but the *thwock* of the underwear's elastic against that round little belly of hers filled him with feelings of longing and domesticity both. Belly. Long underwear. Goosefeather comforter. He yawned and watched Morgan's cat yawn in unison across the room.

He'd have to break into that sealed room some other time, when he wasn't so sleepy. Nobody kept secrets from Vladimir Girshkin. He'd have Jan help him out; Jan loved to smash things in with his shoulder. They were always replacing car windows and such.

And he'd move in with her sooner or later, too. Cohen had shown him Alexandra's confidential report. There was no other way.

AFTER WORK, Vladimir and Morgan would drive into the city and have a kale-and-cabbage lunch at the new Hare Krishna joint, or head for the Nouveau where they drank Turkish coffees and became awake and animated, played footsie to the quick time of Dixieland jazz. But most of the time they spent walking, power-walking, for the November chill was making them brisk. Battling the wind, they would climb to the highest peak of Repin Hill, Prava's loftiest mountain, a green acropolis crying out for a parthenon. At this altitude, the Old Town across the river resembled a garage-sale assortment of bric-a-brac, the powder towers looking like blackened pepper shakers, the Art Nouveau mansions a collection of gilded music boxes.

"It's really something," Morgan once said. "Just look at all those construction cranes by the Kmart. People are going to come here twenty years from now, and they'll never know what it was like when all this happened. They'll have to read your poems or Cohen's poems or Maxine's metaessays…"

Vladimir was not looking at the golden city but rather in the opposite direction, at an ad-hoc sausage stand, a greasy little bratwurst *Imbiß* the locals had quickly set up to feed the hungry Germans. "Sure, it's a special time," he said, eyeing a plump little wurst curling over a slice of rye, "but we must beware the encroachment of…um…you know…the multinationals."

"I feel so remarkably at ease here," Morgan said, ignoring him. "So free of anxiety. There were times in college last year, when I would just stand there in the mailroom and feel this incredible panic.

Just this kind of…unexplained…craziness. Have you ever felt like that, Vladimir?"

"Yes, of course," Vladimir said. He eyed her skeptically. Panic? What could she know of panic? The world lay prostrate at her feet. When one of the big birds, an owl, perhaps, had tried to eat Vladimir in the forest, she had merely to say "Bad!" to the creature in her firm, customer-is-always-right tone, and off it went, hooting miserably into the canopy of trees. Panic? Not likely.

"The blood starts draining from your hands and feet," Morgan was saying, "and then from your head, too, so that you get dizzy. The campus shrink told me it was a classic panic attack. Have you ever seen a shrink, Vlad?"

"Russians are not keen on psychiatry," Vladimir explained. "Life is sad for us and so we must bear it."

"Just asking. Anyway, I would get these panic attacks in the middle of the day, when absolutely nothing was happening. It was strange. I knew I was going to graduate, my grades weren't so bad, I had some pretty cool friends, I was dating this guy, not the brightest, but you know…College."

"Ohio," Vladimir said, trying to create a sense of place for himself. He thought of the progressive Midwestern college he had briefly attended. Nude relay-racing at the workers' solidarity festival, steamy Get to Know You showers at the dorm, the massive spring-break sexual-identity crisis. They had practically invented panic attacks at that college.

"Yes, Ohio," Morgan said. "So what I'm saying is, my life was okay. There was nothing wrong with it. I was doing pretty good with my parents. My mother would drive down from Cleveland and I'd be, you know, just walking her to her car and she would start crying and telling me how lucky I was, how pretty, how perfect. It was kind of sweet, but maybe a little weird, too. Sometimes she'd drive down a hundred and fifty miles to Columbus just to give me a new Nordstrom charge card or a six-pack of soda pop, and then turn around and drive right back home. I don't know. I guess she really missed me. They really fucked up with my brother the year before. Dad sort of press-ganged him into working at the firm one summer and that was just the end...I think he's in Belize now. We haven't heard from him since last Christmas. Almost a year now."

"Mothers," Vladimir said, shaking his head. He reached over to zip up Morgan's jacket against the gathering wind.

"Thanks," Morgan said. "So the shrink would ask me: was I depressed about anything? Was I worried about grades? Was I pre-law? Was I knocked up? And, of course, it was nothing like that...I was just this good kid."

"Hmm." Vladimir was vaguely paying attention now. "What do you think it was?" he asked.

"Well, he told me, basically, that the panic attacks were sort of a cover-up. That what I really felt was this incredible anger and that the panic attacks just prevented me from really lashing out. They were like a warning sign, and if I didn't have them I would do something inappropriate. Maybe, like, vindictive."

"But that's not you at all!" Vladimir said. He was genuinely confused now. "What the hell could you have been lashing out at? Look, I don't know much about the mind, but I know what modernity teaches us: whenever there is some kind of trouble, the parents are usually to blame. But in your case, the mama and the papa sound like perfectly reasonable people." Yes, from what she told him, they lived in a split-level house on South Woodland Boulevard where they raised Morgan and two other Midwestern children besides.

"They sound pretty all right to me too," Morgan said. "They

only really pressured the boys in the family, even though I was the oldest."

"Aha!" Vladimir said. "And your other brother, is he also hiding out in Belize?"

"He's at Indiana. A marketing major."

"Perfect, then! There's absolutely no kind of pattern we can discern here." Vladimir sighed happily. He was getting a little panicky himself. If there was something wrong with Morgan, what hope was there for a Soviet Jew–child like Vladimir Girshkin? She might as well have been saying that Tolstoy was wrong, that all happy families were *not* alike. "Now, Morgan," he said, "these panic attacks, would you say they've gotten better recently or worse?"

"Actually, I haven't had any since I came to Prava."

"I see...I see..." Vladimir clasped his hands together in the manner of Dr. Girshkin contemplating an inquiry from the Department of Health & Human Services. This was a difficult moment in its own right, although it was hard to say why. They were just talking. Two expatriate lovers. No pressure.

"So now let us recall what your psychiatrist said..." Vladimir pressed on. "He said your little panic attacks were some kind of cover-up, that they prevented you from, I believe you said, 'lashing out.' Tell me, since you arrived in Prava, have you been doing anything, hmm, to borrow your words, 'inappropriate' or 'vindictive?'"

Morgan thought about it. She looked out over the mythic skyline of the city and then looked to the bare earth. Another of her silent moments, it seemed, was upon them. She was playing with the zipper of her jacket, reminding Vladimir of the Russian word for zipper, *molnya*, which also meant "lightning." A pretty word. "Have you been lashing out?" Vladimir prompted her again.

"No," she said finally. "No, I haven't." Suddenly, she embraced him, and brushing against his prickly cheek he felt the familiar dime-sized hollow at the tip of her chin, an indentation that Vladimir had somehow perceived as being inherently sexual, but now considered a telling imperfection, a little pothole he could smooth over with his love and analytical bearing.

"There you go, sugar cane," he said, kissing the giant dimple. "So what we've learned today is that your psychiatrist—probably second-rate, anyway; I mean, no offense, but what kind of shrink practices in *Ohio?*—yes, we've learned today that your shrink was completely wrong about everything. The panic attacks did not bottle your anger, did not prevent you from acting irrationally, else how to explain their sudden disappearance here in Prava? Perhaps, if I may infer, what you needed was some fresh air, so to speak, some time away from the family hearth, the alma mater, and— would it be too presumptuous to suggest?—a new love affair? Am I right? Eh? Am I? Of course, I'm right."

He shook all over with the manic feeling of being right. He threw his hands up in the air, hallelujah-style. "Well, thank God for that!" he said. "Thank God! So now we will go celebrate your complete recovery at the Stolovan Wine Archive. Yes, the Blue Room, of course. No, people like us do not need reservations...What a thought! Come on!" He grabbed her arm and started dragging her down Repin Hill where Jan was waiting with the car.

She seemed reluctant at first, as if the transition from amateur psychology to a night getting horribly drunk at the Wine Archive was somehow inappropriate. But Vladimir could think of nothing he wanted to do more. A drink or two! Enough of this talking. Panic attacks. Lashing out. The mind was sovereign. Faced with the most horrible circumstances, it could say: No! I'm in charge here! And what were the horrible circumstances in Morgan's case? A young woman's unease at the prospect of graduating from university? A mother's loneliness for her daughter? A father who wanted the best for his boys? Ach, Americans were too keen to invent their own troubles. To paraphrase an old Russian expression, they were wild with their own fat.

Yes, it was rather disgusting. All through the ride to the Wine Archive, Vladimir was developing a distinct sense of anger toward Morgan. How could she do this to him? He remembered the tent in the forest as if it had happened half a century ago. Normalcy. Arousal. Affection. That was her implicit promise to him. And now this unsettling talk, and now she wasn't letting Vladimir move into her apartment. Well, screw her. Normalcy was on its way. The familiar plush, almost pneumatic banquettes of the Wine Archive would soon be sighing meaningfully under his ass. Grant Green would be strumming along on the stereo. A bottle of port would be brought over by some ponytailed Stolovan. Vladimir would give Morgan a nice brief lecture on how much he loved her. They would go home and sleep together, drunk impotent sex having a charm all its own. It was settled.

But Morgan wasn't through with him yet.

28. AMBUSH
AT BIG TOE

THE STOLOVAN WINE ARCHIVE WAS FOUND RIGHT BY the Foot, in the shadows of the so-called Big Toe. The Toe was the site of daily protests by angry *babushkas* brandishing portraits of Stalin and jerry cans of gasoline, threatening to immolate themselves on the spot if anyone ever tried to knock down the Foot or cancel their beloved Mexican soap opera, *The Rich Also Cry.*

Nu, as far as Vladimir was concerned, the country's senior citizens needed to keep busy, and their discipline and dedication were kind of cute. The self-proclaimed Guardians of the Foot were divided into several divisions. The feistiest grandmas were out in front, waving their high-concept placards ("Zionism = Onanism = AIDS") at the patrons of the Stolovan Wine Archive and the local Hugo Boss outlet, the two institutions that ironically thrived astride the Big Toe. Looking at the *babushkas'* jowly red faces and subtracting some slack and residual anger, one could almost see them as brownnosing young pioneers back in the forties, plying their teachers with potato dumplings and copies of working-class president Jan Zhopka's love poems, *Comrade Jan Looks at the Moon.* Oh, where did the years go, ladies? How did it come to this?

Behind these chanting grandmas, a lesser cadre was assigned the task of caring for the dachshunds of the agitators, and these grannies also performed admirably, spoiling the tiny agit-pups with bottled spring water and bowls of the choicest innards. Finally, in the third and last rank, the artistic *babushka*s were building a giant papier-mâché doll of Margaret Thatcher, which they burned voraciously each Sunday while howling the former Stolovan national anthem, "Our Locomotive Hurtles Forward, Forward into the Future."

NEEDLESS TO SAY, alighting from a chauffeured BMW in front of the Wine Archive was guaranteed to drive these old folks out of their thick, wooly minds, but then Vladimir always enjoyed getting them a little riled up before ascending the stairs to the Blue Room to slurp down oysters and muscadet.

They had made their way through the Old Town in silence, Morgan still playing with her jacket's zipper, rearranging her legs this way and that, rubbing her haunches against the car's sleek Montana leather. Perhaps she was thinking about what she had said up on Repin Hill, all that nonsense about her panic-stricken university days; perhaps she was finally accepting just how much worse Vladimir's life had been than hers. He could certainly tell her some stories; that could be an interesting dinner topic right there. Should he start her off with the Wonders of Soviet Kindergarten or go straight to his Floridian adventures with Jordi? "Triumph over adversity," he would conclude. "That's the story of Vladimir Girshkin, or else he wouldn't be here wiping chutney mayo off that button nose of yours…"

BUT THAT CONVERSATION wasn't to be. Here's what happened instead.

Immediately upon their pulling up to the Archive, the car was

surrounded by grandmas screaming for blood. The *babushkas* were
livelier than usual today, stirred up by the recent change in weather,
the need to keep warm through agitation. Vladimir could make out
a few of their chants, including that old chestnut "Death to the
poststructuralists!" and the crowd-pleasing "Epicures, go home!" It
was remarkable how so many cumbersome words had found a
ready home in the mouths of peasants, how communist slogans
sounded perfectly similar in any Slavic language.

Morgan opened her door. There was a moment of relative calm
as she made her way out of the auto, a moment Vladimir used to
note that Morgan—despite all her absurd talk of panic attacks and
lashing out—was really just a quiet, steady woman in cheap dress
shoes. This realization made Vladimir feel soft-hearted and protective. He was reminded of the Ohio driver's license he had found in
her wallet. Portrait of a high-school girl with a Big Dipper of acne
arching across the nose, a teenager's gloomy hue, shoulders hunched
over to conceal the embarrassing contents of a baggy suburban
sweatshirt. He felt a new font of tenderness opening up for her. "Let's
go home, Morgan," he wanted to say. "You look so tired. Let's get you
some sleep. Let's forget all this."

It was too late.

Just as Vladimir slammed the car door behind them, one of the
grandmas, the tallest of the Foot Guardians, a long, canine face, a
tuft of chin hair, a red medal the size of a discus around her neck,
shouldered her way past her colleagues, cleared her throat, and spit
the warm results at Morgan, the sizeable spew floating right past
her shoulder to land on the Beamer's tinted window.

A gasp of amazement. A German auto worth two million
crowns had been so cleverly defaced! The counterrevolution had
begun in earnest! History, that slut, was finally on their side. The
Guardians of the Foot stood up on their toes, the hero-invalids

leaning forward on their crutches. "Speak, Baba Véra!" the crowd encouraged the spitter. "Speak, lamb of Lenin!"

The Red Lamb spoke. She said but one word. An entirely unexpected, uncalled-for, and decidedly uncommunist word. "Morgan," Baba Véra said, the English name coming off her tongue rather naturally, both syllables intact. More. Gahn.

"Morgan *na gulag!*" another old woman shouted.

"Morgan *na gulag!* Morgan *na gulag!*" the rest of the grannies picked up the war cry. They were jumping now like youngsters on a May Day float—oh, happy days!—spitting freely at the car, tearing at their sparse hair, waving around their spiffy woolen caps, all except for one sad-eyed, bedraggled *babushka* who was quietly trying to sell Vladimir a sweater.

What the hell was this? What were they saying? Morgan to the Gulag? It couldn't be. There must have been a terrible misunderstanding. "Comrade Pensioners!" Vladimir started to say in Russian. "On behalf of the fraternal Soviet people…"

Morgan pushed him back.

"Stay out of this," she said.

"Sugar cane," Vladimir mumbled. He had never seen her like this. Those dead gray eyes!

"This isn't about you," she said.

Everything was about him. He was the king of Prava, and she was, by extension, its denim-clad queen. "I think," Vladimir said, "I think we should go home and rent—"

But there would be no Kurosawa tonight. In a flash of bared teeth, Morgan had turned on her tormentors. It all happened so fast. The tongue was pressed firmly against the upper palate…The letter *R* was thoroughly trilled…There followed several frothy explosions in the guise of *Č, Š,* and *Ž*…

The grandmothers pulled back in horror.

It was as if some devil, some kind of Slavic devil with a horrible American accent, was speaking through Morgan. "Shaker Heights," Vladimir whispered, trying to console himself with geography. *South Woodland Boulevard.*

But he was thinking of someone else, another Morgan, because in place of that warm, nature-loving creature, a far-fetched, worldly one was now shouting at the grandmothers in remarkably fluent Stolovan, dropping the word "polemical" as easily as the real Morgan drove tent stakes into the topsoil.

"*Š mertí k nogù!*" the sham Morgan was hollering, her face twisted into unlikely anger, a white-knuckled fist raised in solidarity with some mysterious non-Ohioan life-force. *Death to the Foot!*

"Eh," Vladimir said, instinctively making his way back to the car.

Meanwhile, Baba Véra, all bad teeth and vitriol, her red Medal of Socialist Labor flapping in the wind, had come snout-to-snout with Morgan and was conveying any number of sentiments Vladimir could not quite make out. The name Tomaš kept coming up and Vladimir assumed *blyat'* meant "whore" in Stolovan as well as in his native tongue.

"Morgan!" Vladimir shouted in exasperation. He was on the verge of asking Jan to start up the Beamer and spirit him away to the Joy or the Repré, someplace full of velvety throw cushions and fuzzy expats, someplace where the entropy factor was nil and everything was primed to go Vladimir's way.

Because, to be honest, he could no longer abide this impostor who spoke an obscure Eastern European language, who dueled communist grannies to the death over a hundred-meter galosh, who maintained (sexual?) relations with some mysterious Tomaš, who kept a sealed, secret room in her *panelak* apartment, and whose life clearly extended beyond dating Vladimir and teaching English to hotel clerks.

"Morgan!" he cried once more, this time without any conviction.

And then, just as Morgan was turning to face her befuddled Vladimir, Baba Véra ambled up and pushed her with one gnarled paw.

Morgan stumbled back a little, there was a moment when her balance seemed lost, but in the end those strong twenty-three-year-old legs kept her aloft. The next thing Vladimir realized was that Jan had somehow made his way between Morgan and the old woman. There was the sound of hard against soft. A shriek. Vladimir's eyes did not react as quickly as his ears. It took him some time to register the situation on the ground.

Baba Véra was on her knees.

There was a collective rumble of disbelief.

A shiny black object.

Baba Véra touched her forehead. There was no blood. Just a circle of red, a smaller version of the medal cradled between her breasts.

The Guardians of the Foot were wordlessly backing away from their fallen comrade. The wiener-dogs were yapping their tiny lungs out.

Jan lifted up the shiny black object in his hand as if to strike her again, but Baba Véra was too dazed to even flinch. "Jan!" Vladimir said. He could only think of his own grandmother tying a red handkerchief around his neck, feeding him a prized Cuban banana for breakfast. "Jan, no!"

Jan had hit her with his radar detector.

IN THE NEXT MINUTE OR SO, the earth continued to revolve around the sun. Jan continued to tower over the toppled grandmother. Baba Véra continued to kneel before him. Vladimir continued to retreat to the safety of the BMW, although his car was now lost in a different, non-Bavarian dimension. And Morgan...Morgan was standing there, chin up, fists curled, nursing her vast and incomprehensible grudge, momentarily silent but ready for more.

They were all bound up now in a single gesture.

A FEW MINUTES LATER Vladimir was dismally eating his oysters, Morgan helping herself to a large pitcher of lukewarm sangria. Vladimir's personal table was located beneath the Blue Room's skylight, so that when he looked up he could see a billowy coal cloud settling over the Foot like a flared trouser. It was uncanny: The damned Foot was determined to follow him wherever he went. He felt like one of those blighted rural folk who keep imagining black U.N. helicopters chasing them during their interminable possum hunts.

The maître d', a slick, modern man of Vladimir's age, kept coming by the table to apologize to Morgan and Vladimir "on behalf of all the young Stolovans." It was he who had ended the showdown at Big Toe, sprinting out of the Wine Archive with a knotted rope and quickly lashing the grandmas into a panicked retreat. "Ah, the old … The old are our misfortune," he said, shaking his head, pausing to check the mobile phone holstered to his belt. "Dear grandmothers! It is not enough that they stole our childhood. Not enough for them … Only the whip they understand."

Soon a complimentary roast boar was placed between Vladimir and Morgan, but the disturbed Vladimir spent the entrée portion of the meal picking at his laminated teeth, leaving the little pig-carcass to slowly suffocate in juniper oil and truffle foam. He was trying to modulate his anger, guide it toward the realm of sadness, wondering how much of an outburst he could get away with within the dignified sanctum of the Blue Room.

Only by dessert time, when their deep silence had become more uncomfortable, did Vladimir open his mouth, did he ask her what it meant: *Morgan to the Gulag?*

She spoke without looking at him. She spoke in a begrudging tone not terribly different from the tone she employed with the Guardians of the Foot. She spoke in the guise of the Other Morgan, the Morgan who evidently found Vladimir untrustworthy, unsympathetic, or, worse yet, positively irrelevant. Here is what she told Vladimir: She told him that she had a Stolovan friend, his parents jailed under the old regime, his grandparents executed in the early fifties. Once her good friend had taken her to the Foot, and they had a terrible fight with the grandmothers. The *babushkas* had been itching to purge her ever since.

Was her friend named Tomaš, perchance?

She answered his question with more questions: Was Vladimir implying she could not have friends of her own? Did she need his approval now? Or was she obliged to spend all her time listening to Cohen and Plank whine about their fat little lives?

Vladimir opened his mouth. She was right, of course, but nonetheless he found himself oddly protective of the Crowd. At least a soft and rudderless fellow like Cohen was not capable of betrayal. Cohen was Cohen and nothing more. He had mastered the American art of being entirely himself. And speaking of betrayal, *where did she learn such flawless Stolovan?*

She allowed herself a tiny victorious smile and informed him that she had taken many classes in Stolovan at that polyglot Ohio university of hers. Was Vladimir surprised that she could master a foreign language? Did he have a monopoly on being foreign? Did he think her an idiot?

Vladimir shuddered. *No, no. It was nothing like that. He was just asking…*

But what Vladimir was doing was this: He was losing her. He

was groveling for her reassurance in a scorned lover's voice. The familiar aphorism "in love there is always someone kissing and someone being kissed" came to mind.

Yes, he imagined it was all over. It was time to forget the holy trinity of Arousal, Affection, and Normalcy, to forget their little sojourn in the tent, the way she had brushed the thistles off his person, unzipped his janitor pants, hoisted him atop of her, pushed him forward. To forget the way she had handled his weaknesses, with kindness and complicity both.

Instead, he was left now to mull over a new word, a word that practically annulled the past three months with this woman. The word was "distance," and as he stirred his espresso and poked at his pear strudel, he was thinking of ways to use it in a sentence. *I'm becoming increasingly aware of a distance*... No, that wouldn't do.

There's a distance between us, Morgan.

Yes, there certainly was. But even that was an understatement.

And finally it came to him. The words he couldn't say.

Who are you, Morgan Jenson? Because I think I've made a mistake.

Yes. Right. Once again. On a different continent, but with the same blind, stupid vigor, with the same debilitating faith of the Jew-walking beta immigrant.

A mistake.

BEFORE THINGS GOT BETTER, THEY HAD TO GET WORSE.
The day after the debacle with the Foot, it was time for an evening
of pain and uncertainty, the long-awaited *Night of Men*—Plank,
Cohen, and Vladimir out on the town with their Y chromosomes,
facial stubble, and early 90s white-male ennui in tow. Looking for
beer.

In truth, Vladimir was not averse to this manly endeavor. After
the previous night of kissing and not being kissed, he wanted,
once more, to embrace whatever embraced him back, and at this
point the Crowd was it; the last bastion of no surprises. That
morning, however, there had been a sign of hope on the Morgan
front. After flossing and gargling for work, she had come over to
Vladimir (he was sitting glumly in the bathtub sprinkling his chest
with soapy water) and kissed his tiny bald spot, whispering "Sorry
about last night," and helping him rub his daily dose of minoxidil
into the bare bull's-eye of his crown. Vladimir, shocked by her
unexpected affection, squeezed her thigh a little, even pulled, in a
desultory way, a clump of pubic hair peeking out of her robe, but
said not a word in response. It wasn't time for that yet. Sorry,
indeed.

———

AS FOR THE NIGHT OF MEN, the chosen venue, a bar, was Jan's suggestion and a good one. As Stolovan as the New, Improved & Euro-Ready Prava could get in those days, with tables of thin, pimpled conscripts and off-duty police officers accounting for most of the patronage. All were still in uniform, swilling good beer poured from a row of spouting taps, which had been so well trained in the art of dispensation that even in the "off" position they continued to gush. There was no decor, only walls, a roof, and a minimal outdoor garden where folding chairs were scattered about, creaking under the weight of the military and security organs that occupied them. A plastic statue of a pink flamingo brought back by "the first modern Stolovan to visit Florida," according to the barmaid, stood watch on one leg over the clinking of mugs, and the cheerful trading of insults.

Cohen and Plank at first seemed uneasy about the local scene. Vladimir could see them clutching their American Express cards inside their trouser pockets as if they feared being eaten alive by the natives after failing to cover the tab. An understandable fear, as the soldiers looked hungry and the kitchen was closed. But as the tab built, the boys let their shoulders stoop and took their unused hand—the one not handling the mug—out of their pockets, setting it on the bar next to the beer where it tapped along to Michael Jackson's entire oeuvre as it unfolded from the sound system. He still sounded good after all those years, that strange bird.

On their own they didn't get past some perfunctory grunts, and "Boy, this beer is good," but then the conscripts next to them, a Jan and a Voichek, started passing around German pornography and practicing their English. Quickly the nude women got to Cohen and Plank; they sighed in unison each time a page was turned by the leering Jan or his giggling, younger companion. "She looks just

like Alexandra," they said, and then tried to explain to the conscripts in a combination of English, Stolovan, and Masculinity, that
they knew a woman just as gorgeous and desirable as the one on
display. Jan and Voichek were greatly impressed.

"Like this?" they said, pointing at breasts and labias and then
looking back awed at the Americans who, at least in the female
company they kept, still seemed the citizens of a great world power.

What amazed Vladimir, who contributed little to the conversation beyond some simulated slobber, was that the German
Valkyries in the magazine did not resemble Alexandra in the slightest. The models were blond and impossibly tall, with legs spread
out like pincers to expose the uniformly hairless run of pink held
open by several fingers. Alexandra, while not short or heavy, was
hardly towering, or blond, or paper-thin. Her Portuguese fore-
mothers had bequeathed her a healthy Mediterranean fullness of
hips, lips, and breasts. The only criteria satisfied by both her and the
women in the magazine was that they were all desirable.

For Plank and Cohen that was enough. Anything would have
been enough to get them hot and upset. Soon the particulars of
Plank's and Cohen's malaise dawned on the conscripts and they
excused themselves claiming they had to go pick up their girlfriends "for the prophylactic work."

"Okay, gents," Vladimir said, when standard English had
returned to their corner of the bar. "Another round, what do you
say?"

Grunts of approval as enthusiastic as the lowing of cows.

"All right," Vladimir said. "Look, I have a thing for Alexandra
too."

Happy amazement. Him too! A universal dilemma! "But what
about Morgan?" Plank asked, scratching at his enormous shaved
head.

Vladimir shrugged. What about Morgan? Could he unbosom

himself to the boys? No, it was out of the question. They were too fragile and set in their ways. The news of Morgan's double life could easily give each a stroke.

"It is possible to love two women," Vladimir declared in answer to Plank's question. "Especially when you only sleep with one of them."

"Yes, I believe that's right," said the scholarly Cohen, as if these laws were codified and available for perusal at the Rimbaud Institute of Desire. "Although sooner or later things start to fall apart."

Vladimir ignored that, pressing on like a concerned den mother: "What you boys need is to chase after someone else. And I mean really chase and not just wait and mope." There was laughter. "I'm serious. Look at the position you find yourself in: You're on top of the world here. You're more respected than you'll ever be…"

He hadn't meant it quite so truthfully. "You're more respected in the context of being young and not yet aware of the full range of your artistic proclivities," he clarified, although it was not necessary. They knew they were great. "You can have just about anyone you want in this town!" he shouted.

"Just about," Cohen said, sadly chewing on his beer.

"I hear you, brother," Plank mumbled to Cohen.

The boys tried to smile and shrug good-naturedly, as senior citizens from the Old World are bound to do when informed that their daily meal of fondue and blood sausages can have repercussions.

Vladimir, for one, was prepared to spend the whole evening hammering in his message and draining the prodigious taps. Unbeknownst to him, however, there were rumors, broadcast to the whole neighborhood by patrons staggering home, of a group of strangely dressed American dandies loitering in the local watering hole, and these rumors soon yielded a visitor.

———

HE WAS A RATHER STRIKING STOLOVAN—tall and built, it would seem, from the same millennial bricks that had gone into the Emanuel Bridge. The hair was cropped short and adorned with a cowlick, as was the emerging fashion in Western capitals; and the clothes, a gray turtleneck and a vest of black corduroy, were also close to the latest style. Not to mention that he was in his early forties and men of that age group could be given some leeway as far as their wardrobes were concerned; that is to say, points could be given for effort alone.

"Hello, dear guests," he said in an accent so slight it approximated Vladimir's. "Your glasses are almost empty. Permit me!" He shouted orders to the barmaid. The glasses were filled.

"My name is František," he said, "and I am a longtime citizen of this city and this neighborhood. Now allow me to guess where you're from. I have a natural gift for geography. Detroit?"

He was not completely wrong. Plank, as has been established before, was indeed from a suburb of the Motor City. "But what about me says Detroit?" the dog-breeder wanted to know with outright indignation.

"I notice your height, lankiness, and complexion," František said, unhurriedly sipping his beer. "I deduce from these attributes that your ancestry is of this part of the world. Not exactly Stolovan, but are you, by chance, Moravian?"

"Partly, I believe," Plank said. "I like to think of myself as more of a Bohemian."

This joke went unappreciated. František continued: "So I think of parts of the States with big concentrations of Eastern Europeans and immediately I think of big Midwestern cities, but, for some reason, not Chicago when I look at you. So…Detroit."

"Very good," Vladimir said, already trying to draw a map of their new acquaintance's social complexion to better account for his remarkable sagacity. "But, in my case, as you can plainly see,"

Vladimir said, "my ancestry is not of this part of the world, and hence, it is unlikely that I am from Detroit."

"Yes, perhaps you are not from Detroit," František said, keeping his good form. "But, unless I am a complete fool, which is surely possible, I do believe that your ancestry *is* from this part of the world, because you look to me a Jew!"

Cohen bristled at the use of the last word, but František continued: "And furthermore, your accent says to me that it was *you* and not your ancestors that left this part of the world or, to be more precise, Russia or the Ukraine, for sadly we don't have any Jews left here except in the cemeteries where they're stacked ten to a grave. So, then, New York is where you resettled, and your father's either a doctor or an engineer; and by the looks of your goatee and long hair you are an artist or, more likely, a writer; and your parents are aghast, because they do not consider it a profession; and university is so expensive in the States, but still it is doubtful they would have settled for anything but the most expensive college, since you are likely the only child; obviously so, since most cosmopolitan Muscovites or Petersburgers (is that where you're from?) have one child, at most, two, in an effort to concentrate meager resources."

"You are a professor," said Vladimir, "or else a traveler and voracious reader of periodicals." He was not surprised to find himself easily replicating the voice and tone of the Stolovan. He was that infectious.

"Well," said František. "I am not a professor. No."

"Fine then," said Cohen, seemingly satisfied that the man was not an anti-Semite. "I'll get the next beers if you entertain us with the story of your life."

"You get the beers and I will buy shots of vodka," recommended František. "They complement each other perfectly. You will see."

So it was done this way, and while the vodka did not go down smoothly at first, the gentle American palate soon adapted, or rather, was bypassed, as inebriation set in. Meanwhile, the Stolovan gentleman related his story with great cheer—it was obvious he relished the opportunity to tell it to young, devil-may-care Americans; older Americans, particularly those not schooled in modern irony, might have been less amused.

As a youth, the handsome František studied at the faculty of linguistics and was a star pupil, as could be expected. This was almost half a decade after the Soviet invasion of 1969, when so-called normalization had set in nicely and Brezhnev was still waving at tractors from atop the mausoleum.

František's father was big at the Interior Ministry, the kind of chipper place where faceless and hairless bureaucrats sent helicopters to hover meters over the open graves of dissidents during their funerals. František's father was particularly fond of that maneuver. His son, however, had picked up some sense of moral disquietude here or there, most likely at the university, where such things generally lurk. But it was a quiet sense of disquietude, in that while František refused a fast-track career at the Interior Ministry, he nonetheless could not bring himself to sneak around with samizdat pamphlets, attend clandestine meetings in sulfur-smelling basements, or to be reduced to a job as, say, an attendant at a municipal water-closet—the basics of dissident activity.

Instead, he got himself a job as assistant deputy editor of the regime's favorite newspaper, the appropriately named *Red Justice*. There were quite a few assistant deputies, but no matter. František with his talent, towering good looks, and a father in the Interior Ministry soon wangled for himself the enviable position of covering "culture," which meant traveling abroad on the heels of the Stolovan Philharmonic, the opera, the ballet, and any art exhibits that made it out of Mayakovsky Airport.

Abroad! "My life revolved around the export calendars of Prava's better institutions," František said, turning to stare wistfully in the direction of what used to be the free world, or so one would imagine. "And sometimes even the provinces coughed up something worth sending to London, although [sigh] more often to Moscow or, God forbid, Bucharest."

František loved the West like the mistress one gets to see only after her mindful husband gets sent to balance the books in the Milwaukee office. He loved Paris especially, a not-uncommon love affair for Stolovans, whose early-twentieth-century artists had consistently looked to Gaul for inspiration. Once free of the silly commitments at the local embassy and the actual performances, he would roam freely without particular destination in mind, exchanging taxis for the metro, aimless rambles along the Seine for getting totaled in the Montparnasse, all while avoiding the significant Stolovan expatriate community that would likely roast him up along with their carp and dumplings.

But with actual Westerners he was a big success. After the Soviet invasion there was no shortage of sympathy for "a young, oppressed Stolovan, let out for just a glimpse of freedom, only to be corralled back into his Stalinist pen." And when the lithe French women begged, and indignant British chaps demanded that he defect, he would wipe his tears and tell them about his mama and papa, the hard-pressed, sooted chimney cleaners, who would surely spend their remaining years in the gulag if he missed his two o'clock flight.

"If you read writers like Hrabal or Kundera," František said, while toasting wordlessly in conjunction with a newly arrived round of Polish Wybornaya, "you will see that sex is not unimportant for the East European man." And then he went into some of this sex that took place in Hempstead Tudors and TriBeCa lofts; and just looking at this healthy, wide-faced buck one could picture him, without too many acrobatics of the imagination, with almost any woman and in nearly any position, but always sporting the

THE RUSSIAN DEBUTANTE'S HANDBOOK

same enthralled and determined expression, his body properly soaked and bruised.

Here Plank and Cohen descended into reverie, staring happily into the depths of their shot glasses as František enumerated his assignations. Vladimir was pleased that they took all this in with a sense of healthy wonderment. Perhaps they weren't imposing the Alexandra template—the way they had done with the ludicrous German pornography—on Cherice the political activist and Marta the performance artist who had both shared a room in Amsterdam's Jordaan district only to share František during the world tour of the Prava Children's Puppet Theater. Who knew what accounted for their budding interest: perhaps Vladimir's earlier pep talk, or the beer mixed with vodka, or the charm of the former apparatchik gushing over his international delights with, still, a sense of boundless possibility?

But, of course, the cultural beat wasn't all Dutch tulips and Godiva. There was also the domestic front, and they watched František take an extended swill of beer in preparation for this portion. "Oh, how they would come," he said. "From every region of every district of every goddamn Slavic country... 'Citizens, now we are pleased to present the Stavropol Krai Peasant Chorus!' All the bloody peasant choruses! All those fucking balalaikas! And always singing about some Katyusha picking boysenberries on the river bank and then the local boys spot her and make her blush. I mean, really! Try writing a review of *that* minus the cynicism. 'At the Palace of Culture last night, our socialist brethren from Minsk demonstrated once again the progressive peasant culture that has kept local ethnographers enthralled since the heady days of the Revolution.'"

He reached into his shot glass and sprinkled some vodka in his face. "What can I tell you," he said, squinting. "That was the hell of it, but then it all fell apart anyway..."

"No more *Red Justice*?" Vladimir asked.

"Oh, no, it's still there," František said. "Some of the older people still read it. The ones on a fixed income who can't afford sausages and are getting really pissed on that score, the so-called Guardians of the Foot, you might have heard them wailing by the Big Toe. Yes, they pay me to write something now and then. Or I give a speech on the cultural-glory days of Brezhnev and our first working-class president Jan Zhopka for the geezers at the Great Hall of People's Friendship. You know, that huge place with the old socialist flag hanging out the window like somebody's dirty laundry."

"Where is that again?" Vladimir asked. "It sounds familiar."

"It's on the embankment facing the castle, right by the most expensive restaurant in Prava."

"Yes, I've been to that restaurant," Vladimir said, coloring at the thought of his Cole Porter revue with the Groundhog.

"But it's not fair," Plank said. "You're so bright and well-traveled. You should write for one of the new papers."

"I'm afraid that's impossible. After our most recent revolution they published a lengthy directory of who did what during the lost years, and it would seem that my family has a whole chapter devoted to it."

"Maybe you could write for the *Prava-dence,*" suggested Cohen.

"Oh, but it's such crap," František said. (Thankfully Cohen was too pickled to take umbrage.)

"What I really want to do is open a nightclub," he said.

"That's a wonderful idea," cried Plank. "Sometimes the night life here really rubs me the wrong way." He stopped. "Excuse me," he said. "I don't feel good."

They let him pass by without much concern. "Yes," František said. "Your weak-stomached friend is right. Right now there's only ABBA here. ABBA and some very poor attempts at modernity. When I was..." Again he looked wistfully in some unspecified direction, perhaps this time of the airport. "When I was traveling around, you know, I always got taken to the latest discos with the most attractive men and women, such as yourselves, of course. Now my mouth waters for a good, what is it now?..."

"Rave," Cohen said helpfully.

"A good rave. Ah, I even know a terrific Finnish disk jockey. MC Paavo. Have you heard of him? No? He's successful in Helsinki, but not very happy there. Too clean, he says, although I don't know, I've never been."

"He should come here!" Cohen said, smashing his shot glass against the bar. Vladimir quickly dropped a hundred-crown note for the damage.

"I think he'd like to, but he needs a sure thing, a contract. He's got the needy former wives and then also the little MCs running around in the Laplands. The Finns are very familial, which is why perhaps they enjoy the world's highest rate of suicide." He chuckled and signaled for another round, pointing to Plank's empty stool and shaking his finger as if to say, "minus one."

"Well, did you know that Vladimir is the vice president of PravaInvest?"

"Um," Vladimir said.

"There's actually something called PravaInvest?" The Stolovan contained his mischievous smile, but clearly with effort and a lot of blinking. "Do post me a prospectus immediately, gentlemen."

"Oh yes!" Cohen said, oblivious to the apparatchik's sarcastic tone. "PravaInvest is gargantuan. I understand it's capitalized with over 35 billion dollars."

František looked at Vladimir long and straight as if to say, "One of *those*, eh?"

"Um," Vladimir said again. "It's no big deal, really."

"Well, don't you see?" Cohen was exasperated. "He'll fund your nightclub! Just bring over the Finn and we're set."

Vladimir sighed at the rashness of his young associate. "Of course, nothing's that easy," he said. "In the real world there are impediments. The skyrocketing price of real estate in central Prava, for example."

"That I wouldn't count as a problem," František said. "See, if you opened it up in the town center you would get basically the rich German tourists. But if you operate on the city outskirts and at the same time you're convenient to public transportation or a short taxi ride from the center, then you get a more exclusive, sophisticated clientele. I mean, how many truly trendy clubs are there on the Champs-Élysées? Or on Fifth Avenue in Midtown? It's just not done."

"He's right! He's right!" said the irrepressible Cohen. "Why don't you just invest in this thing, hmm? Come on, do us all a favor. You know there's no fun left at the Nouveau or the Joy on a Saturday with all those fucking papa's girls and mama's boys and that shit they play…That shit! How can they play that shit and still charge you fifteen crowns for admission?"

"That's fifty cents," Vladimir reminded him.

"Well, be that as it may," Cohen said, now talking almost exclusively to František, the way a child turns to one parent after being refused by the other, "but that's still no reason not to start this thing, especially with MC Pavel on board."

Vladimir lifted his beer up to his twitching face. "Yes, but you see, Mr. František, PravaInvest is a very concerned, socially aware multinational. Its philosophy is to concentrate on essential needs based on a country's conditions on the ground, in a Cartesian sense, of course, at what we call 'point of entry.' And, believe me, this country needs a good locally produced fax modem more than it needs another dance club or casino."

"I don't know about that," František said. "Maybe not casinos, which are, on the whole, quite desperate places, but a nice, new dance club could be, how is it they say in America…A 'morale booster'?"

Perhaps it was František's accent returning after so much alcohol, the way Vladimir's was prone to do, but when their new Stolovan friend said "casino," Vladimir could picture it only with a *K*, which led him naturally to the Kasino in his *panelak,* and, by extension, to the friendly Russian women who entertained there, and by the furthest of extensions, to the tremendous waste of potential space therein. A nightclub.

He accepted yet another shot from the barmaid who, in the poor light and the long-settled darkness, wore an expression that couldn't be gauged; it could only be surmised that she spoke with expressiveness about something. "This round is free," František translated, smiling with pride at the generosity of his countrywoman.

"Morale booster," Vladimir said after the vodka had gone down and burned his insides with the compressed fury of the thousand Polish potato fields that had been depotatoed to produce this vintage. "So how good is this MC Paavo when compared to what they have in London and New York?"

"He's better than Tokyo," František said with the surety of a connoisseur and tipped his bar stool toward Vladimir so that their eyes, red and moist from the festivities, were as close as etiquette allowed. "I like the way you talk, Mr. Conditions-on-the-Ground," he said. "And I know about your little business with Harry Green. Perhaps we should meet and discuss further possibilities."

Meanwhile, the stereo was running out of Michael Jackson. Outside, in the frigid air and by the light of the moon, the soldiers were singing some sort of a local song with an oom-pah-pah beat that clearly could have benefited from the deployment of an actual band. Plank could be heard producing unsettling sounds in the bathroom. "Ah," František said, moving away from Vladimir slightly, as he knew that Westerners did not like to share breath.

"Speaking of peasant choruses, there's one. It's about a little mare who is very upset at her master because he sent her to the smith to get cobbled. And now she refuses to give him a kiss."

Cohen nodded to Vladimir, his eyes narrow with understanding, as if there was a lesson in there for everyone. They heard Plank struggling with the lock of the bathroom and cursing himself, but they sat drunk and motionless, until the barmaid came to his rescue.

HOW IT HAPPENED THAT THEY MISSED JAN AND THE car was for Vladimir a bitter lesson in the downside of alcoholism. Apparently he and Cohen had stumbled into the beer garden and there took the wrong pathway out; that is, instead of walking into Jan and the car they walked into a silent, charcoal-stained street whose silence was broken by the jangle of a tram bell and the screech of rails. "Ah!" they cried, mistaking the passing tram for some kind of heavenly sign, and they staggered after it, waving their arms as if they were bidding adieu to an ocean liner. Soon enough, the yellow-lighted warmth drew closer, and they climbed aboard on all fours, shouting *"Dobry den'!"* to the dusty factory workers snoozing in the back.

It was only after they had gone several neighborhoods down toward somewhere or other that Vladimir remembered Jan and the BMW. "Oh," he said, butting Cohen in the side, in response to which Cohen took out a sparkling bottle of vodka. This was a gift František had given them along with his phone and fax numbers before he departed the beer garden, dragging the incapacitated Plank along to a nearby pad for a refresher course in sobriety. Vladimir had been unsure about the last part. He held a tainted view of visiting older men and their sleeping quarters, especially when the whole scene had been stirred with alcohol. But what to do?

"Ve drink," Cohen said, failing at a Russian accent.

"We're drunk," Vladimir said, uncapping the bottle nonetheless. "Where are we?" he said, pressing his nose to the cool window pane, watching the drooping lindens, the small apartment houses peeking out from behind manicured hedges. "What the hell are we doing here?"

They turned to look at one another. It was a serious question at three in the morning and they tussled for the bottle in exasperation, a struggle which, for the sake of clarification, was not conducted with the energy of, say, two farm boys just coming into their pubescent strength.

The tram had crossed the river and had started mountain-climbing. They had barely reached the middle plateau of Repin Hill, where the Austrians were building a family entertainment complex around a cartoon character named Günter Goose, when the tram suddenly shuddered to a halt.

Outside the tram window, two heads bobbed in the night, their scalps as white as the moon, the few randomly sprouting hairs passable for the outlines of craters and other such lunar geography. Two skinheads, their relative height and size forming approximately the ratio between Abbott and Costello, got on board, their many chains jangling against their belt buckles, which were replicas of Confederate flags. They were laughing and pretending to punch each other, managing in the interim of their playfulness to swig from bottles of Becherovka liquor, so that Vladimir first assumed they were Stolovan gays who had mistaken the Confederate flag for just another symbol of Americana. After all, the bald look had long become de rigueur on Christopher Street.

But when they saw Vladimir and then turned to Cohen, the laughter stopped. Two pairs of fists appeared, and in the overabundant light of the tram their naked scalps, acne, battle scars, and twitching sneers formed a distinct roadmap of adolescent hatred.

There was a crash against the window to Vladimir's right and immediately there was alcohol in his eyes, shards of glass stinging against his skin like so many little shaving accidents, and the unmistakable smell of the pumpkin liquor; the short, fat one must have thrown his bottle. Vladimir couldn't open his eyes. When he tried, there was only the muddled indistinction of eyedrops just applied and, anyway, he really didn't want to see. In the darkness, an amorphous series of thoughts were coalescing around the concepts of pain, injustice, and revenge but what it all came down to was the therapeutic qualities of his grandmother's coarse, old Russian pillow—hard, but yielding—on which he had first practiced his amorous ways. That was the thought of the moment. With the instinctual, life-affirming panic submerged in vodka and Unesko beer, only the sadness concerning the impending loss of life and limb—this sadness that should have emerged only as an afterthought—rose to the surface. It had to have been so, because Vladimir said only one word in response to the bottle attack. "Morgan," he said, and he said it too quietly for anyone to hear. He could see her, for some reason, carrying her fugitive cat across the courtyard, cradling the rebellious animal like a mother all too ready to forgive.

"*Auslander raus!*" screamed the short one. "*Raus! Raus!*"

Cohen had Vladimir by the hand, his own palm cold and wet. Vladimir was dragged up to his feet and then he hit what must have been the sharp edge of a tram seat, but he tried hard not to lose his balance, for, at that moment, the reality that he was his parents' only child, and that his mother and father could not possibly go on with him dead dawned on Vladimir. And so, finally, he panicked—an eye-opening panic that showed him quite clearly the tram steps, the still-open door, and the black asphalt beyond.

"Foreigner out!" shouted the other skinhead in English; between them they had clearly mastered the right words in the right European languages. "Back to Turk-land!"

The wind gusting off the river slammed into their backs like a concerned friend leading the way. Behind them they could hear the laughter of their assailants as well as that of the newly awakened factory workers, and the fading, patient voice of the tram recording: "Please desist entering and exiting, the doors are about to close."

They ran broken-field past the parked Fiats and randomly lit street lamps, toward the familiar darkened hulk of the castle in the far distance. They ran without looking at one another. Several blocks later, Vladimir's sense of panic gave out, and the sadness returned and physically manifested itself in the shape of a giant ball of mucus rising up through his stomach and lungs, past his racing heart. His feet folded beneath him, rather gracefully, and he wound up first on his knees, then on his palms, and then twisted over on his back.

VLADIMIR RECOVERED to the sound of a great automotive roar. Two police cars beaming electric-blue and red against the valley of pink Baroque where Cohen and Vladimir had come to rest had pulled up to within inches of Vladimir's snout, and the boys were immediately surrounded by sweaty giants. They could see the outlines of night sticks bouncing against trousers, smell the beer and pork-loin breath overpowering the street's coal-and-diesel reek, and hear the laughter, the great rumbling free-for-all of the Slav policeman at three in the morning.

Yes, they were a merry lot, prancing atop of our fallen heroes while the strobe lights of their cars reinforced the carnivalesque atmosphere—it seemed as if a rave, the very one František had been hoping to conjure up a few hours earlier, was really underfoot.

Vladimir lay crumpled in a nest he had instinctively made out of his parka and heavy sweater. *"Budu Jasem Americanko,"* he halfheartedly pleaded in the only Stolovan he knew. "I am an American."

This only contributed to the general merriment. An additional squadron of police Trabants pulled out from the converging side streets and a dozen more officers joined the ranks. In no time at all, the latecomers were chanting the expatriate mantra: *"Budu Jasem Americanko! Budu Jasem Americanko!"*

A few had taken off their caps and had started humming the opening bars of "The Star-Spangled Banner," picked up from years of watching the Olympics.

"American businessman," Vladimir clarified, but even that did not raise his estimation in the eyes of the law. The policemen's ball continued with reinforcements arriving by the minute until it appeared that every member of the municipal forces assigned to night duty was involved. Some even brought cameras and Vladimir and Cohen soon found themselves under a barrage of photo flashes; a bottle of Stoli was thrust into Cohen's limp hands and he modeled it half-consciously while muttering all the Stolovan he had ever learned: "I'm an American...I write poetry...I like it here...Two beers, please, and we'll split the trout..."

And then very quickly there was the screech of walkie-talkies, superiors shouting orders, and car doors being slammed. Something was happening somewhere else and the boulevard began to clear. The last to go, a young recruit in an oversized red-and-gold cap initialed with the fearsome Stolovan lion, came by to ruffle Cohen's hair and yanked the bottle out of his arms. "Sorry, American friend," he said. "Stoli cost money." He also did something nice: he picked up the boys, one in each arm, and moved them off the tram rails (ah, so that had been the sharp pain in Vladimir's back) and onto the sidewalk. "Bye, businessman," he said to Vladimir, his

358 GARY SHTEYNGART

sincere little mustache twitching as he spoke, then got into his Trabant and took off, siren blaring into the terminally disturbed night.

IF THE NIGHT HAD ENDED right there, that would have been
one thing. But no sooner had the *Politzia* left and Vladimir and
Cohen started breathing again than an additional convoy of automobiles appeared to take their space, this time a trail of BMWs
flanked on both ends by American Jeeps.

Gusev.

He scrambled out from the flagship car, overbundled for the
weather in his shiny full-length nutria coat, looking like a deposed
king fleeing an onrush of peasants with guns, or like a bald disco
promoter past his prime. "Disgrace!" he shouted.

Behind him were several men, all former Interior Ministry
troops, dressed the part in fatigues and night goggles. It must have
been that kind of night for them.

"Psh, psh," the soldiers were saying in the background, their
heads raised to the sky, as if they were too embarrassed to look
down at Vladimir and Cohen, the latter with his head folded fetally
into his stomach, looking like a half-rolled sleeping bag.

"We heard it!" Gusev shouted. "The talk on the radio scanner!
Two Americans crawling across Ujezd Street, one of them dark-
haired and hook-nosed... We knew immediately who it was!"

"Look at them... How drunk!" one of the soldiers said, shaking
his head as if it was something fantastic to behold.

Vladimir, a young gentleman in many ways, and one raised to
appreciate proper bearing and the importance of seeming sober,
genuinely considered becoming embarrassed. His associate Cohen,
in particular, cut a pretty poor figure at this point, all balled up and
moaning something about "hating it, absolutely hating it." But then
for Gusev and his men to castigate Vladimir after they probably

just got back from neutering some Bulgarians or the like struck Vladimir as something of an injustice. "Gusev!" he said, struggling to achieve in his voice both control and condescension. "Enough of this. Get me a taxi immediately!"

"You're in no position to dictate orders," Gusev said. He flicked his wrist dismissively; it would seem his advance staff had never informed him that this particular expression of absolute power had become passé about a century ago. "Get inside my car immediately, Girshkin," he said, shaking the collars of his coat so that the indistinguishable remains of dead nutrias shimmered in the street light. It was clear that in a different world, under a different regime but with the same armed men at his disposal, Mikhail Gusev would have been a very important man.

"My American associate and I refuse!" Vladimir said in Russian. He felt a swirl in his stomach, the undulation of his daily intake of gulash, potato dumplings, and booze, and hoped to God that he wouldn't throw up right then and there, for that would certainly mean losing the argument. "You have embarrassed me enough. My American associate and I were on our way to a late-night meeting. Who knows what he thinks of us Russians now."

"It is you, Girshkin, who have made us into the laughingstock of Prava. And just when we have cemented our understanding with this city's police. Oh, no, no, friend. Tonight, you ride home with me. And then we'll see who whips the Groundhog in the *banya*..."

Cohen must have sensed the malice in his voice, for despite his utter incomprehension of Russian, he made a mooing sound from within his fetal ball. "No!" Vladimir translated Cohen's mooing into Russian for Gusev's benefit. He was becoming all the more frightened himself. Just what was Gusev planning to do with him? "Your insubordination is noted, Gusev. If you refuse to call for a taxi, give me the mobile and I will do so myself."

Gusev turned back to his men who were as yet unsure whether

they should laugh or take this small drunkard seriously, but after
Gusev gave them the nod the laughter began in earnest. Smiling
solicitously, Gusev began his approach.

"Do you know what I am going to do to you, my goose?" Gusev
whispered to Vladimir, although his thick Russian sibilants were
loud enough for the entire block to hear. "Do you know how long it
takes to solve a crime in this city when you have friends at Municipal House? Remember that leg they found in the sock bin at the
Kmart? I wonder who it was we dismembered that day. Was it his
excellency the Ukrainian ambassador? Or was that the day we cir-
cumcised the minister of fishing and hatcheries? Would you like
me to tell you? How about I look in my log book? Better still, how
about I snuff you and your little friend? Why waste a hundred
words when one bullet will do between you two pederasts?"

He was close enough for Vladimir to smell the intense shoe-
polish reeking off his motorcycle boots. Vladimir opened his
mouth—what was he going to do? Recite Pushkin? Bite Gusev's
leg? He, Vladimir, had done something to Jordi back in the Floridian hotel room...He had...

"Opa, boys!" Gusev shouted to his men. "Can you see the article
in the *Stolovan Ekspress* tomorrow? 'Two Americans Die in Suicide
Pact Over Rising Price of Beer.' What do you think, brothers? Tell
me I'm not a funny one tonight!"

A debate began between Gusev and a gun-toting associate over
a proposal to throw the two foreigners off the Foot. Vladimir suddenly found himself strangely weary. His watery eyelids began to
close...

With the passing minutes, the voices of the men became gradually indistinct, sounding more like the insistent honking of geese
than the rapid hooligan Russian that Gusev's fellows preferred.
And then...

———

THERE WAS AN UNEXPECTED SOUND. The make-believe sound of a Hollywood fairy tale. The sound of a getaway car squealing around a street corner and swerving into the narrow space between Gusev and his troops.

Jan got out of Vladimir's Beamer looking like a domesticated loon in an ensemble of coarse-wool winter pajamas. "I have orders," he shouted to Gusev and then to the former Interior Ministry troops. "Orders directly from the Groundhog. I'm exclusively authorized to take Girshkin home!"

Gusev calmly took out his gun.

"Move aside, sir," Jan said to Gusev. "Let me help Mr. Girshkin up. As I've said, I have orders…"

Gusev grabbed the young Stolovan by his shoulders. He spun him around, then took hold of his pajama collar with one arm, sandwiching the gun into the folds of his neck with the other. "What orders?" he said.

For some time then, only the churning of his stomach reminded Vladimir of the passing of time, each revolution indicating yet another temporal unit in which he remained alive while Jan remained in Gusev's grasp. Finally, his driver, not a small man but small beneath Gusev's inflated face, reached into a leather holster wound beneath his pajamas and, hand shaking only slightly, took out a mobile phone. "The Groundhog has been following your whereabouts on the scanner," Jan said to Gusev, his usually halting Russian now true and precise. "To speak truthfully, he is worried over Mr. Girshkin's safety at your hands. If you would like, I will dial the Groundhog directly."

The silence continued except for the metallic click of a weapon either being decommissioned or readied for combat. Then Gusev let go. He turned away quickly, leaving the defeat in his face to Vladimir's imagination. The next thing that registered with Vladimir was the slam of a car door. A dozen motors started up, all nearly at once. A lone *babushka*, her voice as frail from sleep as from age, had opened up her window from across the street and started shouting for silence or she'd send for the police one more time.

Arranged horizontally in the back seat of his car, while the propped-up Cohen rode shotgun, Vladimir willed himself to pass out, if not into eternal sleep then at least into a subset of eternity. It was not possible. His head was a Central Casting of acne-scarred skinheads, hysterical policemen, fatigue-clad Interior Ministry braves, and, of course, the odd Soviet customs agent with sturgeon breath.

"You'll be back, Yid," the customs agent had said to Mother.

PART VII

WESTERNIZING

THE BOYARS

31. STARRING VLADIMIR
AS PETER THE GREAT

HE WAS BACK.

Sure he had given fleeing some thought. And why not? His DeutscheBank account did contain around fifty thousand dollars—his commission from the Harold Green scam—which would last him awhile in someplace Vancouverish. But, no, that would be an overreaction. Not to mention cowardly.

A knowledgeable Russian lazing around in the grass, sniffing clover and munching on boysenberries, expects that at any minute the forces of history will drop by and discreetly kick him in the ass.

A knowledgeable Jew in a similar position expects history to spare any pretense and kick him directly in the face.

A *Russian Jew* (knowledgeable or not), however, expects both history *and* a Russian to kick him in the ass, the face, and every other place where a kick can be reasonably lodged. Vladimir understood this. His take on the matter was: Victim, stop lazing about in the grass.

He woke up the next day to find himself lying beside Morgan's ethereally pale back, the sides of her breasts rounding out beneath her like little pockets of rising dough. His darling was completely unaware of her Volodechka's curious night.

His darling was completely unaware of many things. Because

no matter what acts of political or romantic inanity she was performing with her Tomaš (likely some impoverished young Stolovan reeking of wet shoes and garlic), no matter the winged lion or
minotaur or gryphon that lived in her sealed secret room, and no
matter those fashionable American panic attacks that gave her the
license to misbehave—ultimately, it would be Vladimir's world,
with its moral relativism, its animalistic worship of survival, that
would leave Morgan short of breath.

In some ways it was a repeat of Vladimir's grand battle with
Fran, a battle between the luxury of ideas and the refugee's fore-
most responsibility of staying alive, a battle between nebulous historical notions (Death to the Foot!) and the complicated facts on
the ground—the Gusevs and their Kalashnikovs, the men with the
shaved heads cruising the streets of the continent. And it was precisely Vladimir's realism that made him a better person than Morgan, that coated him with the patina of tragedy, that excused *his*
deviations from Normalcy and condemned Morgan's deviations
from the same.

Was he a good person or a bad person?

What a childish question.

HE MOVED.

Half an hour after he had awoken, five hours after he was nearly
killed, Vladimir was at the Groundhog's. Didn't call, didn't knock,
just came and made himself known—let the whole world know
who is this Girshkin that he doesn't have to call or knock.

Visiting his boss was now a crosscultural experience. The Hog
had left the "gangsta" compound, along with his latest girlfriend
and secondary and tertiary consorts, for a new development
hideously developing itself in a green corner of Greater Prava: the
Brookline Gardens. Those familiar with the real Brookline, the one

in Massachusetts, would not be disappointed. The Prava version was the apotheosis of North American upper-middle-classdom distilled in ten rows of dark brick townhouses and archways trellised with vine. An enormous sloping lawn at the entrance had been planted with pink, red, and white peonies to spell out "Welcome" in English; while in a far corner, a self-contained Food Court was already under construction, spreading out its feelers for the rest of the hypothetical mall. The only concession to local reality was the fact that the whole place would fall apart by the turn of the millennium.

Into this rarefied habitat came Vladimir with arms crossed and scowl at the ready. Peerless Jan (knighted, beatified, given a sweet bonus) dropped him off at the Groundhog's unit on the corner of Glendale Road and MacArthur Place. The entrepreneur's bodyguards were asleep in a station wagon parked in the driveway, their arms hanging out of the rolled-down windows like pinstriped tentacles. As promised, Vladimir did not knock. He walked right through the empty living room, his mobile phone at the ready, its antenna fully extended like a modern-day broadsword, to find the Groundhog breakfasting in his little breakfast nook.

The Groundhog looked up from his cornflakes. "Ah! Surprise!" he said, although that was clearly not what he meant, unless he was describing his own state of affairs. "*Bozhe moi!*" he said, which was closer to the truth. "What are you doing here?"

"It's got to stop," Vladimir said. He pointed his phone's antenna into the triangle of flesh and hair laid bare by the Groundhog's bathrobe. "I can be on a plane for Hong Kong tomorrow. Or Malta. I have a thousand schemes. I have a million connections."

The Groundhog tried to appear incredulous. He came closest to the expression of Mr. Rybakov's portrait directly above him. The middle-aged Fan Man, dressed in full military uniform, was trying to look dignified for the photographer, but already the lunacy of Soviet life was evident in the feral glint of his eyes, as if he was trying to say, "Put away your camera, civilian! I'll give you something to remember me by!"

"Vladimir, stop," the Groundhog said. "What is this madness?"

"Madness! Would you like to hear about madness? A convoy of armed ex–Interior Ministry troops in jeeps running around an almost-Western city, this to me is madness. Their commanding officer threatening the life of the vice president of a major investment company—this, once again, to me is madness."

The Groundhog grunted and stirred his cereal. For some reason he had been eating it with a heavy wooden ladle, the kind more suited for a bowl of thick Russian porridge than American cornflakes. Through a pair of French doors slightly ajar, a woman's rosy backside could be seen cavorting about the wood-and-chrome kitchen beyond the breakfast nook.

"Okay," the Groundhog said, presumably after his stirring had rearranged the cornflakes just so. "What do you want from me? You want these Americanisms and globalisms? You want to take control? Then do so! Gusev won't give you any problems. I can take away his jeeps and guns like that…" He forgot to snap his fingers. His eyes were glued to the service end of Vladimir's mobile and they looked tired and dim, as if the only thing still keeping the Groundhog awake was the possibility of the antenna poking him in the eye.

"I want training sessions on becoming an American businessman for everyone in the organization," Vladimir said. "Starting tomorrow."

"Exactly as you want it, that's how it will be."

Vladimir tapped his antenna against the dining table, a half-moon of ashwood and computer-perfected design. It seemed that something remained unresolved, and, lost as he was in the Groundhog's flurry of concessions, Vladimir couldn't quite remember what it was. "Oh," he said finally. "We're opening a nightclub."

"Wonderful," the Groundhog said. "We could all use a nice disco." He looked thoughtful for a minute. "Vladimir, please don't hate me," he said, "but if we are talking truthfully, then I must speak from the heart. Vladimir, my friend, why are you so distant from us? Why don't you ever spend time with your Russian brothers? I'm not talking about Gusev and his kind, but what about me, what about the Groundhog? For instance, they tell me you have an attractive American girlfriend. Why have I not seen her? I love to see pretty girls. And why haven't we gone out together, you and your girl and me and my Lena? There's a new restaurant with an American flavor they're opening here at the Food Court next month. It's called *Road 66* or something like that. Surely your girl will feel at home in such a place, and my Lenochka loves milkshakes."

This indecent proposal floated in the air between them, finally settling on the ergonomic dining table between the corn flakes and the Air France coffee mug. A double date. With the Groundhog. And Morgan. And a creature named Lenochka. But before Vladimir could politely refuse the Groundhog's invitation, a second consideration presented itself: Morgan to the Gulag! He was thinking, of course, of revenge. Revenge for Morgan's Foot fetish, revenge for her homicidal *babushka*s, revenge for her slippery Tomaš. Yes, the time had come to teach his pampered little agitator a few useful facts about the cruel and hollow universe around her. And so—a double date! A little sampler of Girshkin World. A proper antidote to the Shaker Heights High School prom. My Dinner with Groundhog.

"You know, my girl is actually very curious about my Russian friends," Vladimir said.

"So then we're agreed!" The Groundhog happily slapped his shoulder. "We will toast her American beauty together!" He turned to the French doors leading to the kitchen and moved them apart with his feet, both shod in forest-green Godzilla slippers. "Have you met my Lena yet?" he asked, as more of his friend's back became visible. "Would you like her to make you some porridge?"

BACK IN HIS *PANELAK* **FLAT,** Vladimir paced his living room in a kind of angry stupor. Globalisms? Americanisms? What the hell was he talking about? Did he actually think he was going to introduce Gusev to the finer points of business-to-business marketing and public relations? What insanity!

The way things stood, only one man in Prava could help him. František. The happy apparatchik Vladimir had found during the Night of Men.

"Allo," František picked up. "Vladimir? I was just about to ring you. Listen, I need to unload three hundred Perry Ellis windbreakers. Black-and-orange trim. Practically new. My cousin Stanka made some sort of an idiotic deal with a Turk...Any ideas?"

"Er, no," Vladimir said. "Actually, I have a bit of a problem here myself." He explained the nature of his predicament in a loud, frightened voice.

"I see," František said. "Let me impart some advice. And remember, I've dealt with Moscow all of my adult life, so I know Gusev and his friends pretty well."

"Tell me," "Vladimir said.

"The Russians of this caliber, they only understand one thing: cruelty. Kindness is seen as a weakness; kindness is to be punished. Do you understand? You're not dealing with Petersburg academicians here or enlightened members of the fourth estate. These are the people that brought half this continent to her knees at one point. These are murderers and thieves. Now tell me, how cruel can you be?"

"I have a lot of anger in store," Vladimir confessed, "but I'm not very good at expressing it. Today, however, I lashed out at the Groundhog, my boss—"

"Good, that's a good start," František said. "Ah, Vladimir, we are not so different, you and I. We are both men of taste in a tasteless world. Do you know how many compromises I have made in my life? Do you know the things I have done..."

"Yes, I know," Vladimir told the apparatchik. "I do not judge you."

"Likewise," František said. "Now, remember: cruelty, anger, vindictiveness, humiliation. These are the four cornerstones of Soviet society. Master them and you will do well. Tell these people how much you despise them and they will build you statues and mausoleums."

"Thank you," Vladimir said. "Thank you for the instruction. I will lash out at the Russians with my last strength, František."

"My pleasure. Now, Vladimir... Please tell me... What the hell am I supposed to do with these goddamn windbreakers?"

THE AMERICAN LESSONS began the next day. The Kasino was set up school auditorium–style, with rows upon rows of plastic folding chairs. When the seats were filled, Vladimir did a double take: the Groundhog's people numbered as many as parliamentarians of a sizable republic.

Half of them Vladimir had never met. In addition to the core groups of soldiers and crooks, there were the drivers of the BMW armada; the strippers who supplied labor to the town's more elicit clubs; the prostitutes who worked the Kasino and, in lean times, covered the nightly beat on Stanislaus Square; the cooks for the common mess-hall who ran an international caviar-contraband operation on the side; the young men who sold enormous fur hats with the insignia of the Soviet Navy to Cold War aficionados on the Emanuel Bridge; the petty thieves who preyed upon older Germans straying from their tour groups—and that was only the personnel Vladimir could identify by their distinguishing combination of age, gender, demeanor, and gait. The majority of the congregants remained to him just so many other units of Eastern European refuse in their cheaply cut suits, their nylon parkas, their rooster haircuts, and teeth blackened by filterless Spartas, three packs per diem as life prescribed.

Forget Gusev. Forget the Groundhog. From now on they would all belong to Vladimir.

Vladimir took them by surprise. He ran out from the wings and kicked the oakwood lectern that had been stolen from the Sheraton and still bore its illustrious seal. "Devil confound it!" he shouted in Russian. "Look at you!"

The general incredulity and merriment that had pervaded the gathering stopped right there. No more giggling, no more loud slurping of the imaginary last drop out of an empty Coke can. Even old Marusya woke up from her opium nap. Gusev, seated alone in the last row, was glowering at Vladimir and fingering his holster. His troops, however, had been moved up front with the Groundhog. *Yes,* thought Vladimir, smiling at Gusev imperiously. *Now we'll see who whips the Groundhog in the banya...*

"We've really done it, beloved countrymen," Vladimir shouted, his whole body shaking from the adrenaline building up ever since the first ray of sun snuck in through the blinds and woke him, irrevocably, at 7:30 in the morning. "We've embarrassed ourselves in front of all of Europe, we have truly shown our simple nature... For seventy years, we have been diligently licking clean an asshole, and it turns out to have been the wrong one!" Silence except for a spurt of laughter on one side, but one quickly nipped in the bud by surrounding colleagues. "What can account for such a gaffe, I ask you? We gave the world Pushkin and Lermontov, Tchaikovsky and Chekhov. We've embarked thousands of gawky Western youths on the Stanislavsky Method, and if truth be told, even that damned Moscow Circus is not half bad...So how do we now find ourselves in this situation? Dressed so ludicrously, a provincial from Nebraska would have cause to laugh, spending all our money on elegant cars just so we can butcher their insides with our bad taste, our women dressed in raccoon furs strolling Stanislaus Square giving all that young girls can give—their very girlhood—to the same Germans at whose hands our fathers and grandfathers perished in defense of the Motherland..."

At this mention there was predictable patriotic fervor among the ranks: bearlike rumbles of discontent, spittle hurtling to the concrete floor, and, here and there, mutterings of "disgrace."

Vladimir picked up on this. "Disgrace!" he shouted. His mind was still ringing with František's lecture on the four cornerstones of Soviet society. Cruelty. Anger. Vindictiveness. Humiliation. He took out a pocket pack of Kleenex, the only item in his vest pocket, and threw it on the floor for effect. He spat on it, too, then kicked it clear across the stage. "Disgrace! What are we doing, friends? While the Stolovans, the very same Stolovans who we ran over in '69, are out there building townhouse condominiums and modern factories that work, we're snipping Bulgarian balls like radishes! [laughter] And what did the Bulgarians ever do to deserve this, may I ask? They're Slavs like us..."

(*Slavs Like Us: The Vladimir Girshkin Story.* Thankfully the crowd was too agitated to make light of Vladimir's lack of Slavonity.)

"Well, you're going to learn and you're going to learn the hard way what it means to be a Westerner. Remember Peter the Great shaving Eastern beards and disgracing the Boyars?" Here he looked, just a glance, at Gusev and his closest men, who barely had the time to react. "Yes, I suggest you review your history texts, for that is exactly how it will be done. *Those who are not with us are against us!* And now, my poor, simple friends, here's what you're going to do first..."

And he told them.

IT WAS A DAY commemorating the transition from November to December, with the local trees hanging on to the last of yellow, the leaden sky cut with lines of ethereal blue where the whipping winds had cleared a swath through the pollution. The Russians, dressed in the black-and-orange Perry Ellis windbreakers that Vladimir now required of all employees, were sitting around the clearing (the same clearing where Vladimir and Kostya staged their athletic drills) like a ring of dark butterflies. In the background, an armada of twenty BMWs and a dozen jeeps were being cannibalized by a team of German mechanics in smocks.

Out came the zebra-striped seats, the woolly cup holders, the shocking Electric Plum ground effects—all tossed water-brigade–style past a line of bobbing blond heads and into the circle of the clearing. There, the personal offerings to the God of Kitsch were already assembled: the nylon tracksuits, the Rod Stewart compilations, the worn Romanian sneakers, everything that had qualified the Groundhog's vast crew as Easterners, Soviets, Cold War–losers—all would be kindling for the flames.

As those lowest on the totem pole splashed gasoline across this burial ground of rosy-cheeked nesting dolls and giant lacquered soup ladles, some of the older women—Marusya, the opium lady, and her clique, in particular—began to whimper and make soft clicking sounds of regret. They wiped their eyes and adjusted each other's head scarves, often collapsing into mournful embraces.

In a matter of seconds, the fire began its crackling susurrations.

Then something unstable (perhaps it was the giant can of brilliantine with which Gusev's men slicked back their thinning hair) exploded with a trace of orange into the darkening sky, and the crowd gaped at the pyrotechnics, the more adventurous young men bringing their hands forward for warmth.

The Groundhog, sighing with the entirety of his soft chest, took an impressive swig out of his vodka flask, then reached into the pocket of his windbreaker and took out the two fuzzy dice that had previously bounced one against the other from the rearview mirror of his BMW, like two puppies with just each other for amusement. He rubbed them together as if to create another fire, then sunk his nose inside one of them. After a few minutes of this melancholia, the Hog leaned back, smiled, closed his eyes, and cast both dice into the flames.

THROUGHOUT THE PROCEEDINGS in the auditorium and in the woods, those of an inquiring nature could turn around to see an attractive middle-aged gentleman with a PravaInvest visitor's tag sitting apart from the herd and doodling in his little memo pad. In a white shirt and corduroy vest, with a gentle, bemused expression on his face, he appeared rather harmless. And yet despite the organization's closely followed axiom that harmless people should always be sent to the hospital, no one dared approach this strange professorial man who chewed on his pen and smiled for no reason. He was more than harmless. He was František.

And he was impressed. "Brilliant!" he said to Vladimir, leading him away from the clearing and toward a wrecked suburban highway where Jan and the car were waiting. "You really are Postmodern Man, my friend. The bonfire and the self-denunciation contest...I must say, you are clown and ringmaster all at once! And thank you for helping me get rid of those infernal windbreakers."

"Ah," Vladimir said, clasping his hands to his bosom. "You don't know how happy you're making me, František. I can't tell you how incomplete I was without you. I've been working on this stupid pyramid scheme for four months, and all I could get was a paltry quarter million out of some daft Canadian."

Jan opened the car door and the two slipped onto the warm back seat. "Well, that will soon change, young man," František said. "I have only one curious problem..."

"You have a problem?"

"Yes, my problem is that I am a sufferer of visions."

"You suffer from visions," Vladimir repeated. "I can recommend a doctor in the States..."

"No, no, no," František laughed. "I am a sufferer of good visions! For instance, last night I had this dream... I saw a local congress hall being rented out for a caviar brunch... I saw a promotional film about PravaInvest broadcast on a screen of enormous proportions... By morning, I dreamed of twenty such brunches at five hundred persons per brunch. Ten thousand English-speakers, roughly one third of the present expatriate population. All the children of mamas and papas from happier lands. All potential investors."

"Aha," Vladimir said. "I see such wonders as well, but I don't quite understand how this film will be financed."

"Now, it is fortunate for you," said František, "that I have friends in this nation's vast and underemployed film industry. Furthermore, my chum Jitomir manages a gargantuan conference center in the Goragrad district. As for the caviar, well, I'm afraid you're on your own regarding the caviar."

"No problems there!" Vladimir said and he acquainted František with the international caviar-contraband venture the Groundhog's men had put together. As he divulged the dark and grainy details, the weather outside the car turned fickle, playing first with a palette of loose baby-pink clouds, then clearing the canvas to sear the approaching Golden City with brilliant sunshine. Each brightening and darkening made Vladimir all the more excited, for it confirmed that change was on the way. "Dear God!" he cried. "I believe we are ready to proceed!"

"No, wait," František said. "That was hardly the sum of my visions," he said. "I see more. I see us buying an industrial plant. A failed one, of course."

"There's one I've seen on the outskirts of town," Vladimir said. "The FutureTek 2000. That one looked like it failed a century ago."

"Yes, yes. My cousin Stanka bought a piece of the FutureTek. It's a chemical plant that not only failed a century ago but actually exploded last year. Perfect. I must have supper with Stanka. But I see still more. I see that night club we talked about…"

"I see that, too," Vladimir said. "We'll call it the Metamorphosis Lounge in deference to Kafka and his mighty grip on the expatriate imagination. 'Lounge' is also a popular word these days."

"I hear Drum N' Bass music. I see a soft, fuzzy, highbrow kind of prostitution. I feel something up my nose. Cocaine?"

"Better still," Vladimir said, "I have learned of a revolutionary new narcotic, a horse tranquilizer, which we can get in bulk by way of a French veterinarian."

"Vladimir!"

"What? The horse tranquilizer is too outré?"

"No, no…" František's eyes were still closed; the veins on his forehead were bulging with high concepts. "I see us listed on the Frankfurt Stock exchange!"

"*Bozhe moi!*"

"I see NASDAQ."

"God help us."

"Vladimir, we must act soon. No, forget soon. Today. Right now. This is a magical moment for those of us lucky enough to be in this part of the world, but it is no more than a moment. In three years Prava will be history. The expat crowds will be gone, the Stolovan nation will become a Germany in miniature. Now is the time to be alive, my young friend!"

"Hey, where are you taking me?" Vladimir asked, suddenly aware that they had crossed the New Town and were going to some mysterious burned-out district beyond.

"We're going to make a movie!" František cried.

VLADIMIR'S FAVORITE Cold War coincidence? The uncanny similarities between the Soviet architectural style of the eighties and the cardboard sets of *Star Trek,* the grand American kitsch program of the sixties. Take, for instance, the 1987-built Gorograd District Palace of Trade and Culture which František had procured for his weekly caviar brunches and for screenings of *PravaInvest: The Movie.* Captain Kirk himself would have felt at home in this giant approximation of a twenty-fifth-century radiator. He would have plopped himself down on one of the orange plastic space chairs, which filled the auditorium's starry interior, then looked on in exaggerated horror as the enormous viewing screen crackled to life, the voice of a fearsome enemy space creature announcing the following:

"In its six years of existence, PravaInvest, s.r.o., has become, by far, the leading corporate entity to arise from the rubble of the former Soviet Bloc. How did we do it? Good question."

So now the truth would be revealed!

"**Talent.** We've united seasoned professionals from industri-

alized Western nations with bright and eager young specialists from Eastern Europe."

There they were: Vladimir and an African actor in a golf cart,
swinging by an enormous white wall on which the words
FutureTek 2000 were printed in futuristic corporate script. The
wall ended and the golf cart pulled into a grassy field where
happy workers of many ethnicities and sexual orientations
cavorted beneath an ever-rising inflatable phoenix, PravaInvest's
rather shameless corporate symbol.

"**Diversity of interests:** From modernizing film studios in
Uzbekistan to our brand-new high-technology industrial
park and convention centre—the FutureTek 2000—coming
soon to the Stolovan capital, PravaInvest has left no market
uncornered."

How about those Uzbek film studios! And the scale model of
the tree-lined FutureTek campus, that postindustrial Taj Mahal!

"**A Forward-Looking Mentality.** Have we mentioned the
FutureTek 2000? Of course! The vanguard of technology *is
the only place to be* whether you're running a modern high-
rise hotel in the Albanian capital of Tirana, a vocational
school for the Yupik Eskimo in Siberia, or a small but con-
sequential literary magazine in Prava. And PravaInvest's
ideals are as solid as our reputation for prudent investment. We're committed to building lasting peace in the
Balkans, cleaning up the Danube, *and* issuing the most
exceptional dividends to our investors. We have our cake
and eat it too, *every single day.*"

Before a Bosnian was shown eating his torte, and after the Yupik Eskimo waved to the camera with their T-squares and protractors, Cohen and Alexandra were caught leaning over *Cagliostro* proofs engaged in heated (and, thankfully, silent) discussion. The camera made Cohen seem fat and thirtyish, while Alexandra, with her round face and dark curving lashes, looked positively Persian. A great cheer greeted the literary pair, a cheer that extended way beyond the Crowd (gorging itself on caviar in the first row) to all the youthful precincts in the auditorium. Even Morgan—her relationship with Vladimir still choppy and unsettled—looking tonight like a bored young embassy wife stuck in some Kinshasa or Phnom Penh, had to pick up her hands and clap at the image of her dear friend Alexandra. Yes, *Cagliostro* had been a stroke of genius, a marketing tool to be studied at Wharton. Too bad the damn thing still didn't exist.

"So what are you waiting for? Shares of PravaInvest stock have been circulating on the Tanzanian stock exchange at approximately U.S. $920 per share. We are now pleased to offer them for nearly half the price in an effort to 'give something back' to those who have enabled our meteoric rise: the residents of the former Warsaw Pact. For information on our current schedule of dividends please call Vladimir Girshkin, Executive Vice President, at our Prava headquarters: tel. (0789) 02 36 21 59 / fax 02 36 21 60. Or call his associate František Kral at (0789) 02 33 65 12. Both are fluent in English and more than happy to assist you.

"Now it's your turn to **GIVE SOMETHING BACK!** *Prava-Invest, s.r.o.*"

MEANWHILE, courtesy of the poet Fish, a package arrived from Lyon containing twenty vials of liquid horse tranquilizer, cooking instructions for transformation of said into snorting powder, and the most God-awful poetry to appear in an Alaskan literary journal. Vladimir took this loot to Marusya and explained the situation to her. She shook her balding head as if to say, *"Nu,* what's in it for me?" Vladimir knew it wasn't a matter of her antidrug principles. She tended to the opium garden with loving grace and surely skimmed off the top both in the garden and at her little concession stand. Hell, by nine in the morning when Vladimir went off for his jog with Kostya (Vladimir looking as cheerless as a conscript in a labor brigade), old Marusya was already tweaked enough to fumble on the obligatory *dobry den'.*

So a hard-currency compromise was reached, and Marusya, limping ahead like a blighted hobbit, took him down to the main building's basement where several gas-fired stoves were lined in a row awaiting some devious purpose. They didn't have to wait long. Inside their cracked ceramic interiors, the liquid horse tranquilizer was cooked at a tremendous temperature in an assortment of pots and pans. Once cooked, Marusya would flip the resulting wafer as gingerly as if it were a blin and set it to cool on a metal tray. Afterward, she'd go at it with a mallet until the wafer was reduced to a small mountain of snortable powder, which she would wrap into a little cellophane log and set out for Vladimir's inspection. This she did while beaming with the pride of workmanship, her mouthful of gold teeth gleaming in the basement's dusty air.

Vladimir assembled a nice stack of the little tranquilizer logs, although for the time being he didn't know where to push them, what the right segue would be for offering up the fifteen-minute lobotomies to the Crowd and beyond. For that he would need his club, the Metamorphosis Lounge.

———————

MC PAAVO arrived a few days hence on a little turbo-prop bearing the Finnish cross on its tail. He couldn't shut up even before he got off the plane. They heard his deep voice knocking about in the cabin while they waited on the tarmac: "MC Paavo in de haus! In de pan-European 'hood! Got de Helsinki beat, y'all can't fuck wif!"

He was no older than František, only he hadn't kept well at all: wrinkles carved deep to the order of the San Andreas Fault, a hairline in recession and not in the graceful arc of male-pattern baldness, but instead a jagged line, like soldiers beating a piecemeal retreat from the front. To maintain his youth he jabbered like a fifteen-year-old on crack, and sniffed at his armpits as if a great youthful elixir flowed from each. The Finn, only marginally tall, hugged František, ruffled his hair, and called him "My boy-ee," while the former socialist globetrotter, unfamiliar with hip-hop expressions but never one to be left out, responded with "My girl," and here the hilarity crested for a bit.

They took Paavo to the Kasino, where he dropped to his knees and crawled about a bit, citing amps and wattage and other technical specifications lost on our Soviet-bloc friends. "Great," he said. "Knock out the two floors above and we ready to start pumpin.'"

This request actually gave Gusev's men something constructive to do: They went after the glue-and-cardboard floors with electric staple-guns and machetes, with axes and grenade launchers, with protective goggles and a Russian's unshakable hope that from destruction the Lord will create anew. By the time they were finished, not only the two floors above the Kasino were removed, but a skylight was knocked through the sixth floor as well. Vladimir, a resident of the Kasino building, found himself temporarily homeless, forced either to squat in Morgan's pad or take a room at the Intercontinental. Despite his problems with Morgan, he resigned himself to the former.

The Russians' hopes of providence, however, were not entirely unfounded. The Lord didn't provide, but Harold Green did. The Canadian's funds paid for a gorgeous, loopy discorama flanked by enough theme lounges to keep the saddest drunk happy. It was christened, as we already know, the Metamorphosis Lounge.

A NIGHT TO REMEMBER at the Metamorphosis Lounge? Good luck. You'll need three omniscient narrators to cobble together half a narrative. But, what the hell, let's try to maintain some dignity and recall what happened on night X, hour Y, in the main room, the Kafka Insecuritorium.

On that particular night the dance floor is hogged by the new *arriviste* crowd, Prava's temporary "it" thing by dint of their impressive numbers and some sort of media-publishing party connection they share in New York–Los Angeles, with a stopover in London–Berlin. There they are: white people in chamois lounge suits and bug-eyed sunglasses, falling apart on the dance floor to the thumpa-thumpa of MC Paavo and the whirl of his techno fog. One gets up, another falls down. One takes off his shirt to reveal himself flabby and old, just as his girlfriend, sweaty and young, is waking up and putting on her bra: a miscommunication. Now they're crying and hugging. Soon enough they're waving to the captain's table, shouting, "Vladimir! Alexandra!"

At the captain's table the wave is returned. "Sure, I wouldn't want to risk sending any of our men to Sarajevo right now," Harold Green is shouting to Vladimir over MC Paavo's twenty beats per second. Harry's webbed face is further creased with concern as he is likely thinking about PravaInvest's "bright and eager young specialists" dodging enemy fire behind the rump of a U.N. armored personnel carrier.

"Have another drink, Harold. We'll talk Bosnia tomorrow."

Speaking of Bosnia, there's Nadija. She's from Mostar or there-
abouts, her face as chiseled as a constructivist bust of Tito, her body
as long and purposeful as that of a socialist-worker heroine, the
mother of a nation. There she goes, leading by the chin a small,
bearded liberal-arts specimen with an eager hamster expression, a
pouf of red hair, and a tragic limp. She's not taking him to the Ministry of Love, though. Its twenty bunkbeds, truncheons, and prized
Israeli water cannon are for a different, later part of the night. No,
first, the pale gentleman must do away with modern malaise: It's
time for a visit to Grandmother Marusya's Infirmary, where there's
borscht for colds, opium for headaches, and horse tranquilizer for
overactive imaginations.

BACK AT THE INSECURITORIUM ... At the Captain's Table, is
that ... Could it be? Alexandra and Cohen necking? Yes! Marcus the
rugby runt, Alexandra's ex-boyfriend, is gone—Daddy stopped
wiring him funds, so it's "back to naffing England for me, mate." A
closer look reveals Alexandra looking great tonight, formal in a
spaghetti-strap dress and with her hair up. But the pouches under
her eyes have the texture of leather, and then there's the red
swelling around her nostrils, a swelling from which sprout dark little hairs as thick and straight as dry grass. Someone's been grazing
at the horse stables one time too many.

But just look at her new beau. Cohen's taken a beautiful old
Armani sports jacket and roughed it up so that it is no longer a
tool of oppression. He's trimmed his beard and hair so that he
looks five years older, with a doctoral thesis in the hopper. And
now he's wrapped his big arms around Alexandra and is telling her
to calm down, that it's all right, that she can drop her nightly
dosage in the toilet, they'll go to Crete next week to dance among

the sheep, to drink mineral water and talk about themselves until it all makes sense. It's hard to hear him above the bird squawks and jackhammer noises slipping off of MC Paavo's turntable, but one can be sure that Cohen's telling her that he loves her and he always has.

AND WHAT ABOUT VLADIMIR? At the other end of the Captain's Table, there he is, watching Cohen neck with Alexandra, as Harold Green begins his latest series of mind-bending lectures on his Soros Foundation in the sky. Vladimir takes a long look around the Metamorphosis, this terra incognito that he and František and MC Paavo have wrought in the biblical span of forty days. It's a late hour, much too late for a Monday—and it's usually around this time that Vladimir starts to ask himself the questions that cannot be answered with a healthy application of horse tranquilizer or a sip of one of the U.S.$5.50 Belgian lagers that have made the Metamorphosis so hip and solvent.

For instance: What would Mother think of his clever new venture? Would she be proud? Would she consider his little pyramid scheme a cheap alternative to an MBA? Has he inadvertently created something that will please her? Come to think of it, is there really any difference between Mother's corporate colossus and his scrappy PravaInvest? And was it true what they said, that childhood was destiny? That there was no escape?

Finally, the one question Vladimir Girshkin has been trying to avoid all night by waxing nostalgic about Mother and fate and greed and his own strange, inglorious path from victim to victimizer:

Where was Morgan?

32. DEATH TO
THE FOOT

MORGAN WAS HOME.

Morgan was home a lot. Or she was teaching. Or she was wrestling with crazy old ladies. Or she was fucking Tomaš. It was hard to say. They didn't talk much, Morgan and Vladimir. Their relationship had entered the stable, mutually dissatisfying stage of an old marriage. They were a bit like the Girshkins, each devoted more to their own tiny personal joys and vast private terrors than to each other.

How could they live like this?

Well, as we have seen, Vladimir, for the past month or so, has been working overtime to make PravaInvest the pyramid scheme to end all pyramid schemes forever. As for Morgan, she asked few questions about Vladimir's flourishing *bizness* and she never made it out to the Metamorphosis either, claiming she wasn't one for ear-popping Drum N' Bass, and that she found Vladimir's new pal František "a little creepy" and the whole horse tranquilizer scene deeply disturbing.

Fair enough. It was.

Now as for their intimacy, it continued. Prava is a fairly warm place in the fall and spring, but by mid-December the temperature inexplicably drops to Siberian levels, and members of the populace

THE RUSSIAN DEBUTANTE'S HANDBOOK

like to "get down" with one another—people of advanced age making out fearlessly in the metro, teenagers rubbing their butts together in the Old Town Square, and, in the freezing *panelaks*, to be without a partner blowing warm, beery breath up your crevices could mean a certain death.

So they pressed against each other. As they were watching the news, Morgan's nose would sometimes be parked in between Vladimir's nose and cheek, a particularly tropical place as Vladimir's feverish body averaged 99.4 degrees on the Fahrenheit scale. And sometimes, on a cold morning, he would warm his hands between her thighs, which, unlike her cold cheeks and icicle ears, seemed to retain most of her warmth; by Vladimir's calculations, a polar winter could pass quite comfortably with his various extremities lodged between her thighs.

As for sweet nothings, the words "I love you" were said exactly twice in the course of five weeks. Once, inadvertently, by Vladimir after he had climaxed into her hand and she was casually wiping herself with a sandpapery Stolovan tissue, her expression peaceful and generous (remember the tent!). And once by Morgan after she had unwrapped Vladimir's thoughtful Christmas present, Vaclav Havel's collected works in Stolovan, with an introduction by Borik Hrad, the so-called Stolovan Lou Reed. "I guess it's important to believe in something," Vladimir had written on the title page, although his own shaky handwriting left him unconvinced of that sentiment.

So, as implied, along with jealousy, there was coitus. Why? Because for Vladimir, the possibility that Morgan might have been sharing her afternoons with Tomaš, while maddening in its own right, only increased his vigor in bed. Much as with Challah during her dungeon days, he was inspired by the idea that the woman he wanted also wanted to be with others. It's a simple equation that exists between many lovers: He could not *have* her and so he *desired* her.

But, apart from his intimate needs, his anger at Morgan continued to grow apace, the lust and hurt sometimes working at cross-purposes and sometimes, as when he had to perform in bed, working in tandem. He felt powerless. What could he do to convince her that she loved him and not Tomaš, that she must renounce her murky secret life in favor of normalcy, affection, and arousal, that one must always be on the right side of history, eating roast boar at the Wine Archive instead of freezing to death in the Gulag?

But she wouldn't understand him, stubborn Midwestern girl. So he worked on two fronts: To alleviate his lust, he crawled into bed beside her, but to alleviate his hurt, the best he could hope for was revenge. The best he could hope for was a certain double date. Hence when the Groundhog called to announce that *Road 66*, the restaurant in the Food Court of his townhouse estate, was ready to dish out hot curly fries in exchange for American dollars, Vladimir happily accepted on Morgan's behalf.

THERE WAS ONE terribly cute thing about Morgan: Despite being nominally upper-middle-class, she owned only one formal outfit, the tight silk blouse she wore on her first date with Vladimir. Everything else in her closet was rugged and "built to last," as they say in the States, for unlike Vladimir, she did not come to Prava to be the belle of the ball.

When they pulled up to *Road 66*, Morgan nervously tugged on the sleeves of this important blouse to make sure it covered her body just right. She smudged at her lipstick for the third time and scratched a front tooth for no apparent reason. "Shouldn't it be called *Route 66*?" Morgan asked, upon scrutinizing the flashing restaurant sign. Vladimir winked mysteriously and kissed her cheek.

"Hey! Stop it," she said. "I've got blush on. Look what you did." She reached for her purse once again and Vladimir had to fight those unproductive feelings of tenderness as she blew her nose and repowdered her cheeks.

"Well if you, Morgan Jenson...ever plan...to motor West," Vladimir sang as they walked arm-in-arm past the ten-acre gravel ditch that would soon become an American-style mall and toward the restaurant's giant neon pimiento, "just take my way...that's the highway...that's the best."

"How can you be singing?" Morgan said, once more blotting at her lips with a napkin. "I mean, we're having dinner with your boss. Aren't you, like, scared?"

"Get your kicks," Vladimir crooned as he pulled at the door handles shaped like two plastic rattlesnakes, "on Route...Sixty-six."

An awesome vista of cheap mahogany and American-themed tackiness greeted them, as the restaurant, just like the song, wound its way "from Chicago to L.A....more than two thousand miles all the way," with tables marked St. Louis, Oklahoma City, Flagstaff, "don't forget Winona...Kingman, Barstow, San Bernardino..."

The Groundhog and his girl were holed up in Flagstaff tonight. "Volodya, I got the cactus!" the Groundhog shouted to Vladimir across the vast restaurant. The Flagstaff table was indeed graced with a mighty glowing artificial cactus, much more imposing than, say, the ridiculous six-foot Gateway Arch of St. Louis or the deserted Geronimo Trading Post several tables into Arizona.

"They tell me there is always a waiting list for cactus," the Groundhog soberly informed them in English while the introductions were made and the chocolate milkshakes ordered. As part of his Western training, Vladimir had forced the Hog to buy ten black turtlenecks and ten pairs of slacks from a specialized slacks company in Maine, and tonight the Groundhog looked like he was headed for a liberal-minded Upper West Side Thanksgiving dinner.

As for the love of his life, Lenochka, well, an entire novel could be written about her, so there is only time to discuss her hair.

Let us say this: in the early 1990s, the Women of the West were favoring short cuts, pageboys, and curt little bobs, but Lena continued to celebrate her hair in the old Russian style. She refused to commit to wearing it either up or down, so she did both: A great mane crowned her shoulders, while an additional fifteen pounds of violent strawberry hair was pulled up by an enormous white bow. Beneath the cascades of hair there was a *mil'en'koe russkoe lichiko,* a pretty little Russian face with raised Mongolian cheekbones and a pointy nose. She wore exactly the same turtleneck-and-slacks outfit as the Groundhog, giving them the look of honeymooning tourists.

The Groundhog kissed Morgan's hand. "Very much pleasure," he said. "Tonight Lenochka and I practicing English, so please to correct Groundhog expression. I think in English I am called, eh, 'Groundhog,' but dictionary also saying 'Marmot.' Do you have such little animal in your country? Vladimir say everyone must speak English now!"

"I wish I remembered my Russian from college," Morgan said and smiled in encouragement, as if Russian was still a global language worth learning. "I know a little Stolovan, but it's just not the same."

They were seated, the couples facing each other, and the Groundhog made himself appear manly by ordering food for everybody—garden burgers for the ladies and ostrich burgers for the men. "Also, three plates of curly fries with hot sauce," he demanded of the waitress. "I love such shit." He smiled broadly to his companions.

"So…" Vladimir said, unsure of how to get this little Revenge Dinner started.

"Yes…" Groundhog said and nodded at Vladimir. "So."

"So…" Morgan smiled at Lena and the Groundhog. She was

already cracking her knuckles under the table, poor thing. "So how did you two meet?" she asked. A great double-date question.

"Mmm..." The Groundhog smiled nostalgically. "Eh, is big story," he said in his broken but strangely adorable English. "I tell it? Yes? Good? Okay. Big story. So one day Groundhog is in Dnepropetrovsk, so he is in Eastern Ukraina, and many people are doing to him bad thing and so Groundhog is doing to them also *very* bad thing and, eh, time goes tick tick tick tick on the clock, and after two revolvement of clock needle, after forty-eight hours passing away, it is Groundhog who is alive and it is enemies of him who are...eh...dead."

"Wait," said Morgan. "Do you mean..."

"Metaphorically speaking, they're dead," Vladimir interjected somewhat half-heartedly.

"So," the Groundhog continued, "is finished bad business, but Groundhog still very lonely and very sad..."

"Ai, my Tolya..." said Lena, adjusting her bow with one hand and directing her milkshake straw with the other. "You see, Morgan, he has Russian soul...Do you understand what it is, *Russian soul?*"

"I've heard about it from Vladimir," Morgan said. "It's like..."

"It's very nice," Vladimir said. He gestured for the Hog to continue, knowing full well where his employer's little tale was headed. Very nice, indeed.

"So, okay, lonely Groundhog has nobody in Dnepropetrovsk. His cousin kill himself last year and Dyadya Lyosha, distant relative, he die from drink. So is finish! No family, no friend, nothing."

"*Bedny moi surok,*" said Lena. "How do you say in English...My poor Groundhog..."

"You know I can totally understand you," Morgan said. "It's so difficult to go to a strange town, even in America. I went to Dayton once, I was in a basketball camp..."

"Anyway," the Hog interrupted. "So Groundhog is alone in Dnepropetrovsk and his bed is very cold and there is no girl for him to lie down on, and so he is going to, how do you say, *publichni dom*? The House of the Public? You know what this is…?"

Lena dipped a lone curly fry into a pool of hot sauce. "House of Girl, maybe?" she suggested.

"Yes, yes. Exactly such house. And so he is sitting down and Madame is coming in and she is introducing Hog to such and such girl and Groundhog is, like, Tphoo! Tphoo! He is spitting on the ground, because is so ugly. One, maybe, has face black like Gypsy, another having big nose, another speaking some Pygmy language, not Russian…And Groundhog is looking for, you know, special girl."

"He is very cultured," Lena said, patting his enormous hand. "Tolya, you should declaim for Morgan famous *poema* by Alexander Sergeyevich Pushkin, called, eh…" she looked imploringly at Vladimir.

"The Bronze Horseman?" Vladimir guessed.

"Yes, correct. Bronze Horseman. Very beautiful *poema*. Everybody knows such *poema*. It is about famous statue of man on horse."

"Lena! Please! I am telling interesting story!" the Hog shouted. "So Groundhog is leaving House of Girl, but then he hearing beautiful sound from room of love. 'Okh! Okh! Okh!' It is like wonderful Slavic angel. 'Okh! Okh! Okh!' Voice tender like young girl. 'Okh! Okh! Okh!' He is asking Madame: 'Tell me, who is making Okh?' Madame is saying, oh, is our Lenochka making such Okh, but she is only for *valuta*, for, you know, hard currency. Groundhog is, like: 'I have dollar, Deutsche mark, Finnish markka, *nu*, what you want?' So Madame is saying, okay, sit down on divan for twenty minutes and soon you will have this Lena.' So Groundhog sitting and sitting and he is hearing this beautiful 'okh' sound like bird singing to another bird, and he is suddenly becoming, eh...How do you say, Vladimir?"

He whispered a word in Russian. "Well..." Vladimir looked to Morgan. Her face was ashen and she was nervously twisting a drinking straw around one white finger as if applying a tourniquet. "Engorged, I guess," Vladimir translated, softening the hard meaning a bit.

"Yes! Groundhog is becoming engorge in the foyer and he shouting, 'Lena! Lena! Lenochka!' And in the room of love she is shouting 'Okh! Okh! Okh!' And it is like duet. It is like Bolshoi opera. Shit! And so he get up, still gorged, and he run down quickly to local *laryok* and he is buying beautiful flowers..."

"Yes!" Lena said. "He is buying scarlet roses, just like in my favorite song, 'A Million Scarlet Roses' by Alla Pugacheva. So I know God is watching us!"

"And also I am buying expensive chocolate candy in shape of ball!"

"Yes," Lena said. "I remember, from Austria, with each ball having picture of Wolfgang Amadeus Mozart. I once study music in Kiev conservatory."

They looked at each other and briefly smiled, mumbling a few words in Russian. Vladimir thought he heard the endearment *"lastochka ti moya,"* which meant roughly "you're my little swallow." The Hog quickly smooched Lena and then looked back at his tablemates, a little embarrassed.

"Aaa..." the Groundhog said, losing the thread of his tale for a moment. "Yes. Lovely story. So I run up to House of Girl and Lena is already finish with her bad business, and she is washing up, but I don't care, I open door to her room, and she is standing there, wiping with towel, and I have never seen this...Oh! Skin white! Hair red! *Bozhe moi! Bozhe moi!* Oh, my God! Russian beauty! I am getting down on my foot and I give her flower and Mozart ball, and,

and…" He looked to Lena and then to Vladimir and then back to his beloved. He put his hand to his heart. "And…" he whispered.

"And so four months later, we are here with you at table," the practical Lena summed up for him. "So tell me," she asked the near-catatonic Morgan, "how did you meet Vladimir?"

"At a poetry reading," Morgan mumbled, looking around the room, perhaps trying to find a fellow law-abiding American to connect with. No such luck. Every second customer was a horny Stolovan *biznesman* in a double-breasted purple jacket, a pleasant twenty-year-old companion on his arm. "Vladimir is a very good poet," Morgan said.

"Yes, he is maybe poet laureate," Lena laughed.

"He was reading a poem about his mother at the Joy," Morgan said, trying to take the high road. "It was about how he went to Chinatown with his mother. It was very beautiful, I thought."

"Russian man loves his mother." The Groundhog sighed. "My mama died in Odessa, year 1957, from death of kidney. I was only little child then. She was hard woman, but how I wish I could kiss her good night one more time. All I have in entire world now is papa in New York, he is sailor-invalid. This is how I hear of Vladimir. He help my papa get U.S. citizenship by making crime against American immigration service. So he is also criminal laureate, my Volodechka!"

Morgan put down her *Road 66* garden burger and glared at Vladimir, a bead of ketchup on her upper lip. "Yes, what can I say?" Vladimir said, shyly addressing the Groundhog's charge of criminality. "There was some intrigue with the INS. I helped out as best I could. Oh, what a long, strange trip it's been."

"Groundhog one day tell me funny story," Lenochka said, "about how Vladimir take money from rich Canadian and then he sells horse drug to Americans in club. You have very clever boyfriend, Morgan."

Morgan painfully nudged Vladimir's shoulder. "He's an *investor*," she said. "He *invested* Harold Green's money into a club. And he's not dealing drugs. It's that Finn. MC Paavo."

"Take, invest, what's the difference?" Vladimir said. But he made a note to ease up on the jolly candor, lest it imperil his pyramid scheme. Morgan, after all, remained friends with Alexandra and, by extension, the Crowd, PravaInvest's trendy cornerstone. Still, when he leaned over to wipe the ketchup off Morgan's shaky upper lip he also managed to whisper into her ear, "Morgan to the Gulag!" and "Death to the Foot, honey!"

He just wanted to let her know where things stood.

THE FIGHTING STARTED in the car, right after Vladimir's final wave to Lena and the Groundhog. Jan was cruising past the darkened townhouses of the Brookline Gardens (some homes still wearing their holiday wreaths and "Merry Xmas" signs), trying to find Westmoreland Street, the smooth, paved artery which connected the Groundhog's suburban fairy tale with Prava's pot-holed municipal highway, its dying factories, and crumbling *panelaks*. Meanwhile Morgan was loudly exploring her feelings.

"He met his girlfriend at a whorehouse!" she was shouting as if that had been the most egregious news of the evening. "He's a fucking gangster... And you! And YOU!"

"Quite a surprise, eh?" Vladimir said in an ambiguously low tone. "It's terrible when people aren't honest with one another."

"What does that mean?"

"I don't know, Morgie... Let's see. Tomaš. Death to the Foot. What do you think?"

"What does Tomaš have to do with anything?" she shouted.

"You're fucking him."

"Who?"

"Tomaš."

"Oh, please."

"Then *what*?"

"We're working on a project together." She pulled a used soda can out of a cup holder and began crushing it with all of her considerable strength.

"A project? Do tell me more…"

"It's a political project, Vladi. You wouldn't be interested. You're more into stealing money from poor Canadians and getting your friends hooked on that horse shit."

"Mmm, a political project. How fascinating. Maybe I can help. I'm a pretty civic-minded guy, you know. I've read Lenin's *State and Revolution* at least twice in college."

"You're a beautiful man, Vladimir," Morgan said.

"Oh, fuck you, Morgie. What's the project? You're going to blow up the Foot or something? There's dynamite in that sealed room of yours? You and Tommy are going to light the fuse during the May Day parade? Dead *babushka*s as far as the eye can see…"

Morgan threw her empty soda can at Vladimir where it momentarily stung his left ear and rattled off one tinted window. "Boy and girl, please be good to expensive car," Jan remarked from the driver's seat.

"What the hell was that?" Vladimir hissed at her. "What the hell did you do that for?" Morgan said nothing. She stared out her window at the pyrotechnics of an overturned oil truck in the middle of the highway, firemen in Day-Glo jackets waving Jan onto a side road. "Are you fucking crazy?" Vladimir said.

Morgan remained silent and this silence made Vladimir both enraged and a little giddy. "Oooh, was I right?" he taunted, scratching his offended ear. "You gonna blow up the Foot, eh? Little Morgan and her platonic buddy Tommy gonna blow up the Foot!"

"No," Morgan said.

"I beg your pardon?"

"No," she said once more. But the "No" repeated twice would be her undoing.

No, Vladimir thought. What the hell did that mean? He took her first "No" at face value, then he added the second "No" and then he threw in her long silence plus the brutal attack with the soda can. What was he thinking now? But it couldn't be. Death to the Foot? No. Yes? No. But how?

"Morgan," Vladimir said, suddenly serious. "You're not going to blow up the Foot, are you? I mean that would just be..."

"No," Morgan said for the third time, still looking away. "It's nothing like that."

"Jesus Christ, Morgan," Vladimir finally said. Sealed room. Crazed *babushka*s. Semtex? That one clichéd word announced itself uninvited. "Semtex?" Vladimir said.

"No," Morgan whispered, still looking outside her window at the dregs of urban Prava, an abandoned railroad station, a television tower lying on its side, a socialist-era swimming pool filled with dismantled tractors.

"Morgan!" Vladimir said, reaching over to touch her but deciding otherwise.

"You don't understand anything," Morgan said. She covered her face with her hands. "You're just a little boy," she said. "An *oppressed* immigrant. That's what Alexandra calls you. What the hell do you know about oppression? What do you know about anything?"

"Oh, Morgan," Vladimir said. He couldn't help but feel a swift and ambiguous sadness. "Oh, Morgan," he repeated. "What have you gotten yourself into, honey?"

"Give me your mobile..." Morgan said.

"What?"

"You want to meet him...Is that what you want? Mr. Vladimir Girshkin. Criminal laureate. I can't believe what you just put me through at that dinner. That poor stupid woman. 'Okh! Okh! Okh!' I can't believe any of you people...Give me your phone!"

AND SO IT WAS DONE. A connection was made. Two hours later. Half past midnight. Back at Morgan's *panelak*. He came with a partner. "This is my friend," Tomaš announced. "We call him Alpha."

Waiting for the Stolovans, Vladimir had helped himself to several vodka shots and was on the verge of becoming boisterous. "Hey there, Alpha!" he shouted. "Are you part of a team? Like Team Alpha? Oooh...I love you guys already."

"I have no money," Tomaš said to Morgan. "Taxi is waiting outside. Could you..." Without a word Morgan ran off to pay the taxi.

"How about I fix you a drink, Tommy," Vladimir said. "Alpha, what are you having?" Vladimir was recumbent in his usual place on the sofa, while the two Stolovans remained standing across the room, their postures hunched and guarded as if Vladimir was a wild ocelot that might attack at any moment.

"I'm not a drinker," Tomaš said, and by Vladimir's estimation he wasn't much of anything. A slight man with pink, scaly patches of psoriasis on his cheeks and a thicket of receded yellow hair that formed a natural mohawk, he was dressed in an old trench coat with thick glasses that verged on safety goggles, and a bright shirt, possibly of Chinese origin, which peeked out of his coat. Alpha looked rather similar (both had their hands jammed into their coat pockets and were blinking a lot), except Tomaš's sidekick was entirely missing a set of eyebrows (industrial accident?) and had a telephone cord tied around the waist of his trench coat. Without knowing it, the two gentlemen were actually on the cutting edge of

fashion, wearing what in New York would soon be called "Immigrant Chic."

"I thought, or rather, I am thinking now," Tomaš declared, "that
I am to blame for problems here. I should have come to you forthly.
Yes? Forthly? Excuse my English. In affairs between man and
woman, honesty *must* be the lodestar by which we navigate."

"Yeah," Vladimir said as he loudly sucked on a lemon.
"Lodestar. You said it, Tommy." Now why was he being so mean to
this unfortunate man? It wasn't exactly jealousy over Tomaš's affair
with Morgan. It was... What? A sense of overfamiliarity? Yes, in
some way, this pockmarked Tomaš was like a long-lost landsman.
What a thought: for all his posturing, very little separated Vladimir
from his ex-Soviet brethren, from the childhoods spent lusting
after cosmonaut Yuri Gagarin, drinking endless cups of homemade
yogurt for dubious health reasons, and dreaming of someday
bombing the Americans into submission.

Tomaš, for his part, ignored Vladimir's remarks. "I was privileged," he said, "to be Morgan's companion from 12 May 1992
through 6 September 1993. On the morning of 7 September, she
ended our love relationship and we have been since then steadfast
friends." He looked imploringly toward Vladimir's vodka bottle
and then down to the pair of broken moccasins on his feet. As soon
as he spoke with those awkward gooey lips, his red ears flapping
along to the sound of each consonant, Vladimir knew it was true:
Tomaš was no longer in the running. Poor guy. There was something indubitably unsettling about having to confess one's failure
as a lover. Then again, Vladimir tried to picture the little Stolovan
with the big flattened nose and ruined skin on top of Morgan and
immediately felt all the more sorry for her. What the hell was she
thinking? Did she have some sort of a fetish for Eastern European
sad sacks? And if so, where did that leave Vladimir?

"What do you think of all this, Alpha?" Vladimir asked Tomaš's partner.

"I have never known love," Alpha confessed, tugging at his telephone cord. "Women do not think of me as this type of guy. Yes, I am alone, but I do many things to keep busy . . . I am very busy with myself."

"Wow," Vladimir said sadly. Being with these two made him feel lost and disoriented, as if his traditional outsider's place in the social hierarchy had been completely usurped. "Wow," he repeated, trying to imbue the word with a kind of empty Californian inflection.

Morgan came back into the flat, averted her eyes from her lover and ex-lover, and busied herself with taking off her snow-covered galoshes. "You know, I'm actually starting to like your friends," Vladimir told her. "But I still can't believe that you and Tomaš here once shared a bed . . . He's not exactly . . ."

"To you I am so-called drip," Tomaš said plainly. "Or, perhaps, nerd or bore." He bowed a little as if to show how comfortable he was with his identity.

"Tomaš is a wonderful man," Morgan said, taking off her sweater, dressed now only in the famous silk blouse. The three Eastern Europeans paused to examine her silhouette. "There's a lot you could learn from him," Morgan continued. "He's not an egoist like you, Vladimir. And he's not even a criminal. How about that!"

"Maybe I'm missing something here," Vladimir said, "but I thought that blowing up a hundred-meter statue in the middle of the Old Town constituted a crime."

"He knows about the Foot destruction!" Tomaš shouted. "Morgan, how you can tell? We are bound by blood!" Alpha, too, looked shaken by this news. He pressed his hand to his breast pocket, where a Stolovan–English dictionary and some computer diskettes likely resided.

"He'll keep his mouth shut," Morgan said in a tone so blasé it was scary. "I'm privy to some info on his PyramidInvest—"

*He'll keep his mouth shut?...Privy?...*Oh, this Morgan was hardboiled! "Tell me," Vladimir asked her, "wasn't it a little danger-ous for us to live here in this shoddy *panelak,* the very earth shak-ing from the tremors of our fucking [slight look of discomfort on Tomaš's part] while hundreds of kilograms of Semtex were stowed in the next room?"

"Not Semtex," Alpha said. "We prefer C4, American explosive. We trust only American. Nothing good left in our world."

"You fellows are ready for the Young Republicans, I do believe," said Vladimir.

"C4 is very good explosive to control," Alpha went on, "and also strong with TNT equivalency of one hundred eighteen percent. Placed at, mmm, such and such interval within Foot and activated by external source, I think result will be that the top of Foot implodes...What I am meaning is that top of Foot will collapse inside hollow of Foot itself. Most important caveat: Nobody get hurt."

"I take it you're the munitions expert," Vladimir said.

"We are both students at the Prava State University," Tomaš explained. "I am studying at faculty of philology and Alpha study-ing at faculty of applied science. So I am working out theory for destruction of Foot and Alpha designing explosion materials."

"Exactly," Alpha said, fluttering his hands inside his coat pock-ets like an anxious bird. "How do you say? He is the intellectual and I am the materialist."

"I don't get it," Vladimir said. "Why don't you two just get jobs at one of those nice German multinationals on Stanislaus Square? I'm sure you're both quite handy with computers and your English is *primo.* If you learn to speak a little office Deutsche and maybe pick up some new tennis shoes at the Kmart I'm sure you'll be rak-ing in the crowns."

"We are not averse to working for this company you mention,"

Tomaš said, as if Vladimir had just offered them a job. "We would like to live nice life and make babies too, but before we can make this future we must take care of the sad history." He looked meaningfully to Morgan.

"I see," Vladimir said. "And by blowing up the Foot, you're…taking care of that…Ah, that pesky history!"

"You don't know how their families have suffered!" Morgan suddenly said. She was staring at Vladimir with those dead gray eyes, her political eyes, or perhaps the eyes of some greater unhappiness.

"Oh, yes," Vladimir said. "How right you are, Morgan. What do I know? You see, I was actually brought up by Rob and Wanda Henckel of San Diego, California. Yes, a healthy childhood spent watching the Pacific surf crash at my big suntanned feet, a four-year stint at UCSD, and now here I am, Bobby Henckel, senior brand manager of Flo-Ease Laxatives for the Eastern region…That's right, Morgan, please do tell me more about what it's like to be from this part of the world. It all sounds so damn exotic and, jeez, kinda sad, too…Stalinism, you say? Repression, eh? Show trials, huh? Wowsers."

"It's different for you," Morgan muttered, glancing at Tomaš for support. "You're from the Soviet Union. Your people invaded this country in 1969."

"*It's different for me,*" Vladimir repeated. "*My people.* Is that what you've been telling her, Tom? Is this the world according to Alpha? Ah, my dear stupid fellows…Do you know how similar we are, the three of us? Why, we're the same proto-Soviet model. We're like human Ladas or Trabants. We're ruined, folks. You can blow up all the Feet in the world, you can rant and rave through the Old Town Square, you can emigrate to sunny Brisbane or Chicago's Gold Coast, but if you grew up under that system, that precious gray planet of our fathers and forefathers, you're marked for life.

There's no way out, Tommy. Go ahead, make all the money you want, hatch those American babies, but thirty years later you'll still look back at your youth and wonder: What happened? How could people have lived like that? How could they have taken advantage of the weakest among them? How could they have spoken to each other with such viciousness and spite, much as I'm speaking to you right now? And what's that strange coal-like crust on my skin that clogs the shower drain every morning? Was I part of an experiment? Do I have a Soviet turbine instead of a heart? And why do my parents still quake every time they approach passport control? And who the hell are these children of mine in those Walt Disney World parkas running around making noise like there's nothing to stop them?"

He got up and walked over to Morgan, who shifted her gaze away from him. "And you," he said, recovering some of the anger he had lost during his speech to the Warsaw Pact duo. "What are you doing here? This isn't your battle, Morgan. You have no enemies here, not even me. That pretty Cleveland suburb, that's for you, honey. This is *our* land. We can't help you here. Not any of us."

He finished his drink, felt the surge of its lemony warmth, and, quite unsure of what he was doing, walked out of the apartment.

WIRY GUSTS OF WIND were prodding frozen Vladimir forward, jabbing at his back with sharp-nailed fingers. He was wearing nothing more than a sweater, a woolen pair of winter janitor pants, and some long underwear. And yet the deadly circumstances of being caught coatless on an icy January night did not bother Vladimir. A steamy river of alcohol ran through him.

He tumbled ahead.

Morgan's building was an isolated structure, but further in the distance, beyond a ravine that concealed an old tire factory, there decamped a regiment of condemned *panelak*s, which, with their rows of broken windows, looked like short, toothless soldiers guarding some long-sacked fortress. Now, there was a sight! The five-story concrete tombstones, perched on a little hill, were slouching toward the ravine, one building having shed its facade entirely so that the tiny rectangles of its rooms were exposed to the elements like a giant rat maze. Chemical flames emanating from the tire factory in the gorge below lit up the building's ghostly recesses, reminding Vladimir of grinning holiday jack-o'-lanterns.

And once again, the undeniable feeling that he was home, that these ingredients—*panelak,* tire factory, the corrupted flames of industry—were, for Vladimir, primordial, essential, revelatory. The truth was that he would have ended up here anyway, whether or not Jordi had taken out his member in that Floridian hotel room; the truth was that for the last twenty years, from Soviet kindergarten to the Emma Lazarus Immigrant Absorption Society, all the signs had been pointing to this ravine, these *panelaks,* this sinking green moon.

He heard his name being called. Behind him, a small creature was steadily advancing, bearing in its arms what seemed to be another creature, which on closer inspection proved to be only a dead coat.

Morgan. She was wearing her ugly peacoat. He heard the crunch-crunch of her footsteps in the snow and saw clouds of her breath puffing skyward at regular intervals like the effusions of an industrious locomotive. Other than her footfalls there was complete silence, the winter silence of a forgotten Eastern European suburb. They stood facing each other. She handed him the coat and a pair of her fluffy purple earmuffs. He figured it must have been the brutal cold that was filling her eyes with steady tears, because when she spoke it was in her usual collected manner. "You should come back to the house," she said. "Tomaš and Alpha are getting a taxi. We'll be alone. We can talk."

"It's nice here," Vladimir said, slipping on the earmuffs, gesturing at the ruined buildings and smoky ravine behind him. "I'm glad I took a walk...I feel much better." He wasn't sure what he was trying to say, but already his voice was lacking in malice. It was hard to think of a reason to hate her. She had lied to him, yes. She had not trusted him the way lovers sometimes trust one another. And so?

"I'm sorry about what I said," Morgan said. "I talked with Tomaš."

"Don't worry about it," Vladimir said.

"Still, I'd like to apologize..."

Vladimir suddenly reached out and rubbed his hands on her cold cheeks. It was the first contact they had had in hours. He smiled and heard his lips crack. The situation was clear: They were two astronauts on a cold planet. He was, for his part, a gentle dissembler, a dodgy investment guru with his hands in many pockets. She was a terrorist who drove tent stakes into the ground, who cradled mewing stray cats in her arms, not to mention the poor Tomaš. Vladimir was weighing his words to best describe this arrangement, but soon found himself speaking rather indiscriminately. "Hey, you know, I'm proud of you, Morgan," he said. "This thing, this blowing up the Foot, I don't agree with what you're doing, but I'm glad you're not just another Alexandra editing some stupid lit mag with a funky Prava address. You're like on a...I don't know...some kind of Peace Corps mission...Except with Semtex."

"C4," Morgan corrected him. "And nobody's going to get hurt, you know. The Foot's going to—"

"I know, implode. I'm just a little worried about you. I mean, what if they catch you? Can you imagine yourself in a Stolovan jail? You've heard the *babushkas*' war cry. They'll send you to the gulag."

Morgan narrowed her eyes in thought. She rubbed her mittens together. "But I'm an American," she said. She opened her mouth again, but there was nothing more to say on the subject.

Vladimir absorbed her arrogance and even laughed a little. She was an American. It was her birthright to do as she pleased. "Besides," Morgan said, "*everybody* hates the Foot. The only reason it didn't get knocked down is because of official corruption. We're just doing what everyone wants. That's all."

Yes, blowing up the Foot was actually *democratic.* A manifestation of the people's will. She really was an emissary from that great proud land of cotton gins and habeas corpus. He remembered their first date all those months ago, the eroticism of her snug bathrobe and easygoing ways; once again, he wanted to kiss her mouth, lick the brilliant white pillars of her teeth. "But what if you *do* get caught?" Vladimir said.

"I'm not the one that's gonna blow it up," Morgan said, wiping her teary eyes. "All I'm doing is storing the C4, because my apartment is the last place anyone would look." She reached over and fixed his earmuffs so that they corresponded directly with his ears. "And what if *you* get caught?" she said.

"What do you mean?" Vladimir asked. Him? Caught? "You're talking about this PravaInvest shit?" he said. "It's nothing. We're just ripping off a few rich people."

"It's one thing to steal from that spoiled Harry Green," Morgan said, "but getting Alexandra and Cohen hooked on some awful horse drug... that's fucked up."

"It's really that addictive, huh?" Vladimir said. He was heartened by the fact that she was assigning relative values to his misdeeds—drug dealing, bad; investor fraud, less bad. "Well, maybe I should phase that stuff out," he said. He looked to the overcast skies pondering his horse tranquilizer's vast profit margins, substituting horse powder for stars.

"And that Groundhog," Morgan said. "I can't believe you would want to work for someone like that. There's, like, nothing redeeming about him."

"They're my people," Vladimir explained to her, holding his hands up to demonstrate the messianic concept of *my people*. "You have to understand their plight, Morgan. The Groundhog and Lena and the rest of them—it's as if history's totally outflanked them. Everything they grew up with is gone. So what are their options now? They can either shoot their way through the gray economy or make twenty dollars a month driving a bus in Dnepropetrovsk."

"But don't you find it dangerous to be around maniacs like that?" Morgan asked.

"I suppose," Vladimir said, enjoying the furrowed look of concern on her face. "I mean there's this one guy, Gusev, who keeps trying to kill me, but I think I've nailed him pretty good for now . . . You see, I usually whip the Groundhog in the bathhouse with birch twigs . . . It's like this ceremonial thing that I do . . . And Gusev used to . . . Well, for one thing, Gusev is this murderous anti-Semite—"

He stopped. For a few frozen moments the burden and the limitations of Vladimir's life seemed to float along on his breath like cartoon captions. By then, they had been standing on the extraterrestrial surface of Planet Stolovaya for over ten minutes with only their earmuffs and mittens providing life support. The wintry landscape and the natural loneliness it engendered was taking its toll; at once, without prompting, Vladimir and Morgan embraced, her ugly peacoat against his fake-fur–collared overcoat, earmuff to earmuff. "Oh, Vladimir," Morgan said. "What are we going to do?"

A gust of tire-factory smoke disgorged itself from the ravine and took on the shape of a magical jinni just released from his glassy prison. Vladimir pondered her reasonable question, but came up with one of his own. "Tell me," he said, "why did you like Tomaš?"

She touched his cheek with her arctic nose; he noticed that her proboscis always seemed a bit more globular and full-bodied at night, perhaps the work of shadows and his failing eyesight. "Oh, where do I start?" she said. "For one thing, he taught me everything I know about *not* being American. We were penpals in college, and I remember he'd send me these letters, these endless letters I could never completely understand, about subjects I knew nothing about. He wrote me poems with titles like 'On the Defacement of the Soviet Rail Workers' Mural at the Brezhnevska Metro Station.' I guess I took Stolovan and history classes just to figure out what the hell he was talking about. And then I landed in Prava and he met me at the airport. I can still remember that day. He looked absolutely hopeless with that sad face of his. Hopeless and darling and also like he desperately needed me to touch him and to be close with a woman... You know, sometimes that's a good thing, Vladimir, to be with a person like that."

"Hmm..." Vladimir decided that he had heard just about enough on the subject of Tomaš. "And what about me—" he started to say.

"I liked that poem you read at the Joy," Morgan said, kissing his neck with her glacial lips. "About your mother in Chinatown. You know what my favorite line was? 'Simple pearls from her birth-land... Around her tiny freckled neck.' It was awesome. I can totally see your mother. She's like this tired Russian woman and you love her even though you're so different from her."

"It was a stupid poem," Vladimir said. "A throwaway poem. I have very complicated feelings for my mother. That poem was just bullshit. You have to be very careful, Morgan, not to fall in love with men who read you their poetry."

"Don't be so hard on yourself," Morgan said. "It was nice. And you were right when you said that you and Tomaš and Alpha had a lot in common. Because you do."

"I had meant that in an abstract sense," Vladimir said, thinking of Tomaš's psoriasis-scarred face.

"See, here's the thing about you, Vladimir," she said. "I like you because you're nothing like my boyfriends back home and you're nothing like Tomaš either... You're worthwhile and interesting, but at the same time you're... You're partly an American, too. Yeah, that's it! You're needy in a kind of foreign way, but you've also got these... American qualities. So we have all these overlaps. You can't imagine some of the problems I had with Tomaš... He was just..."

Too much of a good thing, Vladimir thought. Well then, here was the scorecard: Vladimir was fifty percent functional American, and fifty percent cultured Eastern European in need of a haircut and a bath. He was the best of both worlds. Historically, a little dangerous, but, for the most part, nicely tamed by Coca-Cola, blue-light specials, and the prospect of a quick pee during commercial breaks.

"And we can go back to the States when all this is over," Morgan said, grabbing his hand and starting to pull him back to her *panelak* with its promise of stale Hungarian salami and a glowing space heater. "We can go home!" she said.

Home! It was time to go home! She had selected her quasi-foreign mate of a line-up of wobbly candidates, and soon it would be time to head back to Shaker Heights. Plus, as an added bonus, she didn't even have to declare him at customs; Citizen Vladimir had his own shiny blue passport embossed with a golden eagle. Yes, it was all coming together now.

But how could Vladimir abandon all that he had achieved? He was the King of Prava. He had his very own Ponzi scheme. He was avenging himself for his entire rotten childhood, swindling hundreds of people who most likely deserved his vengeance. He was going to make Mother proud. No, he wouldn't go home!

"But I'm making money here," Vladimir protested.

"It's okay to make some money," Morgan said. "We could

always use the money. But Tomaš and I are going to wrap it up with the Foot pretty soon. We're thinking maybe April or so for the detonation. You know, I can't wait for that damn thing to explode already."

"Eh..." Vladimir paused. He was attempting, momentarily, to order and catalog her entire psychology. Let's see. Blowing up the Foot was an act of aggression against the father, right? Therefore, Stalin's Foot represented the authoritarian constraints of a Middle American family, *ja? A Day in the Life of Morgan Jenson*, that sort of thing. So her panic attacks were gone because, to quote her campus shrink, Morgan was *lashing out*. At the Foot. With Semtex. Or C4, rather.

"Morgan—" Vladimir started to say.

"Come on," she said. "Walk faster. I'll make us a bath. A nice warm bath."

Vladimir dutifully increased his pace. He looked back once more at the condemned *panelak*s and at the blazing ravine, and noticed the quadruped figure of a stray dog pawing the edge of the precipice, trying to see if it could slip down to the warmth of the tire factory without losing its canine footing. "But Morgan!" Vladimir shouted, yanking her coat sleeve, suddenly worried about the most elemental thing of all.

She turned around and presented him with the Face of the Tent, the halo of sympathy he had found in her eyes after he had climbed on top of her. Oh, she knew what he wanted, this shivering homeless Russian man in a pair of purple earmuffs from Kmart-Prava. She grabbed his hands and pressed it to her heart buried deep beneath her peacoat. "Yes, yes," she said, hopping on one foot to keep warm. "Of course, I love you. Please just don't worry about that."

HE LEARNED NOT TO WORRY ABOUT IT. HE PUT HIS arms around her. He closed his eyes and breathed in deeply. She must have done likewise.

Their devotion to their strange projects was inspiring. They were as busy as New York office workers and Vladimir, for his part, just as productive. By the end of the year the PravaInvest juggernaut had rumbled across the expatriate landscape to collect over five million U.S. dollars through sales of its uncommon stock, its brisk business in veterinarian supplies, and the quick turnover at the Metamorphosis Lounge. The FutureTek 2000 even presented the public with a shiny plastic box labeled "fax modem."

The dedicated staff was mobilized. Kostya took the financial reigns, František ran the burgeoning agit-prop machine, Marusya performed daily miracles out in the opium fields, Paavo dropped "phat" beats with distinction, and Cohen even managed to turn out a spiffy little literary journal.

Yes, a lot had happened to Cohen since the misadventure with Gusev and the skinheads, his much-trumpeted liaison with Alexandra being but one long ostrich feather in his mighty rabbit-fur cap. Recently, for example, Vladimir's friend had delved into *Cagliostro* in a way that, clearly, he had never delved into anything before. Each week he managed to spend at least fifty hours at the computer, surprising himself with what his single-mindedness and organizational skills could accomplish even when creativity failed. Cohen was even planning to use his night of Gusevian woe as a starting point for a long essay on the failings of Europe and, unavoidably, his father.

Satisfied of his subordinates' entrepreneurial zeal, Vladimir allowed himself a month in the West with Morgan. The first week of March found them in Madrid running from club to club with a group of friendly Madrileños who chased after the night's pleasure with the zest of Americans dashing after Pamplona bulls. Weeks two and three were spent in Paris, particularly at a mellow Marais *boîte* where some kind of fusion jazz was served up with a course of cheeses, and much champagne was consumed. By the fourth week Vladimir woke up at London's Savoy Hotel, as if hoping that its proximity to the financial doings of London's City would cure his hangover with a shot of Anglo mercantilism. Sobriety was desperately needed: Cohen had talked him into a trip to Auschwitz some thirty hours later. "For my essays," he had said.

Vladimir spent the day in the bathtub, alternately soaking himself then getting up to shower. It was a beast to behold, this shower: four separate heads that attacked from all angles: a regular spray from on top, a drip by shoulder level, a fountain straight to the hip, and a risqué geyser that rammed into Vladimir's genital area (to be used sparingly, that one). When he was dizzy from shower, Vladimir would sink back into the tub and thumb through the *Herald Tribune*, which thankfully had little to say that day, much like Vladimir himself.

With darkness only a few hours away, Vladimir dried his newly plump little body and started dressing for the evening. Morgan was still passed out, her behind lifting and falling slowly beneath the sheets in keeping with her subdued breath; she was dreaming perhaps of her terrorism or some long-dead family pet. After admiring this sight for a bit Vladimir gazed out the window where he could see a sliver of the Thames and a rain-soaked shoulder of St. James. Part of the view was taken up by a lonely skyscraper off in the distance, which, Vladimir had read in the hotel's glossy literature, was a new development called Canary Wharf, billed as the tallest building in Europe. An architectural nostalgic, Vladimir recalled one of the last times he had spent with Baobab, sitting up on his friend's roof, looking at the lone tower they were building across the East River in Queens.

He watched the Wharf for an indeterminate amount of time, letting himself be taken back to the days when Challah and Baobab could still count as the sum total of his affections; when through their failings he could draw comparative strength; when that childish feeling of superiority had been enough to sustain him. By the end of this reverie he found that his mobile had crawled into his hand. The dial tone hummed, indicating that the phone had been engaged.

He had forgotten Baobab's number, although once it was etched into his memory along with his social security number—both were now casualty to the passage of time and the efficacy of Stolovan spirits. The only connection he was still capable of making across the Atlantic was to Westchester, and for that, too, the time had come.

Mother, woken up from her deep weekend slumber, could only conjure up her requisite *"Bozhe moi!"*

"Mother," said Vladimir, amazed at how superfluous that word had become to his insane life, when only three years ago it had prefaced nearly every utterance.

"Vladimir, get out of Prava now!"

How did she know he had moved to Prava? "Pardon—"

"Your friend Baobab called. The Italian boy. I could not understand him, he is beyond understanding, but you are obviously in danger..." She paused to catch her breath. "Something about a fan, a man with a fan, he's determined to murder you and Russians are involved. Your dimwitted friend has been trying to reach you frantically and so have I, but the operator in Prava knows nothing of you, as can be expected..."

"The man with the fan," Vladimir said. He had wanted to say Fan Man, but it could not be said in Russian precisely that way. "Rybakov?"

"That is what I think he said. You must call him right now. Or better yet, get on the next plane out of Prava. You can even charge the ticket to my American Express account. It's that important!"

"I'm not in Prava," Vladimir said. "I'm in London."

"London! *Bozhe moi!* Every Russian mafioso has a flat in London now. So it's just like I suspected...Oh, Vladimir, please come back home, we won't make you go to law school, I promise. You can live in the house and do whatever you want, I can get you a promotion at the resettlement agency, now that I'm on the board. And, this may come as a pleasant surprise, but we've put away a nice sum of money in the past ten years. We must have, I don't know...Two, three, fourteen million dollars. We can afford to give you a little stipend, Vladimir. Maybe five thousand a year plus subway tokens. You can live at home and do whatever it is you young, listless people do. Smoke pot, paint, write, whatever they taught you at that fucking liberal arts school, devil confound all those hippies. Just please come back, Vladimir. They'll kill you, those Russian animals! You're such a weak, helpless boy, they'll wrap you in a blin and have you for supper."

"Okay, calm down, stop crying. Everything is fine. I'm safe in London."

"I'm not crying," Mother said. "I'm too agitated to cry!" But then she broke down and started weeping with such force that

Vladimir put down the phone and turned to Morgan, her form stirring beneath the blankets in response to the loudness and urgency of his voice.

"I will call Baobab now," he said quietly, "and if there's truly danger, then I'll be on the next plane to the States. I know what to do, Mother. I'm not stupid. I've become a very successful business-man in Prava. I was just about to send you a brochure of my new investment group."

"A businessman without an M.B.A.," sniffled Mother. "We all know what kind of businessman that is."

"Did you hear what I said, Mother?"

"I hear you, Vladimir. You'll call Baobab—"

"And I'm going to be perfectly safe. Forget about this being-eaten-in-a-blin business. Such nonsense! All right? I'm dialing Baobab now. Good-bye…"

"Vladimir!"

"What?"

"We still love you, Vladimir…And…"

"And?"

"…And your grandmother died two weeks ago."

"Babushka?"

"Your father nearly had a nervous collapse between her death and your stupidity. He's upstate right now, recovering with his fish-ing. The medical practice is losing money, but what can you do in such a situation? I had to let him go upstate."

"My grandmother…" Vladimir said.

"…has left for the other world," Mother completed. "They had her on the tubes for a few weeks, but then she died fast. Her face looked like she was in pain when she lapsed into a coma, but the doctors said that it didn't necessarily mean she was suffering."

Vladimir leaned himself against the cold window. Grand-mother. Running after him with her fruit and farmer cheese at their old mountain *dacha*. "Volodechka! *Essen!*" That crazed, dear woman. To think that now the rectangle that had been his family had suddenly, with the subtraction of a single, flat EKG line, been reconfigured into a tiny triangle. To think there were only three Girshkins left. "The funeral?" Vladimir asked.

"Very nice, your father cried an ocean. Listen, Vladimir, get on the phone with Baobab already. Your grandmother was old, life for her was not life anymore, especially with you gone from it. Oh, how she loved you...So, just say a prayer for her soul, and for your father, too, and for my suffering heart, and for this whole wretched family of ours on which the Lord has chosen to heap only calamity these past two quarters...Now go!"

IT TOOK TWELVE RINGS but finally the tired, husky voice came on, sounding as unhappy as a government worker caught at his desk immediately after the five o'clock bell. "Baobab residence."

"Is there a Baobab I could speak to?" Vladimir said. His friend's demented greeting made him smile. Baobab remained Baobab.

"It's you! Where are you? Never mind! Turn on CNN! Turn on CNN! It's starting already! Jesus Christ!"

"What the hell are you yelling about? Why does it always have to be hysteria. Why can't we have a normal—"

"That friend of yours with the fans, the one we had the citizenship for."

"How now?"

"He barged into Challah's, into your old apartment last week. He woke us up—"

"Us?"

Baobab sighed a long, pneumatic sigh. "After you left, Roberta married Laszlo," he explained with aggravated patience. "They went to Utah to unionize the Mormons. So…I guess…Challah and I were both lonely…"

"That's great!" Vladimir said. With all of his selfish little heart he wished them the best. Even the idea of them having sex, the tremor of their two large bodies shaking the already shaky foundations of Alphabet City, inspired in Vladimir only joy. Good for them! "But what did Rybakov want?"

"Dah! It's starting! It's starting! Turn it on! Turn it on!"

"What's starting?"

"CNN, idiot!"

Vladimir tiptoed his way into the living room, where the enormous black monolith that was the television had already been set to the news channel. He could hear the newscaster even before the picture materialized, the words *Breaking News—New York's Mayoralty in Crisis* floating along the bottom of the screen.

"…Aleksander Rybakov," the newscaster was saying in midsentence. "But to most people, he is simply…The Fan Man." The reporter was an unsmiling young woman in a provincial tweed suit, hair tied into a painful bun, teeth buffed into a reflective sheen. "We were first introduced to the Fan Man three months ago," she continued, "when his many letters to the *New York Times* lambasting New York's urban decay came to the attention of the city's mayor."

"Aaah!" Vladimir shouted. So he'd done it. He'd finally done it, that grizzly old loon.

Shot of a gilded banquet room, the mayor—a tall man with a square-set face that even two powerful jaws could not stretch into a smile—standing next to a hysterically grinning Rybakov, looking slim and polished in a three-piece banker's suit. Above them a banner read: NEW YORK CELEBRATES THE NEWEST NEW YORKERS.

MAYOR: And when I look at this man, who has suffered such persecution in his homeland and has traveled three thousand miles just to speak out on the very same issues I believe in—on crime, on welfare, on the decline of civic society—well, I just have to think that despite all the naysayers, thank God for—

RYBAKOV (spitting freely): Crime, tphoo! Welfare, tphoo! Civil society, tphoo!

NEWSCASTER: Mr. Rybakov's brash outspokenness and conservative stances certainly earned him many enemies among the city's liberal elite.

GRAY-HAIRED BOW-TIED LIBERAL (looking more tired than enraged): I object not so much to this so-called Fan Man's simplistic views on race, class, and gender but to the whole spectacle of parading around a human being who is obviously in dire need of help just to serve a misguided political purpose. If this is the mayor's idea of bread and circuses, New Yorkers are not amused.

RYBAKOV shown behind a lectern, cradling a little fan, smiling, his eyes clouded over with pleasure, as he lovingly croons: "Faaan… Faaanichka. Sing 'Moscow Nights' for Kanal Seven, please."

NEWSCASTER: But the end came quickly when the mayor invited Mr. Rybakov to register to vote at an official City Hall ceremony. Television crews from around the country gathered to witness the much-ballyhooed "first vote" of the Fan Man's life. The streets around City Hall were to be sealed off for the day for a "Fan Man Get-Out-the-Vote Block Party" complete with sturgeon and herring stands, the two staples of the Fan Man's diet, provided courtesy of Russ & Daughters Appetizing.

MAYOR (holding a piece of sturgeon between thumb and index

finger): I'm the grandson of immigrants. And my son is the great-grandson of immigrants. And I've always been proud of that. Now I want all you naturalized immigrants to go out there and vote today. If Mr. Rybakov can do it, so can you!

NEWSCASTER: But only an hour before the ceremony was underway, reports leaked out from the mayoral administration that Mr. Rybakov was, in fact, *not* a citizen. INS records indicate that at a naturalization ceremony held last January, he had attacked Mr. Jamal Bin Rashid of Kew Gardens, Queens, while showering him with racial epithets.

MR. RASHID (dressed in kaffiyeh, excited, speaking in front of his garden apartment): He is shouting at me, "Turk! Turk, go home!" And he's hitting me on the head, baff! baff! with his, you know, with his crutch. Ask my wife, I am still not sleeping at night. My lawyer says: Sue! But I will not sue. Allah is all-forgiving and so am I.

Cut to Rybakov at a news conference surrounded by mayor's aides, a REPORTER shouting, "Mr. Rybakov, is it true? Are you a liar and a psychopath?"

Slow-motion shot of Rybakov as he picks up his crutch then sends it flying across the room, where it neatly whacks the offending reporter in the head. Silent shots of melee, Rybakov being tackled by the mayor's staff while the camera scrambles to get it all. Finally, the audio kicks in, and we hear RYBAKOV screaming: "I am citizen! I am America! Girshkin! Girshkin! Liar! Thief!"

NEWSCASTER: Police experts were unable to identify the term "Girshkin," but reliable sources tell us that no such word exists in the Russian language. Mr. Rybakov spent two weeks under observation at the Bellevue psychiatric center, while the mayor's staff attempted damage control.

MAYORAL AIDE (young, harried): The mayor reached out to this

man. He wanted to help. The mayor is deeply concerned
with the plight of crazed World War II veteran refugees from
the former Soviet Union.

NEWSCASTER: But it is today's investigative report by the *Daily
News* documenting the fact that Mr. Rybakov, here shown at
the helm of his thirty-foot speedboat, has been collecting
SSI benefits while living in a palatial Fifth Avenue apartment
that finally threatens to bring down the mayoral administration... We now go live to the mayor's news conference...

"**SEE! SEE!**" Baobab was shouting on the other end. "See what
you put me through! I'm trying to take a nap when Rybakov and
this crazy Serb knock down the door, and Rybakov's screaming,
'Girshkin! Girshkin! Liar! Thief!' And he's got the crutches just like
on TV. And Challah was in the kitchen dialing 911. I mean, this Fan
Man makes Jordi look perfectly reasonable. Hey, how's it going
with you, anyway?"

"Hm?"

"How's it going?"

"Ah," Vladimir said.

"Ah?"

"Ah," Vladimir repeated. "No more. No more, Baobab." He
thought of Jordi. And Gusev. And the Groundhog. "Why fight it? No
more."

"Fight it? What are you talking about? You're three thousand
miles away. Everything's roses. I just thought you should be
warned. Just in case he decides to look for you in Prava."

"Groundhog," Vladimir whispered.

"What?"

"His son."

"What about him?"

"Nothing," he said to Baobab. "Let it go."

"If you're trying to quote Paul McCartney, the correct wording is 'Let It Be.'"

"I have to go," Vladimir recovered. "Say good-bye to Challah."

"Hey! I haven't spoken to you in six months. Where are you going?"

"Concentration camp," Vladimir said.

34. HOW GRANDMA SAVED THE GIRSHKINS

A CONVOY OF BMWS, VLADIMIR'S PREFERRED METHOD of traveling these days, pulled into the parking lot of Stadtkamp Auschwitz II–Birkenau. The lot was empty save for one tour bus, its tourists having long disembarked, its Polish driver idling away the time by lovingly cleaning his boots. Vladimir and Morgan had just flown in from London and Cohen had taken the train up from Prava. Cohen's attempts to replace the BMWs with American autos had run into a snafu. PravaInvest's jeeps were taking part in one of Gusev's so-called readiness exercises, of which both NATO and the remains of the Warsaw Pact presumably were not informed. And so Vladimir and his friends were left to commute the three-kilometer distance between Auschwitz proper and its sister camp in the cars of the perpetrators.

They climbed the steps of the main lookout tower, beneath which ran the railroad tracks that kept the ovens supplied. This was the famous tower, a shot of which is requisite in any movie about the camps. For the sake of exaggerated scale, it would seem, many directors had shot the structure from the ground up. In truth, the tower was as squat and unimposing as a station house on the Metro-North railroad.

From the tower, however, the full extent of Birkenau was up for inspection. Rows upon rows of chimneys minus the buildings they were supposed to heat, stretched to the horizon like a collection of miniature factory stacks, bisected by the sandy path of the once busy railroad. The chimneys were all that remained after the retreating Germans, in their last public-relations gesture, dynamited the rest. But in some quadrants, rows of rectangular, ground-hugging barracks still stood, and it was easy to multiply them by the number of orphaned chimneys and in this manner to fill in the gaps of what used to be.

Cohen, consulting his well-worn guide to Europe's concentration camps, traced his finger against the horizon, and said in an even tone, "There. The ponds of human ashes." This was at the edge of the field of chimneys before a forest of naked trees began. Living figures could be seen trudging against the backdrop of the forest; perhaps this was the tour group whose bus was abandoned in the parking lot.

A lengthy cloud had passed—the late-winter sun redoubled its efforts, and Vladimir squinted, bringing his hand up to serve as a visor. "What are you thinking?" Cohen said, misinterpreting this gesture for a sign of trauma on Vladimir's part.

"Vladimir's tired," Morgan said. She understood something was wrong, but wasn't sure if Auschwitz alone was responsible. "You've been tired all day, haven't you, Vladimir?"

"Yes, thank you," Vladimir said, and almost bowed in gratitude for her intervention. The last thing he wanted to do was to speak to them. He wanted to be alone. He smiled and raised his finger as if to demonstrate initiative, then took the lead in descending the stairs and emerging into the forest of chimneys and surviving barracks.

Cohen and Morgan walked beside the railroad tracks, Cohen stopping every few meters to take a damning photograph. They ducked into the barracks periodically to see the blighted conditions of the camp inmates which, of course, left much to the imagination without the human element. They were on their way to the pit of human ashes lying at the end of the tracks. Vladimir walked alone, staying midway between the main lookout tower and the forest. This was where the ramp was supposed to be located, the ramp where arrivals were separated for death, either instantly by Zyklon B or protractedly by hard labor.

It was hard to recreate this part of the process, since only a narrow patch of dust ran off from the tracks to indicate that something had once been here. Across the tracks a sole structure stood—a rickety, wooden lookout post on a set of stilts, which reminded Vladimir of the house of *Baba Yaga*, the witch of Russian fairy tales. Her house was supposed to be built on chicken legs that would take the *Baba* to wherever she felt havoc needed to be wreaked. The house could also act on its own accord, galloping through the village, trampling honest Christian folk at will.

Vladimir's grandmother had fulfilled the duty of Russian grandmothers and told him *Baba Yaga* tales as an inducement for eating his farmer cheese, buckwheat kasha, and the other insipid delicacies of their country's diet. But as these tales were frightening indeed, Grandma tempered the carnage with helpful disclaimers, such as "I hope you know that none of *our* relatives was ever killed by *Baba Yaga!*" Whether Grandma consciously understood the deeper significance of this disclaimer, Vladimir would never know. But it was true that practically his entire family escaped Hitler's advance into the Soviet Union. It was actually Grandma herself who was responsible for saving the Girshkins from Hitler, although homegrown Stalin proved beyond her capabilities.

Originally, the Girshkins were situated near the Ukrainian town of Kamenets-Podolsk, a town whose Jews were all but wiped out in the early phases of Operation Barbarossa. The Girshkins, even then, were prosperous. They owned not one hotel but three, all catering to stagecoach travelers and thereby constituting perhaps one of the first known examples of the motel chain. Well, certainly in the Ukraine.

A practical clan, the Girshkins kept well abreast of the times. When the outcome of the Bolshevik Revolution seemed a certainty, the family pooled all their gold, threw it into a wheelbarrow (which, to hear Grandma tell it, was practically full), then emptied the wheelbarrow into the local stream and resolutely trampled back home to eat up the last of their sturgeon and caviar. Having thus eluded any aspersions of being *bourgeoisie,* the Girshkins put their best proletarian foot forward, and this particular limb—like the lamb shank at Passover representing the strength of the Lord's forearm—was embodied by Grandma.

Grandma joined the Red Pioneers, then the Komsomol Youth League, and finally the Party itself. There were pictures of her playing each of these venues with her eyes ablaze and mouth crinkled painfully into a smile, looking like a heroin addict granted her fix. Looking, in other words, like the paragon of Soviet agitprop, especially with her pendulous peasant bosom and the broadest shoulders in her province, said shoulders kept aloft by a posture that, all by itself, had won her a prize in high school. And so, with these attributes in tow, Grandma left for Leningrad. She managed to get herself admitted to the infamous Institute of Pedagogy, where the most stalwart comrades were instructed in the science of indoctrinating the first generation of revolutionary toddlers.

After graduating the institute with top honors, Vladimir's grandmother became a resounding success at an orphanage for emotionally disturbed children. While the frilly Petersburg women shunned the traditional disciplinary aspects of child-rearing, Grandma singlehandedly beat the crap out of hundreds of wayward young boys and girls, who in a matter of days were on their knees, singing "Lenin Lives on Forever." This when they weren't repolishing the balustrades, waxing the floors, or combing the neighborhood sidewalks for scrap metal, which Grandma convinced them would somehow be recycled into a tank they could all take for rides about town. Within a year, this no-nonsense approach, fresh from the cane-wielding, belt-swinging provinces, had yielded such spectacular results that nearly all the children were deemed no longer emotionally disturbed. Indeed, many of them achieved prominence in all walks of Soviet life, the majority with the military and security organs.

After her tenure at the orphanage, Grandma was given a cheap plastic medal and an entire grammar school to lord over. But the most enduring aspect of her success was her ability to get the Girshkins out of bleak, industrializing Kamenets-Podolsk and into a spacious clapboard house on the outskirts of Leningrad. This first move spared the family a confrontation with the SS and their cheerful Ukrainian cohorts, while Grandma's second move, evacuation of the family before Leningrad fell under siege, saved the Girshkins from starvation and the shells of the Wehrmacht. How Grandma managed to pull the right strings and get all thirty Girshkins on the train to the Urals, where a partly-Jewish cousin, thrice removed, peacefully herded sheep in the shadows of an ore-smelting plant, was anyone's guess. The old woman guarded the truth like an NKVD file, but it was no mystery, really. Anyone who could reform an entire orphanage, or, more significantly, push Vladimir's dreamy and forgetful father through ten years of Soviet medical school (granted, it usually took five), could easily secure passage across the choked rail arteries of wartime Russia.

AND THAT, thought Vladimir, was the woman who had kept his family out of Stadtkamp Auschwitz II–Birkenau. If he possessed even the trace of doubt of an agnostic, now would be the time to mumble what he remembered of the Mourner's Kaddish. But with Hebrew school resolving the last enigmas of the empty heavens above, Vladimir could only smile and remember the feisty Grandma he once knew as a child.

He looked down the tracks where Cohen was on his knees taking a picture of a passing cloud, an unremarkable cirrus shaped as if it were sketched expressly for a meteorology textbook, its immortality assured only through the wild Polish luck of having passed the former concentration camp on the day of Cohen's visit. By this time the tour group had reached the tracks and started toward them at a leisurely pace—perhaps the pond of human ashes had had a debilitating effect and the worldly tour group was beating it back to the barracks.

Perhaps he was being judgmental.

Oh, it was high time to get out of here! Every thought inappropriate, every gesture a heresy. Enough! Look how his grandmother had escaped the gas and the bombs, investing body and soul in the Soviet system that ultimately took as many lives as the Teutonic evil streaming through the borders in columns of panzer and precision-strafing from above. Her lesson to Vladimir was as clear as it should have been for his fellow Jews interned in the pond of ashes down the track: *Get out while you can and by any means necessary.* Run, before the *goyim* get you, and get you they will, no matter how many laps you cover with Kostya and how much they claim to love you while the absinthe flows.

Vladimir turned to the main lookout tower, the direction from which the trains came with so much of their human freight already perished, from Bucharest and Budapest, Amsterdam and Rotterdam, Warsaw and Cracow, Bratislava and...could it be?...Prava. His golden Prava. The city that had treated his ailing ego as kindly as the springs of Karlsbad once treated gout. *Get out!* But how? And to what salvation? He thought of Grandma, forty years after Stalin died, huddled over volume seven of the Social Security Regulations with sleepless eyes, her magnifying glass at the ready, trying to figure out the meaning of "residual functional capacity."

Oh, to hell with this twentieth century that was almost at an end, with all its problems still intact and flourishing, and the Girshkins, once again, the brunt of the joke, the epicenter of the storm, the clearinghouse for global confusion and uncertainty. To hell with... Vladimir heard the singular sound of a zoom lens extending behind him and then the snap of a shutter. He turned. Behind him the tour group was paces away. A ruddy-cheeked middle-aged woman, as tall, thin, and neatly groomed as the poplars that surrounded Birkenau, was scrambling to deposit her camera into her crowded handbag, her eyes darting everywhere except in the direction of Vladimir. She had taken a picture of him!

The rest of the Germans also skirted the ground with their light-hued eyes, some glancing back at the offending photographer with likely malice. Amazingly, most of them looked to be in their seventies—large and healthy, with becoming wrinkles and just the perfect white cardigan sweaters for an informal afternoon—that is to say, they were old enough to have been in Birkenau in a different capacity some half a century ago. Should Vladimir, then, have spread out his chest, raised his head high to show off his dark Semitic curls, and then have said to them with a sardonic smile, "Cheese?"

No, leave such gestures to the Israelis. Our Vladimir could only smile shyly as the Germans approached, his shoulders hunched forward submissively, the way his parents had once approached the sour-pussed immigration officials at JFK.

Their tour guide was a handsome young man not much older than Vladimir although certainly younger-looking. He wore his thick hair long, and the granny-glasses lost amid his square, salubrious face likely contained plain, noncurative glass. There were pockets of loose flesh around his still-muscular chest and belly, giving the impression of a strapping country youth idled by a string of poor harvests. That was, in fact, the impression he gave Vladimir: a sensitive provincial man who had learned of liberalism and the German debt from a galvanic local teacher, a hippie from the time when hippies held sway over the land, and now he had himself joined the progressive ranks and took the blighted older generations to see the handiwork of their times. What a concept, thought Vladimir, neither impressed nor appalled.

His eyes met those of the tour guide who smiled and nodded as if this meeting had been prearranged. "Hi," he said to Vladimir, his voice trembling even for the duration of that minuscule syllable.

"Hello," Vladimir said. He brought up his hand in a formal gesture of greeting. He tried to recall instantly what it meant to look "grave," but knew he couldn't pull it off on the spot, not with the tumult of the past few days under his belt. He continued with his shit-eating grin.

"Hello," answered the tour guide as he filed past Vladimir. His elderly charges followed. With the ice seemingly broken by their leader, they were now able to look Vladimir briefly in the eye and even manage a little sympathetic smile. Only the middle-aged woman, the one who had dared to photograph Vladimir, the Live Jew of Birkenau, had increased her pace while staring resolutely ahead.

Thank you, come again, Vladimir thought to say, but instead he sighed, looked once more at the departing mane of the thoughtful young tour guide—his better in every aspect, despite the rotting branches of the German's family tree—and considered yet again his own relative loss of place in this world; his irrevocable perdition.

Ah, and where now, Vladimir Borisovich?

He began his long, pensive trudge to the pond of human ashes, where his friends were already waiting for him, Cohen aghast by

both the tour group and the ashes, Morgan solely by the ashes. Perhaps she could get Tomaš and Alpha to blow up the remains of
Birkenau as well. Just a few more kilos of C4 and they could *really*
take care of history.

And then his mobile phone rang.

"Well, well," said the Groundhog.

"Please don't kill me," Vladimir blurted out.

"Kill you?" The Groundhog laughed. "Kill my clever goose? Oh,
please, friend. We all knew what kind of character you were from
the start. Anyone who can bamboozle half of America can surely
fuck over my old man."

"I didn't mean to," Vladimir whimpered. "I love your father. I
love—"

"Okay, can you please shut up," the Groundhog moaned. "All is
forgiven, just stop crying. Now, I need you back in Prava. We've got
a strange new scheme going here."

"Scheme," Vladimir mumbled. What the hell was going on in
the Hog's little mind? "A strange new scheme…"

"Strange precisely because it isn't a scheme. A *legitimate* venture," the Groundhog explained. "A brewery in South Stolovaya that
looks ready to expand into West European and American markets."

"Legitimate venture," Vladimir repeated. His mind was barely
functioning. "Did Kostya advise you of this?"

"No, no, it's all me," the Groundhog said. "And you can't let anyone know about this, not even Kostya. Especially about the fact that
it's aboveboard. I don't want to be a laughingstock." He then
invited Vladimir to come out the following week and look over the
brewery. "Without your professional opinion no venture can be
consummated," he said. "Legitimate or otherwise."

"I will never betray you again," Vladimir whispered.

The Groundhog laughed once more, a soft chortle far removed
from his usual boisterous braying. Then he hung up.

PART VIII

GIRSHKIN'S

END

ON THE WAY TO THE SOUTHERN BREWERY THEIR CARA-
van had passed seemingly the entire unremarkable oeuvre of the
Stolovan landscape. Only one mountain, a compact trapezoid
indistinguishable from its neighbors, drew Vladimir's attention, for
Jan announced in a proud, instructive tone that this was the mountain on which the Stolovan nation had originated. Vladimir was
impressed. What a comfort to know the mountain from which
your kind had once come hollering down! He imagined that if the
Russians had had such a mountain it would be a great, sweeping
Everest out in the Urals on which a military surveillance base
would promptly be built, its RKO-style antennas arching into the
heavens, announcing that the sons and daughters of the Kievan
Rus had laid claim to the taiga and its grizzly bears, the Baikal and
its sturgeons, the shtetl and its Jews.

The only other point of interest on their way to the brewery was a
half-built nuclear power plant on the outskirts of town, its cooling
towers rising over a vast field of failing carrots in long spirals of unfinished skeletal grating, as if the meltdown had already occurred.

The brewery town itself was a charmless little burg where the
steeples of Gothic churches, the mansions of the leading mer-
chants, indeed the town square itself had long been cleared away

for a claustrophobic quadrant of graying buildings, each nearly identical, even if one was a hotel, the other an administrative center, the third a hospital. They drove straight to the hotel, its lobby a furry seventies affair crammed with prickly recliners, stale air, naked legs, and, in an homage to the leading employer of the locality, a sparkling vat of the local beer rising out of the shag carpeting like a lone Easter Island–head statue. But upstairs, in the Executive Wing (as the rooms with the *brass* doorknobs were designated), Vladimir felt a thrill of apparatchik camaraderie—these rust-colored, bric-a-brac-less quarters surely must have housed their share of Light Bulb Factory #27 directors and similar happy-go-lucky communist officials. If only František was here!

Not that Vladimir lacked Soviet residue among his traveling companions: He was accompanied by the Groundhog, Gusev, and two fellows who routinely passed out before the meat course was served at the *biznesmenski* lunches and were rumored to be the Groundhog's best friends from his Odessa days. One was a small hairless fellow who kept badgering Vladimir about the efficacy of minoxidil. His name was Shurik. The other one was called the Log, and looking at his withered, combative face—nine-tenths scowl, one-tenth eyebrow—one could easily see him floating lifeless down a river, belly up, blood trailing from the nail-thin indenture in the back of the head.

Perhaps better company can be had if one knows where to find it, but Vladimir, newly happy and secure, was as excited as the first-time hostess of a slumber party. Why, even Gusev, who had once almost killed him, seemed a lion tamed as of late. On the ride in, for example, he had bought Vladimir a pastry from a roadside restaurant. Then, with all the grandness and civility befitting the Hapsburg Court, he had let Vladimir cut in front of him on the line for the pissoir.

And so, with the world once again revolving in his direction, Vladimir was seen running about the hallways as if on spring break, shouting in a sparkling Russian: "Come see, gentlemen...A Coke machine that also dispenses rum!"

His room came with a pair of twin beds and Vladimir half hoped the Groundhog would split it with him so they could stay up late, smoking noxious Mars-20 cigarettes, drinking from the same bottle, shooting the breeze about NATO expansion and loves lost. And indeed, with collegiate bravado, the Groundhog soon stuck his head into the doorway and said: "Hey, wash up, you little Yid, and we'll hit the bar across the square. We'll rape and pillage, eh?"

"I'm there!" cried Vladimir.

THIS WAS SOME BAR. It was run by the local union in the basement of the former Palace of Culture and was habituated by the workers who were laboring on the nuclear power plant, and had probably been doing so since around the time Vladimir was born. Seven o'clock and already mad, hallucinatory inebriation had set in across the board. And then, as if the limits of human endurance were not yet pronounced exhausted, the whores were sent in.

The *prostitutki* in this part of the world formed a stylized labor brigade. Every one around five feet, nine inches in height, as if that particular span had been adjudged most convenient for the local boys; hair hennaed till it had the consistency of a well-worn mop; breasts and bellies, stretched by births bulging corsets a dirty mauve in color. They shimmied up to the dance floor without much enthusiasm and then, in a tradition that has become *diktat* in the eight formerly Soviet time zones—Lights! Disco ball! ABBA!

Vladimir's crew had only uncapped their first beer when the whores arrived and disco fever struck. The Groundhog and his boys immediately got giggly on the scene, fingering the Polo insignia on their shirts, mumbling, "Oh, the country folk," as if they were having a Chekhov moment of their own.

"These women have thighs that can squeeze the life out of you," noted little Shurik, not without appreciation.

"But this beer," Vladimir said. "It tastes like they keep a rusty nail in the bottle. *This* is the brewery that will export to the West?"

"Pour some vodka into it," the Groundhog said. "Look, it even suggests it on the bottle."

Vladimir looked over the label. Part of it did seem to read: "For best results add vodka, 6 ml." Or maybe this was the complex name of the brewery, one could never tell with the Stolovans. "Fine," Vladimir said and went to get a bottle of Kristal from the bar.

An hour later he was dancing to "Dancing Queen" with the prettiest *fille de nuit* in the house. She was the only one that did not tower above Vladimir, and that wasn't all that set her apart from her colleagues: She was young (although not "only seventeen," like the dancing queen of the title), she was lanky and especially lean in the chest, and, most significantly, her eyes did not have that staged good-humored look of the other whores. No, these were the clear, disinterested eyes of a New York debutante with poor grades sent to a college in West Virginia, or else a teenager in a contemporary advertisement for jeans. Even through his considerable inebriation—for do not think that vodka, when deposited in beer, creates a neutralizing reaction— Vladimir felt an affinity with this young, damaged apprentice to the trade. "What's your name?" he shouted.

"Teresa," she said in a mean, hoarse whisper, as if she was spitting the name out of her mouth forever.

"Vladimir," he said and bent down to kiss her speckled neck, aiming for a slot between the carefully spaced hickeys left by others.

But he didn't get a chance to pounce. The Groundhog had swept him aside with one apelike swoop, and attached him to the dancing triad of Groundhog, Gusev, and the Log. They had left their three prostitutes behind (all substantial middle-aged ladies drowning in blush) and were asserting their Russianness with a kind of abbreviated Cossack dance. Crouch together, rise together, kick out one foot, kick out the other... "Opa!" shouted the prostitutes, their faces as redand-white as the Polish flag. "Faster, little dove!" they encouraged Vladimir.

But it was out of Vladimir's hands. The force of the drunken Groundhog, pulling, pushing, swinging, squatting, was entirely responsible for Vladimir's own sorry movements. The Groundhog was a florid mass with a coherence all its own, giving generously to the reverie around him, shouting, "One more time, brothers! For the Motherland!"

At his first opportunity, Vladimir yelled, "Bathroom!" and ran for cover.

In the piss house, the union had just installed automatic flushers from Germany and mirrors over the urinals. Taking advantage of this march of progress, Vladimir groomed himself: He pushed down his wild hair and tried to string the most wayward locks into loops behind his ears; he opened his mouth and examined his slick, ivory teeth; he pulled back his hairline and promised to himself to sacrifice a goat to the makers of the hair tonic minoxidil. He said to himself: *Of course, I'm not going to fall in love with a prostitute*, and headed out.

By this time the ABBA selection had settled on "Chiquitita," which, drunk or not, is a terribly difficult song to dance to. Consequently, the ranks of dancers were decaying; the picniclike tables around the dance floor began filling up with the *prostitutki* and their men. But nowhere could Vladimir spot the Groundhog and his crew, not to mention his young whore. Feeling abandoned and with no place to invest his excitement, Vladimir went to refill his bladder at the bar. *"Dobry den',"* he told the tanned young bartender dressed in a tank top depicting an alligator playing with an American football.

"Hi, friend," said the barkeep in near-perfect English, as if the waves of the Pacific were stroking the sands of Malibu outside. "What can I do for you?"

Vladimir enumerated a lengthy list of booze while the bartender carefully looked him over. "Tell me, where did you come from?" he finally asked.

Vladimir told him.

"I have been there," the barkeep said and shrugged, obviously not impressed by the City on the Hudson. He moved on to another customer, a worker wearing nothing but a desperate grin and a cap of a striking blue color.

When he returned with the beer portion of Vladimir's request, Vladimir asked about his friends. "Went for a smoke outside," said the globetrotting mixologist. He bent down to Vladimir's level and now a most non-Californian scent could be detected from beneath his lanky arms. He said: "I have a note for you. But it's not from me, you understand?" He said this in a tone grave enough to indicate that Vladimir's response was necessary before the note was given.

"I understand," Vladimir said with the same gravity, only inwardly he was excited, for he believed it to be a love note from his prostitute, and he was deeply interested in the kind of seductions she would deploy and in what form and language. He took the small, folded ribbon of purple paper from the barkeep, who immediately galloped off to the other end of the bar, and unfurled it. A carefully drawn gunsight stared back at Vladimir, and beneath in boxy letters the familiar bilingual legend:

AUSLANDER RAUS! FOREIGNER OUT!

It was signed collectively, "The Stolovan Skinheads."

Vladimir did not say, "Ah…" He was on his feet and walking toward the exit. The soft flesh of prostitutes, the pungency of their perfume and hair, was an obstacle course he negotiated with partial success, saying along the way, "pardon, pardon, pardon…" But he was thinking, *Skinheads? Where? Who? The workers? They have hair.* A pace or two from the door he finally saw them out of the corner of his eye—the black military jackets, the camouflage pants, ankle-high boots; the faces didn't even register.

Outside, the familiar darkness disturbed by smog and the distant grumble of dysfunctional Trabants, an empty dirtyard facing the rump of a low, gray municipal building, the only illumination provided by the light trailing from the bar's open door. In front of him two skinheads appeared from different directions, both coming from outside his line of sight, coming together as if they were going to meld into a single unit, as if he was suffering from double vision and there was really only one set of gritted teeth, one pair of busted lips, and only one black swastika painted on an orange T-shirt below.

Vladimir turned around. The space between him and the bar door was rapidly filling up with young men and determined expressions; it was evident that the workers and the prostitutes in this town were not the only ones who formed identical cadres, for the enforcers of local ethnic purity resembled one another to the last detail. Perhaps they were all fathered by the same bald, slightly overweight man with his fists always squeezed by his side, and one eye permanently squinted as if against the oncoming glare of the African sun.

Then their ranks broke to admit one who was surely their leader—a head taller, broad-shouldered but thin, with a pair of contemporary wire-rims and the urgent, piercing gaze of a young German intellectual let loose in an American graduate program.

The tall one looked down at Vladimir's head as if it were a breeding ground for baby hydras and said, "Passport!"

Vladimir exhaled for the first time. He remembered, for some reason, that he didn't have a Soviet passport where his nationality would be listed as "Jew," and from this particular fact he allowed himself the idea of a loophole. No, it wasn't going to end like this. An entire life, a special little creature, an existence whose precariousness was its very leitmotif, extinguished at the hands of morons! "No! No passport!" he said. "Groundhog!" he shouted in Russian, in the direction of the bar.

The leader looked toward his men. *"Jaky jazyk?"* he barked. This was similar enough to Russian for Vladimir to understand: "What language?"

"Turetsky," one of the skinheads happily said, smashing a fist into his palm. Turkish.

The intellectual fixed his gaze on Vladimir once again. He was starting to work on a smirk of his own, which considerably united his appearance with those of his comrades. "You are from Arabia!"

Arabia. *Arabia!* Could it be they were looking for a different kind of Semite? "No Arabia!" Vladimir shouted, waving his hands dangerously close in the direction of the leader. "America! I am America!" He happily remembered the extremist fervor of some of his Zionist classmates in Hebrew school. "Arabia, *tphooo!"* He spit—unfortunately, on his shoe. "Islams…" He brought a mock trigger to his head and shot himself, "Boom!" although really he ought to have been shooting somewhere else, in the direction of the imaginary Arab, perhaps. Laughter broke out among the ranks at this self-indicting gesture, but it quickly got lost amid a volley of inimical snorts and a tightening of the ethnic-cleansing *cordon sanitaire* around Vladimir. Some of the hooligans were already spreading their legs apart, the better to keep their balance during the one-serving pogrom to come.

"Look," Vladimir said and, with hands shaking and vision blurred from the tears he could no longer control, tried to extricate his wallet from his jeans. "Give me a minute...Please, what will it hurt you... Look... American Express...*American Express*...And this is a New York State driver's license. You gentlemen ever been to New York? I know plenty of skinheads there. We go raise hell in Chinatown sometimes..."

The leader examined Vladimir's exhibits and then, in what Vladimir saw through his betraying tears as a foreboding gesture, put them into his own wallet, stepped back an inch, and nodded to the ground where he once stood.

"Please," Vladimir said in Stolovan. He was ready to say it again.

A fist landed above Vladimir's right eye, but before that pain was fully realized there was the sensation of flight and then the feeling of his body breaking up against the ground, his tailbone emitting a crack as the pain radiated outward from a hundred terminuses, and then a great cheer went up, although he didn't understand the exact word (hurrah?), then a girder, it would seem, landed against his ribcage and then one, two more on the other side, flashing in bright childhood yellows then receding to darkness and the aftershocks of pure pain, and then someone had jumped on his clenched fist and—*bozhe moi, bozhe moi*—there was that cracking again, the cracking you could feel in the back of your mouth, the cheering again (hurrah?), Morgan...wake up in Prava, *shto takoie?* which language? *pochemu nado tak?* my God, not like this, *svolochi!* you have to breathe, *nado dyshat',* breathe, Vladimir, and your mama will bring you...*zhirafa prinesyot*...a stuffed giraffe...*ya hochu zhit'!* I want to live! to continue to exist, to open your eyes, to run, to say to them, "No!"

"No!" Vladimir raised a broken fist into the air and swung it at a target that wouldn't present itself. His eyes opened simultaneously and he saw two figures standing in the direct light of the bar.

For a second his eyes focused, then unfocused, then, through an extraordinary ripple of pain charging through his spine like current, focused once more. He couldn't make out their expressions exactly, only that Gusev was nodding, while the Groundhog was looking straight ahead. And then, Vladimir let his fist drop. He saw a boot's wedge of steel making its way expressly toward his face and said, in two languages at the same time: "Come on."

"*Davai.*"

HE IS WALKING FROM HER DORMITORY; IT IS THE FIRST time they have slipped their hands into each other's pants. He is walking through the town square, a meticulously planted conglomerate of trees, lawns, and flowerbeds, which the Midwestern college maintains to remind itself of its less progressive Eastern brethren. It is morning. The clouds extend practically to the tops of the leafless oaks and a light drizzle sweeps in out of nowhere as if to remind the pedestrian of what clouds are all about. And yet, in one of the vagaries of Midwestern weather, this overcast February morning suddenly achieves an unlikely springlike temperature, conveyed through a wind as warm as the gust of a hair dryer.

He is wearing a heavy brown overcoat bought by Mother in anticipation of this bedeviling climate. Today, unlike frigid yesterday, he has unbuttoned it to the hilt and stuffed his scarf in his pocket, ignoring his mother's decades-old advice to "never let your guard down when warm weather suddenly appears, Vladimir. It is a silent killer, like venereal disease." But Mother is nowhere in sight, and he is free to catch both cold and gonorrhea.

This thought, in particular, makes him smile, and he stops in the middle of the square and puts his hand up to his nose, the one that had recently gone inside his new lover's utilitarian cotton underwear, had even gotten a rash from rubbing against its harsh elastic strap, then sniffs his other hand to compare. What animal smells she harbors, that sleek, soignée Chicagoan with her fashionable pageboy cut and strong Marxish opinions.

Ave Maria! It is the first time he had put his hand inside there. He has always imagined the first time would be with some castoff, a large, insipid girl even more scared then he was. Now everything has changed. Now he is standing in the middle of the square, rethinking it all, calculating his bounty with different functions: subtracting Leningrad, dividing by Baobab, adding the Chicagoan, and multiplying it all by his nascent ability to shed his past and become Educated American Man, one bored but ultimately happy superhero.

That pleasant moment in the town square lasts so long that he will remember it even when the particulars of his first tussle with another's genitalia will lose their distinctness. He will remember it just so: the birds confused by the weather chirping away, clinging to the leafless trees whose branches creak and tremble under the birds' weight as if they, too, are being reanimated by the warmth; the bare copses, regal and long, stretching the length of the college's ivied, pink-granite cathedral, recently reformed into a godless student union; the neo-Victorian turrets of the humanities building, once bustling with Pynchonites and Achebians, now abandoned to the intellectual ennui that settles in by spring term. Yes, this apparition, this beautiful and unlikely flora and fauna are finally his. Vladimir College, founded 1981, by the last wave of hopeful Leningrad Grain Jews disembarking at JFK and penetrating a thousand versts inland to mingle their sons and daughters with the new world's soft and fuzzy liberal elite. Thank you Momma and Poppa Girshkin for the $25,000 per year in tuition and costs. It will all work out in the end. I will not be a disappointment.

He makes sure he is the only person standing in the square's brief morning light, then embraces himself tightly the way he imagines the Chicagoan will do all night when she falls completely in love with him, when they begin to hammer out their plans of marriage after graduation. So far, they have spent their first night in a supine position, mostly out of the embarrassment of facing each other in bed, and he has developed all sorts of aches from the unfamiliarity of her grounded mattress. But he takes the pain in stride as evidence of his adventure, and, for the time being, he cannot imagine love's other malevolent pains, the vast penalties for casual infractions and trust misplaced. Although, truth be told, this particular ache hurts like hell too. And so he decides to head to his own dormitory, to his kind and sedulous Jewish roommate from Pittsburgh who will not be loath to fire up the bong on a special occasion like this. And then to get some sleep, finally.

HE OPENED HIS EYES for a moment of incalculable brevity, then closed them as the weight of his eyelids had become oppressive. In the darkness the pain seemed disseminated, a condition common to every part of his body as opposed to the several sites that through cast and bandage had been designated ground zero. But what he saw, in that burst of light and cognizance, was more than he needed to see. A cracked, mildewed tile, its hue a green, which undermined all greenness. Imagine a plant has been taken to a dank factory basement and there taught to reject all it once treasured—the air, the dew, the light and the chlorophyll—until the wilted thing resigns itself to making friends with the basement boiler. And then, in that instant, over that chipped, malformed tile, the outline of a fan blade passed with an anguished whoosh. A slow and ancient fan, its contours bulbous like the rear of a Studebaker.

He knew then the reality of the matter. Not the Midwest's gray sky above him, but Stolovaya's. And he remembered his last thought before he had lost consciousness, the graceless final option of a man without a country: *Escape.* He could already imagine his getaway plane, which, under the influence of the dated ceiling fan, had become a silver Trans-World stratoliner, its four propellers buzzing past sepia-toned clouds with thirty passengers and five crew members, headed for La Guardia Field.

His woke up to find his wrist warm, as if a localized fever had struck. This feeling was particularly disconcerting because south of the wrist lay a heavily anaesthetized void: his hand, likely a jumble of straight things twisted and smooth enclosures undone, no Trans-World stratoliner, rather the modern wreckage of a Boeing in a scrub field, bodies scattered about.

Morgan had slipped a hand around his wrist. She was pressing her index finger into it, measuring the pulse. She had on a straw hat with a daisy, beneath which her face was not just sad, but of a sadness—that is, sad and luminous. Her unpainted lips were chapped from worried nail-biting, a distant approximation of Vladimir's lips split by a boot. Immediately, Vladimir deduced that the hat with the daisy was as much an effort to seem unaged by this experience as an attempt at levity for his benefit.

"Morgie," he said. And then he remembered what this was all about. "I live."

"You're going to live a long time," she said, maneuvering around the bandages to kiss his nose. "We're both going to live a long time. And be happy, too."

And be happy, too. Vladimir closed his eyes and considered this. It almost didn't matter if she was right or wrong. He took in a deep breath, as deep as he could with his lungs brushing against surfaces ruptured and organs impaired. She smelled salty and vital. Her hat fell off as she leaned over him and a curtain of hair brushed against his face, some getting trapped in his hungry nose.

"I live," Vladimir said, squeezing tight the fist that had survived.

TWENTY MINUTES into his visit, Kostya was still pulling out apricots and bananas, along with dozens of mortally wounded local violets and gardenias from the outdoor market. He set up this harvest on the sills of Vladimir's twin windows, which looked out onto a silent New Town back street, bowing all the while as if he were offering sacrifices to a gilded Buddha.

Kostya had already apologized, professed his innocence, and crossed himself a thousand times. He had read Vladimir a letter from the Groundhog, written in a half-literate Russian, a letter whose gist was: "We men, if we must to be called men, must not let slights go unpunished."

The slight was then specified: "My poor, sick father… How could you betray him? And after all he has had to live through: Marriage and immigration, the Soviet navy and the American projects, the Stalin years and the early 90s recession. And I was no blessing as a kid, either, as you can imagine."

A settlement was offered: "We have fixed each other good, Vladimir. But now everything is solved and ended. Now we have work to do. There must be no more hurting and beating, only friendship and respect. You will heal and then we will go to the restaurant where you sang so well and I will pay for the dinner and wine."

And finally a postscript: "I could have had them kill you."

Kostya removed the last piece of fruit from his gym bag. He polished the apple with his hankie and carefully placed it on Vladimir's stomach. "Eat it immediately," he said. "This kind of apple quickly turns brown on the inside." He must have seen in this a fitting analogy for himself, for he clasped his hands to his powerful stomach, as if shoring up his guts, and said, "My God, those animals! They will suffer tenfold for this when their time of reckoning comes. And they will suffer eternally. Although it must be said, if one is to speak truthfully, that you have sinned against them as well, Vladimir. You have betrayed the trust of an old man. Of an invalid! And as for the Groundhog... he pays us handsomely, no? For all his pathologies, he is a kind man in his own right. And mostly he treats us like brothers."

Vladimir moved a fraction so that the apple rolled off the side of the bed and sent Kostya scrambling. He wanted to be surrounded by friends, not by the man who had trained his body for eight months only to allow for its destruction within minutes. "Tell the Groundhog to forget it," Vladimir said. "I will have nothing more to do with this organization. I am leaving the country. And you better get out of this business as well, before they nail you to the cross like your friend there."

"Please don't talk like that, Vladimir," Kostya said, polishing the apple with renewed vigor. He looked very Western these days in his tattersall Brooks Brothers shirt and tan chinos, but his frightened eyes reminded Vladimir of an old, toothless peasant, the kind he had only seen in picture books of Russia. "Now is the time to renew faith, not deny it," Kostya was saying. "And I wouldn't think of leaving the country if I were you. The Groundhog will certainly not allow it. There's a guard outside the room and the front and back entrances to the hospital are also guarded. I've seen it myself, Vladimir. They won't let you go. Have an apricot, please..."

"I will call the American embassy!" Vladimir said. "I am still an American citizen. I know my rights."

Kostya looked at him askance. "That will only create problems, don't you think?" He said this a little too forcefully, without his usual pious restraint, leaving Vladimir, for the first time, in question of his allegiances. "Besides, there's no phone in this room. Now, here, let me get the curtains. What an astoundingly beautiful day it is outside. If only you could go for a walk."

"Please get out," Vladimir said. "You and your fucking religion, and this fruit...What am I supposed to do with all this fruit?"

"Vladimir!" Kostya pressed the apple to his heart. "Say no more! God can only forgive so much! Cross yourself!"

"Jews don't cross themselves," Vladimir said. "We're the ones that put Him up there in the first place, remember?" He single-handedly drew the rank bed sheets over his head, a painful maneuver that brought to fore the sum of his injuries. "Now get out!" he said from beneath his linen fortress.

A DAY PASSED into night, then the situation was reversed.

A young Slovak nurse, her eyes and hair dark like a gypsy's, came to administer painkillers every couple of hours or so; to return the favor, Vladimir let her eat Kostya's fruit. This nurse was as sturdy as a sausage. She flipped Vladimir over without a sigh, mindful of his fractures, then pressed the needle deep into his rear, a pain Vladimir had come to enjoy as it signified the onset of sweet giddiness.

With an entire socialist pharmacopoeia coasting through his veins, Vladimir spent his days either laughing maniacally as he tried to build an airplane out of the institutional wax paper, or, when the effects of the drugs were at their nadir, dolefully mooing to a bedside picture of Morgan, whose four-hour daily visits were obviously not enough. The times in-between he spent chattering away to himself in both Russian and English, chronicling his child-hood and the end of his childhood, often pretending there was a bevy of grandchildren, small and furry, surrounding his bedside. "And when I was your age, Sari, I lived with a dominatrix in a con-demned Alphabet City flat. Later, she went with my best friend Baobab, but by this time I was already a mafioso in Prava. What a business!"

But soon enough, in a week, say, Vladimir's grandchildren

became tall and beefy, their features lightened, the tips of their noses curled upward, and sweatshirts with the names of American sports teams suddenly appeared. Vladimir guessed at their lineage. He knew he was reaching some sort of a decision.

"It'll be the perfect place to recover," Morgan said. "You'll see where I was brought up, the *real* America. And Cleveland's so nice in the summer. And it doesn't smell at all anymore—they've cleaned up the Cuyahoga River. And if you want, my father can give you a job. And if we don't like it there, we can move someplace else." She lowered her voice: "By the way, Tomaš and I are almost finished with our work here. Just so you know…"

"Let me think about it," Vladimir said, even as a whiff of hardy Midwestern air wormed its way through the shut windows.

And if we don't like it there, we can move someplace else.

The next day an adventuresome Vladimir ate a dish of soggy dumplings along with a trace of gulash minus the paprika (for health reasons, according to his doctor). He was able to flip himself over for the nurse, who said several encouraging words in her language, then slapped his butt kindly.

The nurse brought in copies of the *Prava-dence,* and here Vladimir could not escape Cohen's raging commentaries about anti-Semitism and racism in Mittel Europa, in response to which Cohen was speedily organizing a march to the Old Town Square under the banner EXPATRIATES, LET YOUR DISGUST BE KNOWN! Swastikas would be burned, folk music played, and the Mourner's Kaddish recited by a visiting dignitary for "a certain fallen friend."

"But I'm not dead," Vladimir reminded him when Cohen arrived along with František.

"No, no," Cohen mumbled. "Although…" He did not elaborate, but instead blotted at his red eyes with both palms, creasing the unshaven portion of his face below. "Let's have a beer," he said and took out a bottle, which, with a great deal of clumsiness and running foam, he eventually uncapped and placed in Vladimir's good hand.

The beer did not seem like a good idea to Vladimir, what with all the exotic drugs pumped into his posterior, but he took a few sips nonetheless. Over the course of the past nine months he had shared so many beers with Cohen that drinking this final one was akin to a memorial, and looking now at his haggard friend brimming once again with righteous energy, Vladimir was sad to think they might never see one another again. "Well, I hope your march goes as well as your work on *Cagliostro*," Vladimir said. "You have a knack for these things, Perry. I'm glad you were my mentor."

"I know, I know," Cohen said, brushing it off, embarrassed.

"And now, gentlemen, I must ask you to help me to my feet."

They looped their arms under his shoulders, and with František's considerable heft accounting for most of the propulsion, lifted him off the bed while he grunted and said "Ach!" On his feet, he was quickly impressed by his mobility. The feet were, with the exception of a few bruises, remarkably undamaged. His attackers had obviously been more concerned with juicier areas and most of the fractures were concentrated among his ribs, which made him feel as if his torso was a package bulging with broken glass. When he held his posture erect and did not breathe excessively, he could commute from the bed to the door easily, but any time his locomotion required a shift of the body or an extended inhalation, things got a little blurry and dark at the edges.

"I'm ready to leave," Vladimir told them.

Cohen instantly voiced his intention of staying and fighting until every young man with a shaved head was tied up for nine hours and forced to sit through a screening of Claude Lanzmann's *Shoah*, but František merely shook his head (his eyes, too, now had a hard look and were ringed underneath) and said: "Perhaps you are not aware of the situation outside. The guard here and the two guards by the entrance."

Vladimir turned to František and spread out his good hand, palm-upward, in the famous *"Nu?"* gesture.

"Nu?" František said. "What can I do? You understand now what our adversaries are capable of." Then he sighed tremendously. But as the sigh exhausted itself, his face took on the pleased, royal appearance of Son of Apparatchik II. "All right, I see something, yes...But perhaps we should wait until your physique improves."

"No," Vladimir said. "It has to be now. Tell me, František...How much money do I have?"

František shook his head sadly. "That fool Kostya has frozen your DeutscheBank account. As a preventative measure, I was told."

"I thought as much," Vladimir said. "So what's left for me here? Nothing."

It was clear that his two friends had never expected to hear those words from Vladimir Girshkin, for immediately they came together and put their arms around his body, as gently as two men without children can do.

"Wait!" Cohen said. "What do you mean 'nothing'? There must be *something* we can do! We can press charges. We can alert the media. We can..."

"Your girlfriend," František whispered into Vladimir's unbandaged ear. "She says they're going to blow up the Foot this Friday at three o'clock precisely. The explosion will serve as a decoy." František allowed himself a slight squeeze of the fractured former King of Prava.

"Be prepared to run," he said.

VLADIMIR HAD AN INTERESTING DREAM. In this dream he ate dinner with a normal American family that took up an enormous dining table over which hung three well-spaced chandeliers—that's how big this normal family was.

During the meal in the dream they ate St. Peter's fish, which was chosen for its low caloric content and not for any religious reasons. This was explained to Vladimir by a man named Gramps, who, quite normally, sat at the head of the table. Gramps had lived a long time and was knowledgeable about many topics, especially about great, big wars. He was also the only person at the table to have a face, although it wasn't the kind of face that, by itself, could imprint itself on the collective memory of a nation, in the manner of Khrushchev or the Quaker Oats Man.

It was an old man's beetle-browed, double-chinned, wine-reddened face, a face that had clearly seen more good than bad through the years, even when you factored in the great, big wars—*especially* when you factored in the great, big ones. Yes, Vladimir never thought he would enjoy hearing about duty and courage and biting the bullet so much. And he was very polite to Gramps: When the old guy spilled gravy over the sleeve of Vladimir's cuffed white shirt, Vladimir made a very appropriate joke, which was not in the least offensive to anyone present and seemed to put Gramps at ease. The dream ended right after Gramps had been put at ease.

Vladimir woke up pleased with his pleasantness at dinner, his stomach still purring under the gentle weight of the imaginary goy-fish. Sunlight flooded the room while a playful wind knocked at the windows. His nurse was wheeling in the breakfast cart. She was very animated, constantly pointing out the window and evidently saying a lot of nice things about the day outside. "*Petak!*" she said. Friday!

Vladimir nodded and said "*Dobry den'*" to her, which besides being a form of greeting also happened to mean "good day" in Stolovan.

She took out his breakfast—a single boiled egg, a piece of rye bread, and black coffee. Then, without ceremony and still gesticulating about the bountiful weather, she took out of the tray's bottom compartment a briefcase, which she placed next to Vladimir's good arm. *"Dobry den',"* she cheered and, smiling like a dark, Indo-European angel, wheeled the breakfast tray out of Vladimir's life.

At first Vladimir admired the briefcase itself. It was a handsome affair of taupe patent leather monogrammed with Vladimir's initials. He even thought of Mother and wondered if the first letter of the monogram could be changed in her favor.

Inside, there was an amusement-park-for-the-adult set. The first item Vladimir noticed was, of course, the revolver. It was the only gun he had ever seen that was not attached to a cop or to one of Gusev's men, and the idea that it was in his possession proved more hilarious than frightening. *Still-life of V. Girshkin with Sidearm.* The gun came with a diagrammed set of instructions, scribbled in hasty pencil: "Gun already loaded with six bullets. Release safety. Aim. Hold gun steady. Press trigger (but only after you have aimed directly at target)." Hey now, thought Vladimir. Accent or not, I am a child of America. I should know how to blow someone away instinctively.

Next to the pretty gun were stacks of hundred-dollar bills, a hundred to a stack, ten stacks in all; his U.S. passport; a plane ticket for that day's 5:00 P.M. nonstop to New York; and a brief note: "When the nurse knocks twice, the guard outside your room has been distracted. The Foot will explode two minutes later. Run for the nearest taxi (two blocks down is Prospekt Narodna, the closest thoroughfare). Your friend will be waiting for you at the airport. Do not waste time explaining yourself to the hospital staff—they have been taken care of."

Vladimir clasped the briefcase shut and moved one foot off the bed, aiming for his tasseled loafer from Harrods.

Just then there were two knocks at the door.

...Out the door Vladimir went, galloping madly, good hand around his body, a body which seemed ready to fold up like an army cot at any minute. He was rounding corner after corner, through miserable green corridors that seemed no more than an extension of his room, past innumerable older nurses with breakfast carts paying him no heed, all the while following the magic red sign bounded by an arrow and an exclamation point that surely must have meant EXIT!

Outside! into the Prava spring! a street curling away hopefully toward Prospekt Narodna, lined with ancient, bloated Fiat ambulances...A familiar BMW stood directly across the way from the hospital steps; two associates of the Groundhog's, Shurik and Log, were being entertained by a trio of elephantine nurses, whose hair—three bales of loose blond straw—was lifted behind them by the wind, potentially obscuring Vladimir's escape. It would seem the gang was clowning around with a hypodermic needle.

Three o'clock on his watch. The second hand moved five seconds forward. An orange ball overhead. A displacement in the sky. The Old Town shook. The New Town shook. The earthquake had begun.

Morgan!

Vladimir knew he had to move quickly but he could not take his eyes off the burning Foot. It was oddly reminiscent of the torch held aloft by the Statue of Liberty, except this torch was far grander, blowing beautiful swirls of gray smoke over the Tavlata and into the open courtyards of the castle above. Toward the back of the Foot, where the elevator and power cables ran alongside the Heel, electrical sparks blazed into blue-white spirals of lightning, which lashed out—harmlessly, one would hope—at the Baroque forms of the Stolovan Wine Archive and Hugo Boss outlet below. Alpha had been right in his calculations: the Foot imploded, its top two-thirds collapsing into the hollow of the bottom third. This truncated, smoking Foot was truly a landmark, the proverbial "ash heap of history" around which former Cold Warriors and the economics faculty of the University of Chicago would soon gather to warm their fleshy hands.

She had done it, Morgie! She had set the skyline on fire!

But there was no time to feel pride for his strange beloved. Caught in the aftershocks of the explosion, the city continued to rumble beneath his feet, as if an endless metro train was winding its way underground. Vladimir looked to the BMW. The Groundhog's men were crouched on the ground alongside the Stolovan nurses, looking up to the giant flaming limb. Vladimir briskly walked away from the scene, swinging his briefcase resolutely. In his pressed trousers and *Prava-dence* T-shirt, having shed his hospital gown, he was the consummate American businessman shunning taxi rides in favor of exercise, even if his left hand was bandaged into a fuzzy white ball, while a thick strip of gauze adorned his forehead. He breathed evenly at restful intervals in order to build energy for the next exertion, just the way Kostya had once instructed.

This was wise. As he approached the street's curve, which would definitively take him out of the Russians' line of sight, the twin banks of sooty buildings echoed Shurik's unhappy voice: "HALT!"

Exert!

And he was gone, the architecture scrolling around him, an engine swiftly firing up a dozen meters behind. Now he could only feel his head and his two feet—one, two, one, two—carrying aloft the rest of his ridiculous body, like Kostya bearing his cross. And the wind! The damn wind blew the wrong way down the neverending street like a reprimand, slamming into Vladimir's unfortunate chest, knocking out his air supply.

A reprisal! Like a nesting doll, the side street bore a side street. Following the rules of escape, Vladimir ducked into it. But the alley must have harbored some obscure museum, for it was chock-full of melancholy school children being siphoned through, like a slow-motion running of the bulls.

Vladimir stopped, regained a single breath, and shouted: "The

Russians are coming! Run!" This warning proved especially legitimate since it was shouted in Russian and against the background of a steadily exploding hundred-meter statue of Stalin's Foot. Pandemonium broke out, with the kiddies bleating, school bags flying through the air, teachers pushing their plumpness forward into children, children squeezed into the gray plaster of buildings, falling like toy soldiers into the vestibule of a new subterranean pizza parlor. Waving his hand in the air like a flag of national resistance, Vladimir charged through, still screaming his warning; he managed to knock down only one kid—a slow, sad-looking little Kafka who reminded Vladimir very much of himself as a child. He was sorry to see him go.

Forward! Ahead, a great light spilled into the side street, a light born of uncluttered space, of an enormous boulevard, of Prospekt Narodna—the Avenue of the Nation! Still screaming his dated warning, Vladimir careened into a crowd of peace-loving lunchtime strollers, all craning their necks to see the carnage of the Foot, caught up in the universal mood of astonishment and joy.

Behind him, his pursuers let loose the klaxon to clear the side street of third-graders. Not an easy task, since the alleyway was about as big as the BMW itself, and the sidewalks could accommodate only so many little Stolovans.

Feeling time was on his side, Vladimir pushed through the knots of businessmen in purple suits and white socks and leapt into the middle of the street. Once again, he ran. Only now there was no duality of smashed torso and Olympian legs. There was only pain and speed! Now, the happy wind was on the right side of history, and it spoke louder than the clang of the long-beaked tram heading in his direction: VLADIMIR VICTORIOUS!

He altered his course by a hair and brushed past the cream-and-orange streetcar, catching sight of the terrified *babushka*s clutching their Kmart bags within, for up ahead was the storied store itself. But Vladimir couldn't even contemplate escaping into men's casuals, just as in his frenzy he had lost sight of his original goal: finding a taxi, of which surely a dozen green exemplars by now had passed, alongside a procession of police cars, lights ablaze, rushing toward the burning Foot.

One! two! one! two! with the legs, not stopping even for a breath until the counting became a singular onetwooo, when suddenly the Prospekt Narodna concluded itself and he had to apply the brakes.

Ahead, the hazy blue of the Tavlata and a bridge spanning its length. The thought of being trapped on the bridge with nothing but the murky river below did not appeal; Vladimir turned right on the embankment, but at this point suffered a brief convulsion. His ribs scraped against each other with the imagined sound of cutlery and an immense ball of blood anchored in phlegm rose up to coat his mouth with metal. Bent over with pain, his former speed unthinkable, Vladimir made slow progress up the embankment toward the castle in the distance.

He passed the famed restaurant where he had eaten with the Groundhog, and briefly considered taking refuge in its international quarters. Any place with nymphs on the walls and Cole Porter on the piano could not possibly play host to an afternoon assassination. But the building next to it was by far more intriguing. An enormous Stolovan tricolor hung from the ground-level window; it was distinguished by the socialist star, long since banished from similar flags. Indeed, if one strained one's ears against the hum of the city, the "Internationale," shrill and raspy, could be heard from within like a painful birth. Of course! The Great Hall of People's Friendship! This was where František delivered his well-paid speeches to the old communist faithful.

In the distance, where the Prospekt Narodna lapsed into the river, the auto of Shurik and Log ground itself to a full and complete stop with smoking tires and all the appropriate sounds.

Vladimir turned to the other direction, the direction of further escape, to catch the monstrous, sloping hood of the Groundhog's customized Beamer easing its way onto the embankment. And so his fate was sealed.

Past a thick velvet curtain lay the bottom floor of a spacious villa converted into an auditorium. A marble Lenin towered over an empty podium. The podium itself looked out over rows of folding chairs occupied by the Sons and Daughters of the Radiant Future—those crisp octogenarians—the grandmas still dressed in blue work dresses, their revolutionary spouses now sporting significant bosoms to which their many insignia were pinned.

Toward the front of the room, by Lenin's left toe, to be exact, Vladimir caught sight of the youngest person in the joint save himself. His question mark of a cowlick had always been a dead giveaway in a crowded bar. František, with the benefit of his height, noticed Vladimir as well and quickly started making his way back, managing to shake every single hand that was offered him, like a rabbi during a break in the minyan services. "What the hell?" he said, pushing Vladimir back toward the velvet curtain and the street outside.

"I couldn't get a cab!" Vladimir shouted.

"*Jesusmaria!* How did you find this place?"

"The flag…You told me…" Vladimir closed his eyes and remembered to breathe at any cost. He breathed. "Look, they've surrounded the two streets, this way and that way. They're going to start going into buildings. Do you see what I mean?" He looked around to see if any Guardians of the Foot were present, fearful they might recognize him from Morgan's showdown at Big Toe…But all the *babushka*s looked the same to him.

"What about the Foot?" František said. "I felt the ground shaking. I thought—"

"It's gone," Vladimir said. "Finished."

His voice carried all too well. Gray heads were turning, chairs squeaking backward, and the hall was soon suffused with amazed whispers of "Trotsky!"

At first, František did not pay these rumors any notice, probably figuring that anything at all could have stirred up the waves of senility fiercely undulating through the room. Instead, he was trying to calm Vladimir, reminding him that they were in this together, that they were both fellow travelers, "men of taste in a tasteless world," and that he would do anything to save Vladimir. But by then the disparate whispers of "Trotsky!" were united into a single proletarian chant, and the two could no longer ignore the gathering momentum. With embarrassed smiles they turned to face the People and affected a little wave of the hand.

"Interesting," František said, as he energetically massaged his bare temples. "How very Menshevik of them. I would never have imagined...But all right...Never mind. Shall we try for Plan Z, then? I take it you still know your Marxism-Leninism, *Tovarishch* Trotsky?"

"It was my major in the Midwestern col—"

"Then please follow me."

"But, of course, whatever you're thinking is madness..." Vladimir started to say, but in the meantime he followed the madman faithfully to the front of the room. A flawless hush settled over the congregation, well-trained after forty years of marching happily into the future and never bowing to facts.

With arms swinging in martial fashion and chin set firm, František mounted the podium. "Dear friends of Glorious October," he said in perfect Russian. "We have a guest today the caliber of which we have not seen since that Bulgarian with the funny parrot last year...Yezdinsky, was it? Only thirty years old, but already thrice a Hero of Socialist Labor, not to mention the youngest person ever to receive the Order of Andropov for

Heroic Operation of a Wheat Combine... Comrades, please welcome the General Secretary of the Central Presidium of the Liberal Democratic Worker-Peasant Alliance of Unrepentant Communists and a serious contender for Russia's presidency in the next election... Comrade Yasha Oslov!"

The geezers rose to their feet in an enormous polyester wave, cheering "Hurrah, Trotsky!" even though Vladimir's alias had by now been established. Noticing his injuries, some of the grandmas were shouting: "What ails you, Trotsky? We'll fix you up!"

Vladimir waved to them solicitously as he climbed the stairs, nearly losing his fragile balance in the act. He set his briefcase full of greenbacks on top of the lectern and adjusted the microphone with his working hand, waiting for the applause to subside. "Stalwart comrades," he shouted and immediately stopped. Stalwart comrades... Um, and then what? "First let me ask you, is it acceptable that I speak in Russian?"

"But of course! Speak, Russian eagle!" the audience said as one.

My kind of audience, Vladimir thought. He breathed in all his doubts once, felt the pain of breathing, then dispelled them into the air, thick with the smell of groceries going bad and cheap suits worn on a warm day. "Stalwart comrades!" he shouted into the silence. "Outside it is a warm April day, the sky is clear. But over the mausoleum of Vladimir Ilych," he turned for emphasis to the statue of Lenin, "the sky is a perpetual gray!"

"Woe, poor Lenin!" moaned the crowd. "Poor are his heirs."

"Poor, indeed," Vladimir said. "Just look what has happened to your beautiful Red Prava. Americans everywhere you turn! (The crowd roared its opposition!) Performing lewd sexual acts on the Emanuel Bridge as if to laugh at the sanctity of the Socialist Family and to spread their AIDS! (Roar!) Shooting up their marijuana with dirty needles in the Old Town Square, where once a hundred thousand comrades thrilled to the words of Jan Zhopka, your first working-class president. (Roar! Roar!) Is this why for forty years you have toiled in the fields and melted all that metal...melted all that metal into steel, built those wonderful trams, a subway system that is the envy of the Paris Métro, public toilets everywhere...And let's not forget the human element! How many faithful, energetic young comrades have we produced, like Comrade František here..."

He waved to František in the front row and presented the crowd with both an upturned thumb and a victory sign (he wasn't about to skimp on them). "Franti!" cheered the crowd.

"Yes, Comrade Franti has been dispensing *Red Justice* since he was in diapers! Keep beating up that counter-revolutionary element with your mighty pen, dear friend!" Oh, he was starting to like this! He paced before the lectern like an agitated Bolshevik, even touching the cool marble of the Big Daddy of the Revolution for support. "Look at my hand!" he shouted, waving the bandaged package in the air with his other hand. "Look what they've done to it, the industrialists! I spoke my mind at a rally of Negro workers in Washington, and the CIA put it through a meat grinder!"

At the mention of the meat grinder, a comrade in a frumpy mink and floral headscarf could no longer contain herself. She sprang to her feet and waved a segmented string of sausages around her head, lasso-style. "I paid forty crowns for these!" she shouted. "What do you think of that?"

"Yes," the crowd picked up the rallying cry. "What do you think of that?"

"What do *I* think of that?" Vladimir pointed to himself as if he were surprised that they would solicit his opinion. "I think that the store owner responsible for charging forty crowns for those sausages should be shot!"

The entire crowd was now on its feet; its ovation must have

been heard over at the restaurant next door. "I think his family should be forced to leave Prava as enemies of the people," shouted the incorrigible Vladimir, "and his children never allowed to attend university!" Hurrah! answered the crowd.

"His cat should be turned into cat food!" Hurrah!

"And what do you think of twenty crowns for a carp?" another inquisitive *babushka* wanted to know.

"Disgrace! Why have we let the labor camps of Siberia go idle? And what about those nice Stolovan uranium mines? Comrades, when the Liberal Democratic Worker-Peasant Alliance of Unrepentant Communists takes control, these new entrepreneurs will *really* have their work cut out for them!"

The crowd lapsed into cheerful laughter and applause, gold teeth sparkled across the room, and more than one hand reached to calm the overexcited beating of a faulty heart. "We will take care of them one by one, dear *tovarishchii*. We will strangle the life out of them with our own bare hands, those fat bourgeois pigs in their pinstriped Armani suits!"

Now, what can one say about coincidences? Either one believes in a higher power or one just shrugs. Looking back, Vladimir would concede that at that moment he was tempted to believe, for no sooner had the words "fat bourgeois pigs in their pinstriped Armani suits" escaped his mouth, than the Groundhog parted the velvet curtain and burst into the room, trailed closely by Gusev and the Log. Yes, they all had on their Armani pinstripes and were looking more porcine than ever, although perhaps the power of suggestion played some part in that.

"There they are!" shouted Vladimir, pointing, he thought, directly into the Groundhog's solar plexus. "They've come to disrupt our dignified meeting! For the honor of the Fatherland, tear those pigs to shreds!"

The Groundhog tilted his head and sucked in his cheeks in amazement, as if to say, *"Et tu, Brute?"* Then an enormous kielbasa landed on his head and the crowd charged.

Vladimir did not witness all the weapons at their disposal, suffice to say crutches played a big part, but for him the most enduring scene of the melee, like war footage that gets played over and over again on the networks, was the sight of a plump matron in heels stabbing at Gusev's heart with the business end of a sturgeon, shouting: "Is that hard enough for you, you crook?" while her confused victim pleaded for mercy.

And so, as old soldiers heaved metal chairs against the intruders, and sausages circled overhead like Sikorsky choppers, František hurried Vladimir toward an alternate exit to the embankment. "Brilliant!" was the single word he said, as he pushed him out into the noon light and slammed the door shut behind him.

Still full of revolutionary fervor, but now reminded of more pressing matters, Vladimir ran down the embankment chasing a departing taxi. "Halt, comrade!" he was shouting out of habit.

The taxi squealed in compliance and Vladimir heaved himself inside with a crack of something internal. "Oh, for the love of God..." He sneezed, and two gushers of blood were released, one per nostril, the way one imagines a winning racehorse lets out fire at the finish line.

The driver—a teenager by the looks of him, his shaved head tattooed with the anarchist's goofy "A"—caught sight of this bloodbath in the rearview. "Out, out," cried the anarchist driver. "No blood in auto! No HIV! Out!"

A stack of a hundred hundred-dollar bills hit the back of the driver's head (Vladimir had thrown it with such force that it left a momentary red trace on that great moony surface). The driver looked down at the stash. He threw the little Trabant into gear.

The way to the airport required a quick U-turn, which a car any larger than a Trabant could not perform. In this respect, Vladimir was fortunate. In the respect that the U-turn took him straight into the Groundhog's armada of BMWs and *mafiyosi* in retreat from the octogenarian Red Army, he was not.

His driver pressed on the horn dutifully and cursed as well, but with all the confusion up ahead he could not help but hit a large object, which Vladimir to his dying day would believe was Log. However, considering the glare of the afternoon sun and the blinding red flashes exploding around his corneas, he could have been wrong. It could have been a friend of the Log.

Nevertheless, the force of the impact steered the Trabant into the railing of the embankment. The Trabi, knowing a greater physical force when it crashed into one, bounced back into the street, saving Vladimir and his driver from a lapse into the river. A remarkable car, the Trabant! Such shyness and humility, such understated presence. Mother had always wanted Vladimir to marry a girl just like this Trabi.

"Car is dead!" the driver moaned, even as they made exceptional progress up the embankment and onto the bridge that snaked off from Prospekt Narodna. "Pay me!" Flustered and at the teenager's mercy, Vladimir hit him with another ten thou, in response to which the driver pulled a confetti of wires and a single lightbulb out of the dashboard. This immediately sent the Trabant into heat: with terrific gusto and a transparent lack of regard for traffic signals they bounded through the Lesser Quarter and around Repin Hill.

A curtain of gray smoke rising from the Foot now blanketed the city, smoke as thick as the scalloped clouds one sees looking down from an airplane window. A premature night had descended upon Prava, coloring the spires and domes of the Old Town with an eerie industrial beauty.

By this point, the pain in Vladimir's ribs was becoming acute.

He broke down in a fit of coughing. There was something in his throat, a thick string of coagulated blood, and he pulled at it, pulled until the whole food chain unwrapped itself from within his stomach and landed on the driver's bald pate.

For a second his cause seemed lost; for a second it looked like he would have to walk it to the airport. But all the driver said, in the meek, bewildered way of a proud local boy suddenly covered in a Westerner's innards, was, "Pay me." When the money fell alongside him, he gunned the engine once more.

Looking down at the city below them, Vladimir could see the BMW caravan making its way up the hill, one car on the heels of the next, forming a dark-blue river not unlike the Tavlata, except flowing a great deal more energetically and up the slope of Repin Hill. Vladimir shuddered, amazed at the power of the organization to which he once belonged, although a chain of luxury German automobiles was perhaps its most potent manifestation. Unless, of course, every link in that chain was strafing you with gunfire.

This happened a good ten minutes hence. The Trabant had quit the other side of Repin Hill and emerged onto the main highway leading out of the city. Vladimir was suffering from a dizzying attack of blood and tears. He was leaning his head back to keep the blood down and whispering to himself his father's "no-tears" manifesto, when a bullet took out the back window of the Trabi. The tiny shards of glass drew fine red lines on the back of the driver's head, complementing (rather befittingly) the tattooed "A," symbol of the anarchists. "Ah!" shouted the driver. "Artillery is shooting to death car and Jaroslav! Pay me!"

Vladimir crept down into the pool of his own blood. The driver, Jaroslav, swerved into a no-man's land between the guardrails and the freeway proper. The thin Trabant squeezed past a trailer truck in front of them bearing the logo of a Swedish modular-furniture company.

Shell-shocked, Vladimir crawled back up to look through the nonexistent window behind him. The Swedish furniture truck now separated their car from the Groundhog's shooting party like some kind of ad hoc U.N. reaction force. But the Hog's men apparently had no respect for Swedish furniture. With a singlemindedness common only to former Soviet interior-ministry troops and first-year law students, they continued to shoot as the truck swerved madly to stay on the road. Finally, their labors produced results—with an audible whoosh, the back doors of the truck blew away.

A houseful of Krovnik dining tables in assorted colors, Skanör solid-beech glass-door cabinets, Arkitekt retractable work lamps (with adjustable heads), and the daddy of them all—a Grinda three-piece sofa ensemble in "modern paisley," came sailing out of the back of the truck and onto the flotilla of BMWs to settle once and for all the Russo-Swedish War of 1709.

THEY PULLED UP to the departure terminal. Vladimir, in a gesture of last-minute good will, threw another ten grand at Jaroslav, who slapped Vladimir's sweat-soaked back, and, his own eyes now tearing, shouted: "Run, J.R.! One car still follows us!"

He ran, absentmindedly wiping the blood off his nose onto the already bloodied hand bandage. He slapped his passport on the desk of the half-awake security team guarding the departure gate. At that formal moment, his briefcase, stuffed with about fifty thousand dollars and a gun, came to mind. "Oh, pardon me," said the ever-vigilant Vladimir. He hobbled over to the nearest trash can, sheepishly took out the gun, and, with a shrug of the shoulders, deposited that useless item within. "Don't even ask about the gun," he said to the nice, walrus-mustached gentlemen in dark green. "What a long day!"

"American?" said the security commandant, a tall individual, fit and lean, a shock of white hair beneath his beret. It was more of a statement than a question. With a minimum of malice, he told Vladimir to keep his blood-soaked hands off the spotless white counter, then stamped a childish picture of a departing plane into the passport and waved Vladimir through the gate. With ten minutes until departure, Vladimir prepared for a final sprint.

Directly behind him, Gusev and the Groundhog were running up to the security counter, buttoning up their double-breasters, straightening their ties, and shouting in Russian: "Stop the criminal in the bloodied shirt! The little criminal, stop him!"

Vladimir stopped, as if frozen by these hurtful words, but the security detail hardly turned around. "We don't speak Russian here," the commandant announced in Stolovan as the others laughed approval.

"Stop the international terrorist!" Gusev was hollering, still in the wrong tongue.

"Passport!" the chief hollered back at them in the international language of border police about to get more than a little surly.

"Soviet citizens don't need passports!" cried the Groundhog, and, in a final suicidal gesture, leapt for the departure gate and Vladimir.

Vladimir continued to stand there, transfixed by the gaze in the eyes of Mr. Rybakov's son, the crooked gaze of the same hatred, lunacy, and, in the end, hopelessness, that his father, the Fan Man, had worn like a badge . . . And then the eye contact was broken by so many swinging batons, well-aimed kicks in the groin, and an older man in uniform bent over the Groundhog and Gusev shouting revenge for the Soviet incursion of 1969.

"Oh, my poor people," said Vladimir suddenly as the violence commenced. Why had he said this? He shook his head. Stupid heritage. Dumb multicultural Jew.

Among the few last passengers ascending the stairs, he did not even recognize Morgan. Foolishly, he was looking for her bright face to stand out with the luminance of a supernova, for a great, preternatural shout of "Vladi!" to shake the tarmac. Lacking all of the above, he ran nonetheless... Ran the way he was taught by Kostya and by life, ran toward her, toward the hum of jet engines, the sparkle of the sun on metal wings softly shaking, the unbearable sight of yet another landscape falling away beneath him as if none of it had ever happened.

He ran—there was not even the time to lie to himself that he would be back. And lies had always been important to our Vladimir, like childhood friends with whom one never loses an understanding.

I am playing an accordion
on a busy thoroughfare

It's too bad that
happy birthday
comes just once a year.

—The Russian Birthday Song *(as sung*
by a cheerless cartoon crocodile)

IT HAD BEEN IMPOSSIBLE TO SLEEP THROUGH THE
night. A summer storm had been steadily fortifying itself outside,
trying to beat its way through the storm windows and stucco with
a baleful announcement of Vladimir's thirtieth birthday, just what
he would expect from Nature's cruel Ohio franchise.

Now, morning in the kitchen, barely seven o'clock, and sleepy
Vladimir is eating his cereal with fruit. He spends half an hour
watching the strawberries bloody his milk, while submerging his
banana with perverse glee. One of Morgan's gigantic brown hairs,
trapped in the doors of a kitchen cabinet, is blown in an upward
arc by a draft from the window like an index finger beckoning
Vladimir.

Mornings are lonely nowadays.

Morgan, on leave from the clinic where she interns, is still asleep, her hands wrapped protectively around her spherical belly, which already seems to rise and lift independent of her breathing. Her eyes are teary and swollen from pollen season, her face is getting fuller and perhaps a little less kind in preparation for the third decade of her life. Unable to hear her from the kitchen, Vladimir listens to the house breathe, enjoying, the way his father always did, the imagined safety of the American home. Today, it is the inspired hum of some sort of electrical generator buried deep in the house's subbasement, a hum that sometimes pitches itself into a roar, making the dishes chime in the dishwasher.

"Time to go," Vladimir announces to the kitchen machinery and the curtains billowing with embroidered sunflowers over the sink.

HE DRIVES AROUND THE TATTERED ENDS of his neighborhood where the overbearing single-family dwellings of the kind in which he lives give way to the rowhouses of the interwar era—charcoal black either by design or by the industry ringing the city, who can tell? Already, scraps of morning traffic are filling up the intersections; the Ohioans slowing down to let mommies and children cross. Vladimir, in the plush cocoon of his luxury utility vehicle, is listening to the scratchy wail of the Russian bard Vladimir Vysotsky—it is his favorite morning song, set in a Soviet mental asylum where the inmates have just discovered the mystery of the Bermuda Triangle on a television variety show and are full of disturbing suggestions. ("We shall drink up the Triangle!" cries a recovering alcoholic.)

And then, with a cloying twitter, the harbinger of annoyance, his car phone rings. Vladimir looks at it with uncertainty. Eight o'clock in the morning. It is time for the familiar birthday greetings, Mother's annual *State of the Vladimir* address. From atop her glassed-in skyscraper in New York, the celebratory shouting begins: "Dearest *Volodechka!* Happy birthday…! Happy new beginning…! Your father and I wish you a brilliant future…! Much success…! You're a talented young man…! We gave you everything as a child…!"

There is a long pause. Vladimir expects her to start wailing, but Mother is full of surprises this morning. "See," she says, "I'm not even crying this year! Why should I cry? You're a real man now, Vladimir! It took thirty years but you've finally learned life's most important lesson—*when you listen to your mother, everything turns out all right.* Remember how I protected you in kindergarten? Remember little Lionya Abramov, your best friend…I used to feed you boys Little Red Riding Hood chocolate candy. So delicious. And you were such a quiet, obedient child. I could have wrapped you up in my love back then. Well, have they made you partner yet?"

"Not yet," Vladimir says, minding the approach of an aggressive dairy truck. "Morgan's father says—"

"But what a stupid whore he is," Mother muses. "You married their family, you should be partner. Don't worry, I'll teach him a lesson when I come for the *bris.* And how is Morgan? You know, when I saw her last autumn, she wasn't even pregnant, but I couldn't help noticing…She was already a little fat. The thighs, especially. You should say something, in a very gentle American way, about the thighs…And if only she were a little blonder…Just think, the child would have brown hair and a nice round face…But who knows what God has in mind for us!"

"Every week you start with the hair," Vladimir says, nervously combing over his dark curls with a free hand. "Is there nothing else to talk about?"

"I'm old, my treasure! I repeat things! An old woman! Almost sixty."

"That's not so old in this country."

"Yes, but the hardships I've faced. The details. Always with the little details...I can't sleep at night, Volodya...I wake up and the details are choking me. Why is my life so difficult, tell me, treasure?"

Vladimir examines a billboard advertisement for a newly built tire store. He suddenly wants to have his tires changed, to talk to the mechanics in blue smocks about his impending fatherhood and how he should conduct himself throughout the whole affair. He wants to join the simple brotherhood of America's white men. And why not? As part of their new life, Morgan has already surrounded herself with a natural selection of young, attractive, child-bearing women who effortlessly mobilize the kitchen with their coffee-brewing as they glance at the passing Vladimir with a mixture of shyness and disbelief. "Mmm..." he says to Mother.

"Oh, what a healthy American boy you will have," Mother continues. "I've seen one at a neighbor's house. They even crawl differently here. Very energetic. Maybe it's the diet."

Vladimir puts the phone down on his lap and listens to the gentle trilling of Mother's speech, waiting for her voice to descend into the reproachful whisper that signifies she has said all she needs to say. "Well, it's time for me to go," Mother sighs just as he picks up the phone once more. "These calls cost money. Always remember that we love you, Volodya! And don't be scared of Morgan's father. We're stronger than these people. Just take what you want, *sinotchek*..."

They kiss each other good-bye, the sound of their puckers echoing through the ether. Vladimir drives on for a few silent kilometers. Despite the morning storm still massing overhead, the inept Ohio sun has managed to break through the clouds to blind Vladimir with its phony summer glare. The roads are lonesome and dry.

And then, as if the entire populace has simultaneously risen from slumber and finished gargling, the morning's traffic begins in earnest. Vladimir fights his way onto a highway, the main artery leading into the city's center, where a new vista slowly materializes, of gutted industry mixed with Orthodox onion domes supporting crosses as tall as smokestacks... And then, and then...

Downtown Cleveland. Its three major skyscrapers standing above the cosmopolitan wreckage of factories aching to be nightclubs and chain restaurants; the squat miniskyscrapers that look as if they have been cut short in their prime; the hopeful grandeur of municipal buildings built at a time when the transport of hogs and heifers promised the city a commercial elegance that had expired along with the animals... But, somehow, this city has persevered against the unkind seasons and the storms that gather speed over Lake Erie. Somehow, Cleveland has survived, with her gray banner unfurled—the banner of Archangelsk and Detroit, of Kharkov and Liverpool—the banner of men and women who would settle the most ignominious parts of the earth, and there, with the hubris born neither of faith nor ideology but biology and longing, bring into the world their whimpering replacements.

Yeah, good old Cleveland. And who is Vladimir if not its captain? His office is at the top of a skyscraper that surveys the entire domain, land and sea, suburb and metropolis. And there, under the ornery direction of Morgan's father, accountant Vladimir will shepherd the financial futures of so many small businesses throughout the Ohio Valley.

Until, that is, the inevitable happens. At least once a week. Usually after a dressing-down from some clean-cut superior with his flat Midwestern vowels and army haircut. Vladimir locks his office door, closes his eyes, and dreams of ... A scheme! A provocation! Pyramids! Turbo props! The Frankfurt exchange! The old Girshkin something for nothing! What did Mother say? We're stronger than these people. Just take what you want...

But he can't. It's all gone, that youthful instinct. This is America, where the morning paper lands on the doorstep at precisely 7:30 A.M.—not the woolly dominion Vladimir once ruled.

So he'll open his eyes and unlock the door. He'll put in his ten-hour workday. He'll chat up the secretarial pool and use his spare minutes to ascertain the standing of the local sports teams in the back pages of the *Plain Dealer,* statistics necessary for the firm's bizarre afterwork buddy rituals. (Vladimir is, as has been mentioned, partnership-track material.)

And then, finally, the day will be replayed backward and he will return to Morgan...to the tiny trickle of breath issuing from her mouth, to the ears flush with warmth as if burning coals are concealed within, to her pregnant body embracing him in the night with the concern of a pending mother.

And what of this child?

Will he live the way his father once did: foolishly, imperially, ecstatically?...

No, thinks Vladimir. For he can see the child now. A boy. Growing up adrift in a private world of electronic goblins and quiet sexual urges. Properly insulated from the elements by stucco and storm windows. Serious and a bit dull, but beset by no illness, free of the fear and madness of Vladimir's Eastern lands. In cahoots with his mother. A partial stranger to his father.

An American in America. That's Vladimir Girshkin's son.

To Chang-rae Lee, with warmth and appreciation, for launching me into the world of letters. To Diane Vreuls, for the earliest encouragement. To John Saffron, of Haimosaurus University, for endless patience and for cracking the whip. To Denise Shannon of ICM, for superior representation and advice. To Cindy Spiegel, for invaluable editorial guidance and a keen understanding of the immigrant's experience. To Millys Lee, for everything.

GARY SHTEYNGART was born in Leningrad in 1972, and came to the United States seven years later. His novel, *The Russian Debutante's Handbook,* won the Stephen Crane Award for First Fiction, was named a *New York Times* Notable Book, and was chosen as a best book of the year by the *Washington Post Book World* and *Entertainment Weekly*. His work has appeared in the *New Yorker, Granta* and many other publications. He lives in New York City.